CHASING SETH

TRUE MATES: BOOK ONE

J.R. LOVELESS

S ETH Davies stared up at the front of the clinic in front of him, a satisfied smile lighting up his soft features. It'd taken six weeks to finalize everything for the sale, and he could barely wait to get started. Senaka, Wyoming, was exactly the kind of place he needed to be able to heal.

His mind automatically slammed the door shut on those memories, and he sighed as he entered the front of the clinic. The receptionist, Chessie Fox, stood behind the counter, talking on the phone. She smiled welcomingly at him, and he gave her an equally warm grin in return.

"Good morning, Chessie," he said as he walked toward her desk.

Chessie dropped the phone back into its cradle after bidding the person on the other end good-bye. "Good morning, Doc. Your first appointment is already waiting for you in Exam Room One."

"Do you have—?" he started to ask when she handed it to him. Seth liked her. She was efficient, friendly, and very outgoing. He also thought her to be very pretty, with her dark olive-toned skin, dark-brown eyes, and long dark-brown hair. Chessie was Cheyenne and looked every bit of it. If he had found women attractive, he definitely would have taken an interest in her. "Thanks, Chessie, for deciding to stay on with me."

"Oh, it's no problem, Doc. I like working here, and I'm glad that you wanted me to stay!" Chessie exclaimed. Her heart beat hard against her chest at the gorgeous man in front of her desk. He was absolutely beautiful: a slender face with a slightly pointed chin, dimples deep as oceans, his eyes just as blue, and thick hair so black it looked almost unnatural. Seth kept it in a neat cut, slight tendrils brushing the nape of his neck. The top of her head just reached his chin. What really fed her lust for her boss was the single earring that dangled from one ear. A sterling silver feather no longer than the width of a penny twinkled at every move of Seth's head.

"Well, I'm still grateful you decided to stay. I wouldn't even begin to know where to look for the files or know who Dr. Redfern's clients were." Seth glanced down at the name on the folder, opened it, skimmed over the contents of the animal's history, and then looked back at her. "Is my day full, Chessie?"

"Mostly, Doc. You have a gap between appointments around one and three, though. But you never know around these parts. Folks have animal emergencies quite often." The phone rang, interrupting anything else Chessie would have said.

Seth wandered into the examining room, smiling at the older woman and noting the small poodle on the table. "Hello, Mrs. Whitedove. I'm Seth Davies, and I guess this would be Samantha?"

The woman smiled back at him, her eyes studying him intently and almost causing him to squirm. He felt certain Mrs. Whitedove would also be able to claim Cheyenne as her background. Most of the residents of Senaka were Cheyenne, so it was a pretty safe bet for him to make. Her face looked weathered but wise. Deep lines traced her heart-shaped face, and gray had started to streak through her black hair. He had a mere few inches on her in height. "Heard Doc sold his practice. You're a bit young, aren't you, Doc?"

"Oh, please call me Seth, and I may look young, but I am quite experienced at taking care of these little guys," Seth said with confidence, moving closer to the table the dog sat on. A pretty, shockingly white poodle, she whined at him and licked his hand. "What seems to be the problem with Samantha, Mrs. Whitedove?"

"Well, she's been off her food lately. She won't eat and doesn't even play with her toys," Mrs. Whitedove explained, her eyes clouding over in worry and concern.

Seth scratched the poodle behind her ears before putting the earpieces of his stethoscope in and placing the chest piece against the poodle's chest. His eyes slipped closed as he listened to her heart. The sound of a minor irregularity caused him to frown. His free hand smoothed over the poodle's side slowly, gently. The poodle whined again, pressing closer to him.

Mrs. Whitedove watched in fascination at the emotions that flitted over the doctor's features. Concern had been evident at first, but it slowly dissipated to a peaceful, almost serene countenance. "Is everything all right with Sam, Doc?" Fear weighed heavily in her voice.

He didn't respond right away. A tiny drop of sweat broke out over his forehead, but then his eyes opened. He gave her a strained smile. "She'll be fine, Mrs. Whitedove. She just has a bit of upset stomach. I'll give you some Pepcid AC for her, and you may want to adjust her diet for the next couple of days to help with the nausea and the discomfort she's feeling. Just some plain rice and a bit of chicken without the skin.

Why don't you take Sam into the waiting room, and I'll get that for you right away."

Mrs. Whitedove gave a sigh of relief and smiled enthusiastically at him. "I'm so glad, Doc. I was frightened something was really wrong with her. My son, Kasey, bought her for me as a gift after my mother passed away."

"She's going to be just fine," Seth murmured, stroking the dog along her nose briefly. His fingers gripped at the edge of the exam table until his knuckles turned white as he waited for the woman to leave the room.

The instant the door closed behind her, he raced into the back toward the bathroom, where he promptly vomited into the toilet. A dark substance stained the white porcelain as he slumped down onto the floor. He rested his forehead on his folded arms across the seat, waiting for the shakiness and dizziness to fade. When he finally felt he could stand without falling over, Seth pushed up from the floor to go fill the prescription for the poodle.

Chessie stood talking to Mrs. Whitedove when he exited the back. He handed the small bottle to Chessie. "Just give her a half in the morning for the next five days, and she'll be just fine, Mrs. Whitedove. If you have any questions or concerns, please feel free to call me. My cell number is on my card. I'm available anytime you need me."

"Thanks, Doc," she said, smiling, paying Chessie before walking out of the clinic with a very happy bounce to her step. Seth smiled weakly after her.

Chessie gave him a worried look, coming around to place her hand on his shoulder. "You all right, Doc? You look a little pale."

Seth nodded. "Yeah, I'm fine, just a little tired. It's been a long six weeks."

"If you're sure," she replied uncertainly. "Your next appointment should be here in just a few minutes." Her gaze was troubled as she watched him go into his office at the back of the building. She could sense that he hadn't been completely honest with her.

Seth sank down into his desk chair, leaning his head on the desk in front of him. His eyes closed as he struggled to gain control of his body. It wasn't but a few moments before the intercom buzzed and Chessie let him know his next appointment had arrived. Taking a deep breath, he stood, walking into the front to grab the file he needed.

By the end of the day, he felt exhausted and wobbly on his feet. Chessie left an hour before he did, and he was just about to lock up for the night when he heard the bell above the door tinkle. Sighing, he stepped into the hallway from his office, stopping short when he saw the most gorgeous man he'd ever laid eyes on standing there.

The man was the walking epitome of sex. Black hair, held back from his face, shone brightly in the overhead lights. Strong, high cheekbones and a firm, rounded chin gave him a rugged appearance. The olive-toned skin clearly showed his relation to the other locals. He stood at least six feet, with big, wide shoulders that could surely hold a mountain of weight on them. A sheriff's uniform hugged his muscular body in all the right places.

Swallowing hard, Seth walked toward him, a slight smile on his face. "Is there something I can help you with?"

Instantly, a hostile look came into the dark gaze staring at him. "You're white," the man snapped.

Seth lifted an eyebrow at the man. He decided right then he didn't really like him. He peered at the tag on the uniform, eyes widening slightly at the name. "Gee, I'm glad that's been sorted out. Now my confusion has cleared. What can I help you with, Sheriff Whitedove?"

A scowl settled between the elegant arched eyebrows. "Doc never said he was selling to a white man."

The small smile that had been on Seth's face had died long ago. He could tell the man was a prejudiced bigot. "Look, you're obviously not happy about the fact that I'm not Cheyenne, but you'll have to deal with it, because I can't change who I am," he ground out, very angry suddenly. "Now, is there something you needed, or are you just going to stand there all night telling me I'm white? I'm exhausted and would like to go home."

Sheriff Whitedove pulled himself up to his full height, towering over Seth, but Seth didn't back down. He merely glared at the man. "One of my horses is having a difficult labor, but I don't need a white man touching my horses. Your kind knows nothing about animals."

"So you'd rather your horse suffer and possibly die because I'm white?" Seth demanded harshly, his heart aching at the obvious hatred coming from the other man. He'd never admit it, but it hurt. "And I know more about animals than you think, Sheriff, but if you'd rather your horse died instead of having a white man helping, then I suggest you remove yourself from my clinic." His breathing had grown ragged from the anger surging through him. Bastard. Who the hell did this guy think he was?

The skin around the sheriff's mouth grew white with how tight he had his lips pulled together. "Fine, let's go, but know this, Doc, if my horse dies, I'm holding you responsible."

Seth didn't respond to the threat, but he whirled around to go back into his office to grab his emergency medical bag. The sheriff still waited impatiently by the front door of the clinic. Seth felt more concern for the horse than he did for how the man seemed to dislike him for being white. "I'm ready," he said in a serious tone.

The sheriff didn't say a word, just slammed out of the office to the sheriff's department pickup in front of the clinic. Seth shut and locked the door behind him before sliding into the vehicle. The sheriff barely gave him the chance to fasten his seat belt before tearing out of the parking lot. Tense and quiet, the ride seemed longer than the ten minutes it actually took. Seth couldn't stop himself from giving a small sigh of relief when they pulled up in front of a large ranch-style home just outside of town.

"This way," the sheriff practically growled at him.

A horse lay in the straw in one of the stalls. Seth rushed forward, dropping to his knees beside the horse. Everything else disappeared. Not even the sheriff mattered at that moment. His hands slid down the broad side of the dark chestnut horse. The foal was in trouble and fading fast. He knew if he didn't get the foal turned quickly, both the mother and the baby would die.

Moving quickly, he shoved the sleeves of his dress shirt up to his elbows. He didn't take the time to slip on the gloves like he normally would have. He could feel the fear and pain radiating from the horses, adding to his own worry for them.

Reaching into the horse, he carefully grasped the front legs of the foal and tugged slowly, gently. Inch by excruciating inch, the foal began to turn. Seth made a small grunt of triumph as the baby fell into place and began to slide forward. The horse let out a neigh of excitement as she felt the foal moving.

Kasey Whitedove hovered but didn't say anything, instead merely studying the man who had taken over the animal clinic in his town. He could see it was as if nothing but the animal existed for the dark-haired vet. The play of emotions, from worry to relief, across his features fascinated him. He felt a twinge of regret for how he'd spoken to the man at first but viciously shoved it away. Either way, the man wasn't Cheyenne. White men knew nothing about animals. They used them and destroyed them for their own personal gain.

His lips flattened even further in anger at the previous doctor. What had Redfern been thinking?

Seth pulled his hands free of the horse's body and let her finish the work. The baby slid out in a rush of fluids to land in the soft hay. A wide smile split Seth's face at the sight of the beautiful black foal that was already struggling to stand. He carefully moved backward to watch as the mother started cleaning the baby. "Very nice," he said almost under his breath.

When he knew they would both be okay, he looked toward the large Cheyenne, but he didn't expect praise. He merely asked, "Is there somewhere I can clean up?"

"There's a small room at the back of the barn," Kasey replied roughly.

Seth stood, brushing past the sheriff, not noticing the way the man stiffened. He located the room, turned on the faucet, and grabbed the bar of soap resting on the edge. It was a good thing he hadn't needed to worry about another episode, because he couldn't trust someone who obviously didn't trust in his ability. If only the man knew. His mouth turned down at the corners at how much he actually seemed to care what the sheriff thought. It didn't matter, he told himself sharply. The man was a bigot.

Suddenly, he felt more exhausted than he had in months. It had been a long day, and the tense emotion between him and the sheriff was heavy, weighing him down like lead. When he exited the small washroom, the sheriff wasn't inside the barn. Seth gathered his things, exiting the barn. He didn't see the man anywhere out front, either. Sighing, he was wondering if he would have to walk back to town when the front door opened. The sheriff stepped out onto the front porch, his boots scraping the wood floor. "You ready?" the man demanded.

Seth's jaw clenched, but he merely gave a short nod. Not a

word breached the silence between them during the ride back, and Seth was so happy to see his clinic. Even more so than he had been that morning. "Good night, Sheriff."

"Night," the man bit out.

Seth watched the truck roar out of the parking lot, shaking his head. Stubborn, foolish man.

Seth slid into the front seat of his car, heaving a tired sigh. His body hurt, ached with a fierceness that always came after he expended energy healing. Since he'd been a child, he'd had the unnatural ability to see inside animals to find whatever illness they suffered, and he was able to remove that illness, but not without paying a price. His body absorbed the bad energy causing the disease or sickness and had to eliminate it once he'd finished. Most of the time it was a simple matter of dispelling the energy by vomiting, but sometimes, if the sickness were severe enough, his body would need to find another outlet. Usually through bloodletting. Either way, it left him exhausted and fragile.

A yawn broke free as he started the car, and he knew if he didn't get home soon, he would be in danger of falling asleep at the wheel. The little house he'd rented, perfect for just himself, rested on the edge of the forest: two bedrooms with one and a half bathrooms, a small living room but a wide open kitchen, was more than enough for one. He loved to cook, so the kitchen was one of the features that had drawn him to the little house.

When he pulled into the driveway, he smiled when he heard his golden retriever, Bullet, barking at the door. He'd found Bullet as a puppy bleeding to death from a gunshot wound. Even his ability wasn't able to remove a bullet, but despite all odds saying that the puppy would die, he'd pulled through. Seth had kept him as a constant companion since. That had been three years ago.

Thinking of Bullet reminded him of the sheriff's words

about white men knowing nothing about animals. It was true. There were so many animals in the world that were on the verge of extinction because of how little respect humans had for the creatures. But it wasn't just white men. Almost all humans destroyed animals every day, whether by the simple act of killing one by hitting it with their vehicle or the act of clearing a wooded area to make room for more houses or business complexes. It always left him sad when he heard of such things happening again and again. The sheriff couldn't have been more wrong about him, though.

He ruthlessly shoved those thoughts from his mind. He would not allow the sheriff's words to affect him. Blinded by hate, the sheriff couldn't see that not everyone behaved the same way. Dragging his feet, Seth entered the house, greeting Bullet tiredly. "Hey, boy," he murmured.

Bullet whined and shoved his head beneath Seth's hand. Seth laughed quietly, stroking the big dog behind his ears. "I'm happy to see you too. It's been a long day, though. I promise I will take you with me to the clinic tomorrow, okay, boy? There's a big yard in the back that you can run in."

The dog let out an excited bark, wagging his tail at him happily. Seth refilled the dog's bowls with food and water before collapsing on the couch, which was as far as he got. He immediately fell into a dream-filled sleep.

At first, the sheriff starred in a big way, sending his body into overdrive. Naked bodies twisted together in passion with soft sighs and low moans. Seth shifted in his sleep as his cock pressed uncomfortably against the front of his slacks. But the dream slowly transitioned into the nightmare he'd lived and breathed for months. The one that had haunted him ever since. A whimper cut through the small house at the remembered fear and pain. The sweet scent of blood still stung his nose acridly. There was so much of it, and he couldn't stop it.

Seth shot up with a loud gasp, shaky and terrified. Sweat soaked his clothing while shudders ravaged his body. He ran a hand over his face and glanced at the clock. Already four in the morning. He knew he'd never get back to sleep after the nightmare, so he wearily stood up from the couch to get ready to face the day. A shower revived him slightly, but only coffee would truly erase the shadows hiding behind his eyes.

He dressed swiftly, tugging on a pair of faded blue jeans and a gray T-shirt. Deciding to head to the clinic early, Seth called for Bullet, who immediately started leaping against the front door. Laughing, Seth opened the door, and the dog raced to the car, turning in circles in excitement. "I know it's been a while since you came with me to work, boy. Now remember to behave yourself, okay?"

The dog let out a bark like he was actually answering him. Seth gave the dog a pleased smile before opening the driver's side door and letting him into the vehicle. Seconds later, they were on the road into town.

Since the clinic didn't open until eight, he stopped by the local diner to pick up a cup of coffee to go. He left the windows open for Bullet, commanding him to stay inside. The diner only had a handful of people at the moment, thankfully, because when he opened the door, every head in the place swiveled around to stare at him. He smiled, urging his heart to stop pounding. "Good morning," he greeted the girl behind the counter, quickly eyeing her name tag, "Bridget."

"Well, good morning to you, Doc," Bridget replied, leaning against the counter. Fair skin with light-blonde hair, dark-green eyes, and a large chest made it obvious her lineage wasn't Cheyenne. If he hadn't been a gentleman, he might have laughed at how she pushed her breasts up to make them appear more impressive for him. As it was, he had to hide a smile behind a cough. "What can I get for you?"

"Just a large cup of coffee to go, if you don't mind," he requested, taking a seat at the counter.

"Sure thing, darlin'." She winked at him before walking away.

Seth shook his head and ran a hand through his still-damp hair. He could feel the curious gaze of the others in the diner. Though he'd only taken a quick glance around, he'd been able to take in that there were two men at the table in the back nearest the restrooms. Another table held a small Caucasian woman with two children who were obviously still waking up this early in the morning, as they were actually seated at the table without screaming or throwing things. And a single Anglo male sat at the other end of the bar from him. Tension hung in the air around him, and he felt certain his arrival had caused the strain. They obviously didn't trust him.

"Here ya go, Doc," Bridget bubbled, placing a steaming Styrofoam cup in front of him. "That'll be one dollar and twenty-five cents."

Digging his wallet out of his pocket, he pulled out a five. "Don't worry about the change," he said as he grabbed up several packets of sugar and a small container of creamer.

The bell over the door behind him rang out clearly in the nearly empty diner. He stiffened when he became aware of the sudden hostility behind him. He'd been about to prepare his coffee there, but knowing that the sheriff was there made him change his mind. "Thanks, Bridget," he said, turning to leave.

The sheriff stood there in civilian clothing. Tight jeans molded to his strong thighs, and a white T-shirt plastered itself to his chest like a second skin. Seth's breath hitched in his throat, and he had to swallow twice to bid the man, "Good morning, Sheriff."

The man glared at him but returned his greeting stiffly.

"Morning," he said as he brushed by Seth, heading toward the other end of the counter. Seth caught a glimpse of a tattoo on the Cheyenne's upper arm. He couldn't quite see its entirety, but he could just barely make out a tribal symbol.

Sighing internally, he shoved his way out of the diner. Bullet hung halfway out of the window eagerly. "Come on, Bullet, move over." The dog barked loudly, drawing the gaze of the customers in the diner, including the dark eyes that seemed to bore right through him. He started mumbling under his breath, "I really hoped this would be a place that we could stay, Bullet, but now I'm not so sure."

Chessie's car was out in front of the clinic when he arrived, and she greeted him in her usual cheerful manner. "Good morning, Doc. Oh! What do we have here?" She came around the front of her desk and knelt down, laughing as she accepted the slobbery kisses that the golden retriever laid on her. "What's his name?" She looked up at Seth.

"His name is Bullet. I usually bring him with me to work so he isn't cooped up in the house all day long, but in wanting to get the residents comfortable with me, I didn't have the chance. But he'll be joining me every day from now on. Right, boy?"

Bullet barked and rubbed against Seth, who promptly smiled happily. Having the dog near him always boosted his spirits. Perhaps the reason had something to do with his ability, but he couldn't be certain it wasn't because the dog had saved his life on more than one occasion.

"Well, I think he's just adorable," Chessie gushed, hugging Bullet once again before standing up. "Your first appointment isn't until nine, and it's going to be a little slow today. There are only a handful of appointments."

Seth frowned at her. "Is that usual?"

She tried to hide the flash of chagrin in her eyes, but she wasn't fast enough. He gave her a look, and she sighed. "No.

Usually Doc Redfern was booked most of the day. I'm sorry, Seth, but until you prove yourself to the town, you'll find that most of them aren't very trusting. Especially...." She trailed off, but he was pretty sure he knew what she'd been about to say.

"Especially because I'm white," he said bitterly. Her eyes widened in surprise. "Don't worry, Chessie. I've already had that hammered into my head by the sheriff. He came in with an emergency last night. One of his horses was having a difficult birth. The foal had turned. He almost walked out and didn't want me to treat the horse because I'm white. Make sure you send him a bill for the emergency call." He spun on his heel and stomped to his office. Just when he'd thought that maybe things might work out here, it turned out to be a town full of closed-minded bigots.

The rest of his day went by smoothly. Most of the appointments were for annual shots, and thankfully, none were serious enough to require him using his ability. The last appointment left at just after five, and Seth sank down in his desk chair with relief. Bullet immediately put his head in Seth's lap, whining to be petted. Seth's hand dropped down on the large silky head, and he idly stroked the dog behind his ears. The customers who had been in that day were, in fact, wary of him. It left him baffled at how they could all believe that he knew nothing about animals. He'd spent eight years learning about them. He might be young, but he knew his shit.

The intercom buzzed just then. "Doc, I'm going to be leaving for the day. Is there anything else you need?"

"No, but thanks, Chessie. Have a good night," he bid her.

"You too, Doc." He could clearly hear the concern in her voice, and maybe he should be worried as well. If all of the clients in the area refused to come into his clinic, he'd go bankrupt for sure. He'd put all of his money into this place.

The thought left him more resigned than panicked. Bankruptcy would only add to the weight already on his shoulders.

Bullet whined again, bringing him from his thoughts, and then the hackles on the back of the dog's neck stood up. He started growling, crowding close to Seth. Seth's heart started to pound. The dog would never attack a human, and there had only been one other time that Bullet had reacted like that. Looking around wildly, he looked for a weapon, anything he could use, but there wasn't really anything in his office. Standing, he peered out into the dim hallway while Bullet kept tugging on his pant leg to try and stop him. "Bullet," he reprimanded quietly.

The dog let him go but stuck close to him as he walked toward the front of the clinic. Eerie silence met him in the front lobby. Chessie had locked the door behind her, but Bullet didn't stop growling. He merely grew fiercer. Seth carefully turned the lock on the door and pulled it open, bracing himself. The parking lot sat empty except for his car. Eyes darting in every direction, he took hold of Bullet's collar, locked the door, and started toward his vehicle. "It's okay, Bullet," he murmured, trying to reassure himself more than the dog.

His hand had just settled on the door handle of his car when he heard a sound behind him. A small scream lodged itself in his throat as he whirled around. Bullet let out a vicious bark, crouching low beside Seth. Blessed relief flooded Seth when he saw the sheriff. He slumped against his car, shushing Bullet. "Evenin', Sheriff," he said, cursing the quaver in his voice.

The man stopped, frowning. He could see fear lurking in Seth's eyes. Was he afraid of him, or was something else going on? "Doc," he replied stiffly. "Something wrong?"

Seth shook his head quickly, probably too quickly when

he saw the dark gaze narrow at the edges. "No, it's nothing." Bullet's hackles were still raised, and his eyes were trained on the sheriff. "You just scared me is all," he hedged.

Kasey stared at the man in front of him. He'd long ago learned how to smell a lie, and the vet was lying. Kasey's eyes scanned the area around them, but nothing stood out. Fear rolled off the other male, tangible and harsh. Kasey scowled mentally at the almost protective feeling that struck through him at the thought of someone hurting the dark-haired doctor. "You certain, Doc? You seem kinda jumpy."

"I'm sure," Seth stated quietly. Bullet was no longer growling, but the dog never once looked away from the sheriff. Seth started to turn but stopped, looking back at the man who'd dominated his thoughts the night before. "Good night, Sheriff."

Bullet almost didn't want to get in the car, and Seth had to force him. "What is wrong with you, Bullet?" he muttered as he started the car, very aware of the sheriff still watching him pull out of the parking lot. What was the sheriff doing there, anyway? It seemed strange for the man to just show up outside his clinic without a reason.

K ASEY watched the car's taillights disappearing down the road. His hands clenched at his sides. He'd unconsciously walked toward the clinic. Something about the other male drew him, but he couldn't put his finger on what. He was angry about the clinic being taken over by a white man who couldn't possibly understand the ways of his people, but it pissed him off even more how often Seth Davies entered his mind. Yet the way the man handled the horse the night before had been so gentle, and the horse seemed to calm almost immediately. When he'd seen those small, fragile hands trailing over the heaving sides of his horse, his mind imagined them gliding over his body and touching him. His cock responded to those images in his mind, and that left him angrier still.

With the night growing later, anxiety nipped at Kasey to head into the forest. He'd found his mate. Three nights ago, he'd been unable to resist the urge to run in his wolf form and had entered the forest at his usual place. Not long after, he'd caught the most delicious scent. A scent that called to him so powerfully his cock swelled and the nerves just underneath his skin twitched in excitement. An underlying sweet scent of cinnamon and blood brought him to a clearing where a beautiful black wolf rested under a tree, a mostly decimated hare lying nearby. He had only observed at first, but the sheer joy of finally finding his mate had sent him cautiously into the clearing.

His joy turned to dismay when the wolf picked up his scent and immediately bristled in terror. He could clearly see the lithe, muscular body and the black fur quivering nervously in the moonlight flooding the small field. His mate hadn't recognized him and had bolted, crashing through the bushes into the dense forest. Kasey had given chase, but he had lost the wolf in the overgrown brush.

Each night since, he had returned to the forest, hoping and praying his mate would return. His heart ached that he might have missed his only opportunity to capture his mate. He tried to imagine what she would look like in human form, but the stubborn image of the new veterinarian in town kept straying into his mind. Impossible! He'd never been overly attracted to another male, and the vet did not smell like his mate. He felt certain of it. Besides, even if his mate did turn out to be a man, there was no way in hell his mate would be white.

He started back to his truck, intent on getting to the clearing and looking for the black wolf. His mother had told him that she'd taken Samantha to see the doctor, and he'd told her the dog suffered from nothing more than a mere case of upset stomach, but Kasey knew something was wrong with the dog's heart. His powerful sense of hearing alerted him to the irregularity of her heartbeat. But when he'd smirked at the misdiagnosis on the vet's part, which reinforced his opinion of how little white men knew about animals, he'd listened to the dog's heart again. Only this time there was a difference. Her heartbeat sounded steady and even. The smirk had slowly faded to be replaced by disbelief and confusion. Somehow Samantha's heart defect had disappeared.

Julian, his pack mate, claimed he was getting senile in his old age and he hadn't really heard anything wrong with the dog's heart. He'd promptly walloped the pup on the back of the head. He was positive the dog had a heart murmur, one that would eventually have been fatal. Pride kept him from demanding answers from the dark-haired vet, but he knew something had changed since the visit to the doctor.

It was close to midnight by the time he reached the forest, and he swiftly shifted to his wolf form, eager to find his mate. Nothing could ever compare to the joy he felt as a wolf. He'd never really questioned why he'd been lucky enough to be born wolf, but he'd spent many hours researching his people. The world's definition of werewolves was so skewed that Kasey could hardly believe how the legends had changed from life, light, and acceptance to horror, death, and blood. Their kind didn't mutate and reshape like it was depicted in the movies. The magic caused them to take on another form by mere thought, their clothing hidden along with their human form by the gift of their kind. There was no tearing of cloth, no painful trans-formation, and certainly no brutal attack on humans. Only the Created ones who lived as animals, by instinct and hunger, were likely to kill a human. His kind didn't tolerate the Created in their territory. They were either run out of town or, if they refused to leave, tracked and put down by the pack Enforcer.

The clearing where he'd first come across the wolf wasn't far from where he'd parked his truck, and it only took a matter of minutes to reach it. He lifted his nose into the air, scenting the sweet cinnamon smell of her dark fur, but his hopes were dashed when he found no fresh trail. Warring with himself internally, he debated whether to stay or go, eventually choosing to wait for just a little while longer in case the black wolf did show. He settled his lean, muscular form beneath a tree to wait.

Kasey knew that other wolves existed in the world. There were other packs dotted over the United States, all of Native American descent, but another kind of wolf roamed the earth, a kind that was like a disease upon the land. They were the Created. A wolf changed, not born. From time to time one of the Created came to their town and the pack would do whatever necessary to protect themselves and their secret. The Created were an abomination and not to be trusted.

The legend of the Created ones began with their ancestors thousands of years ago. One of the first wolf shifters was mated to a human, a non-shifter who could only stand by on the full moon and watch as her mate ran with the others. Saddened by his mate's pain at being unable to join him, the wolf prayed to their gods, seeking a way to change his mate to become one of them and grant her the ability to shift. Many moons passed before his answer came, but the winds whispered for him to be careful, for he could lose his mate to the nature of the beast inside. The first Created one was born of the life's essence running through the true wolf's veins and the seed from his loins exchanged on the night of a full moon.

Over time, the Created one began to show signs of the wolf's instincts, and the human side was slowly buried beneath the cunning and agility of the beast. Her aggression toward non-shifters, lack of interest in anything more than hunting and running among the trees, and eventual attack on the human mate of another made the true wolf realize his mate's animal nature was taking over, just as the winds had warned him. When his Alpha instructed the pack Enforcer to destroy her, his soul cried to the heavens, begging their gods to forgive him. With her blood upon his head, he took his own life, unable to bear what he'd done to his mate. A new pack law was passed forbidding the conversion of another non-shifter, and any who defied the law were put to death along with the Created one.

Kasey couldn't help but wonder if it was possible his mate was one of the Created. His heart lurched at the thought. What if she was? What if that beautiful black wolf had originated as human? He gritted his teeth, refusing to believe it. *Never*, he thought fiercely.

The sound of something brushing past the low-hanging branches and through the shrubbery of the forest floor reached his ears. They perked forward as his shrewd gaze peered into the darkness around him. Soft, happy panting sent his heart into overdrive. He didn't move, merely waited for the wolf to come to him. When it entered the clearing, he saw it come to a stop, scenting the air. Dark-blue eyes settled on Kasey lounging beneath the shadows of the tree. The wolf bared its teeth and started backing away.

Kasey stood slowly, trying to show he was harmless. A low whimper issued from Kasey's throat as he lowered his head, peering up at the other wolf. The wolf didn't seem to notice the subjugation in his actions and continued to growl while moving further from Kasey.

He wouldn't lose her now. Some wolves never found their true mates, and he wouldn't let her go, no matter what. He began to walk toward the black wolf that was so similar to his own form. His heart leapt when the wolf stopped, watching him carefully. But when he was within a matter of yards from the other wolf, it turned and ran. *No*, he shouted in his mind, and he gave chase.

Fear wafted off the other wolf in waves, and Kasey wanted nothing more than to comfort and soothe his mate. It broke his heart that she feared him. Kasey knew these woods like the backs of his hands, knew each and every turn, every path and canyon. So when he saw the wolf turn toward one of the cliffs that looked out over a rushing river below, horror flooded him. The black wolf didn't seem to realize the danger. Kasey let forth a warning howl, but the other wolf ignored it or didn't understand his call, merely pushing herself faster. Terror gripped him tightly inside when he saw the black wolf struggle to a stop a little too late and go tumbling over the edge.

Kasey frantically raced to the cliff, managing to stop, and peered over the edge. The black wolf lay on a low outcropping of rocks just above the river. A soft breath of relief huffed from his muzzle before he closed his eyes and shifted back to his human form. He would need both hands to get to her. The wolf lay alarmingly still as he began to make the treacherous climb down to her. His fingers dug into the side of the cliff as he hung on with superhuman strength. His feet searched for purchase on the slippery, dirt-covered rocks jutting from the side of the cliff. The scent of blood reached his nostrils about halfway down, and his heart lurched painfully.

When he dropped down to the outcropping, he crouched next to the black wolf, running his hands over her limbs. Thankfully, as werewolves, they healed faster than normal humans, though it would still be painful as the broken front leg knit itself together again. Several gashes ran the length of the wolf's sides, and there was another large slice along her left cheek. Glancing around, Kasey searched for another way up. He wouldn't be able to carry the other wolf back up to the top of the cliff, and there was no way in hell he'd leave his mate here. The only thing he could do was follow the bank of the river and search for a clear pathway.

Gingerly, Kasey slipped his arms beneath the black wolf. He winced when his mate whimpered in unconsciousness, knowing he was hurting her further but having no choice. His body sang out in joy at the feel of the black fur against his skin. Closing his eyes for a brief moment, he breathed in the strong scent of cinnamon wafting off of his mate, taking it deep into his lungs. His eyes flashed when they opened just before he carefully hefted the warm weight into his arms. His mate felt shockingly dainty and slender. Hardly any weight rested in his arms at all. Frowning, he wondered if his mate had been starving herself.

He couldn't concentrate on that now. The banks of the river were going to be difficult to traverse. When the river swelled and breached its banks, the dirt became miles of mud before the river eventually flooded the entire ravine. Thankfully, the rainy season didn't start for another couple of days, but there was still no guarantee it was safe. He hesitantly began to make the trek downriver.

Over the next hour, his mate never stirred, garnering further concern. If the injuries were severe, she'd need their pack Healer. Relief speared sharply through Kasey when he spotted a steep trail leading back up into the forest. His feet were sure as he climbed it, never faltering under the weight of his mate.

He finally reached his truck and delicately settled the black wolf on the passenger seat, making sure she rested comfortably, and then covered her with an old quilt to ward off any chill. Kasey hurriedly climbed into the driver's seat, heading for the reservation as fast as he dared. The Healer would know what to do. Kasey's hands tightened on the steering wheel as he glanced over at the motionless form next to him. He didn't know why the wolf had been so terrified of him or hadn't recognized him as her mate, but he would do whatever it took for her to accept him.

Almost two hours passed before the pack Healer could examine the injured wolf. Instead of heading to his home,

Kasey turned toward the cabin owned by the pack. It was closer to the reservation and the Healer.

Kasey remained tense as he watched Charlie Blackhawk examining the black wolf. "Is she going to be okay, Charlie?"

Charlie gave a small laugh as he checked on the leg that had been broken during the fall. It was already slowly repairing itself, but with the amount of time between the break and the wolf's arrival, the bone would need to be re-broken and set properly. The wolf had lost a lot of blood as well, which was sure to leave it weakened. "She is a he, and I am afraid that we must break the bone again, Kasey. There is no other choice. If we do not, it will heal improperly, and he will not be able to walk without discomfort and a limp."

Kasey sucked in a breath, his face paling at the thought of having to hurt his mate all over again, but the Healer was right, so he agreed with a reluctant nod. "All right," he muttered, filing away the fact his mate was male for later perusal.

"Come hold him down by the shoulders, Kasey. Hold him tight, because I fear he will wake up when it is done." Charlie waited for Kasey to move into position before gripping the leg close to break. The Healer could sense the wolf stirring, and there was no way the pain would not bring him into full consciousness. Taking a deep breath, he twisted, re-fracturing the half-repaired bone.

Kasey winced at the sound of bone cracking, and the slender body beneath his hands shuddered. A loud yelp of pain suddenly issued from the wolf, and he came awake with a vengeance, struggling to get away. Kasey put as much weight on the wolf as he dared while Charlie, working quickly, realigned the bone and strapped on the splint. Kasey crooned to his mate, trying to soothe him. "Shhh, pup, it'll be okay. The pain is over."

The wolf continued to struggle until he'd exhausted

himself and couldn't move. Charlie examined the other cuts, but only one deep cut on his left side concerned him. "He's your mate, isn't he?" Charlie asked intuitively while working to stitch up the deep gash in the wolf's side.

Kasey could only manage a gentle nod, anguish tightening his throat.

Charlie gave a sigh before saying, "You will have your hands full with this one. His mind is unsettled and filled with much pain and terror. I am afraid that he has suffered some sort of abuse, and it will take all of the patience you lack, Kasey, to gain his trust. If you do not learn to control yourself, you will not be able to get through to him."

"I will do whatever it takes," Kasey swore roughly, his throat raw. Charlie had never been wrong.

Charlie did not tell Kasey what else he'd sensed, for it must be something the other male discovered for himself. He merely nodded, passing a hand over the wolf's side to relieve some of his distress. "Rest, young one. No one here will hurt you. I promise you."

The black wolf calmed slightly, although not completely. His eyes never lost their wary look, and he shuddered at regular intervals. Kasey barely noticed the chair Charlie shoved toward him other than to hook his boot around the leg and pull it closer. He would not leave his mate. The ever-present fear clinging to his mate was like a sting to his skin, pressing into him as if it were needles. The hand not touching his mate clenched upon his thigh. Knowing someone had hurt the black wolf left him battling with the rage he felt at that unknown assailant. If he ever had the chance, he'd rip them limb from limb.

Eventually, he felt the wolf let go and fall into sleep, if not because he trusted that they wouldn't hurt him, then to escape the pain. The bone would be completely healed within the next day or so, but it was a painful process. Kasey knew from experience, having broken several bones over his thirty-two years. He allowed his hand to sift through the soft black fur. It felt so good beneath his palm, and it sent a sharp shaft of arousal through his body. His teeth elongated slightly, pressing into his bottom lip. More than anything, he wanted to claim his mate, but it did not appear he would be able to do so for some time. "I have a feeling you're going to lead me on a very long chase, pup," he murmured, his breath causing one of his mate's ears to flicker.

Kasey allowed his cheek to press against the warm back. His eyes slid closed as he once again tried to picture the delicate male wolf in his human form. A scowl settled between his eyebrows as, once again, the white veterinarian's face popped into his head. Damn it. How could he possibly be thinking about the infuriating doctor when he was actually touching and caressing his mate? If he had anything to say about it, the man wouldn't be staying in town long. He had to find some way to make him leave.

The warmth radiating from his mate and the soft, gentle breathing began to lull Kasey into a light sleep. He drifted, never once relinquishing the gentle hold he had on the other wolf. He was so afraid that the other male would disappear. Nothing would keep him from having him. If patience was what it took, he'd find a way to be patient. He just prayed he could make the other shifter believe he wasn't going to hurt him before he ran off into the forest and never returned.

S ETH struggled out of the darkness, grimacing at the agony coursing through his veins. Why was he in pain? He searched his memory for the details of the previous evening before it hit him. He whined low in his throat at the vivid details of being chased through the forest before stumbling over the edge of a cliff. He remembered the ground rushing up at him, and he'd thought for sure he was dead. Then he relived the pain he'd abruptly woken to as an older man had re-broken his back leg. After it had been reset and put into a splint, he'd heard the deep, throaty voice of the sheriff there as well. The word "mate" echoed over and over inside his head. Mate? He was no one's mate.

A growl rumbled in his throat as he realized the heavy warmth on his side was someone's head. The warmth lifted away, and a strong hand scratched behind his ears. Seth felt his body react in a strange manner, almost leaning into the touch. Horrified, he worked at getting a grip on his actions. Wrenching his head away from the other male, he made to sit up, but the hands were there pushing him down. "No, don't move. You'll only injure yourself further."

He stiffened as the sheriff came into view. How could he have been so stupid? That explained why Bullet had disliked the sheriff immediately. Seth bared his teeth at the other man, who stepped back slightly, lifting his hands in a supplicating gesture. "I won't hurt you, pup. I swear it."

Pup? The man called him pup? Seth moved again, only to let out a fiercely pained whine as the leg he'd broken objected. The sheriff immediately returned to his side, pressing him down. "Please don't move," the man practically pleaded with him.

Seth knew he wasn't going anywhere anytime soon, so he relented and settled back on the soft mattress beneath him. The bone would mend quickly, quicker than a human's. He snarled warningly at the sheriff, whose hands were still on him. The dark-haired Cheyenne pulled his hands away and resumed his seat beside the bed. "I know you can't speak," he said quietly, "and I'm going to take the time I have until you're healed to convince you that I mean you no harm. My name is Kasey, Kasey Whitedove. I'm also a shifter, a werewolf."

He knew that much! After the previous evening's events, he'd kind of figured it out. "You're also... my true mate," Kasey said, with such reverence Seth twitched in discomfort.

He didn't believe true mates existed. He'd learned as much in his past. His ears flattened to his head, and he snapped at Kasey, warning him off. The man's face fell in disappointment, and Seth's heart twinged in his chest. He didn't understand the guilt running through him for hurting the sheriff. Why should he care? He ruthlessly shoved the feeling deep down. Kasey just wanted to use him like all the rest. They weren't mates. Seth's mind demanded he never forget the lessons he'd learned all too well.

"I don't understand why you can't feel it, pup, but it's there. So tangible and real," Kasey insisted. "Some of us search forever to find our mates and never find them. I will show you we are meant to be."

Seth turned his muzzle away from Kasey, deciding to ignore the bigger male. He already knew Kasey hated him. Once he'd shifted back to human form, Kasey would change his mind, and he wouldn't want to be mated to him. Seth wasn't Cheyenne. For some reason, the realization pained him more than his broken leg. A fine tremble worked its way through his body. His eyes burned alarmingly, and he blinked quickly. What the hell was this? It felt as though his heart would shrivel inside his chest. Eyes widening in terror, he lifted his head and searched his body, desperate to know if the sheriff had already marked him as his. But the only marks he felt were the ones from his fall. If the son of a bitch had marked him, he'd kill him.

"I didn't mark you," Kasey said stiffly. "Besides, it wouldn't work unless we mated at the time I made the mark."

Sheer relief caused Seth to slump down to the bed again. He'd been born as a werewolf, and until a few years ago, he'd never known other wolves existed, but he'd learned quickly and harshly about the world of werewolves. His parents had known his secret, shared his secret, and protected him from the world. But they'd taught him to be careful and never to reveal his true nature to anyone. If he had the chance, he must leave here without letting Kasey know his real identity.

"I wish I could talk to you," the man said agitatedly, interrupting his thoughts. "There is so much I wish to know. Were you born this way? Are you one of the Created? What do you look like in your human form? How long have you been on your own? Why are you so frightened of me?" He broke off for a moment, studying the toes of his boots before looking up and capturing Seth's gaze. "I could never hurt you, pup. You are a part of me."

Seth whined and lifted his paw up to press against the ear not resting on the bed. He didn't want to hear this. He was no one's mate. He didn't want to be anyone's mate. Being a mate meant pain and fear and blood.

"I don't know what has happened to you in the past, but I promise you I won't give up. You will come to trust me," Kasey stated calmly and with certainty.

If he'd been in his human form, Seth would have snorted and said good luck, but he merely rolled his canine eyes. It would take at least a day or even two days for his limb to heal enough that he could shift back. He gnashed his teeth together, wondering what he would tell Chessie about why he had just up and disappeared for forty-eight hours without letting her know. What could he possibly tell her?

Kasey's voice cut through his thoughts again. "I was born a werewolf. Most of us are on the reservation. But there are some that are not born that way. We call them the Created. They're an abomination, a travesty. They are not allowed in our territory and never allowed to join our pack. Since I first saw you three nights ago, I've wondered if you are one of them. One of the Created." Frustration entered Kasey's voice.

"Are you one of the Created? Were you bitten and changed? Just... just shake your head no if you aren't."

Seth refused to answer him. Instead, he just closed his eyes and ignored the other male. Even the wolves in this territory were bigots. Were they born hating others? Why would they hate wolves who had been bitten and changed?

A strong hand gripped his muzzle, forcing his eyes to open wide in surprise. Dark eyes glittered fiercely, but pain shimmered in their depths.

"Please... tell me."

Huffing indignantly, Seth glowered at him but shook his head. The stiffness in Kasey's body seemed to desert the older man all at once, bringing him to his knees beside the bed. "Thank God," he breathed.

Seth wrenched his muzzle from the man's grip and bared his teeth in warning. Kasey's hand lay on the bed near his muzzle, but he didn't move it. "You won't bite me," he said confidently.

Arrogant bastard, wasn't he? Seth shoved at Kasey's hand with his paw, attempting to push him away, but that warm, tanned hand wrapped around his paw gently, holding it. Seth tensed as pure emotion slammed into him, twisting his gut tightly. Heat, lust, and affection all slammed into him at once. His head whirled with the strength of it all. He felt as though he knew this man, like he recognized him in some primeval way. No... no, this couldn't be happening. He gave a pained whine at the depth of the feelings swirling through him, his mind and his heart. Angry, he clamped his jaws down on the hand holding him but didn't bite, just held it there, growling a warning.

Kasey didn't struggle to pull away but merely waited for the wolf to release him.

Seth wanted to bite down, wanted to injure this man trying to claim him as his mate. He didn't want this. The sheriff lifted his free hand, and Seth's ears dropped down flat to his head as he flinched. But instead of a cruel fist crashing into the side of his face, the hand came to rest gently on the top of his head. Those long, lean fingers softly traced through the fur on the top of his head, scratching easily.

"I won't hurt you," Kasey murmured, "even if you hurt me. I will never touch you in anger, pup."

Seth whined again in confusion. He'd just threatened to hurt a stronger wolf. Why was there no punishment? His jaws loosened, and he pulled his mouth away from Kasey's hand. What was this man doing to him? He started to struggle to stand, wanting away from him, away from these things he had never wanted to feel for another wolf.

Kasey sighed but moved away. "I am sorry, pup. Forgive me for being overeager. It isn't my intention to make you uncomfortable. For now, I will leave things alone. But once you return to your human form, we will talk."

That's what you think, Seth thought with finality. He would never let Kasey know the truth. He might have pretty words to say now, but if Kasey knew that Seth was the white veterinarian that he despised, he would surely take those words back. *More like choke on them*, Seth thought bitterly. There was no doubt in his mind that Kasey Whitedove would be horrified if he saw Seth standing there when he shifted.

Kasey stood and moved toward the bedroom door. "I'm going to go get you something to eat. You'll need to keep up your strength until you heal."

Seth watched him leave. If he thought he'd make it, he'd stand up and leave, but it would only damage the bone further, so he chose to stay for the time being. His eyes closed as he tried to think of how to get away from the other man. He'd come to Senaka in the hopes of getting away from other wolves. When he'd visited the town prior to moving there, he'd sensed no others in the area. But hearing Kasey talk about his pack had left him shocked so many lived there. Thankfully he'd learned a long time ago how to mask the scent he gave off when in human form. It prevented others from finding him easily. His parents had taught him how to gather his power around him and shield the aura he gave off. When he shifted, the guise dropped, allowing others to identify his true being. Another reason he'd chosen to move to such a secluded town. The woods gave him the chance to run wild and free as a wolf. Or so he'd thought.

It left him feeling cornered and afraid, knowing so many werewolves resided in the area. It also made him sad, because he would need to start making preparations to leave. He liked the small town. It was peaceful, and despite the reception from the sheriff, he felt the people there were good people. And having the forest so conveniently close to his house gave him such a sense of home. For the first time in two years, he'd been able to run free as a wolf without fear of humans or other wolves. But if this was the territory of Kasey's pack, they would not welcome him on their land. If he'd been in his human form, he'd have cried in despair and frustration. He hadn't had a true home since his parents had died.

Twenty minutes later, Kasey returned carrying a tray laden with food. "Thought I'd join you in eating," he said in explanation as he set the tray down on the small nightstand. The smell of food wafted to Seth's nostrils, and his mouth watered. Kasey took one of the plates from the tray and set it on the bed next to Seth. Seth struggled to sit up, almost jumping out of his fur when hands slipped beneath his front legs and assisted him. When he was propped in a way he could eat, he leaned down and grabbed a piece of the lightly browned steak on the plate, chewing enthusiastically.

A husky laugh rumbled in Kasey's throat, but he didn't speak, instead concentrating on his own food.

Seth lapped at the plate when he had finished, licking up the rest of the juices from the steak. A small choked sound came from Kasey's direction, and he looked up, tilting his head at the red flush highlighting the Cheyenne's high cheekbones.

Sighing in satisfaction, Seth relaxed back onto the pillows behind him with a large yawn. His eyes were half slits by the time Kasey finished eating and took the plate from the bed. Exhaustion set in, and his head lolled closer and closer to the mattress. "Good night, pup," Kasey said softly as he exited the room.

3

S HADOWS darkened the room when Seth woke, and he had no idea how long he'd been sleeping. From what little he could see from where he lay, the sky appeared a slightly darker blue. His eyes widened in shock. He'd slept for at least fourteen hours, maybe even longer. He grimaced as he felt his bladder protesting. Gingerly, he tested his leg and found it was almost completely healed. A few more hours, maybe twelve, and he'd be as good as new. He carefully stood on the bed and had moved to the edge with the intent to jump off when he stopped abruptly. Kasey lay facedown on a sleeping bag on the floor beside the bed. Seth sank back onto his haunches and studied the larger male.

The Cheyenne's dark hair had come loose from the twine. It splayed out across the pillow like a black wave. His cheekbones were high and well defined, with a strong chin that sported a small cleft that had Seth wondering how it would taste. Scowling, Seth peered closer and noticed a small, light-brown mole right beneath Kasey's left eye. Sometime after Seth fell asleep, Kasey had taken off his shirt, baring his chest. What a chest, though! Seth's eyes ravished the toned muscles and dark-brown nipples, and he could see the tribal tattoos clearly. Several ran along Kasey's upper arms, while one started on his shoulder and curved around to his back. Seth studied it and realized it was an image of a wolf made from thick and wispy black lines. Seth wondered if there were any meanings behind the markings.

His bladder sent a sharp pain through his belly, reminding him of his urgent need, and he whined as he realized he wouldn't be able to jump over the muscular Native American beside his bed. Kasey must have been a light sleeper, because his eyes fluttered open before Seth's whine had finished. A frown graced his firm mouth, and he sat up quickly. "What's wrong?" Kasey demanded.

Seth saw his chance and hopped off the bed, wincing as his leg gave a twinge of pain. Instantly, Kasey appeared at his side, moving faster than Seth expected. "You can't leave." His voice held a small edge.

Seth glared at the sheriff but kept moving toward the door. Only he wouldn't be able to open it. He looked back at Kasey and woofed at him expectantly. The man moved slowly, hesitantly, to his side. "What is it?"

Seth woofed again, this time more insistently, and looked up at the door handle. Kasey opened the door, and Seth huffed in relief, still limping along until he got to the front door, where he glanced back at the man following him expectantly. Kasey shook his head. "You can't leave," he repeated. "You aren't completely healed yet, and we need to talk first."

Growling, he looked up at the door again. If the man didn't let him out, he'd go right there in the living room. Either way, he had to go to the bathroom. He barked this time and scratched at the door. He felt slightly humiliated that he had to act like a dog to get the sheriff to understand him. Finally, it seemed to dawn on the man what he wanted.

"Aw, hell. I didn't even think of that. Sorry, pup," Kasey muttered as he opened the door.

Seth moved as quickly as he could to the trees. He wasn't stupid and knew he wouldn't make it far with his leg still hurting. The sheriff didn't give him enough credit to be smart enough to know that much. When he was finished relieving himself, Seth returned to the house and walked past Kasey straight to the bedroom he'd been in. He noticed it wasn't a house but more of a one-bedroom log cabin, which explained why Kasey had slept on the hard floor instead of in a bed. Guilt speared him. He'd slept comfortably in a bed while Kasey had spent the night on a sleeping bag.

Stopping beside the bed, he eyed the height, wondering if he could get back into it. His leg wouldn't support the weight yet, so he chose to curl up on the sleeping bag. The instant his body hit the sheet, he groaned. The other shifter's scent surrounded him: a deep, woodsy aroma that spoke of spending long days in the sun surrounded by the trees.

Kasey came into the room a second later and spotted him on the floor. He strode forward, and before Seth could guess his intentions, the man picked him up and settled him into the bed. A warning issued from Seth's throat. Kasey stepped back, giving him an impatient look. "I just wanted to make sure you were comfortable."

Without giving himself time to think about his actions, Seth moved closer to the wall and eyed the tall Cheyenne. His paw slipped out and touched the bed beside him. Kasey's eyes widened in surprise as Seth drew the paw back, but no words were spoken as Kasey carefully slipped into the bed beside him. If he'd been human, Seth would have groaned at how stupid he'd just been. The scent came back full-force, and he could feel the heat radiating off the sheriff's body now. The combination caused lust to spiral through his body. He turned his head away from the stubborn man and buried his nose under the pillow. "Thanks, pup," he heard Kasey murmur beside him.

Seth knew he had to figure a way out of there without revealing his human side, but he would worry about it after his leg healed. He let himself drift back to sleep.

This time his sleep wasn't as deep or restful. Being exposed to an entire territory of wolves stirred up some of the muck of his past, bringing forth one of the many nightmares he endured night after night. He whimpered as he saw the blood, and his body twitched in remembrance of the pain. Teeth sank into his shoulder, causing him to scream in pain. Hands gripped at him, and he began to struggle.

"Pup! Pup, wake up!" a frantic voice sounded close to his ear.

Teeth sank deep into one of the hands, eliciting a sharp intake of breath from the owner of the voice. *Not again*, his mind screamed, *not again*. Tears spilled out from behind closed eyelids, soaking into the fur lining his face. The voice deepened, becoming husky with pain. "It's all right, pup. No one is going to hurt you. Never again. Wake up. Come back to me."

Seth's mind cleared of the terror-filled fog that had clouded it from the moment the dream began. The tangy taste of blood coated his mouth, and he realized his teeth were clamped down on someone's hand. Kasey! Oh shit. He immediately jolted wide awake, releasing Kasey and flying to the end of the bed as quickly as his leg would allow. He stared at the man in horror. Kasey cradled his hand against his chest, where blood started to soak into his shirt. No!

Seth let forth a howl so forlorn it sent shivers down the Cheyenne's spine. "It's all right," Kasey soothed, trying to move closer to where Seth crouched.

He shook his head at Kasey. No, it wasn't all right. He'd hurt someone, even if Kasey was another werewolf. Anger began to simmer in the dark eyes before him. Seth didn't blame Kasey. If their situations were reversed, he would be furious with him too.

Kasey was angry, but not at his mate. Fury at the person who'd hurt his pup stabbed through his veins. His hand throbbed, but the teeth marks had already begun to close over. The beaten, defeated air around the black wolf made his heart ache for his mate. He knew without a doubt someone had abused him. He swore viciously and then berated himself when he saw the other wolf flinch. He immediately regained control of himself. "I'm not mad at you, pup. I'm angry at whoever has treated you so badly. You wouldn't have hurt me if you hadn't been having a nightmare." He kept his voice sure and sincere.

"See? My hand is fine. I know you would never hurt me on purpose. Come lie back down." His hand patted the bed beside him as the black wolf watched him warily. Kasey's jaw clenched at the mistrusting gleam in those blue eyes he'd already come to cherish. He could hardly wait to meet his mate's human side. He was certain the other male had quite a personality with the attitude the wolf had given him already. Smiling disarmingly, he patted the bed again. "Please?"

Elation soared through Kasey when his mate slunk forward and sank down on the bed beside him. He laid his hand on the soft fur at the nape of his neck, earning a slight growl, but his mate did not try to shake it off. Kasey stroked his fingers gently over the black fur, soothing the wolf as best he could. "No one will hurt you ever again, pup. I swear it," he murmured.

Kasey felt the other shifter relax into sleep after a while. His thoughts wandered back over the reactions from his mate. Charlie had been right. It would take a lot of patience to earn his mate's trust. He just prayed he would be able to find the patience inside himself. His pup's scream of pain echoed in his ears, and he could only imagine what had happened to the wolf to cause him to make such a sound of agony. It spoke of such pain that it had almost shattered his heart when he'd heard it.

He knew he wouldn't be able to go back to sleep, so he merely lay there listening to his mate breathe. The leg would be healed by the time he woke again, and even if Kasey had to tie the wolf down, he wasn't leaving until he shifted. He would not allow his mate to leave him without being able to find him again.

When the sun rose completely into the sky, he sat up and moved to the chair nearby. His eyes did not leave the black wolf resting in his bed.

The wolf stirred not long after he'd awakened and lifted his head to peer around the room. "Good morning, pup," Kasey greeted him softly. "It's time to show me your human form."

His mate froze, eyes growing wary and watchful. Kasey sighed. "Come on, pup. I promise not to bite… yet." He grinned seductively at the black wolf.

Seth shuddered at the implication behind that. There was no way in hell he was changing back to his human form in front of Kasey. The man would more than likely want to shoot him or even go so far as to kill him, after Seth had bitten his hand last night, once he knew who Seth was.

Kasey's hand looked fine. There wasn't even a blemish where Seth's teeth had pierced the skin. He licked his lips in memory of the man's sweet taste in his mouth last night.

Unless he jumped through the glass window, he had no way out, and it didn't appear that Kasey intended to go anywhere anytime soon. A whimper stuck in his throat at being trapped again. He whined as he looked at Kasey. He saw the teasing gleam in Kasey's eyes dull as the man sat forward, a serious expression on his face. "I'm not going to hurt you. Please shift back, pup. Please," the man begged him.

Seth felt torn. He wanted to give in and believe what Kasey told him, but the image of those eyes turning from an almost tender look to a horrified one stopped him from shifting. The big Cheyenne wouldn't want a scrawny little nobody, especially a white guy like him.

Wait a minute... what the hell was he thinking? He didn't want this man to want him. Maybe if he did shift back, the man would leave him alone. It might be the only way to get him to stop insisting they were mates. Somewhere inside, the idea seemed to hurt, but he ruthlessly pulled on the cloak of numbness he usually wore around his emotions.

Steeling himself for the hatred the big man would certainly send his way, Seth closed his eyes and made the change. The bright flash of light caused Kasey to look away momentarily, but once Seth was in his full human form, the sheriff sucked in a deep breath. Rage began to glitter deep in those dark eyes. "What the fuck is this?"

Swallowing, Seth kept himself from shrinking back against the wall. He glared at the bigger werewolf. "What the fuck does it look like?"

"You're one of the Created!" Kasey stood, knocking the chair over and causing Seth to flinch when the chair cracked against the wooden floor.

"I am not!" he shouted. "I was born this way."

"You're lying!" Kasey stalked closer to the bed, looming over Seth, who this time could not stop himself from shrinking back against the wall behind him. Fear etched itself all over his face. "You are not Native American. Only my people are born this way! You are a white man."

Seth almost screamed when Kasey's hands wrapped around his shoulders and shook him. "Stop," he choked out.

"You told me you weren't one of them! I won't have one

of the Created for my mate. You're an abomination," Kasey growled, his hands tightening painfully on Seth's shoulders. "You don't even smell like wolf in your human form. That's not possible!"

Hurt punched Seth right in the gut, but he blocked out the pain. He'd known this would happen. Unable to take that punishing grip any further, he brought his arms up and slammed them against the sheriff's bigger forearms, knocking them away. In the blink of an eye, he was across the room, his hands fisted at his sides. "I won't be your mate either way, you son of a bitch. So you don't have to worry about it."

He drew himself to his full five foot eight inches and, hiding behind an icy expression he used to hide his true emotions, said, "Whether you choose to believe me or not is not my concern, Sheriff, but I was born a werewolf. And I don't smell like one because it's the only way to protect myself from assholes like you."

Seth didn't wait for a response. He ripped open the door and raced out of the cabin. The instant he hit the fresh air, he shifted again and, in a blur of black, crashed through the trees. He had no idea where he was, but at that moment in time, he didn't care. His chest hurt. His assumptions the man wouldn't want him afterward had been correct, but what he didn't understand was the feeling of his heart being ground up into a million pieces.

He felt a wet heat running over his muzzle, soaking into his fur, and to his utter disbelief, he realized he was crying. What the hell? He should be happy he'd been right. Now the sheriff would leave him alone. He wouldn't have to worry the man would—

His mind shut down those thoughts immediately. His heart already felt too raw from what had just happened to think about his past.

Kasey's words that he'd never hurt Seth and his endearment of "pup" rattled around inside his mind over and over again. It'd all been a lie. And for some reason, that hurt the most. His mind filled with bitterness at how he'd actually begun to believe the sheriff wouldn't hurt him. The grip on his shoulders had more than proved the man really had lied to him. And the words he'd used: "You're an abomination." Pain twisted deep in his gut. The words jabbed into his chest like knives. He'd always thought the same of himself until he'd found others like him. But now... now he wished he'd never dreamed of finding others, because all they'd ever done was hurt him.

ANGER surged through Kasey as he roared like a lion denied a kill, knocking over the table in the small kitchen area. Dishes shattered as they hit the ground. How could this have possibly happened? His fear of the black wolf being one of the Created had come to be true. And it turned out to be the infuriating veterinarian, to top it all off. Swear words spilled from his lips, turning the air blue.

Needing to burn off some of the rage coursing through this body, Kasey tore out of the log cabin and shifted on the run. A large black wolf leapt through the clearing and bounded into the trees, following a different path from the other wolf. His keen senses picked up the cinnamon scent of his mate. He growled at the thought of those words. His mate. He'd been overjoyed to find his true mate, but now he wished Seth had never come to Senaka.

A long howl shattered the silence as he raged at his gods. *Why? Why did it have to be one of them?*

Seth's dark-blue eyes flashed through his mind. Before the younger shifter had gotten control of his emotions, there'd been such pain in them. Kasey's conscience pricked as he remembered the fear on Seth's face as the vet had cowered beneath him. He'd sworn no one would ever hurt him again, not even himself, and he'd done exactly what he'd said he wouldn't allow. His guilt waged war against his rage. The insult that he, son of the Alpha, had a white man and a Created for a mate stung his pride fiercely.

Yet the knowledge he'd indeed found his mate also swirled around in his mind with all of the other information he'd just learned. Had he not sworn he wouldn't let his mate go now that he'd finally found him? But would his people be able to accept his mate as part of their pack? And what of Kasey being Alpha when his father passed on? He threw his head back again and let forth another howl that echoed through the trees.

His father would know what to do, and he was the only one Kasey could tell that his mate was one of the Created to without the rest of the pack finding out. Kasey loped off toward the reservation, heading for his father.

Kasey's father, Jeremiah Whitedove, held the love and adoration of their people as a firm yet gentle leader. He did not use force unless absolutely necessary. The entire pack loved and respected him. Kasey could only hope one day they would feel the same for him.

The houses on the reservation were mostly empty when he arrived. Most of the others had jobs and left for work early. He knew there would be questions, because he'd been gone for two days. While his mate had slept the night before, Kasey's deputy and pack mate, Julian Greywolf, had come to the cabin looking for him. Kasey had explained the situation to Julian, who'd immediately congratulated him on finding Seth. Julian would most certainly want to know why Kasey's mate wasn't with him when he returned to town.

He shifted to human form on his parents' front porch and entered the house. "Hey, Dad, you home?"

"In the kitchen, sweetie," his mother called out.

Smiling, he headed into the kitchen. His mother was a shrewd woman but one of the kindest you'd ever meet. Emily Whitedove wasn't able to shift into wolf form, but she certainly would have made a beautiful wolf.

Kasey's parents sat at the dinner table, but when his mother saw his face, she sat up straighter and looked him over in concern. "Did something happen, Kasey?"

Kasey scowled. What could he possibly say? With his shoulders feeling as though there were a huge weight on them, he sank down into the chair next to his father. His eyes shifted between wolf form and his human pupils in his agitation.

Jeremiah stared at his son and knew it must be serious with the scent of so many emotions rolling off him. "Is it one of the Created?" he asked sharply.

"Yes. No. I don't know," Kasey snapped. His hands clenched on his thighs. "I… found my mate."

Emily squealed in excitement. "Who is she? Is she beautiful? What's her name?"

"Emily," Jeremiah admonished gently, a fond look in his eyes.

"Don't go giving me any of that, Jeremiah Whitedove. It's my son, and he's finally found his true mate. I want to know everything," she said, fire dancing in her voice. She wasn't as submissive as she seemed when it came down to how fiercely she protected and loved her family.

Kasey ran a tired hand over his face. "It's not a she, Mom. It's a he."

Her eyebrows rose to her hairline in surprise. She frowned. "That means no grandchildren from you. Well, I suppose there is always your brother, Thayne."

Jeremiah looked at Kasey expectantly. "And where is this

mate of yours, son? Or is there something else besides him being male that has you in such a state?"

A humorless laugh fell from Kasey's lips. "You could say that. Aside from him being male, he's also white and a Created."

Horror filled his mother's expression. A Created one? Her son's mate was one of the Created? In all her years, she'd never heard of such a thing. She reached out and gripped his hand resting on the table, squeezing it in reassurance. "Are you certain he is your mate, Kasey?"

Lips twisting in a cruel smile, he nodded. "I'm positive. You've met him already, Mother. He's the new veterinarian in town."

Emily frowned. "But… he doesn't seem like a Created. He doesn't have the usual signs."

Kasey realized Seth didn't appear as the others, and the fact he didn't smell of wolf, either, left him baffled. The Created ones were never able to focus on any one thing too long. They could barely contain themselves around humans, too eager to feed on them, more animal than human. Their eyes, even in human form, had a slight bleed-through to canine pupils. Frustrated, he curled his hand into a fist. "I know that. It doesn't make any sense."

"Are you certain he's a Created?" Jeremiah pressed.

"He's white, Dad. What else could he be? Only our people are born naturally," he replied bitterly.

To the pack's knowledge, perhaps, but Jeremiah had long ago learned otherwise. He knew he would have to reveal the secret he carried. Sighing, he sat back from the table. "Kasey, there is something I have to tell you. As pack Alpha, it is my sworn duty to protect us, all of us, and sometimes secrets are kept in order to do so. Before you were born, a stranger came to our reservation. At first, everyone believed him to be one of the Created. When we attempted to run him from our territory, it became obvious he was different."

A frown appeared between Kasey's eyebrows. "I don't understand. Was he another type of Created? Like a mutation?"

"I am saying he wasn't a Created at all. I didn't reveal my discoveries to the rest of the pack because I didn't want to endanger them. It became a very real possibility one of us may mistake a Created for another wolf." Jeremiah glanced at his wife to find her giving him a "we are going to talk later" look. He gave her a small roll of his eyes. She knew he couldn't always reveal things to her despite the fact he often asked her for advice on some of the pack business.

"So it's possible he told the truth, then," Kasey mused aloud, not really speaking to his parents but more to himself.

"He told you he wasn't one of the Created?" Jeremiah sat up straighter, an intense look in his dark-brown eyes. Kasey's father might be in his late sixties, but he didn't appear to be older than his late thirties, early forties. It would be hard for anyone to accept Kasey was his son if they hadn't been the spitting image of each other. Jeremiah had olive-toned skin, raven-colored locks trimmed just below his nape except for one long strand braided over his shoulder, and a strong, muscular body kept in shape by frequent runs in his wolf form.

"He said he'd been born a wolf. After finding out who my mate was, I kind of lost my temper." Kasey had the grace to look sheepish. "I accused him of lying, and he ran out."

Jeremiah gave his son a stern look and shook his head. "You need to learn to open your mind to things, Kasey, and to control your temper. When you become pack Alpha, you will not have the leisure to jump to anger so quickly. You will need to have much patience. Learn to judge with your eyes, mind, and heart. For only with all three can you come to a fair judgment."

Kasey immediately felt his conscience prick again. Shame flashed across his features for a moment. Only his father could make him feel like a little kid again with so few words. "I'm sorry, Dad," he mumbled.

"I would like to speak to your mate, son. To know of where he came from."

"I don't know if he will want to after how I spoke to him and… frightened him." Dismay washed over Kasey as he realized he'd definitely handled the whole situation wrong. But would he have handled it any differently if he'd known what his father had just told him? He didn't know, but now he'd have to do some pretty fancy footwork to try and smooth over the situation.

"Oh, Kasey," Emily sighed. "How could you? No matter the situation, you should never use your strength or size to harm someone unless the situation absolutely calls for it. You are going to march yourself into his clinic and apologize right away. Do you hear me, young man?"

He gave his mother a tight look. "It's not going to be that easy, Mother." His jaw clenched as he again remembered the look on Seth's face before he'd darted from the house.

"Well, it has to start somewhere," she insisted. "And apologies are the best way to begin."

Jeremiah watched his son's face while his mother spoke to him. He agreed wholeheartedly, and if it turned out this man had in fact been born a natural wolf, then it became a very real possibility there were other packs. "I agree with your mother, Kasey. I think you should go and talk to him. Apologize and explain about the Created ones. It's the only way."

Kasey knew his father could make it an order if he chose to, but he gave Kasey the chance to make the decision for himself. Though there would always be the same outcome.

He would have to speak with his mate and try to make amends. "Fine," he said flatly. "I'll go talk to him, but there is no guarantee he will even agree to speak to you."

The Alpha nodded. "I understand, but you must try. If not for me, then for yourself."

Standing, Kasey went to leave but stopped, turning back to look at his father. "What happened to the stranger?"

"He said he'd been born as a wolf yet had no pack, knew of no others like himself until he came to our territory. I knew it was wrong, but I requested he leave the area. We couldn't accept him into our pack, and if he stayed, the others would surely have questioned my allowing him to do so." Sadness haunted Jeremiah's face. He'd always felt regret he'd sent the stranger away, but it'd been necessary to protect his family, his pack.

"What was his name?"

"Eric. Eric Hawthorne."

Kasey gave a jerky nod and left, shifting and running back to his truck. The knowledge he might have caused irreparable damage to the connection with his mate sat like a giant rock in his stomach. His hands tightened on the steering wheel. This wasn't the way he'd imagined finding his mate. He'd never cared if it turned out to be a man or a woman, but he'd never thought his mate would be the man he had turned out to be.

4

Seth had finally managed to drag himself home. He shifted just inside the edge of the forest before walking the rest of the way. It'd taken him hours to find the town again. If it hadn't been for his canine senses, he would still be wandering around lost in the woods. His skin felt raw, as though it'd been rubbed off by an abrasive sponge that had left behind invisible wounds.

Bullet greeted him enthusiastically, and Seth opened the door, motioning his pet outside. Thankfully, he kept a huge bowl of food and water on the floor for the dog, or he would have been starving by now. Seth had never trusted doggie doors, so he knew there had to be a mess on the floor. He wasn't disappointed and sighed, knowing he couldn't blame the dog for his own stupidity. As he headed to the kitchen to grab paper towels and cleaner, he noticed the light on his answering machine blinking like crazy and cringed as he hit play. Every message contained a very frantic-sounding Chessie. He hit "delete all," picked up the phone, and called the clinic. "Senaka Animal Clinic," he heard come over the line.

"Chessie, it's Seth."

"Oh my God!" she shouted. "Where have you been?"

He thought quickly and realized he could use a bit of the truth. "I got lost in the woods," he said sheepishly.

"For two days?" she exclaimed.

"Yeah…," he admitted reluctantly, knowing she probably thought him an idiot. "I just now got home, but I need to shower and change. Please stall any appointments until I can get there, Chessie."

"Will do, Doc," she said. "Are you okay?"

"Yeah, I'm fine. Just a little worse for wear," he said, laughing drily. "Give me about thirty minutes, and I'll be there." He disconnected the call, cleaned up the mess Bullet had left, and went to take a shower.

Several cars were in the lot when he arrived. Wincing, he rushed into the clinic, immediately apologizing to the clients waiting in the reception area. Chessie handed him the first file, and after a quick perusal, he entered the examining room.

The next three hours flew by nonstop, and exhaustion had set in by the time he had some downtime. He sank into the chair in his office and leaned his head back, heaving a sigh. His leg had healed, but the deep ache inside would take a few days to disappear.

The phone on his desk buzzed. "Yes, Chessie," he answered tiredly.

"The sheriff is here to see you," she said quietly, "and it looks serious."

Seth froze. His heart leapt into his throat, and it took several swallows before he could answer. "Tell him I'm not available," he choked and hung up the phone.

Seth heard Chessie call out to try and stop Kasey, but his door flew open roughly.

Kasey stood there, eyes blazing. "Go back to your desk,

Chessie," he snarled at the still-yelling petite female behind him.

Seth saw her glance at him, and he nodded reluctantly. "It's fine, Chessie. Go on." When the door closed behind the sheriff, the room immediately shrank in size. Seth's chest ached, and he pinched the bridge of his nose.

"We need to talk," Kasey snapped.

"I think we've said enough, Sheriff," Seth replied in a low voice.

Kasey prowled the room restlessly in front of him. Seth couldn't quite read the Cheyenne's face, but it appeared tight with some emotion he didn't want to identify, and he shifted uncomfortably in his chair. "We haven't finished yet, Doc. We need to talk about the fact that we're mates."

"I am not your mate," Seth ground out. He glared at the tall, virile man pacing his small office. "And you don't want me to be, either. You made it blatantly obvious earlier this morning."

The man stopped, shoving a hand through his hair in frustration. "Yeah, and maybe I was wrong."

Seth's mouth fell open in shock. "Excuse me?"

Kasey pinned him in place with a sharp look. "You heard me. Maybe I was wrong."

Seth could clearly see the man wasn't used to apologizing to anyone, and the stiff set of Kasey's shoulders brought a cynical smile to his face. "I think you reacted correctly, Sheriff. But even if you are willing to 'accept' me as your mate, I'm not willing to accept you. Not only do you believe I am a liar, but you also can't stand me because I'm white."

Kasey scowled at his refusal to even listen. "That was before I knew what you are."

"Doesn't change the fact of what I am," Seth pointed out in a strained voice.

Before Seth could blink, Kasey stood next to his chair,

towering over him. Unable to help himself, Seth flinched. The man gave him a harsh look. "I would never hurt you."

"You mean like this morning?" Seth challenged, watching in satisfaction when the older male paled beneath his tan.

"I let my anger get the better of me," Kasey bit out. "I never should have touched you in anger." His eyes took on a strange gleam as he dropped into a crouch next to Seth's chair, surprising the vet. "I'm sorry," he murmured.

The soft words left Seth speechless, not knowing what to say, but his mind whispered to him of his past and caused him to withdraw inside himself again. "Either way, it doesn't matter, Sheriff," he said in a voice devoid of emotion. "Now please leave me alone."

"I can't do that," Kasey said hoarsely. "My father would like to meet you. As another wolf in the pack's territory, if you aren't part of it, they will attempt to force you to leave if they know you're here."

Seth wanted to cry. He'd been so sure this place would be perfect for him, a place to live without fear and pain plaguing his every step, but apparently he'd been wrong. "Fine. Give me a few weeks to get my affairs in order, and I'll leave," he finally stated.

A panicked look crossed the sheriff's face at his words. "No!" Kasey's hand shot out and lightly encircled Seth's wrist, and the vet shuddered at the sheer strength in that hand. "You can't leave. Seth, I—" A growl rumbled in the sheriff's throat when Seth's phone buzzed. "Ignore it," he demanded.

Seth glared at him and deliberately answered it. "Yes, Chessie?"

"Doc, there's an emergency. Mr. Sheffield's dog's been hit by a car and is bleeding pretty badly," she informed him in a crisp voice.

"I'll be right there," he said urgently. He shook off Kasey's hand and stood. "I can't talk about this right now. I'd rather not talk about it at all, but somehow I doubt I'm going to get rid of you that easily."

"You're damn right, pup," the man replied darkly as he watched the vet walk out of the office.

The dog's lungs were laboring for breath, and Seth could tell the dog was on the edge of dying. He assured Mr. Sheffield he would do everything he could to save the dog. Kasey stood against the wall by his office as he rushed the animal into the small emergency operating room, but Seth ignored the man. Focusing intently, he laid the small mixed-breed dog on the table. Seth placed both his hands on the animal's side and reached outside himself. There were severe internal injuries. If he had been anyone but who he was, he wouldn't have been able to save the dog in this bad a shape.

His eyes closed as he sent healing energy through the warm body. The instant he touched the wounds, he knew it would take a lot out of him. It was going to cost him almost all of his energy. He'd be lucky if he could stand afterward. He concentrated on fixing the injuries inside the animal. The outside wounds would need to be stitched so no one was aware of what he'd done. They were superficial wounds, anyway.

Seth felt the pull on his own energy. It sucked at him like an incubus. Perhaps ten minutes passed before he released the energy back inside himself. A gasp echoed through the small tiled room as he sank to his knees, gripping at the metal table to keep from curling up on the floor and passing out.

Using the little energy he had left, Seth shakily stitched up the two deepest wounds and bandaged the rest. He could feel the negative energy eating at his insides as he worked. If he didn't get it out soon, it would render him unconscious. Sweat poured off his body by the time he'd finished. His limbs trembled like he'd been stuck in a blender for an hour and had only just gotten out.

Seth stumbled out of the emergency room, barely aware of his surroundings as he gripped at the wall for support. A loud roaring in his ears drowned out his name being called as he shoved open the bathroom door. He slammed it shut behind him, dropped to his knees, and retched. The amount of black liquid that came out was three times what it had been the other day. His body heaved with convulsions as he released the negative energy from inside him.

It was only after the vomiting stopped that he realized someone else was keeping him from sinking to the floor. A cool, wet cloth pressed against the back of his neck and slid along his cheek and forehead. His body trembled fiercely, like he had an intense fever. Seth struggled to his knees, shakily rinsing his mouth out with the little bit of energy he had left. He'd have slumped to the floor if Kasey hadn't caught him.

"It's all right, pup. I've got you." Kasey's warm, smooth-as-honey voice poured over him soothingly.

He didn't have the strength to fight him, to push him away, so he just lay there dazed in his arms. "Can you stand?" Kasey asked gently.

"No," he croaked out.

A small sound of shock left Seth when he suddenly found himself airborne. Kasey carried him into his office, setting him down on the small couch resting underneath the only window in the room. The sheriff brushed a lock of sweat-soaked hair back from Seth's face. "I'm going to go put Ginger in one of the recovery cages and let Chessie know to cancel the rest of your appointments for the day."

"You… you can't," Seth panted. "Just… just give me a few minutes. I'll be all right."

Kasey's lips flattened. "No. Not only is your body still

recovering from a broken leg, but you're obviously exhausted. And we are going to talk as soon as you are able. I want to know what the hell that was all about. And I know it wasn't because the sight of blood makes you sick." He didn't give Seth a chance to respond and merely stalked out of the room.

Seth lay there, drifting between sleeping and awake. He hadn't expended so much energy in a long time. With not having truly practiced as a vet in two years, his body wasn't used to how much it took to repair such injuries. He kept his eyes closed when he heard Kasey enter the room. "I know you're not sleeping, Seth. I can hear your heartbeat," the sheriff said sardonically.

Sighing, Seth opened his eyes to stare at the older wolf.

"At least now you can't run away from me," Kasey added while pulling up a chair to straddle next to where the doctor lay. "So what the hell was that all about back there?"

Seth rubbed a hand over his face, debating what to tell him. He supposed it wouldn't do any harm to tell him. His lips twisted in a sarcastic smile. "Remember how you said I knew nothing about treating animals, Sheriff?"

"It's Kasey, and yes, I remember," he replied flatly.

"If all I know about animals had been a rattlesnake, it would have bitten you in the ass. I was born with an ability that allows me to heal. I've always had an affinity for animals, which is the reason I became a veterinarian. But healing them does not come without a price." Seth's voice grew rougher as he spoke. "When I heal them, I take the negative energy into my body. It weakens me, and I am forced to release them, or they will send me into a coma. I discovered this in a very real way one day when I was a teenager."

Kasey stared at his mate with an expression of awe on his face. His mate could heal? "So that's how you fixed Samantha's heart," he murmured.

"Samantha?" It took Seth a moment to understand who Kasey was referring to. "Oh, the poodle. Yeah. Her heart was defective. She would have been dead within six months to a year." He yawned tiredly, snuggling into the pillow that he lay against. He could barely keep his eyes open.

A low chuckle issued near his ear, and Kasey said softly, "All right, pup. You get a reprieve for now, but soon you and I will talk."

Seth was so far gone that he couldn't do more than sigh when he felt a warm heat against his forehead. He slipped into darkness, letting it swallow him in its comforting embrace.

Kasey watched his mate sleeping. It'd been a long time since the man had been taken care of by anyone other than himself. The way he didn't seem to know how to slow down when exhausted made it obvious. Kasey's lips turned up in wonder at his mate being able to heal. But it did come with a heavy price. He'd felt helpless as he'd watched the delicate form of his mate shuddering beneath his hands and the way the black liquid rushed from his body.

Kasey was astonished to find such a gift existed, despite the illness it seemed to cause Seth afterward. None of the other wolves in his pack could heal. Charlie had the ability to bring peace among their pack during a fight. Others were able to communicate merely by thought with their mate or with the Alpha of the pack if the Alpha wished it. Seth's gift of healing gave their story an unexpected twist, one he'd never have believed if he hadn't witnessed it with his own eyes.

Over the next few hours, while Seth slept, Kasey had a lot of time to think. His mind shied away from the brutal way he'd treated the smaller wolf earlier. He didn't blame Seth for being mad at him or frightened of him. He hadn't exactly kept his promise. His fingers stroked gently over one pale cheek in a light caress. The vet let out a soft sigh and leaned into it, bringing a smile to Kasey's face. Despite the pup's attempts to deny it, his unconscious self recognized he was in fact Kasey's mate.

His body sang out, demanding he claim Seth, and it left him knowing without a doubt the stubborn, feisty veterinarian was his mate. You didn't get another one. It wasn't like walking into a dating agency and picking a new one. Seth had time to come to terms with it, but Kasey would have this slender, infuriating man in his life no matter how long it took his mind to accept what his heart already did.

He'd already accepted that Seth had told the truth about being born as a werewolf. The only matter at hand still troubling him was Seth's skin color. The whole reason he'd always despised the white men of this world wasn't because of how they'd treated his ancestors, though that would have been a very valid reason, but because they cared nothing for other living beings. Money. They raped forests and destroyed the lands and homes of those animals all for the sake of greed and progress. At the rate they were spreading over the earth, there'd be nothing left in another millennium.

Seth didn't appear to be like the white men Kasey had met. Seeing the ability his mate possessed and how drained it left him made him realize that if Seth were in fact evil or greedy, then he wouldn't hurt himself to help the animals he treated. Kasey warred internally over accepting his mate. His pride raged against the destiny of being bound to the vet, but his heart held more power over his will. The resolve he'd felt in the cabin to claim his mate, to protect him from whatever demons haunted him, came back in full force. Even if it took ten years, he'd find a way to complete the binding of their souls into one. To earn the heart of his mate.

The sun had long since sunk behind the horizon before Kasey switched on a lamp, and its dull glow illuminated the room. He could hear Seth's breathing become uneven as he stirred. The steady, slow pulse of his heart sped up in equal fashion. Seth carefully sat up, lifting a hand to his head. "Headache?" Kasey asked.

Seth jumped slightly before croaking, "Yes. I always get one after."

A frown twisted Kasey's lips. Did the healing actually harm his mate? The tremble in Seth's hand twisted his gut sharply. "Are you certain you aren't causing your body damage by healing?"

"I'm a werewolf, Sheriff. I have accelerated healing abilities, and we don't get diseases, so I highly doubt it does more harm to me than a white throne session and a massive hangover afterward." Seth debated standing but thought better of it and carefully leaned back against the couch.

"Kasey," the sheriff insisted.

"What?" Seth gave him a confused look.

Kasey pushed himself up from the doctor's desk chair and slowly stalked around the edge of the desk toward the couch. "My name is Kasey."

Seth swallowed hard at the husky tone and the strange gleam in those dark eyes.

Kasey sank down on the couch next to him, one hand coming out to touch Seth's face lightly. "You keep calling me Sheriff," he explained further, as Seth still looked confused. "Call me Kasey."

He watched as Seth shook his head at his request. The tip of a small pink tongue sliding across his mate's perfect lips drew his gaze. He almost started in shock at his thoughts. Perfect lips? He could feel the heat coming from Seth's body and knew his closeness affected the other male. "Say my name," he whispered silkily, his breath dusting over those same rosy red lips.

Seth sighed his name just a split second before Kasey's

mouth claimed Seth's. His hand slipped around to cup the back of Seth's head, not exerting pressure, keeping it light to keep from scaring his skittish mate. Kasey followed the line of Seth's lips, requesting access to the warm recesses. Seth's lips parted on a small sound in his throat, and Kasey's tongue immediately flooded the smaller male's mouth. A low moan rumbled in his tanned throat. Seth tasted like sunshine and cinnamon, like the musky scent of rain that clung to the earth after a thunderstorm. Kasey's cock hardened, screaming at him to take his mate.

SETH had only been able to watch as the tall, virile Cheyenne walked toward the couch. *No, make that stalked,* he thought. His mouth went dry when Kasey sat down next to him. It took every ounce of control he had not to lean into the gentle touch on his cheek. Suddenly, he'd found himself giving in to the man's request. "Kasey," he whispered.

Pure heat spiraled through his body at the brush of the sheriff's lips on his. His hands seemed to have a mind of their own as they clutched at the older male's strong forearms. Kasey tasted of such sweet fire and spice. Fire flickered along Seth's skin like a burst of power and left him gasping for more. Everything else fell away from the two of them. Seth forgot his dislike and fear of the other shifter. He became nothing more than a mouth, a tongue, and the hard throbbing between his thighs. He moved slightly, moaning against Kasey's mouth when the movement caused his legs to squeeze his stiff flesh.

Reality crashed back in, though, when he felt Kasey's hand gliding along his thigh. He stiffened and yanked himself away, panting. "No, stop."

Kasey stilled, immediately pulling his hand back from the

supple leg he'd been exploring. He collapsed back against the couch with a sigh. His fingers itched to return to touching his mate, to push higher and feel Seth's straining length through his jeans. "Forgive me. I didn't mean for it to go that far."

"It shouldn't have even started," Seth said roughly. He gathered the little energy he had and moved to the other side of the room. Bracing himself against one of the bookshelves, he leaned his forehead against his arm. He could feel those dark eyes boring into his back but didn't turn around.

"You know you can feel it, pup," Kasey said, his seductive voice rolling over Seth and sending a shudder down his spine.

"No," Seth forced out. He would never admit to it. He couldn't admit to it even though a strange urge inside him wanted him to turn around and go back to the large male sitting behind him. It seemed like a living essence in his stomach, his soul, screaming at him to take what was his. Sweat beaded along his upper lip, and he licked at the salty liquid.

"Yes," Kasey breathed hotly against his ear. Seth nearly screamed as his body tightened with need. He'd been so wrapped up in his own thoughts he hadn't even heard the other shifter approach him. He quivered when he felt Kasey's hands settle on his hips, gently pulling him back against his chest.

"Stop," he pleaded on a whimper, his eyes squeezed shut tightly at the feel of those firm lips on the nape of his neck. "You don't even wa-want me," Seth said, stumbling over his words as his body fought to deny the control his mind had over it.

"No?" Kasey intoned, thrusting his hips forward, grinding his cock into Seth. "You see, Seth, it's as I told you. Despite my stubborn, bullheaded reaction before, you are my mate.

That means I want you more than I've ever wanted anyone else." He scraped his teeth along the delicate skin of Seth's bared throat.

A small keening sound came from Seth, but he forced his body to remain still, not to push into the hot, stiff flesh nudging his lower back or to tilt his head to the side and allow the other male to dominate him. "You… only want me because you think I'm your mate," he gasped out, his nails digging into the wood of the cabinet he held onto for dear life. "Not because you truly want me."

"I don't think you are my mate, pup. I know you are. My body craves you like sustenance. My mind craves to hear your sweet voice like the oceans lapping at the shores. My hands need to feel your skin beneath them." Kasey carefully turned Seth to look at him, locking their eyes together. He traced the line of Seth's lips with one finger as he spoke. "I can only imagine what brought you to where you are now, pup, so afraid and unable to recognize me as your mate. I will bide my time, Seth, and woo you at every chance I get, but one day I will claim you."

Seth bit his lip as he strained his body away from Kasey's. The damned bastard made him feel things he'd never felt with anyone. The slightest touch of the sheriff's fingers drifting over his skin made Seth's stomach muscles clench; his heart began to pound inside his chest at just a simple look from those amazingly dark eyes. The gentle treatment left him confused and torn. Taggart had never treated him so carefully. A small sound of dismay broke free at the thought of that name. He'd learned not to think of him, to lock those thoughts deep inside his mind, because they made him feel ashamed, weak, and useless.

It was taking every ounce of control Kasey had not to ignore the little voice in his head demanding he go slowly with the slender male in front of him. He could feel and smell his mate's desire for him. He knew if he pressed he could override the smaller wolf's objections, but he wanted Seth to come to him willingly, to want to be claimed by him. There would be no sweeter reward than to see Seth submit to him without fear or reservation.

A sound from the vet distracted him from his thoughts. "What is it?" he asked softly.

"N-nothing," Seth stuttered, seeming to withdraw into himself.

Reluctantly, Kasey stepped away from the smaller form, knowing he was crowding the other wolf. He reached down and gently took Seth's hand in his. "Come on, pup. I'll walk you to your car and follow you to make sure you get home all right."

"I'll be fine," Seth insisted, but Kasey just ignored him.

It pleased Kasey when Seth didn't draw away from him. He waited patiently for the blue-eyed doctor to lock up the clinic before capturing Seth's hand in his again. A light rain began to mist down to the dry ground during the short walk to the car. When they reached Seth's small sedan, Kasey found himself hard-pressed to let him go. He lifted Seth's hand to his mouth, brushing his lips over the backs of his knuckles. Lust slammed into him when he saw the most becoming blush flood his sexy mate's cheeks. Stifling a groan, Kasey released him and opened the car door for him.

"Good night, pup," Kasey said huskily as he shut the door once Seth slipped into the front seat. He jogged over to his truck and started it, following his mate from the parking lot. The drive didn't take long, and he pulled up to the curb, watching as Seth hurried into the house. It brought one corner of his lip up into a soft smile when he saw his gorgeous mate glance at him one last time before closing the door.

Rain trickled down the front windshield in rivulets,

growing harder with each passing mile that Kasey drove toward the station. A deep-seated instinct told Kasey that there were many dark secrets in Seth's past, secrets that he needed to know to keep his mate safe, and the only way to do that was to know the details of what had caused so much pain.

It was obvious that Seth wasn't going to tell him anytime soon, and even though the sheriff knew the dark-haired vet would be furious if he ever found out what he was about to do, Kasey couldn't ignore his instincts to dig beyond the surface. He hadn't been elected sheriff just because he was the Alpha's heir. His instincts ran deep and true, and he'd found that if he followed them when they were kicking up the kind of fuss they were right then, they never led him astray. Seth would just have to never find out.

5

S ETH leaned back against the door wearily. Bullet whined at him, and he gave the dog a strained smile. "Hey, boy. I know I should have taken you with me today, but I was in such a rush I didn't have time. Tomorrow," he promised.

Bullet seemed to understand as Seth let him out to relieve himself. Seth rested his forehead against the cool, smooth glass of the window while waiting for the dog to return. Kasey left him confused, aching, and uncertain. He'd never felt these feelings before. He'd thought he would never be able to feel anything again after everything that had happened. Especially toward another werewolf. He needed to be firm where the big Cheyenne was concerned. A shiver raced down his spine at the promise in Kasey's voice about how he would claim him.

He hadn't been raised in a pack environment, and being someone's mate seemed impossible. His mother had told him one day he would find his mate just like she'd found his father. For years, it was all he'd dreamed of: finding the one person he was meant to be with for the rest of his life, finally not feeling all alone in the world. Two years ago that dream had shattered, and now he just wanted to live out his life in solitude, a rogue forgotten by the rest of the world.

A woof at the door brought him out of his thoughts, and Seth opened the door to let his dog inside. The phone rang as he turned the lock. Frowning, he wondered who it could possibly be at this time of night. Maybe it was an emergency. "Hello?"

Silence met his ear, but he heard a slight shift in breathing as the person remained quiet. A sense of foreboding trickled down his nape straight to his gut. "Who is this? Hello?"

Click. They hung up.

Seth carefully placed the receiver in the cradle. He berated himself. *Stop it,* he mentally chided himself. It was probably just a wrong number. *And besides, you know it couldn't possibly be—*

Seth slammed the door on his thoughts. The person had the wrong number. Making sure all the doors were locked, he headed back to the bedroom, happy to have Bullet at his side.

The next day dawned bright and clear, the ground fresh and renewed from the rain overnight. Seth stretched beneath his sheets and gave a small groan just as Bullet perked up and took off down the hallway, barking. He heard the sound of someone knocking at the door. He yawned as he stood, pulling a robe on over his T-shirt and boxers and running a hand through his hair to straighten it at least a little bit. When he entered the living room, his eyes locked on the dark orbs belonging to the man who'd haunted his dreams last night. Sighing, Seth unlocked and opened the door for the sheriff.

Bullet growled and crowded in close to Seth. He dropped

his hand onto Bullet's head. "Shh, it's okay, boy. He's not a bad wolf… I think."

Kasey held a brown paper bag in one hand and a tray containing two coffees in the other. A wince spread over his features at Seth's words to the dog. He forced a smile at Seth. It would take time to earn Seth's trust, but patience had never been his strong suit, unfortunately. "Good morning, pu —Seth. I brought some coffee and donuts."

Seth wrinkled his nose at the endearment cut short. Without a word, he stepped back and motioned Kasey into the house. His hands pulled the robe tighter around his body in an almost protective gesture. "I'll go get dressed," he muttered.

"Oh, you don't have to bother on my account," Kasey drawled wickedly, his eyes sliding down Seth's slender body. Even the vet's toes were sexy! A light dusting of hair shadowed the length of Seth's legs, which were visible beneath the hem of the robe, and Kasey's wolf prowled beneath the surface, begging him to claim his mate before he got away. Reining in his desire, Kasey winked at Seth and almost laughed when he saw red flood the pale cheeks of his mate.

Seth escaped down the hall but not before giving a harsh glare at Kasey for enjoying his discomfort. His face felt hot, and he knew he was blushing. A tingle spread over his skin as he quickly dressed, shaved, and brushed his teeth. The primal, lustful gleam in Kasey's eyes caused his breath to hitch, and flashes of what it would be like to be pinned down and roughly taken by the gorgeous male sitting in his kitchen passed through his mind. A low growl rumbled in his throat as his wolf reacted to the thoughts. His cock instantly hardened, pressing against his fly. "Stop it, Seth," he commanded himself sternly.

He looked up into the mirror and noticed his eyes were

starting to bleed through to his canine pupils. His tongue slid along his upper teeth and found they'd extended slightly as well. His hands gripped the granite countertop, hard. This wasn't how he'd seen his life playing out after moving here. It'd seemed like such a quiet, sleepy town, with no one to bother him. Now he either had to accept Kasey as his mate or leave.

He was so tired of moving. It was all he'd done since he could remember. First with his parents, then by himself. But the thought of allowing Kasey to dominate him also made his throat tighten with screams of terror. How could he give in and allow it to happen again? Flashes of the pain and degradation almost sent him to his knees in agony.

Effectively, his thoughts allowed him to bring his body under control so he wouldn't embarrass himself when he re-entered the kitchen. He stopped in the doorway and lifted an eyebrow at his traitor of a dog. Belly-up in submission to Kasey while said wolf scratched his belly, Bullet panted happily. "I hope you didn't feed him any of those donuts," he said darkly. "Or you'll be cleaning up the mess he leaves behind."

Kasey looked up at Seth with a grin. "Nah, Mom never let us feed our pets human food when we were growing up. We just came to an understanding, didn't we, boy?"

Seth didn't realize his eyes were following the big, firm hand scratching Bullet's belly until the man moved to stand up. Clearing his throat, he slipped into his usual chair and picked up the coffee cup to take a sip. He sighed as his eyes closed in pleasure. One of the most addictive substances on the planet, coffee was like heroin to some people. *Just inject it straight into my veins*, he thought wryly. When he opened his eyes again, he found Kasey staring at him with the same feral expression, but it quickly disappeared behind an easy smile the moment he saw Seth's eyes were open. "So, Doc, where'd you live before you decided to move to Senaka?"

He shrugged. "All over the place. We never lived anywhere longer than a couple of years. After my parents died, I kept the same patterns, moving every couple of years. People start to notice certain things."

Kasey frowned at him. "So you've never had a real home? What about friends?"

"I'd make friends, and then we moved on. Lost touch with most of them. Except for my friend Nick." Seth's face softened as he thought of his friend. Even though his parents expressly forbade him from telling any of his friends he was a werewolf, Nick had figured it out and confronted him. So he'd told him the truth, and Nick had stuck with him ever since. He hadn't cared Seth was a monster. Nick was the only person Seth would ever trust in his life again, the only one who'd been there when he'd needed him most.

"Nick?" Seth heard a tinge of strain to Kasey's voice and looked at him, eyebrows furrowed in confusion.

"Yeah. He's my best friend. He travels a lot for his business. He does graphic design and sometimes has to be overseas in Japan or Australia. Wherever it takes him. He'll be coming for a visit when he gets back." Seth looked forward to having his friend there. Nick would be able to help him figure out what he should do about Kasey.

"Is he wolf?" Kasey asked in a heavy tone Seth couldn't interpret.

Seth laughed and shook his head. "No. He's human. I intend on introducing him to Chessie. She's got her sights set on me, and I haven't the heart to tell her I'm gay. Nick could charm the panties off any woman he wanted. He's good-looking, rich, but not arrogant about it. He's very down to earth and far from wolf."

Kasey stifled a growl at the pure affection on Seth's face as he spoke of this Nick. His hands tightened on the coffee cup, and he had to force himself not to crush it. How had this man gotten past his pup's defenses? "How... how long have you known him?"

"Hmmm... I think going on fourteen years now. I met him when I was fifteen, and we lived in New Harrisburg for a year and a half. He saved me from a bunch of bullies the first day of school. We've been friends ever since." Seth swallowed the last of his coffee and stood. He pushed his chair into the table before looking expectantly at Kasey.

"Answer me one thing before I go, Seth." Kasey also stood and moved over to Seth. He picked up Seth's hand in one of his, studying the fragile bones in his fingers as if they were the most awe-inspiring things in the world. "Does he know what you are?"

Seth jerked in surprise, his eyes widening at Kasey. "He does, doesn't he?" Kasey ground out at the sudden shadowing in his mate's deep-blue eyes. He wanted to howl in anger and sadness. This man, this human, had done what he craved. He'd invaded Seth's heart.

Seth stiffened at Kasey's nearness and question. A proprietary note had invaded the older wolf's voice. Seth tilted his head back and gave Kasey a heated glare. "And if he does?"

A fierce look came into Kasey's eyes, and his lips flattened into a thin, disapproving line. "Humans are dangerous. Telling one of them about us is never a good idea. How do you know you can trust him not to betray you as soon as it's convenient for him?"

"Because he's my friend. And he is the only one who's been there for me in the five years my parents have been gone. He's the one who sa—" He abruptly cut himself off, horrified that he'd almost revealed his darkest secret.

"The one who what?" Kasey demanded. His fingers tightened slightly in his jealousy as a red haze drifted over his mind. No one else could be that close to his mate. Seth was his.

Seth winced at the tightened grip. He wrenched at his arm. "Let go. You're hurting me!"

Kasey's grip immediately loosened, and he grimaced, lifting Seth's abused wrist to his lips to press a gentle kiss against the reddened skin. "I am sorry, pup. I just want you to trust me, to be able to tell me the things you would share with your… friend."

Seth's blue eyes narrowed at the edges, a sharp coldness in them. "If you want me to trust you, then stop crowding me and expecting me to obey you. And don't touch me. Every time you do, it turns out to be a bad thing." His gaze dropped pointedly to where Kasey gripped his hand.

Kasey's heart clenched at his mate's obvious rejection of his touch. His thumb caressed the soft skin on the inside of Seth's wrist. "I'm trying, pup. I really am." His other hand came up to cradle the other's face. "I can't help but be jealous of this man having won you over when getting even an inch with you is like pulling teeth."

Seth made a small sound at the feel of the warm, rough palm on his cheek and the calloused thumb rubbing against his skin. His lips parted at Kasey's actions and words. "Don't…," he murmured breathlessly, almost unable to stop himself from leaning into Kasey's hand.

"Please give me a chance, Seth," Kasey begged shamelessly. "Let me show you I'm not a cruel man. Have dinner with me. Tonight."

A war raged inside of Seth. Part of him wanted to say, "To hell with this!" and run for the hills. The other part, the one that had waited for his mate for so long, wanted him to give in and see where the road in Kasey's direction led. One road, if it could be trusted, could lead to a beautiful sunset on a far-off beach in the middle of summer. The other was a bleak and cold existence, alone. Seth bit his bottom lip, hesitating to answer.

"Please, Seth," Kasey whispered again, dark eyes intense and beautiful.

With a small smacking of his lips as Seth let his bruised bottom lip go, Seth nodded, only to find himself in a tight embrace and his mouth under attack by Kasey's. He gasped at the abruptness of it, and then it ended as abruptly. Kasey stepped back, a wide grin on his face. "Tonight, seven o'clock. I'll pick you up at the clinic."

"O-okay," Seth muttered, fidgeting at what he'd just gotten himself into. He watched in a daze as Kasey left the house. *What the hell are you doing, Seth?* he berated himself. His lungs suddenly felt as though they couldn't get enough air in them.

Seth dropped to the floor, bringing his knees to his chest as he tried to control his breathing like the doctor had showed him. Kasey's face blended in with another's. A face he saw every time he slept. The only way he could escape the dreams was to exhaust himself, usually after one of his healing episodes. His chest felt like it would cave in under the pressure of it all. Tears stung his eyes, and all he wanted to do was curl up in a ball and cry himself to death.

He hated himself for being so weak, for not being able to control these emotions. Just the thought of that man could send him to his knees, cowering like a beaten puppy. A bitter smile twisted his lips. Hadn't he been? Just a stupid, stupid puppy who'd been so happy to find others that he ignored the signs, allowing himself to be treated like a battered wife.

The screams, the smoke-hazed room, the fire burning out of control, and the thought that he was finally going to be granted release replayed in his mind as clearly as the night he'd lived through it. Sometimes he could still smell it, still hear it, even while awake. He'd only escaped the blaze because of Nick. Nick had saved his life. It'd been during one of Nick's infrequent impromptu visits that it all ended. The one man who knew him better than the entire world ever could had seen something was wrong, questioned it, and finally helped end it.

Seth managed to grab enough control to look at the clock. The urge to hear Nick's voice overpowered him. He gripped the counter and pulled himself to his feet. Even though it would be extremely late in Japan, he knew Nick wouldn't mind. The phone rang in his ear, but it sounded hollow. "'Lo," a sleep-roughened voice answered.

"Nick," Seth managed to get out.

Nick Cartwright pulled himself up in the hotel bed, instantly alert, disturbing the hotel receptionist sleeping next to him. "Seth? What's wrong?"

A choked sob escaped Seth, and the whole story came spilling out. Kasey, the other pack of wolves, and his fear, his desire to run. "I don't know what to do, Nick."

Fury consumed Nick. Seth had almost died because of someone else claiming to be his mate. Someone Seth had trusted immediately to be telling the truth. Nick scowled as he listened to his friend practically hyperventilating on the other end of the phone. "Listen, Seth, I'm catching the first flight out of here. I'll be there in less than two days. Whatever you do, just be careful with this guy. Remember how Taggart claimed the same thing."

A whimper issued from Seth at the bastard's name spoken aloud. "I… I kn-know," he stumbled out. "I… it feels different this time, Nick. When… when he touches me, it feels so… right."

Fingers tightening on the cell phone, Nick bit out, "Just don't do anything until I get there, Seth. Okay? I'm coming."

Seth gave a whispered acknowledgement and hung up. He shivered at the echo of Taggart's name in his mind. He felt ashamed of clinging to Nick as a lifeline, but only Nick knew the truth of the shattered mess he'd become. It'd taken him two years to recover even a semblance of himself. Every little thing made him cringe and cower.

It took all of his strength to stand up and finish getting ready for work. The dinner date weighed heavily on his mind.

He found Chessie as bright and cheerful as ever when he arrived to work. The day moved way too quickly for Seth's taste. Before he knew it, the clock struck closing time. He winced when Chessie called him on the intercom to let him know she was leaving for the evening. "Are you okay, Doc? You've been edgy all day," she asked hesitantly.

Thankfully, she couldn't see his face. He could feel the lines of strain around his eyes and the tension in his forehead. "I'm fine, Chessie. Just exhausted. The last few days have been pretty eventful. Have a good night."

"Thanks. You too, Doc."

Seth distracted himself by finishing up some of the paperwork from the day's appointments. Right at seven on the dot, he heard Kasey's sure-footed boots scraping across the wooden floor of his clinic. Seth's fingers clenched on the pen in nervousness and, he reluctantly admitted to himself, anticipation. A part of him wanted to believe in Kasey, to believe Kasey was telling the truth about being his mate and wasn't just another Taggart.

Kasey stopped in the doorway to his office and leaned one broad shoulder against the door. "Evenin', Seth."

"Good evening, Ka-Kasey." He flushed as he stumbled over the man's name.

"Ready to go?" Kasey asked.

Taking a deep breath, Seth nodded and stood, closing the

file he'd been working on and setting it in his outbox for Chessie to put away in the morning. "Where are we going?" he asked as he followed the big Cheyenne from the clinic.

"I thought since we're trying to get to know one another, we could have dinner at my house. I have most of it prepared already. If that's all right," Kasey drawled as he opened the passenger door of his truck for Seth.

Dipping his head to hide his smile at the chivalrous act, Seth replied, "That's fine."

He watched Kasey jog around the front of the truck before sliding into the driver's seat. The sun cast a warm orange glow across the sky as it sank slowly below the horizon slowly. Seth leaned back against the seat and sighed tiredly. "I hope you like Italian," Kasey said, noting the strain around Seth's face.

"Actually, Italian is my favorite," Seth admitted slowly.

Kasey smiled, totally stealing Seth's breath away. "Good. Italian is also my favorite."

Seth bit his lip at the way his heart jumped at the brilliant smile on the sheriff's face. He turned his head to gaze out the window.

The rest of the short ride was made in silence. Seth didn't wait for Kasey to open his door and merely slid down to the ground easily. Because of his height, he'd always been grateful he had the abilities he did as a wolf. Agility and being able to move swiftly had saved him from making a fool of himself on more than one occasion. This moment being one of them, when his feet almost went out from under him at the impact with the ground.

"How's the horse and foal?" he asked as Kasey opened the front door.

"Doing fine. The foal is already getting bigger." Kasey motioned Seth in ahead of him.

The fragrant smell of spaghetti sauce made his mouth

water, and for the first time, Seth realized how hungry he truly was. He'd skipped lunch because of nerves, and his stomach growled loudly. He blushed. "Sorry, I missed lunch."

Kasey frowned at him. "You need to eat," he admonished gently. "We can start on the salad while the pasta finishes."

Again, Kasey did the unexpected and held his chair out for him. Seth swallowed back a smile as he slipped into the seat. "Wine or soda?" Kasey's voice sounded close to his ear, startling him.

It took him clearing his throat to be able to respond. "Soda is fine." He needed to keep a clear head, just in case.

Kasey moved away from him, allowing him to breathe again. Seth looked around at the kitchen. Surprisingly, all of the cherrywood cabinet doors were hand-carved with burnished brass handles. A small island counter made of the same type of wood graced the center of the kitchen, complementing the granite countertops and stainless kitchen appliances. Stainless steel pots hung from a rack over the island counter, complementing the whole look of the kitchen. "Your kitchen is amazing," he complimented.

Kasey set a glass of soda in front of Seth. "Thanks. I carved all of the doors and made the island and table myself."

Seth widened his eyes in awe. "You made all of this? It's beautiful." He swallowed as he noticed the laugh lines around Kasey's eyes and mouth deepen with mirth.

"I like working with my hands," he murmured huskily as he winked at Seth, laughing aloud when Seth flushed for the third time that night. "I also like to cook, and I like having the proper facilities to do so."

Seth took a sip of his Coke before asking, "Where did you learn to cook?"

"My mother. She says it shouldn't be just a woman's job to cook. Luckily for her, I like to cook. Although my brother

Thayne isn't into it so much. He does more takeout than anything," Kasey said wryly.

"You have a brother?" Seth watched as Kasey took a large bowl of salad from the fridge and set it in the center of the table. He placed a white ceramic salad bowl in front of Seth and one at his own seat.

"Yeah. He's younger than me by five years. Currently out discovering himself by traveling around and sleeping his way through half the population." Kasey handed Seth a small gravy boat with Italian dressing in it. "Come, eat. Then we can start on the main dish."

Seth dished some of the salad out for himself, spooned a little bit of dressing on it, and began to eat. Kasey did the same while asking, "You said it was just you and your parents?"

"Yes," Seth replied after he'd swallowed the mouthful he had. "Mom couldn't have any more kids after me. They said it was because of the difficult pregnancy she had with me. She started hemorrhaging while in labor." He would have loved to have had a brother or even sister. Maybe things would have been different and he wouldn't have been so afraid to accept Kasey as his true mate. He wouldn't have felt so alone that he leapt at the thought of Taggart being his mate.

Kasey watched Seth's eyes darken, the essence of memories flitting through them. He didn't want his mate thinking of things that made him sad. He wanted to take him in his arms and make the sadness go away, but he restrained himself, knowing it wouldn't help the situation. "Well, sometimes having a sibling can be great, but other times not so much." He launched into all of the embarrassing things his brother had put him through, including catching him making out with a girlfriend and running to tell his mother.

Seth was laughing hysterically by the time Kasey had

finished and got up to serve the pasta. Seth's blue eyes twinkled merrily. "He sounds like a handful."

"Oh, he's something, all right," Kasey muttered, but he couldn't keep the happiness out of his voice. Hearing Seth's laugh was like a cool spring breeze on a hot summer day. It made his heart sing that he could make his mate laugh. He set a heaping plate of spaghetti in front of Seth.

"I can't eat all this," Seth protested.

"Just eat whatever you can," he said calmly, grabbing a couple of napkins before taking his own seat. His mate was far too skinny. "So, when you aren't fixing animals, Doc, what do you do in your free time?"

Seth shrugged. "Read, mostly. Anything and everything I can get my hands on. I had a lot of free time on my hands for a while, and I started collecting books. The second bedroom of my home is virtually a library. All of the walls have shelves along them, and they are pretty full."

Kasey was dying to ask why he'd had free time on his hands, but he stuffed it down inside. Soon. Once Seth began to trust him. "I'm a bit of a movie buff myself," he replied easily. "Although I don't own quite so many movies as you do books, apparently."

The conversation flowed easily, and the time disappeared faster than Seth could have imagined. After dinner, he found himself relaxing in the corner of the sofa with a glass of soda in one hand while Kasey regaled him with tales of his childhood. He told Seth of his first full change and about learning the ins and outs of being a wolf. As he talked, he drew Seth out as well by throwing in casual questions the man didn't hesitate to answer. Kasey hungered to know everything about his mate, to know of his past, and his parents, to know what made his pup so distrustful.

The clock chimed midnight before Seth realized how long they had been talking. "I think it's time for me to head home," Seth said, yawning as he stood up. "Bullet probably needs to go out as well, since I didn't keep my promise to him yet again. I usually take him to the clinic every day, but I forgot this morning."

"All right, let me just put these glasses in the sink, and I'll take you home, pup," Kasey said, reaching out to pick up both their glasses.

Seth was too tired to protest the endearment and merely grunted while pulling his shoes back on. He waited patiently at the front door for Kasey and then followed him to his truck. The ride home went silently, and he had fallen almost completely asleep by the time the truck stopped in front of his porch. "You need help getting inside?" the smooth-as-melted-butter voice said, gliding over his skin and disrupting his descent into slumber.

"No, no. I'll be fine." Seth smothered another yawn.

"I'll come pick you up in the morning to take you to your car, Seth," Kasey told him quietly, reluctant for the date to come to an end. It'd been an enjoyable evening with his mate. Something he hoped he could repeat again, and perhaps without any clothing on, he thought wolfishly.

Seth's easy agreement was a clear testament to how tired he really was. He was about to slide from the truck when Kasey touched his hand where it rested on the seat. He looked over at the sheriff questioningly.

"Have dinner with me and my parents tomorrow night, Seth?" Kasey held his breath while he waited for an answer, a breath that whooshed from his lungs when the dark-haired vet nodded in agreement.

"Good night, Kasey," Seth bid just before closing the truck door.

"Good night, pup," Kasey murmured, watching Seth walk up the stairs into his house. He restarted his truck and backed out of the drive slowly. Excitement twisted his stomach at how much ground he'd already gained. His lips were curled up in an almost permanent smile the entire ride home.

It surprised Seth when he woke the next morning and found he'd gone through the entire night without one of his usual nightmares. He moaned in pleasure as he stretched before rolling out of bed and heading into the bathroom for a quick shower. He tried not to overanalyze the evening he'd spent at Kasey's or the fact he'd agreed without thinking to having dinner with the man's parents. Nick would be there sometime in the next twenty-four hours, and then he could actually think.

Kasey sat on his front porch steps when he opened the door, leaning against a railing and sipping at a Styrofoam cup of coffee while holding out another one for him. Seth mentally shook his head at how well the other man seemed to understand him already. He took the cup gratefully as Bullet tore by them both, bounding across the grass. "Is it all right if he rides with us to the clinic?"

"Of course. But I think it might be a good idea for you to sit in the middle. Not real fond of dog drool on my uniform," Kasey deadpanned.

Seth blinked owlishly before chuckling and sinking down onto the steps beside him. "I thought he'd ride in the back, if that's all right with you."

"Aw, damn. And here I was thinking I might get a chance to cop a feel," Kasey said dramatically, letting his chin droop down to his chest before he glanced back up and gave a teasing wink at Seth.

A thrill raced down Seth's spine as he suddenly found the most interesting crack in the bottom step. What he wouldn't give to turn back time and know this man before all of it. He sipped at his coffee contemplatively. "So… dinner at your parents'?"

"They aren't going to bite you, Seth," Kasey chided gently. "My dad wants to talk to you, and Mom wants to meet my mate."

Seth gritted his teeth at Kasey's words. "What am I? Something to be shown off? Like a prize, or what?"

Sighing, Kasey set his coffee cup aside and placed his hand on Seth's knee. "No. It's nothing like that. I told you already when one of our kind finds their true mate, it's a special event in their life. My mother is my father's mate even though she is human. It is something to be celebrated in our world. And I want you to be a part of our world, my world. You'll see we aren't monsters, Seth."

"I… I'm just not comfortable being around a lot of… of our kind," he muttered, shifting restlessly.

Kasey squeezed Seth's knee reassuringly. "It'll just be the two of us and my parents, I promise. We'll go straight into the house. You won't have to see or talk to anyone else, all right?"

Seth's eyes locked on the large, tanned hand resting on his knee. Kasey seemed like such a touchy person. It was almost as if he couldn't *not* touch him. Whenever they were close to one another, Kasey had to touch him. Even last night on the couch, Kasey had rested a hand on one of his feet. And even though it frightened him in some ways, it also left him feeling somewhat… protected. Giving a resigned look, he said, "Fine. But if I get uncomfortable, I want to leave."

"The instant you feel like you need to go, we'll go. I'll take you home or wherever you want to go, pup. I promise," Kasey swore fervently.

After letting Bullet into the bed of the truck, Kasey started it up, and they were on their way to the clinic. It wasn't but a few minutes until they were pulling up in front. That was when Seth thought maybe he'd been wrong about not having a nightmare, because the worst one was right in front of him. Chessie stood on the sidewalk in front of the clinic talking to another Cheyenne in uniform. Seth felt as though his whole world could implode in a split second. His breathing went ragged as he looked at the state of his clinic. "No," he whispered brokenly.

6

KASEY swore and hopped out of the cab of the truck. He shouted for his deputy. "Julian!"

What a disaster! The windows had been smashed out, possibly with rocks or maybe even something bigger. The front door hung on its hinges, and Seth could only imagine what the interior looked like. He slowly lowered himself from the truck and, putting one foot carefully in front of the other, walked toward the entrance. His entire future rested on this clinic. Every penny he'd had was invested in it. He'd never be able to afford to fix it. Horrified, he took in the mess before him. Chessie's file cabinets were tipped over, all of the papers scattered everywhere. Chairs and tables had been overturned, while the light fixtures were barely hanging by wires.

Seth's heart broke as he realized the depth of the destruction. "Why?" he moaned, bending over to pick up the frame his license was in. The shattered glass tinkled to the floor as the wooden frame fell apart, splintered in several places.

The walk to his office felt like it took forever, but when he finally pushed open the door, it took only one look to bring him to his knees. "No!" he screamed. "No… oh God, please no."

Ginger, the dog who had been hit by the car, had been brutally gutted. Her blood and innards were smeared everywhere. Seth's nostrils flared at the strong, sweet smell, causing his stomach to churn with nausea. Her head rested right in front of his chair on his desk. From where he knelt, he could see a piece of white sticking out of her mouth. But he couldn't move. His eyes wouldn't look away from the mutilated dog.

"Seth? Seth! What's wrong?"

Strong hands gripped Seth's shoulders just as Kasey saw the gory display inside his office. "Holy shit," he breathed, briefly lost in the horrifying scene that held Seth spellbound. He snapped out of it quickly, though. "Seth? Come on, you shouldn't be here."

Seth didn't respond. He couldn't do anything but stare. His very livelihood was gone. Right then he wanted to just say to hell with it. To hell with living and the pain that always, always came with it. What had he done so wrong that he could never be happy? "Why?" he finally choked out.

Kasey felt helpless at watching his mate suffer. Rage exploded inside him, and his teeth extended while his eyes blended into his canine pupils. "I don't know, pup, but I swear to you, as your mate, we will find whoever did this, and I'll rip them limb from limb. You hear me? It's a promise." He pulled Seth close to him and turned his head away, pressing Seth's face into his broad shoulder.

He felt a shudder wind its way through Seth, and then those slender arms gripped at him tightly. Great, gulping sobs racked Seth's body as he grieved for the animal, for himself, and for the loss of his clinic.

Kasey saw Chessie standing at the end of the hallway,

staring at them curiously but sadly. Instead of commenting, she merely retreated back out of the clinic to wait outside.

Julian came down the hallway a short time later. Seth had managed to calm down by then and just lay there weakly in Kasey's arms. "No one saw or heard anything last night, Kase. We'll dust for fingerprints, but with the amount of people that have been through this clinic, it's going to be almost impossible to pinpoint exactly who did this."

"What about Seth's office?" Kasey demanded. "It's usually just him and me in there. Try there first. And check the cages in the back. The dog came out of one of them."

Julian nodded before going back to get the kit.

Kasey brushed his fingers through Seth's hair soothingly. "Come on, Seth. I'll take you home."

"No," Seth protested vehemently. He extricated himself from Kasey and stood, brushing off his slacks. Anger slammed through him, not just at the person who'd done this but at himself. Instead of standing tall and bearing it like he'd been trained to do, he'd allowed his grief to take over. He felt even angrier for believing that if he found a nice, quiet town, then maybe he could have a good life… but he'd been an idiot to even think for a minute he could have peace. Because of his blindness, an innocent animal had paid the price. "I have to call Mr. Sheffield. He has to know the truth."

Kasey felt bereft when Seth pulled away, but he reluctantly let him. "Seth, I have to be the one to take care of notifying Mr. Sheffield. And you shouldn't be here until this mess is cleaned up."

"It's my clinic," Seth said, glaring at him. "I have a right to be here."

A sigh broke from Kasey, but he didn't argue further. Stubbornly, Seth intended to stay. "Fine, but at least leave this mess to me."

He'd barely finished speaking when Seth strode forward

and snatched the piece of white from the dog's mouth. It was a folded piece of paper. Kasey frowned. "Seth, don't. There could be fingerprints on that!"

Seth ignored him and almost tore it opening it. After that, everything became a blur. The paper fell to the floor. Seth felt as if the ground beneath him had become a deep, gaping chasm ready to swallow him up. *No. It couldn't be.* Seth wanted to howl, to rail at his fate, but even now, after two years, he hadn't escaped it. It had just followed him everywhere he'd gone. His eyes were empty, frozen, lifeless when they looked up at Kasey. "Don't bother with the fingerprints. You won't find any," he stated in a flat, emotionless tone.

"What? How do you know that?" Kasey strode forward and snatched up the paper, but there were no words on it. Just a symbol: black paint smudged into a shape similar to a wolf decorated one side. He looked up at Seth. "What is this? How do you know there won't be any fingerprints?"

"I just do. It doesn't matter now. I have no choice but to leave. My clinic is destroyed. I can't afford to repair the extent of the damages. All of my money was tied up in this place. The insurance paperwork hasn't even been filed yet. I've been too busy with everything else to get the forms completed and filed." Outside, Seth showed no emotion, but panic roiled beneath the surface of his calm exterior. His demons were coming for him, and he didn't know if he could stop them this time.

"You can't leave," Kasey said heatedly. "I'll help you fix it, Seth. Don't talk like that."

Seth shook his head. "No. It will cost too much money."

Kasey kept insisting, but Seth refused. It wouldn't be right to take money from him. And besides, if he didn't leave this place, he'd wind up dead. Either by his own hand or that of the Triad, the group of wolves led by Taggart. The ones who'd made his life a living nightmare for months.

Maybe if they hadn't been so busy arguing, they would have noticed the man standing in the doorway, but Seth denied Kasey at every turn. "Damn it, Seth. You're my mate!" Kasey shouted.

"It sounds to me like he doesn't think so, Sheriff," a deep, Scotch-roughened voice interjected from the doorway.

Eyes widening, Seth whipped around to find his best friend standing in the doorway. "Nick!" he cried and rushed to him, throwing his arms around him and hugging him tightly. He pulled back to gaze up at the one man who'd always been there for him. "You're earlier than I expected."

Nick shrugged one lean, elegant shoulder. "The flight from Japan was only nine hours. I stopped to catch some sleep when I landed in California and then headed straight here on the next flight out."

With an assessing look on his face, Nick studied the dark-haired Cheyenne still standing at the desk with the paper in between his fingers. Kasey stared back, taking in the man who'd earned Seth's trust so completely. Nick wasn't nearly as tall as himself, maybe three or four inches shorter. His body had a lean, wiry build to it but an undeniable strength in the muscles beneath. His nose was wide, not handsome but elegant. A scar sliced through the left eyebrow above those eyes that shimmered the deep green of emeralds. Dark-blond hair was cut short in a neat style that suited his features, outlining his sharp face perfectly. Just then, a familiar yet strange scent assaulted Kasey's senses. His lips parted as if he were about to say something, but Nick gave an almost imperceptible shake of his head, silencing him more effectively than a shout.

"Want to tell me what happened here?" Nick lifted his hand to wave it uncaringly at the mess decorating Seth's office.

Seth stiffened and pulled away from Nick, wrapping his

arms around his own waist. His eyes had a hunted look in them, a look that spoke of a fear so deeply ingrained that it would never be banished. "Just a cruel joke," he replied flatly.

Kasey could sense an underlying tension in his mate. He knew Seth wasn't telling him the whole story. The instant he had a chance to speak with Nick alone, he would demand some kind of answer. He held up the paper for the blond to see it. "They left a calling card."

Nick's eyes widened, and he swore softly and dangerously. His hand settled on Seth's shoulder. "It was always a possibility, Seth."

"No," Seth denied, shaking his head furiously. "He's dead, Nick. I refuse to believe he's still alive." He hunched in on himself, trying to keep from dropping into a hysterical ball.

Nick sighed and squeezed Seth's shoulder. "Why don't you go check on that cute nurse of yours? She looked pretty shaken up."

Seth gritted his teeth, glaring at Nick. "Don't."

Kasey could see some kind of silent war between them. It left him feeling very anxious and angry. His inner wolf sensed competition where his mate was concerned. It took all of his patience, which was very little, mind you, to keep a leash on his canine side. His mate couldn't sense what he'd picked up on the instant Nick had entered the room. Nick wasn't human, as Seth believed. Nick was wolf.

"Please don't," Seth begged Nick, disturbing Kasey from his thoughts.

"You know I would never hurt you, Seth," Nick said quietly. "But the sheriff needs to know what's in his territory and, if he's telling the truth, the danger to his mate. You know if Taggart's still alive, the sheriff might be the only one who can protect you from him."

A wet shine came over Seth's deep-blue eyes, so turbulent they were almost a stormy gray. Kasey instinctively let out a growl, moving closer to his mate. He hovered protectively around the smaller man, practically crowding Nick out.

Kasey's stomach wrenched with emotion when Seth unconsciously huddled closer to him. Dark eyes challenged Nick viciously. "Tell me," he demanded gently.

Something akin to relief flashed through the emerald gaze, and Nick physically relaxed. His shoulders eased down from their tenseness, as if he'd suddenly received an answer he'd been looking for. "Seth, I think you should go check on your nurse, okay?" Nick looked at his friend. "Go."

Kasey didn't want to let Seth leave his sight, but somehow he knew whatever Nick was about to tell him would send his mate into the same hysterics as before, or worse. He nudged Seth gently, his hand on his lower back. "I'm sure Chessie could use some reassurance, Seth. We won't be long."

Kasey's eyes followed Seth as he left his office. His hands clenched at his sides as he focused on Nick the instant the door shut behind the slender back of his mate. "I want to know everything."

Nick leaned against the wall nearest him. His eyes were clear with sincerity. "You might want to have a seat, Sheriff, because as Seth's mate, what I'm about to tell you might bring you to your knees."

"So you believe I'm Seth's mate, then?" Kasey's gut twisted. If Seth's past was as bad as he feared, he could only pray he'd be able to control himself. He knew the pain in his mate's past was what kept Seth from accepting Kasey as his mate.

"I know you are, Sheriff," Nick said confidently. "Aside from me, only his mate could get that close to Seth. His instinctive reaction to be near you when he's afraid showed that even more clearly. I can't believe anything otherwise."

"How does he not know what you are?" Kasey demanded. "And why haven't you told him you're wolf?"

Nick settled his long length into one of the clean desk chairs. He crossed one leg over the other in a careless gesture. "You have to understand that Seth is very special and very rare. Seth is a Rho."

Kasey's breath caught as his lips parted in surprise. Seth was a Rho? Rhos were extremely rare and very special indeed. That explained his pup's ability to heal.

The only things Kasey knew about Rhos were from the stories the elders of his pack had told of their last Rho, who had died over seventy years ago. Rhos were born every 100 years. A pack could go two or three hundred years before they were graced with a Rho again. Rhos were known from birth because they were born in their true wolf form and over the course of the first year of their life slowly shifted to their human shape. It was during their fifth year that the ancestral Mother gifted them with an extraordinary ability. Some of the abilities the elders spoke of included the chance to become a healer like Seth, to take on other forms like those of a coyote or fox. The rarest gift that Kasey knew of was the ability to speak telepathically to more than just one's mate or pack, including humans.

Rhos were highly coveted by a pack because of their unique gifts, and it was common for members of a pack to break out into fights over the right to claim a Rho as their mate. But only a Rho's true mate could rightfully claim them. The mating bond with a Rho would not take unless the Rho chose to take another as their life-long partner.

The protective instinct, already prominent when Kasey thought of his mate, increased tenfold. It meant Seth would constantly be in danger until Kasey claimed him. "Go on."

"Seth's father knew from the day Seth was born that he would constantly be in danger, and he left our pack in fear of the others becoming violent with the need to claim Seth as their own. Our pack sent me to watch over and help protect

Seth from others who would take advantage of him or seek to claim him."

Kasey interrupted Nick. "Why is it you were able to control yourself around Seth if the others weren't?"

Nick's lips twisted in a cynical smile. "I'll admit it wasn't easy, but when your Alpha orders you to do something, you can't exactly say no or go against him. Unless that person is your mate, which Seth was not. After a while, it became manageable and then as simple as breathing air. Seth and I became best friends, and I wouldn't do anything in the world to change that."

"Yet he has no idea who you are? You think it's not going to change anything when he finds out?" Kasey raised an eyebrow at Nick.

Nick grimaced and ran a hand through his hair in frustration. "He knows me. He just doesn't know that I'm also wolf. Would you like to hear the rest or not, Sheriff?"

Kasey scowled but nodded for Nick to continue.

"Seth's father taught Seth how to gather his power around him and use it to project a human scent over the stronger one of the wolf. It is how I have kept myself a secret from him, as well. His father preferred Seth believe they were the only ones in the world able to shift, and the Alpha agreed, ordering me not to reveal my wolf side to him. For a time, it left him able to live a relatively normal life. Until three years ago." Nick's face became hard with rage, and his lips flattened into a line so thin they almost disappeared.

Bitterness rang out in Nick's tone as he spoke. "Our pack has never tolerated the existence of the Created ones. They bring danger to us all. Their animal sides are in control more often than not. Because of Seth's sheltered upbringing, he wasn't aware of others in the world like him or like the Created. One of them found him. An Alpha of a small pack of the Created called the Triad. There were six of them."

A sharp swear word cut through the tension in the room. "They figured out Seth is a Rho." It was a statement, not a question.

Nick nodded, his jaw tightly clenched. "Yes. Taggart found out and, playing on Seth's lack of knowledge, claimed to be his mate. Overjoyed at finding others like himself, including a man saying he was his mate, Seth believed him and spent the next four months in hell. All of the men in the Triad, including Taggart, had been imprisoned at one point or another for armed robbery, rape, or attempted murder. A friend of mine heard rumors around the neighborhood of their 'pack' and eventually word of them having a Rho amongst their numbers. By then I'd been searching for Seth for a couple of weeks, and when I heard that, my blood ran cold.

"They brutalized him. Taggart allowed the entire pack to rape and dominate Seth anytime they wanted. When I finally found him, they had him chained to the wall of the warehouse they inhabited. He was broken, a shattered shell of his former self." Nick's nails lengthened and dug into the arms of the chair, puncturing the leather.

Kasey's heart froze inside his chest, and it took all he had not to howl in rage and pain for his mate. "What happened?" he managed to choke out. His chest felt tight at the things Seth must have suffered those four months. No wonder his mate didn't want anything to do with him and didn't understand the bond between them.

"During an attempt to rescue him, the Triad returned, and some of it is still unclear even now, but somehow a fire started. It spread quickly. It was all I could do to get Seth out before the whole building went up. Taggart and the rest of the Triad were still inside when the building exploded. Or at least, we thought so. Until today." Nick ran a hand over his suddenly tired face. Dark circles made his eyes stand out starkly against his tan features.

"It took me months to get Seth back to even a fraction of who he used to be. These past two years have been hard on him. A lot of moving around and just trying to function again. This clinic was his attempt to return to a normal life. And it would seem that is what Taggart was waiting on. For Seth to come out of hiding. Dammit!" Nick growled low in his throat, his eyes flashing from human to canine and back again. "Two years! If Seth falls into his hands again, I don't know if we can ever bring him back."

A fierce look came over Kasey's face. His dark eyes glowed with power and strength as he spoke. "I'll break him into little pieces before he touches Seth again. I promise you. I want to know what he looks like, what he smells like, what his habits are, everything you can tell me. Because I fully intend to take the son of a bitch down before he can even so much as look at Seth."

Nick smiled. Seth had finally found his mate. Now if only his friend could accept Kasey into his heart and as his mate, then he would truly have the chance to be happy. When wolves mated, they mated for life, and they protected their mates as ferociously as a mother bear protected her cubs. Nick's heart ached that he hadn't found his own yet. He tried to fight off the loneliness with whatever warm body would accept him, but it wasn't the same.

When Kasey growled impatiently, Nick shook himself out of his thoughts. Melancholy didn't suit him, so he never really dwelled on it too much.

For the next ten minutes, Nick pumped out as much information about Taggart as he could remember. Taggart, a mean bastard, was big, tall—about six foot five—with a huge scar across one of his dark-silver eyes, rendering it almost useless, and a nose that was crooked from being broken in one too many fights. Nick had done some research on Taggart's history before he became one of the Created and disappeared from the human world. He'd been a violent man by nature even before being bitten, in and out of jail several times for armed robbery and rape. "The most defining feature is the scar. He got it before he became one of them, so it didn't heal like ours would."

Kasey cataloged each and every detail. He wouldn't allow Taggart within a hundred miles of Seth if he had anything to say about it. "Fine. Now, if you'll excuse me, my mate needs me."

He turned to leave, but Nick grabbed his wrist from where he sat. Kasey glared at the other wolf, growling in warning. "Just take it easy with him, Sheriff. Have patience. He will come to accept you if you just give him the chance. No wolf can deny his mate forever," Nick said, grinning lopsidedly.

A tight nod of his head was Kasey's only acknowledgement of Nick's words, and then he rushed out of the office. No matter what his mate said, he wasn't leaving his side.

Seth sat on the hood of his own vehicle, just staring forlornly at his clinic. The look of desolation on the slender man's features caused Kasey to growl in frustration. He stepped up to the front of Seth's car, practically standing between his mate's thighs. Instinctively, he reached out and brushed a strand of hair that had blown across Seth's pale cheek behind one ear. "Everything is going to be all right," he murmured soothingly.

"How can you possibly know that?" Seth croaked out, ignoring the way his heart leapt inside his chest at the tender gesture from the taller wolf.

Kasey quirked his lips in a soft smile. "Cause I say so. I'm very stubborn, which you will soon find out."

Seth wanted so badly to just give in to it, to let Kasey take care of him, to lean on the older male, but it wasn't what he'd trained himself to do these past two years. He pressed the heels of his palms against his eyes, digging them in. No matter how hard he tried to forget, he couldn't get the image of his office out of his mind. The sweet smell of the dog's blood stung his nose as if he were still standing there. He jerked, startled, when he felt warm hands drop onto his shoulders and start kneading the tense muscles there. "I'll find him, pup. I swear it. He won't get near you again."

Seth tensed even further, knowing without having to ask who Kasey meant. His hands dropped, and he glared at Kasey. "It's none of your business, Kasey."

"It is my business, dammit," Kasey snapped. "Whether you choose to believe it or not, I am your mate." His voice gentled as he cupped Seth's face in his hands. "I will protect you, Seth. I can do nothing else."

Seth's eyes stung, and he blinked furiously. Depression had long since settled over him. It left him reeling, and without thinking, he threw himself against Kasey's chest with a sob. His face pressed into Kasey's throat tightly. "I don't want to go back to him," he cried desperately.

Kasey naturally wrapped his arms around the shaking, slender form of his pup. His hand rubbed over Seth's back. "Shhh. You won't go back to him. I swear to you."

Seth greedily accepted what Kasey offered right then. He knew he should pull away and stand on his own two feet, but he didn't have the strength to push the warm body away. His lungs drew in the sheriff's scent deeply, and his body reacted. The wolf side of him strained to be closer to the other man. He could feel it just there beneath the surface, begging him to let it free. He'd never felt such a sense of "home" when Taggart claimed him. The idea of accepting the feeling of rightness singing out inside of him frightened him.

The uncertainty swirling through him allowed his canine

half a bit of freedom, and his lips pressed to the pulse beating beneath Kasey's throat. He felt Kasey shudder against him, and his arms tightened around him. Seth's tongue slipped out to pass over the same spot, licking wetly, hotly over the smooth, salty skin. Kasey pressed forward between Seth's thighs, urging them further apart. The hard length digging into Seth's belly stripped a harsh groan from Seth's throat.

"Seth?" Kasey questioned hoarsely, his breath stirring the strands of hair atop the dark head.

Seth realized what he was doing and jerked away from Kasey with a horrified look, almost falling off the hood of his car. He would have if Kasey hadn't reached out to steady him. "God, what am I doing?" Seth growled, running a hand through his hair in frustration.

Kasey knew it had been his wolf side coming through, begging to be with its mate, but it still stung that Seth seemed so angry with himself for kissing him. He could smell Seth's arousal from where he stood, and it left his own body hard and aching. "Your wolf was responding to mine," he said flatly, his voice void of all emotion.

Standing, Seth moved away from Kasey. He looked up and could see Nick standing and talking to Chessie. Seth wanted nothing more than to go back to his house and just curl up in his bed. His hands clenched tightly at his sides. "I can't handle this right now. It's too much. I just wanted a peaceful life here. It doesn't look as if I'm ever going to have it," he said bitterly, wearing an agonized expression that ripped through Kasey like a sharp knife.

Suddenly Kasey felt as though his shoulders would collapse in despair. Would Seth ever open up to him? Accept him as his mate? He'd been overjoyed to find him, and he'd never imagined his mate wouldn't know him or accept him. "You will have it, Seth," he replied quietly, still watching his mate with a longing in his eyes he wasn't even aware of. "And I hope someday you'll choose me to be a part of your life."

He didn't wait for Seth to respond before turning and stalking back toward Nick. "Stay with him. He doesn't want me around right now. And I need some time to think."

Nick frowned, tilting his head slightly. "What about what just happened over there? He seemed to accept you easily enough just now."

"He didn't accept me, just the comfort I offered him," Kasey said in a pained tone. It ravaged him, and the pain etched itself deeply into his face. Chessie gave him a sympathetic look, which he ignored. "I'm going to check with my deputies at the station. See if there has been anyone new in town or drifting through town. See if they match the description you gave me. Just… please stay with him."

"Give him time, Sheriff. He'll come around," Nick said quietly. He could only imagine the pain Kasey felt when his mate rejected him so adamantly, but he knew the only reason Seth didn't feel the connection was because of fear. If Kasey treaded lightly enough, Seth would begin to trust him soon enough. "I'll be by his side every minute."

Kasey gave him a tight smile of thanks and left. As the clinic fell from view in his mirror, he couldn't quite shake the feeling that he'd left a part of himself behind, vulnerable and aching. His jaw clenched to hold back the howls of rage and anguish his wolf wanted to let forth. The Created one had destroyed more than his chance to claim his mate, but a piece of Seth's soul Kasey could only hope he would someday be able to return to him. He wondered if the background check he'd placed on Seth had come in yet. There might be information in there that would lead him to Taggart.

Seth watched the sheriff's truck leaving the clinic parking lot. He felt a sense of panic invade him when the taillights disappeared. He tried to shake it off, but his hands trembled.

Why? He looked helplessly at Nick standing at the other side of the parking lot. It felt as though he were drowning in fear. Not fear of Taggart or what they would do to him if they were truly still alive, but the fear Kasey wasn't coming back. It literally drove him to his knees in anguish. His eyes were wild, and his body shuddered. He could hear his name from a long way off. "Seth?"

"Doc?" A soft female voice followed it. Then a pair of strong hands lifted him to his feet. He blinked and focused enough to see Nick holding him up. Seth's teeth were elongated as the wolf side of him fought for dominance, and his eyes had bled into their canine counterparts. "What's wrong with him?"

Nick sighed at his friend, shaking his head. "He's reacting to the sheriff leaving him after such a traumatic event, the big idiot. The sheriff is his mate, and though he hasn't recognized or accepted the fact, his wolf side reacts very strongly to it. His wolf is burying his humanity and attempting to take over. You wouldn't happen to have Kasey's number, would you?"

A whimper tore free from Seth's throat at the mention of the other wolf's name. A suffocating weight dropped over him, blanketing him in a heavy sheet of despair. He felt as though he couldn't breathe. He didn't understand what was going on. "Nick?" he managed to croak out in question once Chessie had gone back inside the clinic to use the phone.

"It's okay, Seth. Let's just get you back to your house for now. Chessie is calling the sheriff to meet us there." Nick didn't launch into an explanation, because he wasn't even sure if he could explain it to Seth enough to make him understand. Once a wolf found its mate, it held on for dear life, and with Seth being a Rho, his instinctual reaction to feeling abandoned by his mate would cause a depression so severe it could literally drive him to take his own life. And if

Nick tried to explain that to Seth, he'd have to tell Seth the truth about himself, because otherwise how else would he know?

Seth allowed Nick to help him into his car, and he leaned weakly against the seat. He found it hard to concentrate on anything. Sounds were muffled to a dull roar, and he could feel the wolf side of him pushing forth, so strong. It felt as though it were the night of the full moon, one of the few nights he couldn't truly leash the wolf inside him. The sense of hopelessness crowding in on him reminded him of being held captive by Taggart and his pack. But it seemed stronger and more intense. His canines elongated further and pressed into his lower lip, cutting into it.

The passage of time had no meaning for him. It could have been twenty minutes or even an hour by the time he found himself in his house. The shifting of his eyes between wolf and human sight was making him dizzy. Would it be easier just to shift? Or would that be worse?

The human items surrounding him made no sense to him in those moments either. The wolf side had no use for them. What did he care for a television set when he felt as bereft and barren as an empty desert stretching on forever?

Not since childhood had Seth's wolf side pushed so hard for control. His skin itched to change, to mold into the canine counterparts that were always there. The smell of the forest called to him. The solitude of the forest screamed for him to embrace it. He dug his nails into his scalp to try and erase the thoughts, to garner a semblance of himself. It wasn't enough. He gave Nick a helpless look. "I'm sorry, Nick," he whispered before he fled out of the house and straight into the woods.

Before he'd even been completely engulfed by the shade of the trees overhead, he'd shifted into his wolf form, racing through the trees and bushes. He wanted to outrun all of his demons, the pain of his past and present, to forget the emotions Kasey stirred in him. A loud howl rent the air around him as it burst forth from him uncontrollably. The unbearable sadness in his wolf consciousness made Seth wonder if maybe Kasey had been telling the truth. A shudder wound its way through him at the thought of letting himself believe it, though. The thought of being vulnerable again terrified him more deeply than the thought of Taggart kidnapping him again.

Like the other day, he found himself just running flat out to burn off the restlessness inside of himself. The muscles in his legs burned by the time he managed to slow down to a trot before eventually collapsing in the same clearing as he had the night he'd first come across Kasey. Somehow he'd instinctively found his way back to this same place. Everything always came back around to Kasey—his thoughts, all of the events of the past few days—and as he lay there thinking of the other man, he knew he felt a deep attraction for the arrogant Cheyenne who had come crashing into his life. He couldn't deny it any longer.

He whined deep in his throat, bringing both paws up to cover his ears. He just wished he'd never come here. It'd taken two years to recover enough of himself to return to the human world completely, and now he was on the verge of losing those fragments again. Only this time to a strong yet amazingly gentle werewolf who didn't know how to take no for an answer. He should have been overjoyed Kasey had taken the hint and left him alone, yet he couldn't shake the feeling of abandonment. To the wolf inside him, it seemed like the end of the world. It wasn't like Kasey wouldn't return, but he couldn't seem to get his wolf to understand.

The sheriff held some kind of pull over his wolf. It was as if it were a hypnotic aura demanding he submit to the older wolf. Whenever he was near Kasey, it took all of his strength not to roll over and show his belly in submissiveness, like a wolf to its Alpha. When he'd felt Kasey's teeth scraping against the side of his throat that night in his office, it had seemed so natural to want to allow his head to tilt further, granting him access. An intense desire for Kasey to sink his teeth into his throat had almost consumed him. He'd never wanted Taggart or any of the others to dominate him. When they'd forced him to submit, there had never been such a deep sense of rightness to it. His body had never sung out for them to touch him. The lust gripping his stomach when he was near Kasey was so strong and fierce that it stole his breath.

The fur along his body rippled with the shudders tearing through him. Heightened emotions always made him this way. Seth didn't like to be in environments that weren't peaceful and calm. Anything else always left him unsettled and restless. Thunder rolled overhead from dark, ominous clouds, the sound almost drowning out another one. He lifted his head when he heard another wolf call in the distance. It caused him to flinch, but he knew it wasn't Taggart. He knew Taggart's call quite well and would never forget it. Instinctively, he recognized Kasey's call, and before he could try to control himself, the wolf once again took control and let forth a joyous howl, calling to the other wolf. He growled at the wolf within him, but the wolf just wagged his tail happily as he waited in eagerness for his mate.

7

KASEY was just looking over the report on Seth when his cell phone rang. He flipped it open without looking at it, barking, "Yeah?"

An anxious female voice came over the phone. "Kase?"

He immediately sat upright in his chair, dropping the file. "Chessie, what's wrong?"

"It's Seth. Nick said you need to get to Seth's house right away. Seth was acting strange. Nick seemed to think he might hurt himself."

A swear word slipped free from Kasey, capturing the attention of his deputy, Julian. "I'll be right there."

Julian lifted an eyebrow at him. "Trouble?"

"Nothing for you to worry about. I'll be back later." Kasey threw his jacket on and raced out of the station. He berated himself for leaving his pup. He should have listened to the instincts telling him to turn around, but he'd just assumed it was because of his wolf not wanting to leave his mate. Of course, it had been that and more.

The drive felt interminable, and by the time he reached Seth's house, his teeth were gnashing together. Nick stood on the front porch waiting for him. "Where is he?" Kasey demanded.

"He took off before I could stop him. He's in the woods somewhere," Nick stated flatly. "His wolf is reacting to being left behind."

"You were supposed to watch him!" Kasey growled before stalking toward the back of the house. He wasn't even inside the woods before he shifted, immediately scenting for Seth and darting off in the direction his pup had headed. With no idea how much of a head start his mate had, Kasey let forth a loud call in the hopes his mate would answer. If the wolf had as much of a hold on Seth as he suspected, there should be an answering call.

He wasn't disappointed. A joyful howl reached his ears, and he grinned, loping off in the direction it came from. Seth's canine side seemed to be fully in control. Kasey howled again, beseeching his mate to return to his side. The other wolf responded again, this time closer than before. Eagerness to see his pup urged his paws faster, covering more ground. Fat drops of rain began to fall from the heavy clouds above as he got closer to the one person, the one wolf, who meant the world to him.

Relief flooded Kasey when he spotted the black wolf rushing toward him. Seth skidded to a stop in front of him, pushing into him affectionately. Kasey breathed in deeply the smell of cinnamon and sunshine, practically purring in satisfaction. They wound themselves around each other, and eventually he had Seth pinned beneath him. He nuzzled Seth's throat affectionately, attempting to soothe his pup. Their fur was soaked through by then, but neither cared about anything except each other and being close to one another.

Shifting back to his human form, Kasey stroked his hands along the powerful muscles beneath the black fur. Rain still fell down on them, but it had lessened to a light drizzle for the moment. "It's all right, pup. I'm here. I told you I wasn't going anywhere. I just wanted to give you some space."

A low whine echoed from Seth's throat, and then he shifted. He lay underneath Kasey, staring up at him with sad eyes. "I don't understand why," Seth whispered, blinking furiously against the drops of water dusting his eyelashes.

Kasey gave him a gentle smile, leaning his forehead on Seth's. "It's all part of being mates, my pup. Your wolf knows we are connected, and it reacted to my leaving after you went through something so traumatic. It felt abandoned. Our wolves are intertwined with each other. You are the other half of my soul, Seth, just as I am yours."

Kasey slid the tip of one finger down the younger wolf's cheek in a light caress. His body leapt at the lust darkening Seth's gaze at his touch. "I am trying so hard not to push you for more than you are ready to give," he murmured huskily, "but when you look at me like that…."

Seth flushed, and his eyes closed, drawing a soft chuckle from Kasey. Kasey rubbed his nose against his pup's teasingly. "You are so adorable."

Blue eyes opened with a flare of indignation, but before Seth could lay into him for saying such a thing, Kasey kissed him. It wasn't a hard or rough kiss like the last ones had been. It was soft and tender, just a light kiss meant to comfort. Kasey probed lightly along the seam of Seth's lips, requesting access to his mate's mouth. A soft moan shuddered through his large form when Seth tentatively responded, opening to him like a flower to the first drops of dew on a cool spring morning. The moan deepened into a lusty growl when Seth's tongue slid wetly over his. Slipping one hand between their bodies, Kasey delicately strummed his fingers over Seth's belly, seducing his mate with a gentle touch. A sigh from Seth flooded his mouth, and Kasey deepened the kiss while sliding his fingers under the hem of Seth's shirt to touch bare skin. Electricity zipped from the tips of his fingers straight down to his groin.

Breathing heavily, Kasey broke the kiss with a gasp, wrenching himself to the side and collapsing among the wet leaves on the forest floor. If he didn't stop now, he wouldn't be able to stop at all. Seth had no idea what he did to him. His cock, hard and aching, dug into the zipper of his uniform, but Seth didn't seem to realize just how thin his control was stretched, for he followed Kasey, splaying his body over the large Cheyenne's. He buried his lips into the hollow at the base of Kasey's throat, swiping his tongue over the skin there. Kasey gasped, gripping Seth's arms lightly. "Seth… stop," he begged.

Whether Seth was in the driver's seat, so to speak, or his wolf was, Kasey didn't know, but his mate ignored his request, sucking on the skin his tongue bathed. Kasey's hips jerked upward, grinding his stiff flesh into the other male's equally hard length. His hands instinctively gripped at the slender wolf's rounded bottom. The storm started to build again, the rain falling heavier and faster. It almost appeared as if the storm were connected to their emotions and sensed the building passion between them.

The moment Seth's smooth, elegant hand cupped him through his uniform, his willpower dissolved, and with a keening cry, Kasey rolled them, pressing Seth into the grass under him. His mouth captured Seth's in a ravaging kiss as he frantically pulled at Seth's clothing. The need to be buried inside his mate ate at him like a deep-seated primal demand he couldn't ignore. Not anymore. He just prayed when it was over Seth wouldn't hate him or feel he'd taken advantage of him in a vulnerable situation.

He almost shredded Seth's shirt in the process of stripping it from the slim, pale chest. Light brown nipples were peaked in desire, and Kasey's teeth found one of them with unerring accuracy. Seth gasped and cried out as Kasey tugged at it while removing his own shirt. Their skin contrasted startlingly, dark tan against soft white. Kasey's calloused hands slid roughly over Seth in a heated caress while his mouth feasted hungrily on those beautiful stiff nubs. Unable to linger there any longer, the need to explore his mate greater, he started nibbling and licking his way down his mate's body, leaving behind small red marks. Seth fisted his hands in Kasey's hair, lost in the ecstasy of Kasey's mouth on him.

Nimble fingers quickly removed the last barrier of clothing from Seth's body, and Kasey drank in the sight of his pup sprawled in naked splendor among the golden-brown leaves and the bright-green blades of grass. His pale skin shimmered wetly, each drop of rain beading on his skin. Seth's cock, a pale pink that made Kasey's mouth water hungrily, stood stiff and jutted straight up from a nest of dark curls that matched the color of the hair on his head. His cock wept with pleasure, a small drop of liquid shining clearly on the very tip. Kasey's tongue flicked out to taste his mate, wrenching a moan from him at how good Seth tasted mixed with the rain. Seth arched his back and gave a small whimper at the feel of Kasey's hot tongue rolling over the head of his shaft.

Another drop seeped out, trickling down the stiff length, and Kasey followed its path using just the tip of his tongue, savoring the feel of the silken flesh. Trailing back up Seth's cock, Kasey swirled his tongue around the ridged tip, circling it before sucking it between his lips. His hands gripped at Seth's thighs, holding him in place as he slowly lowered his head, taking the man's hard flesh deeper. A guttural moan rattled above his head, indicating Seth liked what he was doing. He'd never sucked another man's dick before, but it seemed the most natural thing in the world when it came to his mate. He knew what he enjoyed and mimicked each action perfectly.

Soft sighs of pleasure drifted from Seth's throat, mingling with the wet sucking noises Kasey's mouth made. It made Kasey feel amazingly powerful to know he could cause such pleasure for his pup. He could feel his mate trembling and writhing beneath him. Kasey circled the entrance to Seth's body with the tip of his index finger, feeling the puckered flesh around the opening as he teased at it softly. Seth pressed up against the seeking digit, trying to pull it into his body, but Kasey pulled away, gently scraping his teeth along Seth's sensitive prick in punishment.

"Kasey!" Seth keened wantonly, gripping at his mate's long wet hair.

Kasey hummed at the sound of his name on his mate's lips, wrenching a scream from Seth at the vibrations on his cock. He did it again, relishing the noises it elicited. His finger returned to the puckered opening, exerting more pressure before finally slipping the tip inside. His cock surged lustily at how hot and tight his mate felt around the very tip of his finger. He wasn't sure how he would fit into such a tiny space, and reluctantly he released Seth with a wet popping sound. "Seth… I don't know if I will fit inside you," he said in doubt, disappointment on his face. "I don't want to hurt you."

Seth opened passion-glazed eyes to look down his body at where Kasey knelt between his legs. His lips curved into a trembling smile as he picked up Kasey's hand, slowly pulling one finger into his mouth. Kasey's skin tasted salty and felt calloused against his tongue as he laved Kasey's finger. Seth's saliva gleamed wetly when he pulled the finger free only to suck two fingers into his mouth this time. "I just need to be stretched," he whispered huskily, his eyes shifting in discomfort. He guided Kasey's now very wet fingers down to his hole and carefully pushed the first one inside him. Moaning, he leaned his head back at the sweet pain tingling up his spine.

Kasey didn't make any move to help him as he could only watch in lust as his mate prepared his own body for Kasey's cock. When Seth began to feed the second finger into his ass, Kasey groaned again, licking his lips. Seth's hips instinctively thrust downward onto the invading fingers, riding them eagerly. Seth's hand forced Kasey deeper, causing Seth to elicit a throaty cry as Kasey felt his finger brush over a small bump inside his mate.

Taking over, Kasey removed Seth's hand from his and began to thrust his fingers in and out of the smaller male. Each time he pushed back inside, he made sure to target the spot that seemed to bring his pup such immense pleasure. His cock had grown hard as a rock at how lusty Seth's moans sounded. He yearned to fuck his mate, but he still hesitated. His fingers were gliding in and out easier than they had at first, and lubing his mate with saliva seemed to help. An idea came to mind, and he pulled his fingers free of Seth's hole, diving down between his thighs, pushing his tongue where his fingers had been.

Seth jerked in surprise when he felt Kasey's tongue pressing at his most intimate of spots, but instead of being embarrassed, it merely turned him on even more. He groaned and spread his legs wider, tilting his hips up to grant him better access. It surprised him that Kasey, who knew nothing about sex with another male, seemed to just instinctively know what felt good to him, but perhaps it merely felt this good because it was Kasey. His head whirled with lust and a sense of joy he couldn't describe or begin to understand. It just felt so right to let Kasey touch him like this. His body felt more alive than ever, and he felt overwhelmed by how much Kasey wanted him. It was a heady sensation and made him forget everything—except wanting Kasey to fuck him right then. The feeling of despair had been replaced by a searing euphoria that made his dick throb with hunger. "Kasey…," he panted breathlessly, "please…."

He tried pulling at Kasey's wide shoulders, wanting to feel his body pressing against him fully, but the other male stayed where he lay, lapping at Seth's channel. When the wet muscle suddenly pierced his hole, his body bowed from the earth, and he gave a loud, lusty cry. Kasey's tongue mimicked another part of his anatomy, thrusting into him over and over again. Just when Seth thought he'd go out of his mind with hunger for the big Cheyenne, Kasey suddenly rose above him, kissing him. The musky flavor of Seth's body coated the man's lips, and he could do no more than greedily accept the deep plundering of his mouth, tasting himself on Kasey.

"What do you want, pup?" Kasey demanded softly, knowing what Seth wanted from him but needing to hear it. He needed to know that Seth wanted him too.

Seth was drowning in the craving to have Kasey inside him, to feel them connected in such an intimate way. "Please," he whimpered.

"Please what, Seth?" Kasey murmured, nipping at Seth's bottom lip teasingly.

Seth's blue eyes opened, glittering feverishly. "Take me, fuck me, claim me," he begged.

A loud groan crackled through the clearing when Kasey heard those words. It was all he needed, and he immersed himself in Seth's lips while reaching for the fastenings to his own pants. It seemed as though his fingers were stiff and numb as he fumbled in his urgency to bury himself inside his mate.

Seth could feel Kasey's hands ripping at the front of his

pants, releasing the hard flesh that would soon be inside him. It felt hot and heavy against Seth's thigh as those strong hips settled between his legs, which he immediately wrapped high around Kasey's back. Seth's hand reached between their bodies to grip the stiff cock and help Kasey enter him. He gasped at the sheer, throbbing size in his palm. It seemed as though he held a living spear of fire in his hand. His fingers stroked it several times, but Kasey gave an impatient growl. "No. Time for that later. Need to fuck you, pup. Now."

Hearing those words ignited Seth even further, and he pulled Kasey closer. The flared tip nudged Seth's tight hole, asking for entrance, which he eagerly granted. Both men released a loud groan as Kasey slowly sank inside him, finally connecting them in the primal mating dance their wolves craved. Seth gripped at him frantically, attempting to anchor himself in the violent storm swirling around him and inside him. Thunder ripped through the clearing, almost rattling the ground beneath them. It urged them along the path they'd chosen to follow.

Kasey growled fiercely at the feel of his pup's body embracing his cock so tightly. It was like he'd buried himself in an inferno with how hot Seth's insides felt. "You feel so good, pup," he gasped, burying his face in Seth's neck as he started to thrust ever so slowly, denying the urge to pound his mate into the ground despite how badly he wanted him.

He didn't want this to end anytime soon. It scared him to death how much he needed Seth, how afraid he was at the thought of losing him. Finally being able to claim his mate opened up a maelstrom of new emotions inside him. It made him feel vulnerable in a way he'd never felt in all his life. Perhaps it was merely because Seth was his mate, or maybe it came from Seth being who he was, but he suddenly knew he loved this man more than anyone he'd ever known. Tears stung his closed eyelids, but he held them back, lightly clamping his teeth down on Seth's shoulder as he surged forward into the snug depths of his mate.

Seth raked his nails down Kasey's broad back at the feel of Kasey's teeth in his shoulder. Rapture exploded inside him, and something shifted, changing inexorably forever. "Oh... God," he moaned. "Too much... oh fuck... more... harder... fuck me harder."

If Kasey could have formed a coherent thought aside from how good Seth felt wrapped around him, he'd have laughed at the contradictory words of his mate, but all he could concentrate on was his cock and fucking the stubborn vet. His hips started thrusting faster, plunging in and out of Seth hard and deep. The wet, slick sounds of flesh sliding into flesh echoed off the trees around them, and the heady scent of sex overwhelmed their senses, blocking out all thoughts except of each other.

Bright spots danced behind Seth's eyes as the lust washed over him like a tidal wave sweeping him along in a stormy flood. He thrust his hips upward, meeting Kasey thrust for thrust, accepting his hard cock deeper into him on every plunge. It gave him a heady rush to hear Kasey's pleasure every time he bottomed out inside him, to know it was his body causing him so much ecstasy. He ran his hands up and down the strong muscles of Kasey's back, feeling them ripple with each thrust. They were both covered in a fine sheen of sweat and earthy rain that stung Seth's senses, pushing the flames burning within him even higher, like a forest fire threatening to consume him.

Kasey knew he wouldn't last much longer, and he reached between them, gripping Seth's stiff cock tightly, tugging it in time with his thrusts. "Come... Seth, I need to feel you come for me, around me," he panted hoarsely.

Seth tilted his head to the side, baring his throat to Kasey in submission as he felt himself splintering. He screamed out at the feel of Kasey's teeth sinking into him, marking him. Lightning flashed behind Seth's closed eyelids as hot liquid spilled out between their bodies, his back bowing almost in half, threatening to snap his spine.

The taste of his mate's blood and the aroma of his seed, combined with knowing he'd finally claimed Seth, sent Kasey careening over the edge. He threw his head back, tossing his long dark hair around his shoulders as he came, his hot cream searing Seth's innards. Dark drops of blood glittered on his lips as he collapsed atop Seth, panting and shuddering. Something had changed between them with their mating, binding them forever. Kasey felt whole, as if a part of him had been missing all these years and he hadn't realized it until right then. It slipped into place like the last piece of an amazing puzzle. He just prayed Seth could feel it and wouldn't break his heart by denying it. Passion made people do things they normally wouldn't, and Seth might regret what had just happened. Kasey lay there, unwilling to move and shatter the moment, and quite possibly his heart, just yet.

Seth trembled in the intense aftermath of it all. He couldn't seem to let go of Kasey, just clinging to him like a lifeline. The bite mark on his shoulder throbbed, but he knew it had already healed over. His mind reeled at what he'd just done. It felt so different to be claimed by Kasey than it had been by Taggart. When Taggart had bitten him, it had been nothing but a bite, nothing he'd felt to the depths of his soul like he had this one. His soul felt… complete. The wound pulsed pleasantly beneath his skin, a reminder of Kasey's claim on him. Panic started to wind through him at the realization of what he'd just done and how much he was beginning to need Kasey. He felt agony to the bottom of his heart at the thought of Kasey ever leaving him. If he ever lost the man who lay on top of him, it would shatter his soul into a million pieces, pieces that would surely never be knitted back together again.

Kasey felt the shift in his mate's emotions almost immediately, and sadness engulfed him. The regret rolled off of Seth in a tangible wave, like the drops of rain trickling down his mate's pale skin. "It's okay, pup," he murmured, stroking a shaky hand through his mate's dark locks as he sat up, bringing Seth with him into his lap.

Seth struggled weakly for a brief moment before collapsing into Kasey. "No. It's not okay. I can't… I can't need you," he sobbed.

A warm, calloused hand soothed down Seth's bare back in a gentle caress. "You can, Seth, because I need you just as much as you need me, if not more."

Seth shook his head, denying his words, but his movements stopped abruptly when Kasey lightly cupped his chin, tilting his head back to look up at him. Seth tried to avoid the dark gaze glittering softly down at him, but Kasey wouldn't let him. The rain had stopped, but beads of water clung to Seth's lashes, sparkling on the tips like diamonds in the sand. "Look at me, Seth. Truly look at me."

Tormented blue eyes opened reluctantly, meeting Kasey's. Seth's breath caught in his throat when he saw the depth of emotion shining from the larger werewolf. It was an emotion he'd never seen from another living being. He'd seen the same look between his parents when they'd been alive. His heart beat even harder against his ribcage, pounding like a terrified rabbit trying to escape a trap.

"I know you might not believe me, Seth, or you might think it's too soon, but… I love you. With all my heart. You are the piece of my soul that has been missing all these years. I am not going anywhere, and I will give my life to protect you."

Seth whimpered frantically, trying to pull away, but

Kasey gripped his hands tenderly, lifting them to his lips. "These hands hold my heart, Seth. These amazing, gentle, sexy hands hold my heart so deeply inside them that it will never belong to me again. I know you aren't ready to say it back, but I will be here, pup. As long as it takes. Just know I will always be here, with you."

He could do nothing but stare at Kasey helplessly. Kasey loved him? "I… I can't do this right now," he stuttered out, almost choking on the panic still racing through him.

Kasey sighed, his heart aching, but he'd known Seth couldn't accept it so easily. Seth was his now, no matter how much he wanted to fight it. He wasn't ever going to let the stubborn vet go. Even if it took him a hundred years to earn his mate, he would do whatever it took. "All right, pup. I'll let it drop for now, but it isn't going away. The longer you deny it, the more your wolf will suffer. Your wolf knows the truth that you're refusing to see."

He handed Seth's clothing to him, almost grinning at the missing buttons and the dirt smudges. Pure contentment rumbled through him with the knowledge that he'd claimed his mate. He wouldn't allow any dark thoughts to dampen the euphoria he felt right then. He wouldn't allow Seth to cut him from his life once the Triad situation was cleared up. Seth was his.

On the way back, despite Seth's attempts to wiggle free, Kasey held his hand and lightly whistled while walking. "Nick is waiting at your house. I think he's a little upset, rightly so, if you ask me, that you just left," he scolded gently. He squeezed Seth's fingers affectionately. "Promise me you won't leave either Nick's or my side again. Not while we are still trying to track the Triads, if they are indeed the ones who trashed your clinic."

Tensing at the sound of the name he feared, Seth shuddered, unconsciously moving closer to Kasey's side. Kasey's arms snaked around his waist, pulling him into his body. "We'll find whoever this is, pup. But until then I'm going to be by your side every step of the way."

Seth knew it was unreasonable to believe he wouldn't freeze like a solid block of ice if he did come face to face with Taggart. Despite the past two years of training he'd gone through, just the thought of that bastard's name made his blood run cold. Sheer terror alone would render him immobile. Giving a heavy nod, he allowed the older wolf's strength to seep into his bones. "I know I can't face him alone," he croaked. "But… please give me time to process what just happened."

Kasey tightened his arm around Seth's waist. "You have all the time you need, Seth. I never intended for our first mating to be quite so… ill-prepared," he said, grimacing. "But I don't regret that it happened."

It baffled Seth why he didn't feel regrets about it or anything other than a mind-numbing sense of panic that it was already too late to pull away from Kasey and protect his heart. Seth didn't know what to say, so he remained silent. He could feel something growing between them. Some kind of connection that allowed him to actually feel what his mate felt, but it was more like he was a spectator than the feelings being his own. Pure happiness practically screamed from the other werewolf, and Seth couldn't quell his own emotions answering Kasey's. A small smile curled one corner of his mouth, and he buried his face in the side of Kasey's chest to hide it.

That might have been a mistake, though, because the man's musky scent stung his nostrils, and it sent desire spiking through him. Arousal settled low between his thighs, and he found himself once again semi-erect. Kasey chuckled against him, his strong fingers stroking lightly over Seth's waist, but the sheriff didn't say anything in response to the scent of his lust. Whenever he was near Kasey, it seemed almost impossible to keep his body from reacting. It seemed like he'd been horny since they'd met. Another emotion Seth wasn't used to, either.

Nick stood waiting on the front porch, and the instant he saw them, his bright-green gaze widened. His lips pressed together firmly, and he gave a hardened look at Kasey but didn't say anything, or else he'd give away his own secret before he was ready to. "Where've you been, Seth? Why'd you run out?"

Seth had the grace to look chastised before mumbling, "I had to, Nick. Just to get away for a while."

Emerald eyes traveled over the both of them, noting the leaves and dirt clinging to their clothing. "So… is there something you want to tell me?"

A small sound left Seth's throat as he dropped his gaze to his best friend's feet. "I… uh…."

"We've mated," Kasey said bluntly.

"Kasey!" Seth exclaimed, his cheeks blazing hotly, and he pressed his face into Kasey's shoulder, hiding his expression.

Nick laughed then, breaking the tension. He reached out and clapped Seth on the shoulder. "No need to be embarrassed, Seth. I could tell that even without him saying it. But I'm glad. It means I'll have some help keeping an eye on a certain wayward wolf."

A scowl creased Seth's brow, and he opened his mouth to refute the other's statement, but Kasey smoothly interrupted him. "Why don't you go take a hot shower, pup? It'll help you relax, and then afterward we can talk, okay?"

Seth wanted to refuse, but he'd already been thinking of a shower because of how dirty he felt, not just from his romp in the grass with Kasey but also from being in the office at his clinic. His skin still crawled with the memory. "Fine," he said tersely before stalking past Nick and into the house.

Nick waited until Seth was in the bathroom before he turned on Kasey and snapped at him, "What the hell happened out there? Did you force him?!"

Kasey's eyes narrowed dangerously, flashing between canine and human pupils in his anger that Nick would suggest such a thing. He clenched his hands at his side to keep from slugging Nick. "I'm going to forget you said that. So let's move on to another subject, like what we're going to do about Taggart and the Triad."

Not entirely accepting that Kasey didn't push Seth into their first mating, Nick still had a skeptical look on his face, even though he let it go for now. He would talk to Seth later on when they had a moment to themselves. Turning, he entered the house, clearly expecting Kasey to follow him.

Kasey didn't disappoint and was hot on his heels. The last time he'd been in Seth's house, he hadn't really paid attention to their surroundings. His attention had been entirely focused on Seth and getting through to his mate. What he saw brought him to a standstill.

The house was practically barren inside, with no personal effects to stamp the house as Seth's. Kasey's eyes roved over the empty walls and shelves. The only furniture in the room was a couch, an easy chair, a coffee table, and a small television set. On the bar between the kitchen and living room were a telephone and a rack holding some spices. There were more material items in the kitchen such as pots, dishes, and such, but still no personal "stamp" to it. "Is this… because he just moved in?" Kasey asked the other male werewolf softly, his heart pulsating with an ache that seemed to radiate through his body.

Nick's lips pursed with distaste. "No. He keeps it this way because of the last two years. Moving place to place left him with very little home comforts, if you know what I mean. The only things he doesn't let go are his books. He keeps the spare bedroom as his library. And I think he believes that he doesn't deserve to have a home like most people. He thinks he did something to deserve all of the bad things happening to him. So he keeps it empty, easy to pack up and leave if necessary. His office at the clinic is the first thing in two years that I've seen him actually put effort into, and that bastard destroyed it. I have no doubt Seth is going to revert back to having nothing so he has nothing to lose. Aside from me and Bullet, you're the first person I've seen him get so close to in a long time, Sheriff."

Kasey sank down onto the couch in a daze. Seth lived like a monk because he was afraid. It made him finally understand what Seth had been saying out in the woods. He couldn't need him, not because he didn't want to but because he thought that if he let himself need Kasey, then he'd feel it so much more if he lost him. Kasey's nails dug into the sofa cushion as he realized just what Taggart had stolen from his mate. "I think it's time you call me Kasey," he said suddenly, looking up very seriously at Nick. "Because if you are the one person he trusts most, I need you on my side to make him understand I'm not going to leave him."

Nick's green eyes shrewdly examined the Cheyenne sitting on the well-used sofa. Strength and sincerity shone from Kasey's dark eyes, and the tension Nick had been feeling since the news of Seth finding his mate eased from him. He truly relaxed and gave Kasey a wide grin, emeralds sparkling in his lightly tanned features. "It's about time Seth opened himself up to someone besides me, and I think you're just the right one to make him do it. As a Rho, Seth has an innate need to be dominated. Despite his attempts to make himself stronger, his wolf side won't allow him to do anything but be dominated in the presence of a bigger, stronger wolf. He's peaceful by nature, and fighting has never been something he should have to do."

Kasey nodded. "He won't be fighting at all. And I think you should tell him the truth, Nick. About you. If you keep lying to him, and he finds out some other way than from you, it will hurt him far worse than if you tell him."

A sigh whispered from Nick before he spoke quietly. "Even though my pack sent me to watch over him, and at first I thought it merely an assignment, Seth has been my best friend almost from the moment I met him. He became more than an assignment. He's like my brother."

"If Seth cares about you as much as I think he does, he'll forgive you, Nick. You just have to be honest with him," Kasey replied.

"Forgive him for what?" Seth's voice interrupted their conversation, and Nick visibly tensed.

SETH stood in the doorway, hair still damp from his shower, wearing a pair of soft blue jeans and a gray T-shirt. His eyes darted between them, and he frowned. Kasey's gut twisted at the fresh clean scent coming from his mate, and it was all he could do to keep from going to him and kissing him senseless. He held out his hand for Seth to join him on the sofa. Nick had already claimed the easy chair across from him. Seth hesitated but slowly drifted over to the couch, sinking down next to Kasey just close enough to be able to feel the heat from the other's body. "Forgive you for what, Nick?"

Nick knew there was no way around it and with a heavy heart began to explain what he'd told Kasey earlier. He couldn't bear to watch as the light of betrayal entered those blue eyes, and his gaze dropped to his lap. Dead silence dominated the room when Nick had finished. Seth hadn't said a word, which made Nick's stomach sink even further.

Seth stared at his best friend of fourteen years. His heartbeat sounded loud in his ears as he listened to Nick telling him that their friendship was a lie, that he didn't have to be alone, that he had a pack out there. Somewhere he could have belonged. Nick had been sent by them to watch over him and protect him. "Why, Nick? Why didn't they claim me after my parents died?" he finally asked in a faint voice.

Nick winced and ran a hand over his face. "You're a Rho, Seth. Until you found your mate, fights would break out within the pack over the right to claim you, and they couldn't chance that. It was too unstable of a situation. Once you were born and your parents realized what you were, they chose to leave the pack out of fear for your safety. The Alpha didn't entirely agree with your parents' decision to hide you away, but he also felt the need to think of the sanity of our pack members. Perhaps things should have been handled differently, but they… we thought it would be safer for you if you didn't know the truth. If you were left in the dark until you found your mate, it would be harder for any wolf to tell what you are unless they knew of your healing ability."

"How was I supposed to find my mate when I wasn't around others like me?" Seth blazed, suddenly very angry. He buried the hurt deep inside to be processed later. When he was alone, he could grieve over Nick and their friendship.

"Do you remember your father bringing… strange men home for brief time spans? Always telling you they were people he worked with?" Nick grimaced as he remembered the last time Seth's father had attempted to locate his son's mate. One of their unmated pack members had been invited to dinner, and it hadn't ended pretty. He'd actually had to help keep the man away from Seth.

Seth nodded in response to his question, clearly waiting for a detailed explanation of why he'd mentioned those times.

"They were others from your pack, Seth. Your father tried so hard to locate your mate in order for you all to return home. Only… none of the ones he brought to the house were your mate. The last attempt he made with one of them did not go so well. Do you remember a night where your father had a man named Charles Drakson over for dinner? Your mother pulled you out of the room without warning?"

Shock held Seth immobile as he processed everything his friend told him. His father had been trying all that time to find his mate? "I remember," he murmured.

"The man almost attacked you right there at the dining room table. I had to help your father get him away from you. He would have claimed you right there if we hadn't stopped him." Nick shuddered at how close a call it had been.

"How did you know he wasn't my mate?" Seth asked curiously.

A sad look came over Nick's face. "Because no matter how badly your mate wanted to claim you, they would never hurt you to do so."

"Why did they only try men?" Kasey interjected, frowning. "Why not try female wolves too?"

"Because Seth came out to his parents when he was fifteen. They figured if Seth was gay, it must mean his mate would be male. I guess it never occurred to them to try women. Though it seems that they were right," Nick explained, gesturing at Kasey toward the end.

Kasey's question barely registered as a fine shudder went down Seth's slender frame at the memory of Taggart claiming him, how painful it had been. Perhaps if he hadn't been kept ignorant of it all, he would have known Taggart wasn't his mate. "No matter whether my parents and you wanted to protect me or not, you had no right to hide everything from me. If I had known the truth of my past and who I am, then maybe things would have been different with Taggart!" Seth growled fiercely, shoving up from the couch.

Bullet whined and padded around the couch from where he'd been lying to press against Seth. Seth's hand dropped down automatically to rest on top of the dark-golden hair. "I would have known Taggart wasn't truly my mate! And maybe I would have found the strength to run away."

"You think I don't know that?" Nick asked in an agonized voice, his eyes pained. "You think I don't remind myself of that every single minute of every single day? You're my best friend, my brother, Seth, and if I had only told you the truth and explained to you about mates, the feelings they stir, you'd have known what Taggart was. But I didn't, and I live with my mistake every day. The memory of how broken you were when I finally found you haunts my dreams, Seth. But I can't change the past, only make up for it with the present and the future."

"Then why did it take Kasey telling you to tell me the truth before you did?" Seth challenged, his canine teeth beginning to lengthen in his anger.

"Because… because I feared you'd cut me out of your life, Seth," Nick said softly, his voice taut. "I was afraid you'd think me to be like Taggart and wouldn't want me around anymore."

"You should have given me the chance to make that decision for myself!" Seth shouted. "I'm sick of everyone making my decisions for me, telling me what my life should be and who I should be. Just… just get out, Nick. I don't want you here right now."

Nick flinched at Seth's words. His hands gripped the arms of the chair tightly. "I can't do that, Seth. I can't leave you until we know for sure if Taggart is truly alive, and if he isn't, then who is the one who trashed your clinic?"

A rumbling sound started in Seth's chest, and he glared at Nick. "I can take care of myself."

Kasey couldn't just watch silently any longer, and he stood, moving to Seth's side. His fingers encircled Seth's wrist gently. "We know you can, pup, but we want to help you," he soothed quietly. "Nick cares about you, Seth."

Trembling, Seth felt as though he would be buried beneath the wealth of emotions flooding him. Fear, anger, betrayal, and yet it was tinged by lust and affection for the man standing next to him. He tilted his head back to look up at Kasey. His eyes were wild with all of the thoughts racing through his mind. "I… I just—" He choked off, dropping his head into his free hand.

Tugging slightly, Kasey pulled Seth into his arms, holding him close. "Shh, pup. I know it's a lot to take in, and so much has happened, but everything will be okay." He ran the palm of one big hand down Seth's spine in a brief caress.

Seth leaned his forehead against Kasey's shoulder, and Kasey looked up at Nick. "I think he's had enough for one day. We'll talk about the Triad later. For now just let him rest."

Kasey could feel Seth's jumbled emotions and his exhaustion, not just physically but mentally. He nuzzled at Seth's temple with his chin. "I think you need to get some sleep, pup. You can sleep without fear. We'll both be here to make sure nothing happens."

Nick stood and walked out of the house to the front porch to give them a few moments alone.

Seth shuddered. "It's not the fear he'll come for me that keeps me awake," he whispered. "It's the dreams, the memories."

The shattered way Seth said it made Kasey want to rush out and find the bastard named Taggart. If he was dead, Kasey wanted to drag him back from the depths of the hell he was in and send him right back into the heart of it. But if he was alive, Kasey would drag him from whatever hole he'd curled up in for the moment and rip the son of a bitch apart. But his mate needed him more than he needed a furious werewolf, so he breathed in deep, his embrace tightening. "If you'll allow me to, pup, I'd like to hold you while you sleep. To help fight away the demons I can't see," he murmured quietly into Seth's hair.

To his embarrassment, Seth clung even tighter to Kasey. Why couldn't he be strong around this man? Why did he feel as though he wanted to lay his soul bare to this stranger who'd come into his life so abruptly? A stranger he felt as if he'd known all of his life, and they seemed as deeply connected, if not even more so, than he and Nick were. Was this what it felt like with your mate, he wondered, this insane urge to hold on and never let go?

Kasey must have taken his clinginess as a yes to his question, because the next thing Seth knew, he'd been swept off his feet and into Kasey's arms. A bright flush spread over his cheeks. "I can walk," he protested weakly, ignoring the butterflies fluttering in his stomach at the romantic gesture. *A gesture that usually leads to more than just sleeping*, he thought and immediately chastised himself for thinking such things.

"Let me do this for you without you arguing for a change," Kasey replied teasingly, dark eyes sparkling.

Seth rolled his eyes but relented, hesitantly slipping one arm around Kasey's neck. He felt… warm and… cherished. It wasn't something he was used to feeling, and he shifted in discomfort. Kasey's arms felt strong, like he could lean on them forever.

The words the Cheyenne had whispered to him in the woods echoed inside his mind. Kasey loved him. Seth didn't know why, but he believed him, someone he'd known a few short days. He believed Kasey did love him. The declaration rolled around in his head as he analyzed his own feelings toward Kasey. He knew he was nowhere near ready to put that kind of name to how he felt about the man, but he knew his feelings for the gentle sheriff were growing by leaps and bounds.

Since Kasey had found out Seth was his mate, the hostile edge that had always been around the sheriff in his presence was gone. He treated Seth as if he were a precious gem, something that could shatter at the briefest touch, except during those passionate moments in the woods. Seth's cheeks heated at the memory of Kasey inside him and the warm, calloused hands gripping him so tightly.

Kasey disturbed him from his thoughts when he carefully lowered him to the bed. He watched as Kasey's gaze flitted around the nearly empty room. A strange light came into the man's intensely beautiful dark eyes.

The only furniture in the room was the king-sized bed, a dresser, and a nightstand with a lamp. On the nightstand were a couple of photographs of his parents and him with Nick. Seth wondered what Kasey thought of his barely furnished, barely lived-in house.

Kasey sank down onto the edge of the bed next to him. "When this is all over, pup, I'm going to show you what it's like to have a real home."

Seth jerked at his words. His eyes widened, becoming deep-blue sapphires in his pale features. He opened his mouth to say something, but Kasey laid one tanned finger across his lips. "Take off your clothes, Seth."

Seth's breathing deepened, and his lips parted on a small intake of air. Kasey smiled. "Not for that, pup. I want to give you a massage. To help you relax."

Kasey stood and went into the bathroom to wash his hands and face. Dirt still covered him from their romp in the woods.

Seth quickly stripped to his boxers before sitting down on the edge of the bed to wait for the dark-haired sheriff.

When Kasey returned to the room, he pulled the sheets

back and told Seth to lie down on his belly. Seth wanted to protest at first, realizing how vulnerable a position he would be in, but he took a deep breath and reminded himself Kasey wasn't going to hurt him. The sheets were cool against his skin as he slid facedown, turning his head to the side so he could watch Kasey. "I don't have any massage oil with me," Kasey said regretfully. "It would make it feel even better and help you relax more, but another time."

The implication that there would be more time with Kasey in the future eased some of the tension from Seth, and he let himself relax into the mattress only to tense again when Kasey straddled the backs of his thighs. "Relax, pup. I'm not going to hurt you," Kasey said gently, setting his palms in the middle of Seth's back carefully.

The first strokes of his palms calmed the skittish wolf, and Kasey began to knead the muscles beneath his pale flesh. His eyes devoured the soft skin, learning where each mole and freckle speckled his body. His tanned skin showed starkly against his mate's. He noticed a tattoo on Seth's upper arm. He'd missed it before in his desperate need to claim Seth as his. His fingers brushed over the small paw prints encircling his arm, feeling the slightly rougher skin. "When did you get this?" he asked huskily before returning to the task at hand.

Warmth slowly seeped through Seth, and he started to feel drowsy. It took effort to answer Kasey's question coherently. "When I turned nineteen," Seth answered sluggishly. "Nick and I wanted something to represent our friendship, so we each got a matching tattoo."

Kasey pressed his thumbs into the muscles at the base of Seth's neck, eliciting a groan from the slender male. He couldn't stop his body from responding to the almost sensual moan, but this wasn't about passion. It was about comfort and making his mate feel good. A tinge of jealousy rose up at the realization his mate and another male had made matching marks upon their bodies to connect with each other. His lips turned down at the corners, but he didn't say anything, just continued the path down Seth's spine. The tips of his fingers gently stroked over Seth's shoulder blades before sliding lower. When he reached Seth's lower back, his hands gentled even further as they traced the hollowed indent. He resisted the urge to bend down and press his lips there, instead choosing to knead his way back up to Seth's shoulders.

The way Seth's ribcage stood out against his skin made Kasey wonder if his mate had been eating properly. Seth was so slender and skinny it felt like Kasey could snap the younger wolf's bones with the just the slightest bit of pressure. Concern flitted through him. From now on he would make sure Seth ate properly. He trailed his hands down Seth's arms, amusedly watching the skin twitching. It appeared his mate was ticklish. He filed that bit of information away for later. An image of Seth handcuffed to the bed, helpless underneath him and begging for Kasey to fuck him, flashed into his mind, and his cock throbbed. Kasey shook his head. Seth would never allow him to do it, and he would die before he hurt or scared the fragile vet. The image persisted, though, and his hips rolled forward, grinding his hard-on into the rounded cheeks beneath him. Perhaps he'd discuss it with Seth first, but it definitely left him lusting for the opportunity to make Seth submit.

He could feel the massage taking its toll on Seth. A sense of peace settled over his mate, and he felt his heart swell with love toward his stubborn man. The sound of Seth's breathing deepening as he drifted into sleep made Kasey smile. He carefully moved off the bed, stripped, and slid back in beside his mate, pulling him close to his side. Seth nestled unconsciously into him, one hand, curled into a fist, coming to rest over Kasey's heart. Kasey placed his hand on top of Seth's and closed his eyes, praying they could catch whoever was tormenting his mate quickly so they could concentrate on each other. He wanted the time to woo his mate, to court him without the threat of Taggart or the Triad hanging over their heads.

Seth felt so safe and comfortable. A serenity he hadn't felt since his parents were alive washed over him, and he didn't want to let it go. His eyes refused to open to find out what had caused it in case it disappeared. The warmth pressing into him moved against him, and the memory of just hours before rushed over him. Kasey slept next to him, and their limbs were tangled together. A long, muscular leg rested between his. Eyelashes fluttering, he carefully pried open his lids and found the other's face quite close to his own. The breath from Kasey's lips whispered over his, sending aware-ness spiraling through him. His cock throbbed with desire for Kasey. He experimentally rubbed himself on the hard thigh between his legs, sucking in a breath at the pleasure it caused. He did it again, moaning softly.

What am I doing? he panted internally, practically dry-humping the man in his sleep like a cat in heat or, in this case, a dog in heat. He tried to stop, but it seemed his body had a mind of its own, and his hips thrust forward as his back arched slightly. The feel of Kasey's palm sliding down the outside of his bare thigh was like a hot brand on his flesh. "Seth," Kasey breathed into his ear, and then his lips were gently coaxing Seth's to open under his.

Seth slid his hands into Kasey's long dark hair, winding it between his fingers when he found himself flat on his back with Kasey on top of him. Kasey's hair cascaded over his skin, sending a ticklish sensation along his shoulders and arms. His weight felt warm and heavy but wasn't unwelcome, only adding to the slow, leisurely feel of their touches and kisses. No urgency lay behind their actions. Nothing like several hours ago, where it had been an all-consuming passion to possess one another. Kasey feathered light, soft kisses along Seth's jawline to his ear. The tip of his tongue traced the shell of Seth's ear, learning the curves and ridges of it before he wetly sucked the fleshy lobe into his mouth.

A moan rattled in Seth's throat at the hot wetness on his ear. He gasped when he felt Kasey sucking it into his mouth, clutching at the strands of hair in his hands like they were lifelines tethering him to the earth. Seth had never known his ears could feel quite so sensitive before.

"Did I ever tell you how sexy your earring is? How hot it makes me whenever I see it?" Kasey murmured before moving his mouth to the space just behind Seth's ear, licking and sucking at it, sending delighted shivers down Seth's body.

"Kasey," Seth whined, not even sure what he was whining for.

"I love the way you say my name," Kasey growled low. "So needy." He swirled his tongue down to Seth's throat, nipping at the vein pulsing just under his skin.

The feel of Kasey's teeth scraping over his throat caused Seth to gasp, and this time he allowed his hands the freedom to explore. They smoothed down Kasey's muscular back, feeling the uneven patches where his tattoos marked his skin. "Don't tease me," he demanded weakly, tilting his head back to grant the larger wolf further access.

"But I like teasing you," Kasey taunted, rocking his hips forward, rubbing their aching flesh together. "It makes me so hard to hear you beg for me."

Seth raked his nails down Kasey's back in retribution, but it merely caused a hiss of agonized pleasure to explode from Kasey. The sheriff chuckled against Seth's neck, and he pulled back to look down at his mate. His eyes appeared even darker in the dim light of the waning day. "I like pain with my pleasure, pup. Scratch all you want. It only makes me want to fuck you even more."

A mischievous glint entered Seth's eyes as he said in a rough voice, "Who said I didn't want you to fuck me?"

Kasey's chest rumbled harshly, a feral sound of lust, before he devoured Seth's mouth in a deep kiss. His tongue surged inside, wholly dominating the younger wolf. His nails lengthened into claws, and he shredded the boxers Seth still wore, removing the last article of clothing separating their bodies. "I liked those boxers," Seth pouted breathlessly up at Kasey.

"I'll buy you a new pair," Kasey ground out just as he wrapped his hand around Seth's hard prick.

Seth's breath caught in his throat, and to his utter embarrassment, a mewling noise escaped him. "Oh…," he moaned, thrusting up into Kasey's hand.

Kasey squeezed the hard column of flesh before he began stroking his mate slowly, torturously so. He raked his teeth down Seth's collarbone, then licked at the small wound as his hand moved up and down the stiff cock. His palm rolled across the head, smearing the pearl of crystal liquid seeping from the small slit. He smoothed the hot fluid down the shaft to the base and back up to the top, gathering more of it with each stroke. Needing to see the evidence of his pup's desire for him, he pulled the sheet away from them both and lifted up enough to see the weeping staff. His thumb slid around the very ridge at the top of Seth's cock, tracing the helmet-shaped head. When he heard a moan rattle in Seth's throat, he looked at his mate and licked his lips, drawing Seth's passion-glazed eyes to the pink tongue sliding along his full lips. "Is there something you want, pup?"

Seth's dark head tossed against the pillow, and he gave

Kasey a helpless look. The man teased him even now. "Please," he whimpered.

"Please what, Seth?" Kasey rubbed his thumb on the sensitive indent just underneath the flared tip, causing Seth to shudder. "Tell me," he demanded ruthlessly.

"So… not fair," Seth huffed, his fingers twisting in the sheets. His hips bucked upward when Kasey slid the same thumb down the slit. "Fuck! Suck me already," he snarled, glaring at him.

Kasey tsked at Seth with a humorous expression. "That wasn't very polite," he drawled as he fisted Seth's cock in a tight grip and squeezed again.

"Kasey," Seth sobbed in exasperation, only to let out a loud cry when Kasey suddenly licked the head of his straining flesh. The feel of the slick organ rolling around the tip of his cock almost sent Seth over the edge. He panted heavily in pleasure, unable to keep his hips from thrusting upward, only to be restrained by Kasey's strong hands pinning him to the bed.

Carefully suckling just the knob of Seth's length into his mouth, Kasey made love to it languidly, tonguing it and lapping it over and over again. He eased his mate into his mouth a fraction at a time, enjoying the feel of the silky flesh over hard steel. It took a couple of tries before he could swallow the entire length down his throat. Seth's panting cries caused Kasey's cock to throb with lust to be inside him, but this wasn't about him. It was about the seduction of his pup's senses, the need to drive him so wild that Seth could do no more than beg him to fuck him, and to imprint himself so deeply on Seth that the other wolf didn't want to leave him once they'd caught the bastard who'd hurt him.

He deep-throated Seth over and over again, and when he felt Seth about to come, he released him, the wet sucking noise sounding loud in the silence of the room. Seth growled in frustration, and Kasey secretly grinned before turning his attention to the sac hanging beneath Seth's cock. His tongue weighed each of his balls deliberately. The clean, musky scent of his mate made his head spin, and the knowledge that his mate wanted him just as much—even though he protested—filled his heart to the brim with love for his pup, his Seth. Surprising Seth, he pulled first one orb then the other into his mouth, imbibing the taste of him on his tongue.

Seth's cock was so hard he felt as though it would explode right out of its skin if he didn't come soon. The jerk kept him right on the brink of his orgasm, teasing him and tormenting him. He clutched at Kasey's shoulders desperately. "Kasey, please, I need... I need to come," he groaned, trying to push his hips up.

The slightest touch of Kasey's incredible, hot, wet mouth would send him over the edge. That was all he needed, but Kasey continued to tongue his balls and lave the area just underneath them, above his twitching hole. The teasing slick muscle crept closer to his ass, leaving a wet trail that sent a shiver down his spine when the breath from Kasey's nose wafted over it. The first tentative touch of the slick organ wrenched a loud keening sound from Seth, who tilted his hips and spread his thighs even farther apart.

Kasey licked at the soft, puckered flesh leisurely, not caring that he was driving Seth absolutely fucking insane. Seth's body glistened with sweat as he tossed among the sheets, writhing in the ecstasy of Kasey's mouth on him. When Kasey suddenly thrust his tongue into his hole, Seth growled, "If you don't let me come soon, I'm going to kick your ass."

Laughing softly, Kasey looked up at his mate, a merry twinkle in his eyes. "That right, pup?"

"Yes," Seth whined before his voice softened. "Please, Kasey. Let me come."

"Since you asked nicely…." Kasey trailed off as he engulfed Seth inside his mouth again. Just a few suckles sent Seth careening over the edge with a loud cry while he frantically clutched at Kasey's dark head. Stars exploded behind his eyelids and blood roared in his ears as his body trembled through the most mind-blowing orgasm he'd ever had.

Greedily drinking down the bitter, salty come, Kasey hummed in satisfaction at his mate's taste. Nothing could be more intimate for him than giving his lover such ecstasy. It brought his mate just a little bit closer to him. He lapped at Seth until he'd completely softened. It was only then that he released him from his mouth. Kasey licked his lips, grinning widely. "That was fun."

Weak and dazed, Seth could do nothing but glare without heat at his mate. "Fun? God, it feels like my balls turned inside out."

Another husky laugh rumbled in Kasey's chest as he rose up over his pup. His tanned face showed true affection and happiness in the moment. Lying there in his mate's arms, Kasey could forget all of their other troubles and the uncertainties waiting for them outside the bedroom. Nuzzling at Seth's neck, he murmured, "I hope they turn right side out again soon, because I'm still horny, pup." He ground his stiff prick into Seth's soft belly.

Wanting to get some of his own back, Seth heaved a dramatic sigh. "Sorry, Sheriff, but I'm all worn out. You'll just have to go jerk off somewhere."

Kasey bit down on Seth's shoulder, just enough to mar his skin, in retribution, and thrust against Seth again. "So you take your pleasure and that's it, pup? Didn't know my mate was such a cocktease."

Seth grinned into the darkness that had swallowed them

up in the time Kasey had been sucking him off. "Cocktease is such a harsh word, Sheriff. I prefer to think of it as keeping you on the edge of your seat."

Joy tingled through Kasey at the easy bantering. It felt good to hear the smile in Seth's voice and know he'd caused it. He smiled between the light kisses he pressed intermittently along Seth's collarbone and throat. "You certainly manage to do that, babe," Kasey said gruffly, hiding the depth of love in his voice behind a rough tone.

Lightly scratching his nails down Kasey's spine and enjoying the fine trembles it sent through the big Cheyenne, Seth wrapped his tired limbs around the large, warm body and whispered into his ear, "So are you going to fuck me or not, Sheriff?"

Groaning loudly, Kasey plundered Seth's mouth as he lined the head of his hard flesh up with the tight opening his tongue had slickened just enough to ease the way. The tip pushed past the clenching muscles, and he grunted at the way Seth's ass clamped down on him. "God, you feel good, pup," he wheezed out, his hands soothing over the pale vet's body in an affectionate caress.

The feel of Kasey inside him was so fucking amazing. Seth reached down and gripped Kasey's firm bottom, pulling him all the way inside. A small whimper left his lips as the man stretched him wide. Then Kasey retreated, pulling his engorged cock almost all the way out before slamming back home with a hard shove of his hips. Those same words were on Seth's lips, but Kasey knocked the breath straight from his lungs on that deep plunge into his body, and he could do no more than gasp beneath him.

"Does it feel good, Seth?"

He barely heard the words as he held onto Kasey to keep from flying apart. A mere grunt of agreement was all he could manage before his breath became stolen anew.

It felt as though Kasey were buried in a furnace with how hot Seth's body felt wrapped around him. He slowly pushed in and out of his mate, savoring the connection, however brief it might be. He feared once his pup's itch had been scratched, so to speak, he'd revert back to the prickly veterinarian Kasey had met that first night. His lips reverently trailed over the slender bones of Seth's jawline and over the lids closed in pleasure. Maybe he was being selfish, but now that his mate lay in his arms, he didn't ever want to let him go. When they'd resolved Seth's situation, he wasn't sure he'd have the strength not to cage him like the Triad had in order to keep him. Tears stung the backs of his eyes, and he could smell the salt burning in his nose. To keep from showing his weakness to the younger wolf, he pressed his face into the side of Seth's neck and held on for dear life.

At first, Seth was too far gone with how Kasey felt moving inside him to notice the man's distress. He could feel every ridge and bump of the hard cock. It quivered hotly, readying itself to flood his body with its seed, and the heat generated felt so intense he could almost swear it burned the flesh lining his channel. A warm wetness on his neck drew his attention to Kasey's anguish. He made a sound of surprise and ran his hands down the broad, rippling back soothingly. "Kasey?" he questioned breathlessly.

Kasey didn't respond, merely shuddering and panting as his balls tightened closer to his body in preparation to unload inside his mate. Fire tingled in his lower back, and he gave a hoarse cry as his shaft pulsed and sprayed his hot semen deep into Seth, claiming him all over again. He collapsed boneless atop Seth, still trying to stem the tears seeping from beneath his closed lids.

"What's wrong?" he heard Seth ask in concern.

He shook his head, but to his unbearable shame, a sob rattled in his throat.

"Kasey!" Seth sounded frantic this time and embraced him tighter.

To hear such a strong, virile man make a sound of such loss broke Seth's heart, and he didn't know what to do to help him. Seth began to lightly stroke Kasey in gentle caresses anywhere he could reach. He ran his fingers through the long dark hair over and over while whispering soft words of reassurance in the man's ear, anything that came to mind. It could have been five minutes or even an hour before he felt Kasey calming down. There had only been the one sob, but he had still felt the tears drenching his skin. "Shh… I'm here, baby."

The fact that Kasey could let down his defenses and cry in front of him squeezed Seth's heart in a tight fist. It would take some time before he could admit to it out loud, but he was slowly, terrifyingly falling in love with the stubborn, cocky, brash Cheyenne who'd crashed into his life like a Mack truck through a house. Other than the moments after Kasey had discovered Seth's secret, the man had treated him affectionately, tenderly, and passionately. Except for the emotions Kasey stirred inside his heart, he had felt no true fear around him. The need to protect his heart kept him from blurting out the jumbled thoughts racing through his head.

Instead, Seth chose to tilt Kasey's tear-stained face to his and kiss him unhurriedly. He kept it a simple kiss, just lips lightly brushing over lips, but it conveyed more emotion than passion. He followed the traces of tears to Kasey's eyes, pressing a kiss to each lid before drawing back. "All right now?" he asked gently.

Red-rimmed dark eyes opened to gaze at Seth in slight surprise. Kasey lifted one hand to lovingly trace the lines of Seth's lips as he studied his mate. He knew his pup had to be dying of curiosity about his crying, but he was sure if he revealed the truth of how much he needed Seth, how much he wanted to handcuff him to the bed and never let him leave, it would scare his gun-shy lover. Seth might have let him inside his body, but it didn't mean he'd let him inside his heart.

9

"**I**'M SORRY," he murmured in a strained voice, his throat raw from holding back the gut-wrenching sobs he'd wanted to let out.

"For what? Everyone has emotional moments, Kasey. It doesn't make you any less of a man." Seth shifted underneath him, but when Kasey went to move off him, he embraced him tighter. "No. Stay."

"But I'm heavy," Kasey said tenderly, secretly thrilled his mate wanted him to remain. He collapsed into Seth with a sigh and closed his eyes again. Truth be told, he hadn't slept much while he'd been holding Seth in his arms because he hadn't been able to stop looking at him. It would take time, but he knew he could earn Seth's love. The only thing terrifying him was that he wouldn't have the time he needed, and Seth would leave him before he could invade every dark corner of his pup's bruised and battered heart, tying him to him irrevocably.

"No, just right," Seth replied, running his fingers through Kasey's hair. He hesitated for a moment, but curiosity stabbed at him viciously. "Will you tell me why?"

Kasey didn't respond right away. He couldn't decide how much he should say. He hadn't cried since he was a little kid when he'd scraped his knee on the sidewalk one day. It showed how far beyond his defenses his true mate had gotten. Maybe a slightly edited version of the truth would be the best way to go, he decided. "Many of the wolves I have known in my life never found their true mate. They lived their lives and found others to share it with, but a piece of their soul was still missing."

His voice hitched, and he had to swallow to keep talking. "I thought I'd end up living my life that way. Without ever knowing the warmth and touch of my true mate. Until I met you. None of the others in my pack have ever made my heart beat with so much longing that it would surely leap from my chest at the merest brush of their hand on mine."

Seth's hand in his hair stilled, and Kasey closed his eyes, praying his words didn't cause his pup to panic. Too late to take them back now, and he couldn't stop the words from tumbling out. "You do that to me, pup. From the moment I felt your fur beneath my hands, the warm weight of your body as I carried you. When I saw how frightened you were of me, lying here with you is more than I could have ever hoped for. I'm so afraid you're going to decide I'm not worth fighting for, that you'll believe I'm like that bastard and want nothing more than to hurt you, that you'll leave me in a place so dark I won't be able to breathe."

As Kasey spoke, Seth's eyes widened further and further. His heart clenched at the sheer agony in the man's voice. When the words about believing him to be similar to Taggart were followed by fears of Seth leaving him, Seth made a whine of pain in his throat. He clutched at Kasey, hard, and shook his head. "You're nothing like Taggart," he said fiercely. "Even when you were angry, you were nothing like him, Kasey. You are so much more than him. Kind, gentle, caring. He was never and will never be any of those things."

Running his fingers over Kasey's dark brow, Seth studied the tanned features of his lover. Tiny lines of strain around the edges of Kasey's mouth and eyes stood out starkly, and he wondered what it cost Kasey to appear so vulnerable. "I can't promise I know what the future holds for either of us, and despite the fact that you're cocky, stubborn, and a pain in my ass, I… I like you." He rushed on without giving Kasey the chance to say anything when the dark-chocolate eyes suddenly opened to stare at him intently. "And I want to give it a chance."

The silence after his declaration stretched on for what felt like forever, and Seth had begun to twitch in discomfort when Kasey's eyes started to twinkle in amusement. One corner of his firm, sexy mouth lifted in a half-grin. "A pain in your ass, is that right, pup?"

"Oh yeah. Like a splinter that won't come out," Seth breathed. He would cut out his own tongue before he admitted it, but Kasey's endearment of "pup" had started to grow on him now that he knew Kasey didn't mean it in a condescending way but merely as an affectionate term.

Kasey's body shook with suppressed laughter. His once again erect cock nudged Seth's thigh. "I think I like the idea of being a splinter in your ass that won't come out," he teased his blue-eyed mate.

Seth choked on a laugh at his own choice of words. Very aptly put, though. He wrapped his arms around Kasey's neck, grinning up at him. "I kind of like that type of splinter," he purred while giving Kasey a seductive look.

If his stomach hadn't chosen to growl right then, Seth had a feeling Kasey would have taken him again. A flush rolled over his face at the loud noise.

"When's the last time you ate a decent meal?" Kasey asked, a frown marring his forehead.

"Uh… last night at your house." Seth gave him a sheepish look.

"And before that?" Kasey asked as he rolled off of him and stood up, holding his hand for Seth to take.

Thinking, Seth remembered eating a sandwich for lunch a couple of days ago. And of course the steaks Kasey had made for him while he'd been in his wolf form. "I don't remember."

Kasey scowled at him. "No wonder you're so damn skinny. You aren't to skip any meals from now on, pup, or I'll be more than a splinter in your ass."

Seth rolled his eyes at Kasey as he swept by, moving toward the bathroom to clean up. "Yes, Dad."

A swift swat on the ass left Seth gasping with an indignant expression as he whirled around to glare at him. "I won't tolerate impertinence, pup." Kasey smirked.

"I'll give you impertinent," Seth growled, launching himself at Kasey, who caught him easily enough.

Husky laughter rumbled in Kasey's chest as he captured Seth's wrists and dragged him closer to him. "I can see I'm going to have a hell of a time taming you, pup," he taunted affectionately.

Seth sniffed at him in exasperation. "Taming me?"

"Mmm. Then again, I do so like to watch your cheeks flush and your eyes sparkle with anger. You look so damn sexy when you're angry," Kasey mused, walking Seth backward to the bathroom.

Being called sexy stopped whatever retort Seth could throw at Kasey. Seth dropped his gaze to the floor in a fit of shyness. "You think I'm sexy?"

Kasey halted next to the shower, cupped Seth's chin, and tilted his head back to look up at him. "Oh, baby, you have no idea," he murmured in an emotion-laden voice before proceeding to kiss him senseless.

Breaking the kiss long enough to turn on the water, Kasey returned to Seth's lips, drinking deeply of his pup's sweetness. Steam built around them, fogging the mirror and distorting their reflections as they twined together in passion. They stumbled into the shower stall and were instantly drenched in hot water, but neither noticed. There was nothing but the two of them, their hands touching, mouths clinging, moans echoing off the tiled walls. It built to a peak that both of them raced in eagerness to free-fall off the edge of.

They wound up in a tangle of limbs on the floor of the shower, panting heavily and weakly holding onto each other. Seth felt like his bones were made of gelatin, and he couldn't have moved even if his life depended on it. Soap still clung to Kasey's long hair, and Seth gave a shaky grin while running his fingers through it to rinse out the rest. His stomach growled rather loudly, bringing a chagrined look to Kasey's face. "Sorry, pup, food should have come first."

Seth lifted one slender shoulder in a careless shrug. "I've gone longer without food." A stern look flooded Kasey's expression, but Seth clamped his hand down over Kasey's mouth just as he opened it to chastise him. "I know, I know. If I don't start eating more often, you're going to kick my ass."

Kasey lightly gripped Seth's wrist, pulling it from his mouth. "And don't forget it, pup."

Laughing, Seth stuck his tongue out at Kasey in retaliation.

"I have a much better use for that tongue," Kasey growled lustily.

At those words, Seth's blue eyes shifted to the color of storm clouds. Seth hadn't taken the initiative in any of their lovemaking sessions, but the thought of taking Kasey inside his mouth, licking and sucking him, embedded itself in his brain. He was damn sure going to put it to use later. But.... "Food first, Sheriff."

It took a few more minutes before they both could find the energy to stand. Seth yawned and stretched, giving a small moan of pleasure as his joints popped. He frowned when he realized he didn't have any clothing to fit Kasey. "I don't think anything I own is going to fit you, Kasey," Seth called to the man still in his bathroom, pulling out a pair of soft faded blue jeans and a dark green T-shirt.

He jerked in surprise when a pair of tan arms slipped around him from behind, pulling him in against a broad chest. Damn, the man could move quietly. Warm lips nuzzled into his ear. "I think you fit me just perfectly, Doc. But I have a change of clothing in the car that I carry with me in case of emergencies."

Shivering, Seth stilled his hands, resting them on the dresser drawer, and he leaned back into Kasey. "Do you... do you want me to go out and get them?" he asked breathlessly.

"I'd rather save them for tomorrow, pup," Kasey replied meaningfully, gently tightening his hold on Seth while waiting for an answer.

"O-okay," Seth sighed, his heart beating faster at the thought of Kasey holding him throughout the night.

Kasey could hear the sound of Seth's heart rate pick up, and he took Seth's stutter as uncertainty. His smile dropped from his face. "Unless you'd rather I went home...."

"What? No. I said okay." Seth frowned, turning around in Kasey's arms to look up at him. "You want to stay, right?"

"Do you want me to stay?" Kasey countered.

Seth reached up to tug on a strand of wet hair lying on Kasey's shoulder. "Didn't I say that?"

Kasey lifted an eyebrow, his tension easing at the obvious

acceptance from Seth, but not wanting to let his mate off the hook quite so easily. "I didn't hear it, no."

Giving Kasey a perturbed look, Seth stated it plainly: "I want you to stay."

"Are you sure?" Kasey teased, brushing the tips of his fingers along Seth's cheek. He liked watching the emotions playing over his pup's face. It fascinated him to see the way his mate's eyes changed from a bright blue to a stormy blue-gray with the change of his disposition.

Seth pushed at Kasey's chest, heaving a strained sigh, knowing his mate was teasing him. The thought brought him up short, and he froze, his hands still pressed on the warm skin. His mate? When had he started to think of Kasey as his?

When he'd admitted to himself he was falling in love with the man, that's when. But the realization just made him even more afraid. The closer he got to Kasey, the more it would hurt if he lost him.

"I think we should order pizza. It won't take long for them to deliver it," Kasey said, interrupting Seth's thoughts.

He nodded. "That's fine. Nick is probably ready to eat a horse. I can't believe I forgot he was here."

"I should hope you weren't thinking of him," Kasey said dryly. He pressed a brief kiss to Seth's forehead. "Come on, get dressed, and we'll see about ordering pizza. What kind do you like?"

"Pepperoni and mushroom," Seth said in bemusement as he watched Kasey pulling on his clothes and covering up his delicious physique.

"Sounds good. I'll check on your friend and call Franco's. They've got the best pizza in Wyoming." Kasey tossed Seth a grin before leaving the bedroom.

The rest of the house was dark, and after a brief scent of the air, he knew Nick wasn't there at the moment. Somehow, he hadn't expected him to be. He noticed a note on the bar next to the phone and picked it up to read while dialing the number he knew by heart. Ah, so Nick had gone out to give them some privacy. He wondered if it was for a different reason but shrugged it off as he spoke his order into the phone.

Seth lazily ambled his way out to the living room, stopping when he didn't see Nick. "Where's Nick?"

Kasey silently handed the note over to Seth. He walked into the small kitchen and pulled out a couple of plates after searching for a moment. Seth remained quiet behind him. When he turned around, he found Seth staring at the paper as if his heart had been cut out. He set the plates down and quickly made his way to his mate's side. "What's wrong?"

"All this time he's been lying to me," Seth whispered, remembering what Nick had revealed earlier. "How can he be any better than Taggart?"

"Hey, hey," Kasey chided softly. He slid one hand under Seth's chin while the other combed his still-damp hair back. "Nick is your friend. His Alpha commanded him not to tell you, and not many can go against their own Alpha. He cares about you, Seth. He does. I know it hurt you that he didn't tell you, but he's been there to protect you, Seth. If it weren't for him, I'd have never met you, known you. I owe him my life."

Seth's eyes fluttered open in confusion. "Why do you owe him your life? It's me that owes him mine."

Sighing, Kasey looked at him seriously. "You still don't understand, do you, pup? Your life is my life, and mine is yours. If he had not been there for you, you wouldn't have been able to escape Taggart, and quite possibly would have been killed one day by him. Nick saved my life by saving yours."

Tears welled up in Seth's eyes, and his heart twisted painfully inside his chest. He flung himself at Kasey, tightly wrapping his arms around the lean waist while burying his face in the firm chest. The words he wanted to speak so badly stuck in his throat, though. He still couldn't speak them, couldn't open himself to such pain again. Not yet. But Kasey's words cemented the growing love he'd felt, causing it to blossom into the deepest emotion possible. The kind that sends you to your knees and gives your entire being meaning.

Kasey didn't try to get him to talk. He just held his mate in his arms and let him know he was there. It wasn't until the pizza arrived that he released him. "I have to get the door, pup. Why don't you put the plates on the table while I pay for the pizza, okay?"

Seth nodded and reluctantly pulled away from Kasey without looking him in the face. His hands shook as they reached for the plates, shook so badly he was afraid he would drop the plates as he carried them the short distance to the small table. Trotting back to the kitchen area, he grabbed a few napkins and opened his fridge to pull out a couple of beers. Kasey had set the box on the table when he turned around. The fragrant smell of pizza filled the room, and his mouth watered, sending his stomach into another growling fit.

"Pizza and beer," Kasey said, grinning as he dished out a slice on each of their plates. "The staples of men."

It broke the discomfort Seth felt, and he laughed hoarsely. "It's all I've survived off of for the last couple of years. Despite the fact I love to cook, it's hard to have the decent equipment to do it when you move around so much."

Kasey worked on distracting his pup from his thoughts by asking questions about the places he'd been. It surprised him that he'd even been overseas to England and Scotland. His mate seemed to be very well traveled. Once again he found himself captivated by the play of emotions across

Seth's face as he talked. At times he shined so brightly it almost hurt to look at him. At others the light dimmed so quickly it sent a stab of pain straight through his chest. He still didn't know how Seth's parents had died, but he didn't want to bring it up right then. Perhaps Seth would tell him when he was ready. "Will you have dinner at my parents' tomorrow night, Seth?" he asked abruptly.

Seth halted, his second slice of pizza halfway to his mouth. "What?"

"Have dinner tomorrow night at my parents' home. With everything that's happened since the other night, there hasn't been a chance, but they want to meet you. And I'm sure my mom will try to embarrass me by dragging out my old baby pictures." Kasey grimaced at the thought of the one where he wore nothing but a hat and cowboy boots.

The thought of seeing baby pictures of Kasey made Seth smile. Seth couldn't help but wonder what Kasey's parents were like. If the way Kasey treated him was any indication, they must be wonderful people to have raised a son like him. Aside from being prejudiced about white people. "Won't they care I'm not Cheyenne?" he said doubtfully. "You had a problem with me being white at the beginning. Why wouldn't they?"

Kasey blanched at the memory of his reaction to his mate being white, and he gave his pup a sincere, apologetic look. "They aren't stupid assholes like I am," he muttered. "They don't care if you're white, black, Asian, or even if you were purple. They only care that you're my mate."

Eyeing the taller man, Seth ignored the little voice telling him not to go and agreed. "All right, but Nick has to go too."

"Agreed. But you have to make sure to cloak your scent whenever you're outside my parents' home. The pack believes only Native Americans can be true born wolves. And if they know what you are, they may believe, like I did, that you're a Created."

Seth tilted his head to the side in confusion. "I always keep my scent wrapped up in my power."

His statement brought Kasey's eyes sharply to Seth's face. "Even now? This very moment?"

"Yes." Seth nodded. "Why?"

"Because I can smell you. I thought you dropped it because you were around me." Kasey let out a loud expletive and stood, pacing back and forth. Was it possible Seth's scent had changed when they'd mated? But would it matter to the way he covered his scent? "Shit… shit…."

Seth sat there, flabbergasted and pale. If he couldn't hide his scent, he couldn't protect himself. "I… I can't…."

Kasey realized how upset his mate was and immediately went to his knees next to Seth's chair, cupping his cheek in one hand. "Hey, pup, don't panic. I'm here to protect you now. I am a dominant, heir to the Alpha, and I have claimed you. No one can contest my rights to you. There is no need to fear the others will fight over you any longer. As long as I continue to claim you, mark you, then you will be safe. It is not my pack mates I am worried about."

The explanation calmed Seth down enough that he could relax slightly. "Then what are you worried about?" he asked fearfully, afraid of the answer.

"It is what I said before. If you cannot cover your scent, then the others will believe you're a Created one. Fear makes others do stupid things. And I will not lose you when I just found you," Kasey growled, eyes flashing angrily. "We will wait until your friend returns to the house and see if he is able to smell you. If he can detect you are wolf, then we must figure out why."

Seth stared at the hard, angular features of his lover, thinking of what could have possibly changed. When Kasey claimed him, had it changed something in his physiological makeup? Did his DNA alter or change? Mutate, perhaps? "The only thing that's changed since my arrival was mating with you." His cheeks flushed, but he went on, "Perhaps when you c-claimed me, it altered my scent in some way? Or is it possible that because you are my… my mate you can smell me in my human form when others can't?"

Kasey didn't miss the way Seth's voice cracked when he called him his mate. But what really grabbed his attention was the light entering his pup's eyes when he said it. It took all he had not to grin joyfully. Seth had begun to accept they were mates. It would only be a matter of time before Seth accepted it all, accepted him. "Unfortunately, we've never had this happen before," he said in a thoughtful voice.

"Maybe Nick will know something?" Seth's expression shone in hope and eagerness. "It could possibly be something the pack I'm from has seen before."

"Perhaps. We'll ask when he returns, but until then, eat," Kasey instructed, standing from his kneeling position beside Seth and returning to his own seat.

It was hours before Nick returned. When Seth heard the front door open from where he lay wrapped up in Kasey's arms, he carefully sat up, extricating himself from the larger man. He padded barefoot out to the living room to see his friend staring broodingly up at the ceiling. "Nick," he said softly.

Nick rolled his head slightly toward the entrance of the hallway, and his emerald-green eyes, sorrowful and unhappy, opened to look at Seth. "Hey, babe," Nick replied gently, almost hesitantly.

Seth dropped down onto the couch next to his best friend and put a hand on his forearm. "I'm not mad anymore, Nick. I understand you had no choice in lying to me because you were ordered to do so. But you were only appointed my bodyguard, nothing more. You didn't have to be my friend all this time, listening to me, helping me in other ways."

Some of the sorrow dissipated from Nick's expression, but not all. Seth could practically feel the despair emanating from his friend. It seemed almost like a tangible breath wafting across his skin. "Nick? Did… did something happen tonight?"

A pained laugh rattled in Nick's throat. Seth noticed Nick's shirt then, ripped and bloodstained. "Nick!" He sat up straight in horror.

"It's fine, Seth." Nick waved his hand carelessly. "It's already healed."

"What happened?" Seth demanded, his eyes flashing fiercely with the thought of someone hurting his friend.

Nick shook his head ruefully. "You know, I never thought by coming here it would really change anything. But I guess you can't always guess how your life is going to go. I never wanted it to be like this. I certainly never pictured it would be this way."

"What the hell are you talking about, Nick?" Seth moved to sit on the coffee table in front of his friend so he could see his face. A pain he'd never seen before shone from those emerald-green eyes. He made a low noise in his throat and lifted his hand to touch Nick's cheek. "Tell me what happened."

"I found—" Nick's voice cut off when a low growl came from the hallway. His gaze shifted there, and he immediately tensed at the sight of a very angry wolf. "Seth… I think it would be best if you moved away from me."

Seth frowned, glancing toward the hallway as well. His eyes widened at the absolute fury on Kasey's face. The dark eyes had shifted, and it appeared his mate had a very tight hold on himself, his skin trembling finely. Dropping his hand, Seth stood up and walked to where Kasey stood. Kasey immediately crowded him against the wall while still glaring at Nick. Seth sighed and slapped a hand on Kasey's chest. "Hey," he fairly ground out between clenched teeth.

When Kasey still didn't look away from Nick, Seth reached up and turned his mate's face toward him. The dark eyes were in their canine phase. "Nick is my friend. Nothing happened. You are my mate, Kasey. Even if I wanted to do anything with him, I couldn't, because you are the only one I can smell, the only one I can taste, and the only one my body craves. Now snap out of this!"

Each word Seth spoke slammed into Kasey's chest like an invisible arrow, causing his wolf side to start to pull back the longer Seth talked. Seth believed they were mates! When he'd walked out of the bedroom and found the two of them so close together, Seth's hand on Nick's face, not unlike how he'd touched Kasey only hours before, a red haze had drifted over his consciousness. The rage from seeing his pup's hands on another allowed the wolf to slip through unrestrained. He wrapped his arms around Seth tightly. "I'm sorry, pup. I just feel that he has a greater hold on you than me, and my wolf knows it," he muttered into Seth's ear even though he knew if Nick chose to he could hear every word.

"Nick has been my best friend for fourteen years, Kasey. We've only known each other a few days. You have to give me time," Seth chided gently. "And I'm a touchy person. I cannot stop myself from touching other people. Maybe it's the healer in me, but either way, I do it without even thinking about it."

Kasey didn't want to ruin the tenuous hold he had on Seth, but his wolf beat at him, demanding he fight anyone near Seth. He was the future Alpha and whoever touched his mate challenged his claim of the younger man. "I'll try to control myself, Seth, but it's not going to be easy."

"Nothing worth something ever is," Seth growled quietly

into Kasey's ear before nipping at the sensitive lobe with his teeth. He still had not taken control of their lovemaking, but he had learned of some of the hot spots on Kasey's body. It seemed the man loved to have his ears licked, sucked, and nibbled on. Seth grinned lasciviously when he felt the big body resting on his quiver with awareness. The scent of Kasey's arousal stung his nose, and he laughed, gently pushing Kasey away. He took the sheriff's hand in his and tugged him to the couch. "Come on. We need to discuss things with Nick."

Nick gave Kasey an apologetic look. "Sorry, Sheriff."

"It's fine. Not your fault. But I do believe I told you to call me Kasey," he said as he sank down into the easy chair, pulling a disgruntled Seth into his lap.

"I can sit on the couch," Seth grumbled, hiding the fact Kasey wanting him close made him want to grin idiotically. He gave a resigned sigh after a halfhearted attempt to get away and snuggled into his mate.

Kasey glanced at Nick's face and blinked at the pure longing on the man's features. But with a twitch of Nick's eyelids, his expression returned to being the usual placid emotion. Was Nick thinking of Seth just then? Or maybe Nick wanted his own mate. Sympathy flowed through Kasey. He knew how the other felt. The arm wrapped over Seth's legs pulled him in tighter.

"So tell me what it is you need to talk to me about," Nick said, interrupting Kasey's thoughts.

The two of them outlined their conversation from earlier, explaining about the change in scent and the fact Kasey could still pick it up despite Seth's "shield" being in place. When they were finished, Nick frowned, leaning forward. "So you are saying you are fully shielding yourself now?"

Seth nodded vigorously. "Yes. Can you pick up my scent?"

Nick scratched at his nose for a minute, thinking. He'd

never heard of that happening before. With Kasey helping him protect Seth now, he didn't really think it too much cause for concern, but he'd never heard of something similar happening in his pack. "Yeah, I can. I've never been able to detect your wolf when you've been in human form before. To be honest, Seth, I can't really answer why it changed, though. You were the first Rho born to our pack in centuries. And the one born before you was claimed almost immediately by their mate. But since you are here, Sher—Kasey, to protect Seth, then it's not really a big deal now. Right?"

"No. That's not true. It is a problem because it's not just Taggart we have to worry about. We have to worry about my own pack believing Seth is a Created. Remember, I thought the same when I first met him. Until my father told me of another who came to these parts before I'd been born. A man who wasn't a Created. The others in my pack will believe Seth is unholy, evil, and until we can break it to them gently, we have to figure out how to keep them from scenting Seth." Kasey's voice was flat and hard. His jaw clenched tightly against the anger seething beneath the surface. Rage at his father for not telling their pack of the existence of others and how it seemed danger shadowed his pup swirled inside him. And he was still mad at himself for the way he'd treated Seth at the beginning.

"Another wolf that wasn't Native American?" Nick looked up at him, pinning him in place with a sharp look. "Did your father tell you anything about him?"

"Not much. Just that he realized the man wasn't the same as a Created. He could function with awareness while in wolf form, and when in human, his eyes were clear and focused. Oh, and he told me the man's name. Eric. Eric Hawthorne." Kasey felt Seth tense and saw surprise flood Nick's features. "What?" he demanded.

"That... that was my father," Seth replied shakily, his eyes misting slightly at the realization his father had actually been here in this town before. Maybe it explained why he'd been so drawn to it when he'd first arrived only a few short weeks ago.

Kasey lifted an eyebrow. "But your last name is Davies."

"Davies is my mother's maiden name. After escaping the Triad, I changed it as a way of hiding in plain sight," Seth explained bemusedly, still hung up on the fact his father had actually met Kasey's father before. "Hawthorne was my dad's real last name."

Which cleared up why the background check on Seth had come back empty, Kasey thought ruefully. "It's so weird how my dad actually visited here all those years ago," he heard Seth state, awed.

He smiled and nuzzled at the dark crown of hair. "It was fate, pup."

"Do you think your father will remember anything about my dad? I mean, what he did? Why was he here?" Seth sat up eagerly, his eyes shining brightly at the thought of hearing something about his father he never knew. "Did he ever say anything to you, Nick?"

"Afraid not, Seth." Nick slumped down wearily, ready to take a good long nap. "The only way you can disguise Seth's scent would be to practically bury him in yours." He yawned before continuing, "Rub his clothing all over your body before he puts it on. Pretty much almost carry him into the house. Since I can still cloak my scent, I should be fine."

Seth watched his friend nodding off into sleep. He remembered he hadn't been able to press Nick about what had happened tonight. Why he had blood on him and why his clothing was torn. Tomorrow, he promised himself. For now, Nick needed rest. Heavy dark circles under his green eyes stood out starkly in his tanned face, and it made him feel guilty for being angry at him. "I think we should let him rest for now," he whispered to Kasey, standing reluctantly from the warm lap he'd been seated in to grab Nick a blanket and ease him down to a reclining position on the couch.

Kasey took Seth's hand the instant he finished and drew him into the bedroom, where he embraced him tightly. "I have to go in to the station tomorrow, pup. Just for a few hours. I wish I could take you with me, but my deputy, Julian, is a wolf as well and would be able to scent you from a mile away."

Clenching his fingers in the khaki uniform shirt, Seth rested his ear over where Kasey's heart beat beneath the big broad chest. The steady thudding soothed him. He smiled softly as he spoke. "It's okay, Sheriff. I know you have a job to go to. You can't stay by my side 24/7. Besides, Nick is here."

"Exactly." Kasey scowled teasingly, even though Seth couldn't see it.

Seth pulled back and looked up at a Kasey, frustration evident in his expression. "You better get used to the fact he's in my life, Kasey, because he's my best friend. I'm not going to give up almost fifteen years of friendship because you're jealous."

It took a few breaths before Seth noticed the laughter dancing in the man's dark eyes. He wrinkled his nose at Kasey and shook his head. "What am I going to do with you?"

The mirth died away, leaving behind a yearning spark that blazed higher the longer they stood there. Kasey's fingers lightly traced the lines of Seth's face and whispered gently over his cheek before resting on the pulse beating just beneath the skin on his throat. "There is only one thing I need you to do with me, pup," he murmured quietly.

"Oh?" Seth held his breath, his heart slamming against his ribcage. "What's that?"

Kasey slowly walked them toward the bed, never letting

go of his mate or releasing his gaze. When Seth felt the backs of his knees hit the bed, Kasey said, "Just love me."

Unable to utter a word as Kasey's mouth suddenly landed on his, Seth found himself on his back on the mattress. Seth wanted to tell him right then that he already did, but the words became lost in passionate, demanding kisses. Mere moments passed before he became a writhing, shuddering mass of flesh beneath the hard thrusting body above him. He sobbed Kasey's name over and over again, begging him to end the torture and send him flying. The Cheyenne's scent was everywhere around him, in him, Seth's nose drinking deeply of the earthy smell he adored. His hands pawed at Kasey's bare skin, almost attempting to pull him inside himself.

More than animal lust drove them to new heights, and it wasn't long before Kasey spilled his essence inside his mate and Seth's own slick ropes of come sprayed across his bare chest and belly. When the storm faded, they lay in a panting entanglement of limbs, their breathing loud in the dark room. Kasey could just barely manage to move himself to the side without releasing Seth. A soft sound rumbled in his chest when he felt Seth's hand lazily drawing circles in the light dusting of hair on his chest. Contented couldn't even begin to describe the emotion inside him. Warmth spread outward from his chest, straight down to the tips of his fingers and toes. "Good night, pup," he said softly.

"Good night, babe," Seth mumbled almost unintelligibly. Safe, warm, and loved, he'd already reached the half-asleep point.

Kasey grinned tiredly into the darkness before sliding into slumber with his mate tucked in his arms.

1 0

PAIR of warm lips brushing along his forehead woke Seth. He stirred, but a large palm caressed the length of his bare arm. "Just going into work, pup. Go back to sleep."

He grunted and grabbed Kasey's wrist, pressing a kiss into his palm before cuddling back down into the warmth of the blankets. He had no real reason to rush getting up, since his clinic no longer existed. Seth allowed himself to drift for another hour or so before rousing fully. He moaned as he stretched beneath the covers, his muscles feeling a pleasant burn after being in the same position for so long.

Nick, already awake, sat at the small dinette table drinking a cup of coffee. Seth grimaced in distaste. If Nick had made the coffee, it would surely be like axle grease, but his senses screamed for the caffeine, and he gave in. Adding sugar and creamer to cut down on the bitterness, he looked at his friend, who stared off into space, obviously thinking about whatever event had taken place the previous evening. "So you going to tell me what happened to you last night? Why your clothes were torn up?" Seth leaned back against the counter, blowing on his coffee to cool it down slightly before taking a sip.

Nick blinked heavily several times, but what brought Seth upright and to the chair beside his friend was the anguish in his eyes. "Come on, babe, tell me what's going on?"

"I found him, Seth. I found my mate," Nick choked out hoarsely.

Him!? Seth's eyes nearly popped out of his head with how wide they flew open. Nick's mate was a man? Wait, it was a good thing he'd found his mate, right? "If you found your mate, Nick, why are you so upset? Haven't you wanted to find h-him? Or is it because it's a man?"

Shaking his head, Nick admitted, "I'm bi, Seth. I sleep with men or women. It doesn't matter to me that my mate is a guy."

"Wait a minute. Since when have you been bi?" Seth demanded, sitting up straighter.

"Since I realized it at the age of sixteen and wound up having sex with our English teacher," Nick said, looking sheepish.

Flabbergasted, Seth felt his mouth drop open. Their English teacher? Mr. Tyson? "What the hell?! How is it you never told me this?"

"I thought if you knew you might… want to be more than friends," Nick whispered, knowing his friend would go through the roof.

"You arrogant jerk!" Seth shouted, punching his friend in the arm with all his might. A sense of satisfaction stormed through him when he saw Nick wince and rub his upper arm. "What else have you been lying to me about?"

"Nothing! I swear," Nick protested, running a hand against the back of his neck. "Well… there is one thing."

Seth growled, but Nick held up his hands in an innocent gesture. "Before you kill me, let me just say it isn't that bad."

Seth gave him a look, clearly waiting for an explanation. "Well, I wouldn't say I was lying, but it was more of an omission."

"Tell me before I tie you down outside, smear honey all over your body, and let the ants have their way with you," Seth ground out, his arms crossed over his chest.

"Oh, kinky, Seth. Didn't know you were into BDSM. I wonder if the sheriff knows what he's in for." Nick grinned teasingly at Seth.

Seth fought an answering smile but couldn't keep it from spreading across his face. They'd been friends for far too long, and Nick knew exactly what buttons to push to cool Seth down whenever he was angry with his friend. "Just tell me, Nick."

Nick wondered if maybe he should get up and move away from Seth. What he was about to reveal would probably make Seth really want to kill him or at least maim him. "I, uh… kind of scared off that guy Bryan you were interested in."

Seth's eyebrows flew up into his hairline. "Excuse me? You did what?"

Bryan, the first guy who'd ever been interested in him, had worked at the same place as him, a small family pizza joint, as a waiter. Seth had been a busboy clearing the tables. For months they'd flirted and danced around the issue, but just when Seth had thought for sure Bryan intended to ask him out, Bryan disappeared. He'd quit his job and wouldn't answer his phone whenever Seth called. Seth's breathing deepened as he started to get mad, but then the anger faded away. A snort left him, and he clamped a hand over his mouth to stifle the chuckle boiling up in his throat.

Watching Seth about to lose it, Nick quirked one corner of his mouth up in a half-assed grin. "Sorry, Seth, but… he only wanted to get you in his bed. I overheard him talking to one of the other waiters there when I came to get you from work one night. I actually found it kind of funny because he, uh… pissed himself when I warned him off."

Peals of laughter burst from Seth, and he clutched his stomach. Bryan hadn't exactly been a big, strong guy, but he wasn't a weakling either. "How… how'd you do it?" he gasped.

"The next night, I went back. You weren't working, so when he finished for the night, I cornered him in the alley behind the restaurant. At first, I just warned him to stay away from you, but he got nasty about it, and I had to kind of let the wolf come out," Nick said, an almost sadistic grin on his face.

Seth cracked up again. Tears rolled down his cheeks from laughing so hard. Now that he knew Nick's true nature, he could almost picture the entire event. "No wonder he just up and quit without a word," he chortled. "No one could figure it out."

When Seth had managed to settle down again and catch his breath, he looked at Nick. "So tell me why you aren't over the moon at finding your mate?"

Nick blanched as he remembered the events of last night. He ran a hand through his hair in frustration, and something akin to pain reflected on his face. "Like your mate, he's Native American and believes I am a Created. He tried to kill me last night. And he almost succeeded, because I couldn't see past him being my mate. I couldn't hurt him. No matter what he did to me, I couldn't hurt him, Seth. I managed to get away from him, but ever since it's like there is this cloak over me. I can't hear or think of anything but him."

Sympathy flooded Seth, and he moved to Nick, hugging him fiercely. "Once Kasey figures out how to explain us to his pack, maybe things will be different, babe. Maybe he can accept you. Just have faith."

A silent sob shuddered through Nick, and he buried his face in Seth's dark hair, holding on tightly. No tears fell, and the sound was nothing more than a jerky motion of his lean body. Seth couldn't help but wonder if Kasey had felt the way Nick did right then whenever Seth had rejected him. Guilt bit at him despite the fact that he'd been justified at the beginning to reject Kasey. His throat closed over at the depth of anguish roiling off his friend like a tidal wave crashing onto the shore. "Calm down, Nick," he murmured to Nick, stroking a hand down his friend's back.

Nick sighed and pulled away from Seth, brushing a strand of hair behind his ear. A flush darkened his high cheekbones. "Sorry," Nick mumbled.

"It's what friends are for, right?" Seth said quietly. "Things will be okay, Nick. When they explain about me being Kasey's mate, they'll understand we aren't the Created. And he'll be able to accept you."

Nick only grunted in response. He doubted it. The hate on his mate's face as he'd charged at him, shifting mid-jump, had clearly showed his loathing of Nick's claim. His hand unconsciously rubbed at his chest over his heart. "So what time is the dinner with Kasey's parents?"

"Hmm… I think he said we'd be leaving here at five." Seth glanced at the clock and saw it was only noon. "There's a park over on the main street. You want to go shoot some hoops?"

"I don't think it would be a good idea to be around places you could be scented. Remember, you still haven't managed to cover your scent again," Nick pointed out.

Seth sighed and nodded. "Fine. I guess we can just stay here and watch movies or something."

. . .

K ASEY'S skin itched, and he could barely sit still at the desk in his office. His mind wandered to Seth, and he hoped Nick was smart enough to not let him go anywhere. Seth's scent still clung to him, and Julian had grinned knowingly when he'd come close to him. "Smells like someone got lucky last night. You found your mate, didn't you? Who is she?"

He'd shaken his head. "Can't say anything just yet, Jul."

"What? But it's obvious you claimed her. I can smell cinnamon and sex all over you. Besides, I'm your best friend, you've never hidden things from me before," Julian demanded.

"Just drop it, Julian. I can't explain everything right now because my mate's life is in danger," he'd snapped. Only instead of making Julian stop asking questions, it had only made him get worse. He'd finally roared at Julian to shut the hell up before stalking into his office and slamming the door. He decided he had better inform his mother Seth and Nick were coming to dinner.

The phone rang several times before a breathless female voice answered, "Hello?"

"You left the cordless upstairs again, didn't you, Mom? You better be careful on those stairs or you could break your neck," Kasey chided gently.

"Don't you tell your mother what to do, young man," she replied without heat, a smile in her voice. "To what do I owe the pleasure of a call in the middle of the day, sweetheart?"

"I wanted to know if it'd be all right if I brought my mate and a friend of his to dinner tonight at the house."

Mrs. Whitedove grinned widely. So her son had claimed his mate. "Wonderful! I'll make your favorite meatloaf. So you claimed the young veterinarian, did you? Despite the fact he's white, I assume you believe he is not a Created."

"He isn't a Created, Mom. Like the man Dad met all those years ago, Seth was born a wolf. And here's the kicker: the man was Seth's father." Kasey twirled his pencil between his fingers as he listened to his mother gasp in shock and start firing off a dozen different questions. His nerves sang anxiously, the urge to get up and go back to his mate, to hold him in his arms and protect him from whatever the world threw at him, strong. "My mate… Seth… is in danger, Mom," he said softly, his voice strained in fear and worry.

"Why? What do you mean?" Mrs. Whitedove asked, beyond horrified at the thought of Kasey losing his mate just days after finding him. She'd seen others in the pack perish from despair when they lost their mates. Never eating, never sleeping, and eventually giving up and letting themselves fade away.

He outlined the brief details he knew about Taggart and the Triad, the destruction of the clinic, and what he'd since learned of his mate: the other pack out there, the things Taggart had done to Seth, and how Seth didn't entirely trust him yet but was slowly beginning to. It felt good to get it all off his chest to someone he knew he could trust. Some of the tension he'd been feeling eased away, and he actually smiled when he heard his mother declaring her desire to do something unladylike to Taggart. "I'm sure we can handle it, Mom," he drawled, chuckling.

"If he so much as touches my new son-in-law, I'll kick him right where it hurts," she insisted, almost growling it.

Laughing, Kasey soothed his mother by telling her that he already intended to do much worse if Taggart even looked at Seth. "So you'll be all right with two guests for dinner, then?"

"Of course, sweetheart. I'm looking forward to it. Oh, your brother's in town. He came home to rest for a bit. Said he needed a break from all the traveling."

Kasey tensed. His brother knew nothing about Seth.

"That might be slightly difficult. Seth can't hide his scent anymore. Something in his genetic makeup changed when I claimed him."

"Don't worry, Kasey. Your father and I will speak to him about it, explain everything," she stated calmly.

"This is Thayne we're talking about, Mom. He's worse than me when it comes to the Created and white people," Kasey muttered. Thayne, hotheaded and high-tempered, had only gotten worse because of a previous situation with both species. Kasey had never known the true extent of what Thayne had gone through at the hands of a white man who'd been a Created, but if it was anything like what Seth had been through, he could only imagine. "All right, Mom. If Thayne doesn't take it well, at least call me so we can arrange a different night when he's not here."

They spoke for a few moments longer before Kasey disconnected. His office door opened, and a very pissed off Julian stood in the doorway. Kasey sighed and ran a hand over his face. Apparently Julian had decided it would be okay to eavesdrop on his boss. "How much did you hear?" he asked wearily.

"Everything," Julian stated flatly. "What the hell, Kase? Why couldn't you tell me about this?"

"Because if you heard everything, then you know Seth isn't a Cheyenne but still a wolf. Our pack believes white men cannot be werewolves unless they are a Created one. You know that. It will put his life in danger even further. And... I just found him, Julian. I can't lose him," Kasey stated as calmly as he could. His lips flattened into a thin, angry slash across his face, his rage at Julian for snooping under tight rein. "You can't say anything to anyone. Understand?"

"I understand, Kasey. And I'm your best friend. No matter what, I'd stand by you in whatever decision you make," Julian said, hurt evident in his tone.

Julian Greywolf would make a fine Beta when Kasey became Alpha. Loyal and strong, Julian stood at six foot four, with raven's-wing-black hair, broad shoulders, a lean physique from the five miles he ran every morning before coming to work, and golden-flecked dark-brown eyes. Kasey could see no censure in those eyes for Seth being white or distrust at Kasey stating he wasn't a Created. "You should have told me," Julian said quietly, sinking down in the chair in front of Kasey's desk. "You will be my Alpha one day, Kasey, and I trust you. If you say Doc is not a Created, I believe you."

His deputy's eyes were clear and without guile, cementing his words as truth in Kasey's mind. Kasey grinned tiredly. "Thank you, Jul. You have no idea how I've been going out of my mind with how to convince the pack Seth isn't dangerous, that he's one of us. I'm taking him to see my father tonight in the hopes he can find a way to explain Seth's existence to them without causing anyone to panic or try to kill him."

"So tell me everything, Kase. Where did he come from? And his friend, is he also a wolf?" Julian settled into the chair comfortably, clearly not going anywhere until he heard the story. So Kasey repeated everything he'd told his mother and then some. More than a friend, Julian was his confidant, the one person he'd always gone to for advice or support. He laid out his reaction to Seth at the beginning, the things he'd done to Seth and how hard it had been to get the little bit of acceptance from Seth he had now.

Julian shook his head at Kasey. "You're just like your brother sometimes, Kase. Acting without thinking."

Kasey winced. "I know. I couldn't see anything but the impossibility of a white man being anything but a Created one. And the thought of my mate being a Created one was too much to bear. The thought that someone had changed my mate into one of those vile beasts…."

Julian slouched lower in the chair, one long leg thrown over the other. "So there are others like us out there that aren't Native American," he mused. "I wonder if that will open our pack to the possibility some of us won't have to live a life without our mates."

The thought hadn't occurred to Kasey, and his eyes widened in surprise. "True. I didn't even think of that before. Julian, you're a genius!"

"See? That's what you have me for," Julian drawled, smiling.

By the time Kasey finished for the day and headed to Seth's to pick him and Nick up, it felt as though a great weight had been lifted from his shoulders. He felt lighter somehow and more carefree despite the threat of Taggart hanging over all of them. Maybe he could even convince Seth to start building a home that contained more than just a room full of books and a few dishes. Before leaving the house that morning, he'd peeked into the spare bedroom, gazing in awe at the shelves filled with books lining the walls. Nick hadn't been lying about the sheer volume of literature. There were fiction and nonfiction books, even textbooks littering the cabinets. It made his heart ache at how much time his mate must have spent alone to accumulate such a collection.

When he arrived at Seth's home, he found Seth and Nick lounging on the couch in the living room. Seth looked up, and the way his face brightened at the sight of Kasey sent a shaft of joy spiking through him, a bolt of lightning that swiftly shot down to his groin. He dropped a kiss on the top of Seth's head before sinking into the easy chair with a sigh. "You guys ready to head to my parents'?"

Seth could see tiny lines of exhaustion around Kasey's eyes and fought the urge to go to him, to touch him. Nick stood and stretched, yawning widely. "Yeah, just let me use the restroom, and I'll be good."

"I still need some of your clothes or something," Seth mumbled.

A wicked grin crept across Kasey's face. "Oh, I think we can find another, more enjoyable way to put my scent on you."

Seth's breath caught, but he managed to tear his gaze away from Kasey, still slightly fighting his wolf on easily accepting Kasey's touches. "Come here, pup," he heard Kasey's deeply sinful voice wash over him.

He gave a hesitant shake of his head to negate Kasey's request. "Please," came from Kasey this time, and he couldn't deny it again.

Still not looking at Kasey, he stood and moved closer, almost gasping at the pure electricity that raced up his arm when Kasey's large hand encircled his slender wrist. Kasey pulled him down into his lap, his arms sliding around Seth's waist. A sigh of relief wheezed from Kasey, and Seth burrowed into him, wrapping his arms around his neck. "Missed you, pup," Kasey whispered against the side of Seth's neck.

Melting into his mate at those words, Seth felt the nameless tension he'd felt all day ease from his body. "I… I missed you too," he stammered out.

Pure lust slammed into Kasey at those stuttered words, and he growled, "You're lucky your friend is here, or you'd find yourself naked and on your back before you could even breathe."

The discomfort Seth had felt at the joy that rushed through him when Kasey first came into the house had completely faded away. He grinned and pulled back to be able to look at his large Cheyenne mate. "Promises, promises, Sheriff."

Love and affection swamped the lust completely at the happy twinkle in those ocean-blue eyes. Kasey cupped Seth's cheek, rubbing his thumb tenderly along the curve there. "It's not just a promise, pup. It's a guarantee you'll be begging me for it later on tonight," he taunted.

Seth laughed and replied, "I think tonight will be my turn to make you beg."

Kasey's eyes darkened at his words. "Is that a promise?"

"Oh yes," Seth murmured as he leaned in closer to Kasey, his lips parting in anticipation. He fairly quivered with the need to kiss his mate, to feel his hard mouth plundering his and dominating him.

Kasey's eyes became heavy-lidded in desire. His hand moved to grasp Seth's chin, gently encouraging him to move closer. Their lips brushed together softly, again and again, until their hunger for each other demanded more. Seth pressed closer, opening his mouth to accept Kasey's slick tongue deep inside. A soft moan flooded Kasey's mouth as Seth surrendered himself to the kiss, sinking into it like the waters of a warm ocean. Kasey combed his fingers through the soft black strands of Seth's hair, enjoying the taste of his pup. The sound of the bathroom door opening brought Kasey to his senses, and he broke the kiss, leaning his forehead on Seth's shoulder while trying to catch his breath.

"We'll continue this later," Kasey breathed seductively into Seth's ear, grinning in satisfaction when he felt Seth shiver in anticipation. He slapped Seth's hip lightly. "Off you go, pup. Time to meet the 'rents."

The slight tap to Seth's hip garnered a glare and a huff from Seth. "See if we continue this later after that," he threatened.

One of the sexiest laughs Seth had ever heard rumbled in Kasey's throat, and it made his knees almost give out at the heat the sinful sound sent spiraling into his cock. He stifled a groan and struggled to remain standing. "I don't think it will take much convincing for you to change your mind," Kasey threw at him as he walked past him, the back of his hand accidentally brushing against the bulge in Seth's jeans.

Seth wanted to smack him for that as his cock throbbed in need for his mate. He glared at Kasey again, but the man's back was turned to him, and he didn't see it. Kasey asked innocently when he stopped at the door, "Coming?"

He heard Nick stifle a laugh and swung his head to shoot daggers at his best friend. He intended to disown the bastard for laughing at him. It wasn't as if he could hide his arousal. Both of them could smell the drops of liquid soaking into his boxers anyway. Seth didn't respond, not wanting to give them anything more to laugh at him for, and sulked on the way to the reservation. But his nervousness at meeting Kasey's parents grew. He'd already met his mother, but it hadn't been for anything like this, merely for the appointment for her dog. His thoughts shifted back to his clinic.

A sigh slipped free, and Kasey looked at him sharply. "All right, pup?"

"Huh?" He turned his head to glance at his mate for a split second. "Oh, I'm fine. Just thinking about my clinic."

Kasey's expression changed to one of sympathy. "I'm sorry, Seth."

Seth sighed and ran a hand over his eyes, pinching the bridge of his nose between thumb and forefinger. "Literally every single penny I had went into that clinic."

"Well, you are part of the pack now, and the pack takes care of their own," Kasey said flatly. "It'll be repaired, Seth. I promise."

"Oh, no. No. I can't let you do that," Seth protested, sitting straighter in his seat.

"Don't argue with me, Seth. Your clinic is your livelihood,

and you are my mate, which means what's yours is mine, and what's mine is yours. Understand?"

Scowling, Seth slumped down in his seat with his arms crossed. "Well, I don't have to like it," he said petulantly.

Kasey ignored him, flipped on his turn signal, and pulled into the reservation. When they pulled up in front of his parents' home, he looked at Seth. "Stay in the truck. I'm going to come around and practically lean on you, just in case."

He jumped out of the vehicle and raced around to the other side in seconds. Seth took the hand Kasey offered to him and allowed himself to be pulled into the larger man's side, almost completely swamped by his mate. Of course his wolf didn't mind. The energy inside him hummed at being so close to him. Seth twisted one of his hands in the hem of his shirt in nervousness.

"There's nothing to be nervous about, pup. My mother already considers you her new son-in-law, and my father is eagerly waiting to meet you."

"They... they don't care I'm a man and not a woman? I can't give you children," Seth mumbled.

Kasey stopped, waving Nick up onto the porch with one hand while looking down at his mate. "You are my mate, Seth. Man, woman, it doesn't matter." He used the tips of his free hand to tilt Seth's face up toward him. "I would want you no matter what."

Seth blinked furiously. If he hadn't already been in love with Kasey, his declaration would have cemented it. His heart swelled so big it could have burst from his chest. "Thank you," he whispered.

The half-smile Seth adored twisted up one corner of Kasey's mouth. "Anytime, pup. Just don't ever forget and never ever doubt it."

"It mattered to you when you thought him a Created one,"

Nick's voice came from the darkened porch, a pained quality to it.

Frowning, Kasey turned to look at Nick, but his face was shadowed. "Yes, it did, because he would have been a danger to everyone. You know what the Created are like, Nick."

"You didn't even give him the chance to explain anything," Nick snapped angrily. "You spout pretty words now, but I know what it did to him when you rejected him."

Seth gave Nick a warning look to try and make him stop, but he plowed on. "Whether you care to know or not, Sheriff, you devastated him with the way you treated him at the beginning. He was nearly in tears when he called me to come home. You're lucky I didn't beat your ass for the way you've treated him."

Kasey stiffened against Seth, his face seemingly made of stone. "You think I don't blame myself for the way I treated him at first? Or it doesn't haunt me that I've hurt him? I've damned myself more than you ever could for what I did to him. I can only pray he forgives me, and do whatever I can to make it up to him."

Shock kept Seth silent. It never occurred to him Kasey felt that way. Tension and anger radiated from his mate. It washed over him, bringing his inner wolf alert to his mate's distress. A low sound rumbled in his throat as he glared at Nick. "Stop it, Nick," he managed to force out, but it was deep, harsh, and unforgiving. "Leave him alone. You don't have the right to take the pain of your mate rejecting you out on him."

Nick stepped back as if stunned Seth would turn on him, considering their friendship and how long they'd known one another. In fourteen years, they'd never argued or disagreed. "Seth, I...."

Seth's features softened as he realized how he'd sounded. "I'm sorry, Nick. But things are better between me and

Kasey. It's not like that anymore. I know you're hurting right now, but please don't make him feel any worse than he already does." His gaze turned to the tall Cheyenne still wrapped around him. "I don't blame you, Kasey. I know you were upset that I might be a Created one, and I know better than anyone here exactly what the Created are like. I forgive you, Kasey."

Humbled by his mate's easy acceptance of his early treatment, Kasey kissed him, hard but only briefly. His voice sounded a little ragged when he said, "I think we've lingered out here enough. Let's go inside."

A WONDERFUL smell immediately flooded their senses when Kasey opened the front door. Seth felt his mouth water hungrily. "Mom, Dad," Kasey called, shutting the door behind them.

"In the kitchen, sweetheart," his mother called.

The three of them headed toward the kitchen, stopping in the doorway. Kasey's larger form blocked both Seth and Nick from sight. "Well, would you look at what the cat dragged in," Kasey drawled when he saw his brother lounging in one of the chairs at the kitchen table.

"Right before I ate it," Thayne Whitedove replied with a big grin. "How's it going, big brother?"

Seth felt Nick stiffen behind him and turned to see his friend's face ashen. "Nick? Nick, what's wrong?"

Then he heard a cry of "You!" come from behind him.

Seth turned to look at the man Kasey had greeted as his brother. Although a couple of inches shorter and not quite as muscular, he could have been a mirror image of Kasey. He asked Nick, "That's him?"

Nick gave a stunned nod. Thayne tensed as if he were

going to spring himself at Nick. Kasey stepped in between them. "Thayne," he said sharply. "Don't. He's not a Created one." He turned his head to his mother. "Didn't you explain to him?"

"Of course! And he said he understood. What is wrong with you, Thayne?" she reprimanded sharply.

Thayne bared his teeth at Nick, dark eyes cold as ice. A low growl rumbled in his chest and echoed off the stainless steel appliances. Seth backed up against Nick, crouching slightly to protect his friend in case the other decided to attack. "Would you like to tell me what the hell is going on?" Kasey demanded.

"Your brother is Nick's mate," Seth stated flatly. Kasey's mother gasped, and Kasey jerked in surprise. "They met last night, and apparently your brother believed Nick is a Created one. They fought."

"I can't stay here," Nick whispered, turning and racing out of the house. He shifted mid-jump from the porch, tearing through the reservation, uncaring that others might see him, his only thought to get away from the pain exploding in his chest.

"You idiot," Kasey snarled at his brother. "He's not a Created one. Mom explained already. How can you outright reject your mate?"

Thayne drew himself to his full height, a haughty expression on his face. "You're one to talk. Mom told me how you rejected yours before you knew he wasn't a Created. And who says I want a mate? I like being free to do whatever I want."

Seth interrupted them, suddenly furious on his friend's behalf. He didn't care how much smaller than Thayne he was, he pushed himself in Thayne's face, poking him in the chest. "You are a spoiled, selfish prick. Do you even know how much pain you've caused him by rejecting him? You don't even care that you hurt him?"

Kasey stifled laughter at how fierce his mate looked, despite his size and the expression on Thayne's face. He reached out and gripped his mate by his shoulders, pulling him back against him and looping his arms around his waist. "I think you should listen to him, Thayne. I made the mistake of rejecting him and just barely managed to scrape my way back into his good graces."

Thayne glared at Kasey. "I don't care about him or getting back into his good graces. I don't want a mate."

Seth felt sad for his friend. He could only imagine how it would have felt if Kasey had truly rejected him. He shook his head at Thayne. "I feel sorry for my friend to be saddled with you for a mate. I just hope he can accept that you don't want him, because it looked to me as if he'd just found and lost a part of himself all at once."

Thayne gave no response for a few moments, then said, "I can't be here right now. I'm happy you found your mate, bro. You've always wanted him." Thayne darted out of the house, shifting before he'd even reached the forest.

The whole chain of events hadn't been what any of them expected, and it cast a pall on the joy of the occasion. Emily Whitedove chose that moment to step forward and hug Seth tightly. "Mmmm… I'm so glad my son found his mate." She pulled back to look at him, her face wreathed in a giant smile. "Especially one as handsome as you. Even when I first brought Samantha into the clinic, I was absolutely amazed by those eyes."

Seth flushed. "Thanks, Mrs. Whitedove."

"Oh, pooh on the formalities, dear. Call me Mom," she insisted, releasing him and moving back over to the stove. "I hope you like meatloaf. It's Kasey's favorite."

Recovering from being told to call her Mom, Seth took a moment to answer. "Yes, I love it."

"Mom's is the best meatloaf around," Kasey said proudly, throwing a loose arm around Seth's shoulders. "Where's Dad?"

"Out back with that young one, Chase Hunter. The one that's always stirring up trouble." She opened the oven and reached for the pot holders, but Kasey got there first, sliding them on and lifting the pan out of the oven. "Thank you, dear. Why don't you show Seth around the house while I finish up the mashed potatoes and rolls? Your father should be in soon."

"Sure thing, Mom." Kasey grinned, grabbed Seth's hand, and tugged him out of the kitchen. "She always kicks everyone out of the kitchen. She considers it her domain."

"She's really sweet," Seth replied softly. He looked around him at Kasey's childhood home. None of the homes he'd ever lived in were as beautiful. The large wide open spaces and big, comfortable furniture made him smile as he imagined Kasey and his brother chasing each other through the house and jumping on the overstuffed couch. There was mostly wood flooring throughout the house, accented by runners and throw rugs. The living room area had a big mortar and stone fireplace with two wooden rocking chairs in front of it, facing the plush brown couch and loveseat. A dark oak shelf held a multitude of books and knickknacks. On the walls were several seascape and forest paintings done quite skillfully.

But what drew his eye the most was the mantle above the fireplace, filled with dozens of framed pictures, pictures of Kasey's parents, baby pictures of Kasey and Thayne, Kasey graduating high school, and so many more. It took his breath away and left behind a feeling of melancholy. He hadn't really had that, even with his parents. A whole lifetime of friends and family sat on that shelf. Something he'd never truly had aside from his parents and Nick. He supposed it was more than some ever had, though. Seth's eyes zeroed in on one of Kasey astride a black horse, and he moved closer to study it.

Kasey hadn't released Seth's hand since he'd taken it, and he pulled Seth closer to him at the wave of sadness he felt coming from his mate. "I was fifteen. Summer camp and the first time I'd ever rode a horse. I fell in love with the sensation of the wind in my face and a powerful body beneath me. Nothing can touch me when I ride. It's like a whole other world for me."

"I've never ridden a horse before," Seth said wistfully, staring at the picture and wondering how many friends his mate had before, how many girlfriends had come before him. Such happiness sparkled in those dark eyes that it made his heart ache with it. All these years he'd missed out on experiencing the same things and possibly even sharing them with Kasey.

"Then we'll have to remedy that. Let me take you riding?" Kasey asked, squeezing Seth's hand affectionately, trying to distract his mate from whatever thoughts were making him unhappy.

"Really?" Seth's face lit up at the idea. "When? When can we go?"

"What about this weekend? I'm off from the station on Saturday." Kasey thought his mate looked so adorable, seeming to shine at the idea of riding a horse.

Seth nodded enthusiastically. "All right. I can't wait."

They continued on through the house until they reached Kasey's bedroom. Seth was too interested in his surroundings to notice Kasey had closed the door and leaned against it, watching him. The walls were a pale blue. One wall had a mural of wolves and horses running together. Seth trailed his fingers along the detailed lines of a large black wolf in wonder. "This is beautiful," he breathed.

"Thank you," Kasey replied huskily, hungering to feel his mate in his arms. He moved behind Seth and rested his hands on his slender shoulders. "My friend Max painted it when we were in high school. After summer camp."

"Your friend is very talented. Does he paint for a living?" Seth wondered if the man would be willing to do something like this on the wall of his clinic. Once it was fixed up and running again, he thought bitterly.

"He does some freelance work, but he actually graduated from Harvard with a degree in law." Kasey slipped his arms around Seth, resting his chin on top of the dark crown. "Mind-blowing that your friend is my brother's mate, huh?"

Settling into the light embrace, Seth tipped his head back to look up at Kasey. His eyes were troubled. "Do you think Nick will be okay considering your brother doesn't want to accept him? I've never seen him look so… broken."

"He'll be all right, pup," Kasey reassured him, pressing a kiss to Seth's temple. "Thayne just needs time to think. I don't think he expected his mate to be male, and it is still fresh that Nick isn't a Created one. When he's processed it all, he'll come around. He might be stubborn and bullheaded, but he's still wolf. And a wolf cannot deny his mate."

"Did it… did you feel that way when I pushed you away?" Seth whispered, dropping his gaze from Kasey's.

Kasey debated teasing his mate but decided it would just be cruel to do so. "No," he said, noticing with a grin when Seth looked disappointed. "Because I never doubted you'd give in to my charms."

Seth's head jerked up at his words, and he opened his mouth to make a smart remark but didn't have the chance. What he'd been about to say was cut off by Kasey's mouth on his. The words flew from his mind as he became lost in the pleasure of his mate's kiss. Dazedly he felt Kasey turn him in his embrace and start to move them toward the bed. Their lips never parted as they fell across it. Seth nearly groaned when the weight of Kasey's body pressed him into the mattress. Common sense kicked in at a sound from the hallway, and he broke the kiss with a gasp. "We should… ah… go back downstairs," he panted, his head lolling to the side as Kasey blazed a wet trail down his throat.

"I'd rather have you for dinner," Kasey murmured, sucking hotly at Seth's neck just over where the pulse beat beneath it. The scent of Seth's arousal called to his wolf, sending a rumbling growl through his chest. "You taste so good."

Hands entwining in Kasey's hair, Seth pulled him tighter into him. If they'd been anywhere else, he'd have lost all self-control by then and started tearing at Kasey's clothing to be closer to him, skin to skin. But they weren't somewhere else, and he didn't want to disrespect Kasey's parents. "Kasey… stop," he begged. "You'll embarrass me in front of your parents."

Reluctantly, Kasey released the bit of skin he'd been nibbling on. Rising onto his elbows, he gave his mate a rueful smile as he brushed a strand of hair from Seth's cheek. "You make me forget anything else exists, pup."

Blushing, Seth wrinkled his nose up at Kasey. "If we were anywhere except here, I'd forget anything else exists, but I can't forget we're in your parents' home. But we most definitely will continue later when we get home."

Groaning at his mate's lusty expression, Kasey stood abruptly, holding out his hand. "Come on, pup, before I forget my resolve and take you right here, my parents be damned."

Seth laughingly took Kasey's hand and allowed him to pull him from the bed. "I don't think your mom would be too happy if we made love in her house when she only invited us over for dinner."

"Made love?" Kasey asked in a soft tone, a question buried in its depths.

But before Seth could answer his question, Kasey's mom shouted up from the bottom of the stairs, "Dinner's ready, boys."

Kasey almost growled at the interruption but managed to stifle it. They'd continue the conversation later. "Come on, pup. She'll get real impatient if we don't show up immediately."

Seth breathed a sigh of relief inwardly, thanking Kasey's mom silently for the excuse to not answer. He followed Kasey down the stairs to the dining room, where a man, presumably Kasey's father, sat at the head of the table. The man looked young enough to be Kasey's brother, not his father! The same strong chin, the high cheekbones that seemed to be a signature of the Cheyenne, and well-defined nose made him the spitting image of Kasey and Thayne. Shyness overwhelmed Seth then, and he looked at the floor. "Hey, Dad," Kasey bid from beside him before making his way around the table to give his dad a hug.

"So this is your mate," Jeremiah Whitedove said, staring with shrewd eyes at Seth. "My wife tells me your father was Eric Hawthorne."

Looking up in surprise, Seth stared at him. "I told Mom," Kasey explained at his mate's reaction. "Come have a seat and talk to my father. I'm going to go help bring dinner to the table."

Seth swallowed a sound of protest at Kasey leaving him alone with his father. He nervously moved to the seat beside the imposing Alpha. "Ye—" His voice cracked, and he cleared his throat. "Yes, my father was Eric Hawthorne."

Jeremiah sensed the same thing Charlie had reported

almost immediately after tending to the pup. The boy was a Rho. Peace and healing exuded from the young wolf, tangible, almost. "Your father told me there were others out there like himself."

"I wouldn't know aside from my parents, my friend, and everyone I have met since I came to Senaka. They never told me about others. Not even the Created." Seth felt slightly bitter about it. It should have been his choice to hide. They had taken away part of who he was by hiding him all those years, and if he'd known of the Created, been educated about them, perhaps he would have been able to prevent his mistake in believing Taggart to be his mate.

Reaching out, Jeremiah set his hand on top of Seth's. "I may not have known your father long, but I do know he was a great man. A great wolf. And he did what he thought best, trying to protect you. You are a Rho, Seth. Do you know what that is?"

The warmth of Jeremiah's hand on his reminded him of his own father, and it sent a shaft of longing through him. He missed his parents. "Only what my friend Nick told me. I'm supposedly something special among a pack, and there are many who would try to claim me against my will."

"Rhos are very rare. They are only born every so many generations, and each is born with a unique ability. My son tells me you have a healing capability beyond anything he's ever seen. This is an amazing gift, son. And many would try to take advantage of such a gift. Your father must have known this, and though keeping you in the dark about your heritage was not something I agree with, he did it to protect you."

The bitterness melted away, and Seth felt chagrined that he'd thought so negatively of his parents. He knew they loved him and never would have done anything to hurt him. "Thank you, sir," he murmured.

Jeremiah waved away the respectful title. "There is no need to call me sir. You may call me Dad if you wish, or Jeremiah, as you are my son's mate. Sir makes me feel old and stuffy."

"Will you tell me everything you knew about my father?" Seth sat forward eagerly, like a child waiting with bated breath to hear a great tale of heroism.

"First you need to eat," interjected Kasey, a steaming plate of meatloaf in his hands, which he set in the middle of the table. His mother stood just behind him, holding a bowl of mashed potatoes and a plate of biscuits. Kasey gave a stern look at Seth, who rolled his eyes.

"Yes, Dad," Seth replied sarcastically.

"Impertinent pup," Kasey drawled at him, earning a glare. He settled his long frame into the chair next to Seth's and, after placing a couple slices of meatloaf on his plate, passed it to Seth.

Jeremiah hid a grin behind his glass of water, and Emily gave the two of them a knowing look. It warmed her heart to see her son so happy, and though Seth might not have accepted him at first, it clearly showed that Seth had grown fond of her son. The only concern she had now was the Created one terrorizing her new son-in-law.

For the next hour Jeremiah regaled Seth with tales of the interactions between him and his father. Eric Hawthorne had been sent by his pack to seek out others. They were having the same troubles with finding their true mates. Jeremiah had refused the request of having some of the others in his territory, believing it would stir panic and fear in his pack, but it had pained him to do so after getting to know Eric.

"Your father was certainly an Alpha. I am surprised he didn't go off and start his own pack. But I suppose it wasn't possible after you were born," Jeremiah mused.

"Had he already met my mother by the time you met him?" Seth barely noticed Kasey sliding his arm along the back of his chair or the way his fingers teased the strands of hair brushing his collar.

"He hadn't met his mate yet, but about six months after he left, I received a letter from him. I still have the letter if you'd like to see it." Jeremiah could see Seth's adoration for his father. The man would have made a wonderful leader for a pack, kind, generous, and strong.

"Oh yes! I would like to very much."

"You miss your parents." It was a statement, not a question. "If you don't mind my asking, how did your parents pass?" Jeremiah's voice held a sympathetic tone.

Seth's face went void of emotion, and his tone was flat when he said, "They were on a road trip for their anniversary. It was just before Christmas, and they were on their way home. They hit a patch of ice and spun out of control. A witness said my father tried everything to stop the car, but there was nothing he could do to keep it from going over the edge. They were in the mountains in North Carolina. The car exploded on impact."

Kasey stroked the side of his mate's neck in sympathy. The anguish Seth felt rolled off him in waves. Wolves might be able to heal more quickly than humans, but even they could not survive something like that. "I am very sorry to hear it," Jeremiah said solemnly.

"Thank you," Seth replied woodenly. "I do miss them very much."

The conversation changed quickly after to avoid such a depressing topic during dinner. Before long Seth sat laughing as Emily told one particularly hilarious tale about one of the scrapes Kasey had gotten into as a child. Of course the story prompted her to pull out the baby pictures after dinner, when they were relaxing in the living room. "Mom," Kasey groaned and covered his face with his hand.

"What? You were adorable!" She held a picture of Kasey dressed in his skivvies with a pair of his father's underwear on his head. "He was two years old at the time I took that."

Seth wiped tears from his eyes and grinned broadly at Kasey. "You were cute," he teased.

If anyone else had said it, Kasey would have hit them, but he merely let out an indignant huff and tickled Seth in his ribs. "You'll pay for that later," he muttered into Seth's ear, causing him to flush.

Worry about Nick constantly niggled at the back of Seth's mind. Where had his friend gone? He didn't have a key to Seth's home and didn't know anyone else in town aside from Chessie at the clinic. The thought froze him. Would Nick drown his sorrows in Seth's receptionist? *He better not*, he thought fiercely.

When they were in Kasey's truck on the way home, Kasey asked, "Are you okay?"

"I'm just worried about Nick," he admitted quietly.

Kasey took his hand. "He'll be fine, pup. He's a grown man, and I'm sure he just needs time to himself right now."

"I'm sure you're right." Seth bit his lip pensively as he stared out the window at the trees flying by. When Kasey turned onto a small dirt road leading into the forest, Seth was pulled from his thoughts. Seth looked at him curiously. "Where are we going?"

"Well, it occurred to me we haven't had the chance to run together," Kasey explained, turning the truck into a small clearing off the road. "I want to run with you, pup. Will you run with me?"

Though Seth had been in his wolf form with Kasey several times already, they'd never run together. The only time they'd been truly near each other in their true forms was the night they'd mated. Seth's skin itched at the thought of shifting, and he nodded. "I'd like that."

The night air felt cool with a hint of a breeze, and the moon, almost full, shone brightly in the inky blackness overhead. They shifted in the middle of the clearing, and two black wolves, one larger than the other, rubbed against each other before the smaller wolf raced into the trees and the second gave chase. Paws crushed leaves, padding with soft thuds along the forest floor. A long, joyful howl issued from Kasey, and Seth echoed it, truly reveling for the first time in being a wolf.

Kasey felt as if life couldn't be any sweeter. He had his true mate, and his mate was slowly extending him his heart. Though Seth hadn't said it yet, he grew more certain as time passed that the younger male loved him. He could sense it in the way Seth touched him, the way he kissed him. The look in his ocean-blue eyes whenever he gazed at Kasey spoke volumes. The threat of Taggart still hung over them like a black cloud, but he didn't fear the Created one. He would protect Seth no matter what, even if he had to give his own life.

Finally Seth let Kasey catch him, and they wrestled around like two puppies in the empty clearing they'd reached. Kasey growled playfully and nipped at Seth's neck, and Seth responded by rolling him abruptly and pinning him beneath his body. Even though Kasey was bigger and stronger than Seth, he didn't fight it, merely grinned a sappy, tongue-lolling smile up at Seth. He would never use his strength against Seth, even if only in play. The thought of his mate ever being afraid of him sent daggers stabbing between his ribs and straight at his heart.

Sides heaving, Seth collapsed on top of Kasey's prone form and just lay there, his ear twitching occasionally. For the first time in his life, he felt as if maybe everything would work out and he could be happy. God knew he'd never felt as happy as he did right then. He never wanted this moment, however brief, to end. If he could stay right there beside Kasey, he'd never want for anything else.

But their time grew short. Seth nuzzled at Kasey's throat for a brief affectionate moment before dragging himself up and encouraging Kasey to head back toward the truck. Just inside the trees, they shifted back to human form. "You all right?" Kasey asked Seth as he opened the passenger door for him.

"I'm fine," Seth murmured before slipping into the front seat.

Kasey picked up Seth's hand once they were on the main road, entwining their fingers together and letting them rest on his thigh. Tension wafted from his mate. He squeezed his fingers reassuringly. "Nick will be okay, pup. I'm sure he'll be waiting for us at your house when we get there."

Seth gave him a grateful smile and squeezed back. The warmth of Kasey's palm on his and the feel of the hard thigh on the back of his hand reminded him of what he intended to do to Kasey tonight. Anticipation spiraled through him, and he twitched in his seat as he felt his cock respond to his thoughts. He could hardly wait to feel Kasey inside him again.

But those thoughts only lasted as long as the drive, for when they arrived back at the house, several lights were on, and the front door stood wide open. His eyes widened in surprise. Nick didn't have a key, so how did he get in?

Nick stepped off the porch, a strange look on his face, the instant the truck came to a halt. He met Seth as he opened the passenger door. "Stay in the truck, Seth," Nick stated in a strained voice.

"Why? What's going on?" Seth tried to step down, but

Nick shut the door, forcing him back into his seat. He stared in shock at Nick. "Dammit, Nick. What the hell is going on?"

"Stay in the truck, Seth. Don't come into the house," Nick commanded fiercely. "Sheriff, I think you should come with me."

Dread speared Seth's heart like a sharp knife as he watched Kasey following Nick into the house. Something was wrong. He could feel it.

Kasey stopped dead in the doorway and just stared at whatever had caused Nick to act so out of character. *No...,* Seth thought, his hand blindly reaching for the door handle. He ignored Nick's command. His legs trembled as he stumbled toward the house, his face frozen with fear. His blood pounded in his ears, and he didn't hear the profuse swear words Kasey let out when he saw Seth.

"Seth, no, don't!"

He shoved clumsily past Kasey, coming to an abrupt halt before dropping to his knees. An anguished sound ripped from his throat, and he wrapped his arms around his waist. "No," he keened brokenly, unable to speak further as great sobs racked his body.

BLOOD was spilled everywhere, splashed over the white walls of his living room, standing out starkly and searing the message written with it into Seth's brain. It was a message that was clearly a confirmation that Taggart was indeed alive and coming for him: *"You can never escape me."* But where the blood had come from was evident by the gruesome remains of Bullet. Taggart had taken his time ripping the poor creature apart. His legs were thrown on opposite sides of the house, his tail and torso strewn across Seth's couch, and the head placed in the middle of the small coffee table, as if to rub in the fact it was Seth's fault Bullet was dead. Seth rocked back and forth, making incoherent sounds of grief as he stared unblinking and wide-eyed at the horrifying mess that had once been his loving animal.

Strong hands gripped his forearms and lifted him from the floor, but he didn't feel it, didn't notice it. The heartbreaking sorrow filling his chest numbed him to everything else around him. Somehow he found himself back in the truck while Kasey called his deputy and his father. He couldn't seem to pull his gaze from the front door he'd just realized hung haphazardly off its hinges. The door had been forcibly opened by a brutal assault to it.

A hysterical laugh built up in Seth's throat. Taggart would never let him go. The urge to run away again, to keep running as he had for two years, never stopping for longer than a day or two, jabbed at him fiercely. He looked over at the keys Kasey had left in the ignition. He'd been stupid to think he could ever stop running or could ever escape Taggart.

Seth didn't stop to think of what it could do to Kasey if he left or how much he would hurt after leaving Kasey once the numbness wore off. He just slid over the seat and into the driver's, turning the key and throwing the truck into reverse the instant the engine turned over. Kasey's and Nick's heads swung around, and they started shouting, racing after him as he squealed out of the driveway. He spun the truck as he backed out, slamming the gears into drive and stomping on the gas. Kasey and Nick were yelling at him to stop, but instead his hands gripped the steering wheel tightly, almost shattering the thick plastic with his strength.

Infuriated at himself for leaving the keys in the truck, Kasey swore harshly. He'd been stupid to do something like that knowing how unsteady Seth was. But it had never occurred to him that Seth would leave him, would run from him instead of to him. "Fuck!" He spun around on his heel and raced back to Seth's house, grabbing the keys to Seth's car off the island counter. "What the hell is he doing?" he demanded of Nick as he darted past the other wolf.

"Running," Nick called after him. "Like he's always done."

Kasey swore again and tore out of the driveway as if the hounds of hell were on his heels. He sped off in the direction Seth had gone, pushing the little car until it practically shook. It took all of his strength to keep the little car on the road, its size clearly not meant to go at those speeds. He just prayed he could make Seth understand he wasn't going to let Taggart anywhere near him. He'd gut the bastard first. It hurt that Seth didn't know that already, but he shoved the emotion aside to be processed later. The only thing that mattered was getting Seth back.

The taillights of the truck appeared ahead of him on the main road out of town, and he gunned the engine harder, slowly creeping up behind Seth. He flashed the lights to try and get Seth to pull over, but Seth just picked up speed. "You little fool," he growled under his breath.

He pushed the pedal down further, crawling up next to his truck. He slapped the button to bring the window down and started shouting at Seth, "Pull over!"

Tears streamed down Seth's face, and it wrenched Kasey's gut how much pain his mate was in. He shook his head furiously at Kasey, and Kasey scowled in agitation. "Dammit, Seth, pull the fuck over!"

A car appeared ahead of Kasey, the headlights shining brightly in the front windshield. He saw Seth glance at him then, but he didn't pull back, choosing to continue alongside the truck. Seth's gaze turned frantic, and he looked at Kasey again, clearly expecting him to fall back behind the sheriff's vehicle. When he didn't, Seth's expression turned to one of horror as the approaching car got even closer. Kasey's mouth set into a grim line of determination. His trust that Seth would pull over before the other vehicle got to them held firm. Seth would never allow him to get hurt. It was instinctual to protect your mate no matter what.

Seth realized Kasey didn't intend to pull back and let the other car pass by them. The closer the other car got, the harder his heart pounded. His palms started sweating as his anxiety rose even higher. He had to pull over or Kasey would hit the other car head on! He yanked the wheel and slammed on his brakes as he hit the shoulder. The tires fought for traction on the loose soil and grass. Just as the glare of his headlights caught mere feet in front of them, the tires caught and held, kicking dirt up in a high plume behind the truck. Seth shakily put it into park as Kasey wrenched the door open and practically lifted him bodily from the car into a crushing embrace. "What the hell were you thinking?" a gruff voice murmured into his ear shakily.

He clung to Kasey, trembling and overwrought. "I'm sorry," he sobbed, his face pressed tightly against Kasey's chest. His arms were wrapped tightly around Kasey's back, his fingers gripping at the fabric of his shirt. Warm hands traveled up and down his back in a soothing caress as Kasey crooned in his ear to calm him down.

"Don't run from me, Seth," Kasey begged quietly once Seth's body had stopped quivering. "Don't run from us. I need you to trust me."

"I do trust you, Kasey, but I'm scared," Seth admitted hoarsely.

Kasey rubbed his chin on the top of Seth's head. "I will protect you, pup. Until I draw my last breath, I swear it. Please don't run away from me again. If you trust me, trust me enough to keep you safe."

The underlying tone of pain in Kasey's voice brought Seth's head back so he could look up at his mate. "I didn't mean to hurt you," Seth said softly, reaching up to cup Kasey's cheek.

Kasey leaned into Seth's touch, his dark eyes closing at the affectionate touch of his pup. He'd been terrified when he'd thought he wouldn't catch Seth in time. Never being able to touch, to hold, or kiss his mate again seemed worse than death. He had no idea how anyone survived losing their mate. It would be hell on earth never to see Seth smile again. "Let's go home," he said gently.

"I can't go back there," Seth whispered in pain. He

couldn't see the gruesome remains again or the message that chilled him from the inside out.

"I meant to my home. I don't want you going back there. Come on. I'll lock up your car, and we'll take my truck. I can radio Julian and have him drop Nick off at my place." Kasey reluctantly released Seth and went to move Seth's car from behind the truck. He locked the doors and jogged back over to where Seth still stood, leaning against the side of the truck. "In you go, pup," he said, patting Seth's hip.

Seth didn't react as he would have if he hadn't been so shell-shocked and just slid into the passenger's seat from the driver's side. He leaned his head back against the headrest and stared out the window at the trees rushing past the window of the truck. He vaguely heard Kasey speaking with his deputy, but he didn't pay attention to the outcome of the conversation, his thoughts a jumbled mess over everything. Taggart had destroyed Bullet because he knew the dog meant something to him. Would he try to do the same to Kasey? Seth would never be able to live with himself if the sheriff, his mate, was hurt or worse because of him. His heart thudded hard and painfully against his ribcage at the thought of Kasey's lifeless eyes staring up at him from a pool of blood. His teeth sank into his bottom lip at the agony flaring through him.

"Nick is going to stay in town with Julian tonight," Kasey said, disrupting Seth's thoughts.

Turning his head to the side to look at Kasey, Seth nodded in understanding but didn't speak, his throat too tight to force words out. It felt like a lump of rock had wedged there, and he could barely swallow or breathe. Things had been so different before. He'd had nothing to lose. His parents had already been dead by then, and he'd had no one except Nick in his life. Now he'd already lost his dog, but would it only be a matter of time before Taggart took Kasey from him too?

Worry wound its way through Kasey as he saw how quiet his mate had grown, felt how unsettled he was. He carefully wrapped his hand around Seth's, bringing it to his lips to press a kiss to the backs of Seth's fingers. "Seth?"

Fear and anxiety churned through Seth's stomach, twisting it cruelly. He made a small grunting noise to let Kasey know he had heard him. "Tell me what's on your mind," Kasey said gently. Nose scrunching up as Seth suppressed hysterical laughter again, he merely shook his head. "Talk to me, Seth. How can I know what's going on inside that gorgeous little head of yours if you won't tell me?"

"Because it won't change the reality of my situation," Seth croaked, his voice strained as his throat worked to stem his emotions.

"It helps to talk it out, my mate. I want to be there for you. Will you please tell me what you're thinking?" Kasey pulled into the dirt entrance to his ranch, pulled up to the porch, and shut the engine off. Twisting in his seat, he looked at his pup. Seth sat huddled against the door with such a sad expression that Kasey's wolf almost let forth a keening cry.

Seth stared straight ahead, unable to meet the dark gaze locked on him. The feel of Kasey's hand on his was warm and alive. He could feel the beat of Kasey's blood pulsing underneath his fingers. "I never thought I'd find someone I could be happy with after Taggart. I always thought I would be alone because it just seemed I was meant to be." A small smile lifted the corner of his mouth. "Then you came along and everything changed again. No matter how much I pushed you away, you stayed. I fought against it because I was afraid you would turn out to be just like him. That you'd use me too."

Now that the dam had broken, the words kept spilling

out, overflowing from the river of his emotions. "But you haven't. You've been kind to me. Caring. Nothing like him. I didn't know what to do with you. Whenever something went wrong, Nick was the first one I ran to, but now the first person I think of is you. Tonight when I ran, I knew it would hurt you, but I couldn't stop myself, and it only made me feel worse. At first I didn't think you'd come after me, but when you did, I was happy. Happy you cared enough to come after me."

When Kasey went to speak, Seth stopped his words, two fingers against his lips. "But I was scared, too, scared you would be hurt because of me and that what Taggart did to Bullet, he would do to you. I'm still terrified he's going to hurt you, but I can't run anymore." Anguish rattled in his voice, and his lips trembled. "I can't run from you, and I don't want to."

"Thank God," Kasey breathed, yanking Seth over the bench seat and into his lap. He pressed his nose against the side of Seth's neck and breathed deeply. "The pack protects its own, pup. He won't have the chance to hurt me. Dad's going to inform the rest of the pack about you and the Created one tomorrow at a pack meeting. Until then, he's spoken with several of his most trusted members, swearing them to secrecy and assigning them in shifts to run patrols through the forests and surrounding areas until we catch the son of a bitch. Julian already knows about everything. Taggart won't even get within a hundred yards of you before we'll catch him. And you won't be going anywhere without someone guarding you at all times."

Seth's legs stretched across the front seat of the truck from where he sat in Kasey's lap. The fingers of one hand tugged unconsciously at the seam of his jeans, and the other hand rested on Kasey's shoulder. He shifted in discomfort at the thought of others, strangers even, risking their lives for him. "Taggart's cruel," he said softly. "I… I don't like the idea of others risking their lives because of me."

Kasey kissed the skin over the pulse beating against the side of Seth's throat. "You are my mate. I am the future Alpha, and you are the future Rho of this pack. They would die for you."

"That's just it!" Seth cried. "I don't want them to die for me. I don't want anyone to die. I'm tired of all this death and blood."

Cuddling Seth closer, Kasey sighed. "No one is going to die, Seth. Except Taggart if I get my hands on him. No one will be running solo. They run in pairs, pup. Dad will order them not to engage without the others present. Relax. Nothing is going to happen."

It helped Seth relax slightly. He melted into Kasey, burying his face in his neck. "I just don't want anything to happen to you," he murmured.

"Aww, come on, pup. You know I'm too stubborn," Kasey teased. "Besides, if he did succeed, you'd finally be free of an arrogant ass like me."

Seth drew back to glare at him. "That's not even funny, Kasey. I don't want to be free of you, even if you are an arrogant ass. I lo—" He abruptly cut himself off, horrified at what he'd almost said.

"You what?" Kasey demanded, refusing to let Seth try to hide his face from him. He tilted his head back so their eyes were locked together. "You what, pup?" he asked again, this time softer.

Sucking on his bottom lip, Seth tried to think of what he could say, but the hope shining out of the depths of Kasey's eyes made him capitulate. His heart beat faster in anxiety, and his palms started to sweat. Aside from his parents, he had never told another person he loved them. Swallowing hard, he breathed out hesitantly, "I… love you."

Kasey felt stunned, to say the least. His breath caught in a slight hiccup of emotion, and he crushed Seth to him, kissing him fiercely. His chest heaved for air when he broke away, leaning his forehead on Seth's shoulder. His voice sounded rough, and his body quaked lightly when he could finally speak. "I wondered if you'd ever say it, if you'd ever feel it enough to say it. Oh God, pup. Do you really mean it?"

Seth ran his fingers through Kasey's hair, stroking the base of his neck affectionately. "Yes, I mean it. I was afraid to admit it. Loving someone… telling someone you love them gives them a power over you that I wasn't ready to give before. It's why I can't bring myself to run from you anymore. And maybe it's selfish to leave you in danger, but I can't stop myself."

"It would be more selfish to leave me," Kasey replied as he started slowly caressing Seth's body. His hand smoothed along Seth's thigh, around his knee and back up along the inside of it. His fingers began to lightly massage at the hot point he'd found on Seth the first time he'd taken the opportunity to explore his mate's body to the fullest, just at the point his leg met his crotch. The backs of his fingers brushed over the swiftly swelling cock beneath his jeans with each stroke.

Seth moaned and gasped out, "What are you doing?"

A breathless chuckle left Kasey's lips as he nuzzled at the tender spot behind Seth's left ear. "I should think it pretty obvious, pup." His tongue flicked out to lave the sweet skin before his teeth gently scraped over it. "I want to make love to you, Seth."

"But it was supposed to be me in charge tonight," Seth wheezed. His stomach flip-flopped at the love in Kasey's voice. Everywhere Kasey's hands and mouth touched him tingled. The drift of his fingers over his thigh, the moist heat of his tongue behind his ear, and even the hot breath sifting silkily across his skin sent fire licking through his veins. His jeans couldn't hide the obvious effect Kasey had on him.

"Let me take care of you tonight, my mate. Let me cherish every inch of your beautiful, amazing body," Kasey whispered between soft licks and kisses. His nose twitched and flared, filling his lungs with the scent of cinnamon. He'd never known a household kitchen spice could be so sexy. But he had a feeling if it were on anyone else, it wouldn't compare to his captivating pup.

"Not in your truck, outside," Seth groaned when Kasey's hand cupped him through his jeans. "Anyone can see us."

"There are no other houses around for miles," Kasey murmured while continuing to feast on the luscious flesh. His palm felt his mate's hard length throb, and he squeezed slowly, enjoying the long, loud growl Seth released.

"But...," Seth said, arching his back slightly, his hands gripping at the large muscles in Kasey's shoulders, "didn't you say… there were others in your pack…?"

Seth reminded Kasey of his father's promise to send out patrols, even around his own property. Reluctantly, he withdrew his hand from Seth's cock, but not before giving it another squeeze and savoring the low sound Seth made. "Let's go inside, then, pup."

Seth didn't need another word of encouragement. He'd jumped out of the truck and walked around the front before Kasey could gather himself enough to move. Laughing, Kasey slammed his truck door shut and took Seth's hand in his, tugging him toward the front porch. "So eager to have me inside you, Seth?" he teased with a twinkle of merriment dancing in his eyes.

When Kasey stopped to unlock the front door, Seth stood up on tiptoe and nipped at Kasey's ear. "I am eager to have you inside me, hot and hard and fucking me until we both can't move." His tongue slipped in and out of Kasey's ear a couple of times, simulating the act they would be performing in the very near future, before he drew back.

Kasey fumbled with the keys as he shuddered in lust, swearing when he almost dropped them. Seth grinned victoriously, but it was only a short battle, for Kasey would win the war very shortly. He pinned Seth to the door the instant it shut. Growling into Seth's ear, Kasey began stripping Seth of his clothing. He didn't take Seth up against the door like Seth hoped he would. Instead, once he had Seth completely naked, he swept Seth up into his arms and carried him bridal-style up the stairs to his bedroom.

Seth had never been in his bedroom before, but he didn't have the chance to look around, because Kasey covered his body immediately, his still fully clothed. Seth pouted up at Kasey. "You're still wearing clothes."

"I want to savor my gift before I bury myself balls deep inside your beautiful body," Kasey explained. He started pressing hot, openmouthed kisses over Seth's throat, collarbone, and down to his chest. Seth had very little hair on his body. A small sparse sprinkling along his pecs drew Kasey's attention first. He rubbed his face along it, enjoying the slight tickling sensation. But he didn't linger there, moving on to his mate's left nipple.

His pup's nipples were a light shade of brown, just dark enough to stand out against the lightness of his skin. He'd marveled more than once over how dark his skin appeared compared to Seth's. They were as different as night and day, but it didn't matter to him. Seth had quickly become his entire world. In the week since they'd met, things had changed so much. Despite it happening so fast, it felt right to be there, touching him, kissing him.

Kasey slid his tongue over Seth's nipple slowly, teasingly, drawing a swift intake of breath from his lover. The nipple quickly puckered when Kasey blew on the wet skin. Seth wound his fingers through Kasey's dark hair, pulling out the leather string that tied it back. "You're not being fair," he whimpered when he felt his mate gently roll his nipple between his teeth.

"All's fair in love, pup," Kasey said, grinning before he resumed the slick strokes of his tongue. He brushed kisses along the slight indent between nipples and paid the right one as much attention as the left. His eyes caught sight of the tattoo his Seth shared with the other wolf. Jealousy returned. He looked up at Seth and asked, "Will you do the same with me, Seth? Will you mark your body permanently to show the world we belong to each other?"

The jealousy rolled intensely off of Kasey. Seth could feel it, fierce and hot. He smiled tenderly and traced the tip of his index finger over the ridge of his high cheekbone. "Still jealous, love?"

"My true mate and another wolf share a permanent mark signifying a deep relationship between them. Do you think you wouldn't be if it were reversed?" Kasey lifted an eyebrow, still stroking his hand over Seth's soft belly. A secret thrill had gone through him when Seth called him his love. If there was only one thing he'd learned about his mate, pride and loyalty were taken very seriously by Seth. If Seth said he loved him, he loved him unconditionally.

Seth hummed in pleasure at Kasey's touch, but he knew he would be just as jealous if it were him in Kasey's position. "No, I would be insanely jealous," he murmured. "You've handled it much better than I would have."

A triumphant gleam came into Kasey's eyes. He lazily slid his hand lower, letting the small sprinkled trail of hair leading the way down to a great treat tickle his palm. "I like the idea of you being jealous," Kasey smirked.

"Yeah, well, don't get used to public displays of it," Seth said, scowling. He attempted to keep control of his body, but it seemed to want to ignore his thoughts. His cock leapt when Kasey's fingers brushed the base, but the touch merely teased him before the fingers moved away. A frustrated snarl rumbled in his throat.

"Patience, mate. I want to enjoy this night." Slipping down, Kasey licked and kissed each of Seth's ribs, following the line down to his navel. Seth's belly button looked like a perfect O, so pretty and just begging for him to make love to it with his tongue. He didn't disappoint, and the wet hot muscle slipped into the small hole, twirling around the edges of it.

"Just tonight?" Seth groaned out in question, one hand coming to rest on the back of Kasey's head and the other clutching the sheet beneath him.

"Oh, I fully intend to savor this gorgeous"—he kissed the top of Seth's hipbone—"sexy"—his teeth scraped over the sensitive skin—"body of yours every minute of every day for the rest of our lives. But tonight"—his tongue soothed the small mark from his teeth—"tonight is the first time you gave me everything."

A strangled cry echoed through the room when Kasey suddenly sucked the skin between Seth's hipbone and his groin into his mouth. It sent spirals of pleasure shafting through Seth, and his cock grew even harder, pressing against Kasey's cheek. Sweat began to form on his body, glistening in the moonlight shafting through the window. Kasey had left all of the lights turned off when he'd brought him up to his bedroom, and there was only a matter of days before the full moon, leaving it hanging an almost full orb in the sky. The muscles under Seth's skin rippled as Kasey continued to suckle at the bit of skin his mouth had captured. "Kasey," Seth keened.

Seth's cock wept profusely, and Kasey could feel the liquid smearing on his cheek. He ignored his mate's plea and just continued enjoying the way his small body trembled and quaked, the way he panted and sighed. Those sounds were the most precious things in the world to him. They were proof his mate enjoyed what he did to him. He never wanted to hear a sound of fear from his mate when he touched him, when he made love to him.

Once his mouth left behind a love mark, Kasey moved away from the spot. He brushed his lips over the base of Seth's fully erect prick and continued up the shaft, just passing his mouth over it in small butterfly-like kisses. Then Kasey went back down the shaft, using just his tongue. He did it over and over again until Seth became nothing but a moaning, quivering mass of limbs. Kasey's nostrils flared, taking in the sharp tangy scent of his mate's fluids and the salty scent of the sweat dampening the sheets. Kasey swiped at the flared tip, tasting the pearly liquid steadily seeping out of the little slit in the end. "I love the way you taste, pup."

"No more," Seth gasped, his hand tightening in the dark strands of Kasey's hair. "Please... please, Kasey. Take it in your mouth."

"What do you want me to do with it, Seth?" Kasey taunted seductively, rubbing his cheek against Seth's dick. "Tell me exactly and in detail, mate. I'll do whatever you want."

Seth blushed as he whispered, "Lick it."

A flash of pink swiped over the tip of Seth's cock. "What else?" Kasey asked roughly between licks.

"Kasey...," Seth whined quietly. "It's... it's embarrassing."

"I just want to do whatever makes you feel good, pup." Kasey nuzzled his nose at the tight sac under his mate's erect shaft. When a panting moan rattled in Seth's throat, he took pity on the dark-haired vet and rose up enough to engulf the head in his mouth. He hummed in pleasure when he felt Seth's fingers reflexively squeeze his hair even tighter. It made him happy to know his mate enjoyed his mouth on him. Curling his tongue around the shaft, he slowly descended to the base, taking each inch into his mouth and further down his throat. Despite Seth's stature, he wasn't built small. The head touched the back of Kasey's throat, and he relaxed his muscles, taking it all the way in.

"Oh fuck," Seth groaned when he felt Kasey deep-throat him. His hips rose slightly from the bed at the lust spiking through him. His eyes rolled back in his head, and his neck arched gracefully, glistening with a tempting sheen of sweat. The warm moist sucking sent shivers along his spine, but it wasn't enough to trip him over the edge. "Kasey…."

The dark-haired sheriff enjoyed the taste of his lover too much to bring him to orgasm just yet. His large hands stroked along the inside of Seth's thighs, caressing him with roughly calloused palms. Seth's skin felt soft and silky, smooth like warm butter. It almost made Kasey feel ashamed to touch him with such coarse hands. Kasey pushed Seth's legs wider and higher up, resting the backs of his knees on his shoulders. The position gave him access to the tight opening that would soon be sheathing his hard staff, and he eagerly released Seth's cock to tease him further by pressing his tongue against the puckered flesh.

Seth gasped at the first touch of wet heat against his hole. He felt vulnerable and exposed to Kasey right then, his legs in the air and his body bared for the still fully clothed Cheyenne's roving hands and mouth. He licked his dry lips, his breath wheezing in and out of his lungs. Tingles zipped up his body when Kasey's tongue pushed inside him, spreading him open. The longer Kasey fucked him with his tongue, the more relaxed his body became, which allowed Kasey to push two fingers inside him easily. Seth bucked upward and cried out as Kasey's fingers brushed against his prostate. "Kasey…," he rasped, writhing on the sheets. "No more. Please… need you… now."

A low growl emanated from Kasey at the plaintive sound of his mate crying out for him. His cock throbbed, still encased in the tight jeans he wore. He disentangled himself from Seth and sat up, stripping his shirt over his head, surprised when he felt Seth's hands fumbling at opening his jeans. Still on his knees when a greedy little hand closed around his hard flesh, Kasey sucked in a sharp breath and tilted his head back. Seth stroked him in a tight grip, moving the silken sheath over the hard muscle. "Mmm, pup, I love your hands on me," Kasey sighed, his eyes half-slits, pupils glittering lustily.

Seth moved until he could reach Kasey with his mouth. His mate felt large and hot on his tongue. Kasey's hand cupped the back of his head lightly, not forcing him any further, just guiding him as he sucked. The knowledge Seth wanted him as much as he wanted Seth only drove his desire for the adorable little wolf even higher. He never wanted this to end, never wanted to face the reality or gravity of the situation waiting for them outside this very moment. All he wanted to do was bury himself in his mate's body and never let go. Looking down at Seth, Kasey almost shot his load at how erotic his pup looked, cheeks bulging with his hard cock. He pushed Seth off, groaning, "Stop…."

When Seth refused to release him, Kasey forced him away and tumbled them down to the bed. Seth grinned up at him in feigned innocence, sending Kasey's heart into overdrive. "Were you getting close?"

"Yes, and I didn't want it to end before I got to feel your luscious ass," Kasey replied huskily, kissing Seth deeply while sending his hand traveling down the pale body underneath him. A soft sigh escaped his lover when he sank two fingers into the tight channel waiting to be ravished. "Always so tight and hot," he growled lustily, thrusting in and out several times before placing the head of his shaft at Seth's entrance.

The sweet burn of being stretched sent a loud moan drifting into the air. Seth gripped the hard muscles of Kasey's shoulders in an attempt to hold on against the oncoming storm. The need for his mate to be inside him was exquisitely painful. It only eased when the entire length of Kasey had been completely encased in Seth's body. Without a word exchanged, the dance began. Kasey thrust deep into Seth in slow, steady plunges, which Seth met, tilting his hips upward. Their bodies pressed together over and over in their eagerness to crawl inside one another.

Seth's legs were hitched high up Kasey's back, and he trailed his palms down the broad back, feeling the slight roughness of the tribal tattoos littering his back and arms. The man was sexy as sin and all his. A moan broke free from him at a particularly deep thrust from Kasey. The head of his dick jabbed at his sweet spot, sending fingers of pleasure rushing up Seth's spine. "Unnnh… Kasey," he moaned, lifting his head from the pillow to kiss him.

Their tongues twirled over each other without losing the gentle rhythm of their bodies, moving in a primeval way as old as time. Seth tightened his inner muscles around the invading pillar of flesh, wrenching a groan from Kasey. "Teasing me, pup," Kasey asked breathlessly.

"Uh-uh," Seth sighed out, lightly scratching his nails down Kasey's back. "Feels good." His words were nothing but a whisper of sound in the silence around the two of them. Their breathing grew harsher and heavier as their movements became faster and rougher.

"I want to mark you, pup," Kasey panted, leaning forward to nuzzle Seth's throat. His teeth elongated in preparation, but he waited for Seth to accept him, to accept his request. Pure joy exploded through him when he felt Seth's hand on the back of his head, pressing him tighter into the area between shoulder and neck.

A low whine echoed across the room when Seth felt Kasey's teeth sink into his skin. The exquisite pain sent him over the edge, and giving a sharp, strangled cry, Seth spilled his seed between their bodies in hot, heavy jets of fluid.

Kasey felt Seth clamp down on him a split second before the sharp, tangy scent of semen stung his nose. His mate's blood spilled over his tongue and into his throat. He growled low, giving one harsh thrust, seating his cock deep inside his pup, coming mere seconds behind Seth.

The hot length inside Seth throbbed and sprayed its cream along his insides as he tightened his hold on Kasey, closing his eyes in pleasure. He felt stupid for ever believing Taggart was his mate. The connection he felt with Kasey was so much more powerful, more intense, than anything he could have ever felt with Taggart. He breathed in the Cheyenne's woodsy smell, the essence of their coupling, and the light sheen of sweat clinging to their bodies. He belonged here, wrapped in Kasey's arms, and he would fight to keep it until the last bit of strength he had faded. Taggart wouldn't take this away too.

Kasey slumped on top of Seth, shuddering. His ear rested just over Seth's heart, and he could hear it still pounding heavily. He lifted up just enough to press a kiss over it before resting his forehead on his pup's chest. He moved so he could look down on Seth's flushed face. The ocean-blue eyes he cherished so much were closed, but they opened slowly on his next words: "Love you, pup."

Seth stared up into Kasey's dark gaze. The tenderness shining at him took his breath away. He didn't know how he could have been so blind before. He smiled gently as he lifted his hand to cup Kasey's cheek. "I love you too," he said thickly.

He found the air in his lungs suddenly cut off when Kasey sat up abruptly, crushing him to his broad chest. Seth squeaked in surprise but just let Kasey hold him without protest. His slender fingers stroked gently through Kasey's hair. "You're squishing me," he managed to cough out after a few moments.

Kasey's hold relaxed, but he didn't pull away or release Seth. Something warm and wet splashed onto Seth's shoulder blade. Seth's eyes widened, and he rested his chin on Kasey's shoulder. "I'm sorry it took me so long to say it," he murmured.

Swallowing hard, Kasey squeezed his eyes closed tightly. He rubbed his cheek against the side of Seth's neck affectionately. His tears were ones of joy and love. "I wasn't sure you'd ever say it. I hope you know this means I'm never letting you go," he growled softly.

A pleased grin slid over Seth's face. "Good, because now that you know, you're never going to get rid of me."

Kasey laughed and tumbled them both down among the sheets. Not even the thought of Taggart terrorizing his mate could overshadow the euphoria he felt. Seth loved him. His stubborn, sweet pup had finally given in to the inevitable and let himself love him. He pulled Seth close to his body, cuddling him. "I think I'll bring you breakfast in bed in the morning. How does that sound?"

"Hmm… sounds good," Seth breathed as he closed his eyes. He yawned then. It'd been a long day. A twinge of guilt over Nick's situation twisted his stomach, but he knew Nick could handle whatever might happen. Tomorrow he would spend time with him. After all, he'd come here because Seth had asked him to, and they'd barely spent any time together. He felt Kasey press a kiss into his hair as sleep claimed him.

13

KASEY reluctantly slipped free of Seth's embrace the next morning. He nuzzled lightly at Seth's temple for a split second before going downstairs to the kitchen to start breakfast like he'd promised. Though he usually only had coffee in the mornings, he didn't want to make a promise to his mate and not keep it, no matter how small. He grinned in memory of Seth's declaration the previous evening. Finally! He felt slightly embarrassed he'd broken down in front of Seth, but they were mates and couldn't hide their emotions from one another.

Only one thing remained hanging over them before they could be truly free to explore each other fully. He wanted to know each and every detail about his pup. There was still so much he didn't know about the dark-haired, blue-eyed vet. The butter sizzled as it hit the already warming skillet. He hoped Seth ate western omelets. Something else he didn't know about his mate.

His thoughts turned to his brother and Nick as he chopped up peppers and onions. The agony on Nick's face last night when Thayne had once again rejected him had been hard to witness on such a strong and confident wolf. He sensed a bit of Alpha in Nick, no doubt about it. The core of steel beneath the calm, cocky exterior fairly screamed it out. His control around Seth all these years proved it. He'd talk to his brother the next time he had a few minutes alone with him and try to convince him to accept Nick. After being around Seth for only a week, he realized a part of him inside would never have been complete without him. Surely his brother would know the same emptiness and change his mind.

Seth floated in a warm haze for a few moments before opening his eyes. He smelled a delicious scent of eggs and bacon cooking downstairs, and he grinned as his stomach rumbled hungrily. Stumbling slightly out of Kasey's still-warm bed, he picked up the shirt Kasey had worn the night before and slipped it over his head. A small laugh rumbled in his chest at the incongruous sight of him swathed in the fabric of his mate's clothing. Kasey was certainly much bigger. The hem of the shirt fell to mid-thigh but left quite a bit of his legs bare. "You're supposed to still be in bed," Kasey's voice admonished from behind him.

Turning around, Seth smiled happily at the tall Cheyenne standing in the doorway. He held a tray laden with food in his hands, but Seth noticed the way his dark eyes slid down his body. He flushed and gestured to the shirt. "I hope you don't mind I borrowed your shirt."

Kasey bit back a groan at how sexy his pup looked. His body responded to the sight of his dark hair freshly tousled from bed and the pale, cream-colored skin of his thighs. If he didn't have to report to work, he'd strip the shirt right off and—

He stopped his wayward thoughts quickly as his cock began to harden. Swallowing, he replied huskily, "No. I don't mind. Never looked that good on me."

"We can go downstairs and eat," Seth suggested as Kasey gestured for him to return to bed.

"I promised you breakfast in bed last night, and I intend to keep my promise," Kasey said meaningfully. "Now get your gorgeous self back into bed."

The silver feather earring in Seth's ear glinted in the early morning light coming in from the window as he curtsied in a playful manner. "Yes, sir!"

It didn't escape Kasey's notice that his pup felt safe enough to joke around, and a warm sense of peace settled in the center of his chest. He had a feeling his mate's true personality had only just begun to shine through the fear and pain that surrounded him. Kasey set the tray over Seth's lap after he'd situated the pillows against the headboard for comfort. Once he made sure Seth seemed comfortable, he slid onto the bed next to his mate to enjoy his own breakfast. "I'm going to call Julian and have him bring Nick back here to stay with you today, but the others are already patrolling the property. If anything happens, yell and they'll hear you. I'm also going to leave my office number and cell phone number next to the phone."

Seth set his hand on Kasey's forearm, a soft look on his face. "I'll be fine, Kasey. With Nick here and the others running watch, Taggart wouldn't be stupid enough to try anything."

A low growl rumbled in his chest at the sound of the name on his mate's lips. "I cannot help but fear for your safety, pup. You are my mate, and now that I've found you, nothing is going to take you away from me."

Using a piece of toast to hide his smile at Kasey's protective tone, Seth asked, "Do the others in your pack know… about me?"

Kasey could hear the underlying uncertainty, and he picked up Seth's hand, pressing a kiss to his bare wrist. "My father only told the ones who will be patrolling the area. And he swore them to secrecy. They cannot go against a direct order from the Alpha, so you have nothing to fear. I'm sure they are curious, so if you see them close to the property, don't worry. They are only trying to see who the mate of the next Alpha is."

Seth's appetite fled as he realized how much trouble he had caused for Kasey and his family, his pack. How could he stay here when his mere presence endangered their entire life here in Senaka?

It startled him when he felt a warm hand on his chin lifting his face to look up into a pair of very dark, very intense eyes. "Whatever you're thinking in that amazing brain of yours, stop it. Our bond grows stronger every day, Seth. Don't think I can't feel the distress rolling off of you. You belong here, with me and with our pack. So don't even for a single second think of leaving."

Tears stung Seth's eyes at Kasey's use of "our pack," and he blinked heavily, nodding because he couldn't speak past the lump in his throat. Kasey kissed him fiercely, stealing his breath, before pulling back to finish his breakfast. They ate the rest of the meal in companionable silence with an odd comment thrown in here and there.

"Take a shower, enjoy the cable television downstairs. The fridge is stocked, and I do expect you to eat," Kasey said as he gave Seth a stern look.

Seth held up his hands in surrender. "I will. I promise." Giving a cheeky grin, he looked up from beneath his eyelashes at Kasey standing next to the bed. "Besides, you don't think I'm going to miss out on the chance to cook in that outstanding kitchen of yours, do you?"

Kasey laughed deeply and reached out to gently caress his mate's pale cheek. "Is my kitchen the only reason you want me?"

Seth lifted a shoulder in a careless shrug with a you-caught-me expression. "Now that you know, are you going to keep me anyway?"

Leaning down, Kasey murmured into Seth's ear, "You bet your cute ass I am."

An indignant squeak left Seth at Kasey's words, but the tall Cheyenne covered his mouth, quickly erasing all thoughts of anything but the taste of his sheriff.

Kasey groaned when he pulled back reluctantly. "If I don't leave now, I'm not going to work, and I have to today. There's a big meeting with the town council about the Created one."

"Go. I'll be fine," Seth assured him. "Nick'll be here soon, and you said yourself some of the others are patrolling the property."

Kasey still felt strange about leaving Seth, but he figured his wolf merely wanted to stay and protect his mate. "All right. The house is yours. Make yourself at home, pup. I'll be back as soon as I can."

He planted another smoldering kiss on Seth's lips before wrenching himself away and swiftly heading down the stairs two at a time. If he'd stayed a moment longer, he wouldn't have gone anywhere.

On the way to the station, Kasey put in a call to his father to ask that he make sure the others kept a very close eye until he returned.

Seth decided to explore Kasey's house, since he'd only been there once, and he'd been way too nervous to notice anything in particular other than the beautiful kitchen. He started in the bedroom, looking around at the dark furniture —a mahogany dresser with matching end tables, the intricately designed four-poster bed, and stainless steel lamps. On the dresser there were several picture frames that immediately grabbed his attention. He recognized Kasey's parents in a few of the photos, and in another Kasey stood with the brother he'd met last night, Thayne. Seth's teeth elongated at the photo as he remembered Nick's pain caused by the other wolf.

The other photograph had a dark-haired, dark-eyed man almost as tall as Kasey standing beside him. He looked vaguely familiar, but Seth couldn't place him. Their arms were around each other's shoulders, and there seemed to be an almost affectionate look on their faces. His wolf perked up and snarled inside him. Someone else his mate found important. Seth stepped back and turned away, trying to soothe his inner wolf. Kasey loved him, so the past didn't matter.

Wandering out of the bedroom, Seth headed downstairs, slowing to look at the other photos hanging on the wall of the staircase. There were many of Kasey with many other Cheyennes. He wondered if these were pack mates. They must be. His hand trailed along the wooden banister lightly as he continued down to the first floor of the house.

Dark and heavy furniture gave the house a masculine air. A beautiful fireplace dominated the living room, and more framed photos graced the mantelpiece. He knew for a fact the black leather couch in front of the fireplace was extremely comfortable. A large hand-woven rug with tribal symbols on it covered most of the floor between the couch and the hearth. A flat-panel TV hung on the wall above the fireplace, and he could see a built-in shelf holding a DVD player. Another shelf built in on the other side of the TV held a bunch of movies in various genres.

In the back of the house he found a study containing quite a few books, several of which were contained in his own spare bedroom library. Seth couldn't help but be impressed with how well-read his mate seemed to be. He saw everything from Shakespeare to James Patterson. It didn't surprise him Kasey liked to read detective novels, and it brought a smile to his face as he trailed a finger over the spine of one. Aside from horseback riding, what else did his mate enjoy doing in his spare time?

It was too early to start making lunch, so Seth decided to go ahead and get dressed. After dressing in the jeans he'd worn yesterday and one of Kasey's T-shirts, Seth went back downstairs and out the front door. He knew if Kasey found out he'd gone outside the man would have a fit, but he couldn't stay cooped up inside for too long. He'd go stir crazy with nothing to do. Besides, the other wolves were there if anything happened.

Seth looked at his surroundings and breathed in deep, taking the scent of the trees into his lungs. He closed his eyes briefly, giving a small smile. He could definitely get used to this place, peaceful and quiet and so much room to stretch his legs. He just hoped he would get to stay here.

The barn he'd gone into the night he'd met Kasey loomed across the yard, and he headed toward it, intent on checking on the horse and foal. A strong smell of hay and manure assaulted his nose when he opened the barn door to step inside. Horse hooves shifting in the hay drew his attention. The horse let out a small wicker at seeing him and snorted, nervously prancing in its stall. He set his hands on the door, letting the horse get used to his scent. "Hey, beautiful," he murmured. "I'm not going to harm you."

If Seth hadn't allowed his guard down, he might have realized the horse wasn't afraid of him but of something else. As he started to open the stall door, he heard a creaking sound above his head. Seth jerked his gaze upward to see a hulking shadow above him. A scream stuck in his throat, and he whirled around to run, but he didn't get far before something slammed into his back, knocking him to the ground.

Seth grunted as he hit the wood floor of the barn. Hot

breath wheezed over his neck, sending terror straight down his spine. This time he managed to get out a yell, screaming as loud as he could, but the wolf on top of him clamped its jaws down on the back of his throat, crushing him just enough to cut the sound short. Seth's vision swam as he tried to drag in a breath. The beast's claws dug into his back while it attempted to pull him back over the barn floor.

Kasey's horse let out sharp squeals of fear and stamped its feet hard into the hay beneath it. Seth prayed the others had heard him and if not him, then the horse. His consciousness slowly faded, and just before the darkness consumed him, his last thought was of Kasey and how sad he'd be when he found his body.

K ASEY was just attempting to calm the town council after revealing the details of the Created one in the area when a sudden gut-wrenching fear gripped him tightly. Sweat broke out over his brow as the realization that something had happened to his mate jolted through him. Without even saying a word to the council members, he raced down the stairs from the podium and straight out the front door of the hall. His hand reached for his cell as he dashed to his truck. First he tried to call the house, but there was no answer, and his anxiety grew by leaps and bounds.

The next call he placed to his deputy. "Julian," he barked into the radio.

The radio crackled with static for a second before Julian's voice came over the speaker. "What's up, Chief?"

"Did you drop off Nick yet?"

"Negative. An emergency call came through on the way. Heading there now."

Kasey growled fiercely at his deputy's words. The

certainty his mate was in trouble grew by the second. "Get your ass over there, now!"

Nick's voice came over the radio then. "Something wrong, Sheriff?"

"Something's happened to Seth. I can feel it. I'm on my way now." Kasey gunned the engine and turned on his siren, pushing the truck as fast as he could. He also contacted his father, because it was very possible the wolves on patrol were injured or worse.

Anger and fear warred inside him. His wolf rose up fast, demanding he let it take over to protect his mate. If Seth was hurt, there was no telling what it would do. He saw no signs of movement when he reached his property, his truck coming to a halt in a plume of dust. Seth's scent led him straight to the barn. A roar built up in his chest when he caught the smell of blood and saw the evidence of a struggle in the barn. But the barn was empty. They'd taken Seth! His heart squeezed inside his chest when he realized he'd failed his mate. He should have taken Seth to town instead of leaving him there.

Unable to stop himself, he shifted in a quick blur. His wolf grew even more furious when he immediately caught the scent of another wolf, unknown to him. His lupine eyes narrowed just before he set forth a long, loud howl. Tires pulling into the driveway brought his head around. Kasey trotted outside, fur rippling angrily.

Nick and Julian were just getting out of the vehicle when Nick spotted him. "Kasey? Where's Seth?"

The wolf growled low in its throat, causing Nick to step back. "It's just us, Kasey. We would never hurt Seth. We want to help find him."

Kasey lifted his nose to the air to scent for his mate, and another howl broke free when he caught Seth's scent. He darted off into the woods, following the cinnamon smell he loved so much, barely aware of Nick and Julian giving chase, already transformed. Nothing mattered to him except finding Seth and ripping to pieces the bastard who'd dared take his mate.

A few hundred feet into the woods, they came upon the two wolves set to guard Seth for the day. One, badly injured, could hardly breathe. It most likely had a punctured lung. The other wolf had already been killed. Julian came to a halt next to them, nudging at the wolf still alive. He whined, looking toward Kasey and Nick. They would have to continue on without him. Someone needed to help their pack mate.

Nick and Kasey set off after Seth alone. Kasey knew Julian would bring the rest of the pack to help once he'd gotten back to the reservation. Nothing would make Kasey wait any longer to find his pup. The trail couldn't be more than half an hour old, and the more time that stretched between them allowed the Created one to get further and further away with Seth.

Silence reigned in the forest as their feet padded on the mossy floor, twigs snapping with precision beneath them. The birds were silent, as if they sensed something wasn't right inside their home. Seth's scent continued deep into the forest, almost to where he'd tumbled over the ridge the first night Kasey had touched his pup; then it twisted sharply along the ravine. Kasey kept from howling in frustration when the scent abruptly ended just where the path to the bottom began. His lip curled in fury, but Nick head-butted him sharply, shaking his head.

Nick lifted his nose to the air and breathed in deeply. It took several attempts before he could pick up a faint smell of cinnamon. He immediately darted off down the trail into the ravine.

Kasey followed eagerly on his heels, trying desperately to

calm himself. The only way he could save Seth was if he kept a clear head. If he let his anger get the better of him, as it did at times, it might well cause Seth to lose his life. His teeth gnashed together harshly at the thought that he might never again see Seth's smile or feel his supple body beneath him. If there was even a scratch on his pup, the bastard would feel a thousand times more pain than any being in this world had ever felt.

The banks of the river were already at maximum capacity. It would not be long before they broke and the water flooded the ravine. Kasey prayed they would reach Seth in time. His paws dug into the damp earth, kicking up mud as he ran. The sound of the roaring water echoed off the ravine walls and took away any chance they would be able to hear how close they were. Seth's scent was faint, covered by the musty smell of wet wood and rocks.

S ETH groaned as he struggled toward consciousness. Where was he? He realized someone was carrying him over their shoulder, and each step jarred the blinding headache beating against his skull. The noise of rushing water beat at his eardrums, but his hands were tied, and he couldn't cover his ears to drown out the sound. He could only hear his captor's heavy breathing over the roar. He knew trying to get away would be useless at the moment. He would have to wait until his captor set him down and became distracted.

"I know you're awake," his captor growled. What caught Seth's attention was the voice. He frowned as he tried to pinpoint it. It wasn't Taggart's. Taggart's voice had barely been human near the end.

"Who are you?" Seth demanded, trying to sound more ferocious than he felt.

The unknown assailant laughed almost mindlessly. "You do not recognize your own mate, Seth?"

"You are not my mate," he bit out. "My mate is Kasey Whitedove, the sheriff of Senaka."

"No!" the man roared. "I am your mate. You would know it if they hadn't taken you from me!"

Seth would have laughed if it wouldn't have further ignited the stranger's anger. "Who are you?"

Instead of answering, the stranger leapt with preternatural ability onto a large boulder in the center of the river and then across to the other side. Seth groaned as the impact jarred him harshly. His bound hands came up to cradle his head, but his captor continued moving. It suddenly grew dark as they entered some kind of cave. Seth could smell the mold growing on the rocks surrounding them. It stung his canine senses, and he wheezed slightly.

The stranger tossed him none too gently into a corner of the cave. After taking a few precious seconds to collect himself, Seth looked around him. There were supplies stacked in one corner, along with some kind of wrought iron cage. Seth's eyes widened and terror struck him. Not again. He couldn't be caged again. He stood to run, but his captor easily overpowered him in a second, throwing him against the unforgiving rocks. Pain shot through Seth as sharp edges dug into his back before he collapsed to the floor, coughing at the agony flowing through him like pure fire.

The sound of the cage door opening brought a sob to Seth's throat. He stifled it, refusing to allow the bastard to see him weak. He felt a sharp pinprick to his bicep before the stranger picked him up and dumped him inside the cage before slamming the door shut. The lock clicked into place with a snick, leaving hopelessness to invade Seth along with the sense of weakness from whatever the other wolf had injected him with. He tried to push it back. Kasey would find him. He couldn't lose hope that Kasey would find him.

"Just a little something to keep you from attempting to escape, my love. Now, then, shortly we shall deal with the dog who dared claim you as his."

"No!" Seth shouted, shakily pushing himself to stand. He gripped at the bars as best he could, glaring at the stranger. "If you lay one hand on him, I'll fucking kill you," he growled ferociously.

The stranger threw his dark head back and laughed. "Temper, temper, my beautiful mate. You are going to be a spirited thing, I can see. I can hardly wait to tame you."

Seth studied the man, trying to place him. He stood taller than Seth, at least six feet, with dark-brown hair and strangely light-green eyes that sent a shiver of fear down his spine. The crazed look about him suggested he wasn't entirely sane. Something about him struck a chord in Seth's mind, but he still couldn't remember where he had seen the other wolf before. "What do you want?"

"Tsk, tsk, Seth. I would think you'd already understand what it is that I want." The man stalked toward the cage, smiling smugly. "You didn't think you could hide forever, did you? If only your parents hadn't stolen you away from me all those years ago, you would know me as your true mate. Instead you believe that filthy Indian is your life mate."

It clicked inside his head as Seth heard the man's words. He searched for the name Nick had mentioned a few days prior. Charles… Charles Drakson. "Drakson," he breathed out.

"Ah, I see you remember me, then, Seth. You should, as I am your true mate." Charles drew himself to his full height, once again smiling arrogantly. He stepped closer to the cage and reached out to touch Seth. Seth reared back in horror, his skin crawling at the thought of the bastard touching him.

"You aren't my true mate," Seth bit out between clenched teeth, his blue eyes blazing at the deranged wolf in front of him. "Kasey Whitedove is my mate."

Fury flooded the light eyes gazing at him, and Charles snapped his teeth. "No! You are mine. I will make you forget about that dog once I have rid myself of him."

Seth feebly threw himself at the bars of the cage in his own desire to protect Kasey. He wrenched at the bars ineffectively. They wouldn't budge. Tears burned behind his eyes, but he stifled them, refusing to allow his weakness to overcome him when Kasey needed him. "How did you know?" he asked quietly. "About Taggart and the Triad?"

An arrogant smirk curved the corner of Charles's mouth as he prowled the cave restlessly. "Who do you think set the fire that night, Rho? I tracked him to the warehouse. There had been rumors of a Created one mated to a Rho spreading among the other wolves. Taggart bragged about you to anyone who'd listen. Whenever he came into contact with other wolves, he'd tell them all about you."

Shock widened Seth's eyes. They had never been able to figure out why the fire had started, only been grateful it had. Charles gave a bark of laughter. "What? Did you think you managed to escape on your own that night? You and that mutt? As if Nick Cartwright has ever been anything but reckless. Did he tell you Taggart found you because of him?"

"No!" Seth denied vehemently, yanking at the bars ineffectively. "You're lying!"

Charles chuckled with malice. "You really are blind, Seth. Nick was Taggart's original mark. He and Nick engaged in a… shall we say… one-night stand before Taggart became a Created."

Seth's breath caught in his throat. Had Nick bitten Taggart?

Charles waved a hand at Seth's look of horror. "Oh, Nick

isn't the one who made Taggart. But he is the reason Taggart became a Created. Taggart wanted more than one night with Nick. He wanted Nick to continue being his fuck buddy, as you young ones call it nowadays. Only it wasn't what Nick wanted. Taggart stumbled into a den of rogue wolves one night and ended up fodder for them. Except he didn't die. He managed to survive and became a Created."

Trembling at what Charles's words meant, Seth shook his head with sheer disbelief. "It's all lies," he whispered.

"Nick led Taggart straight to you, Seth." Charles cocked his head to the side, a pitying look on his face. "Did you really think Nick cared about you? He only stuck around because he felt responsible for you. The pack decided Nick had watched over you long enough and relieved him of the duty a few years back. They needed him back in the fold."

A few years back? Seth's heart leapt as he realized if Nick hadn't truly cared about him, he never would have stayed after rescuing him from Taggart. Nick had been there every step of the way as Seth pushed through the pain and fear. If it hadn't been for Nick, he never would've met Kasey. It wasn't Nick's fault Taggart had fixated on him. Seth gritted his teeth as he stared at the bastard who had tormented him over the last week. "You were the one who destroyed my clinic and killed Ginger and Bullet!"

Charles lifted a shoulder in a slight shrug. "I needed you to run again. I figured the only way you would is if you believed Taggart was alive. Oh, he died in the fire that night along with the rest of them, but you couldn't know that for sure. I used the fear you still have of him to coax you into leaving town. You almost did too. If it hadn't been for your stupid mutt, you'd have run, and no one would have been hurt."

A growl built in Seth's chest, rumbling deep and harsh. He had to get out of this cage. It was the only way to help

Kasey. Closing his eyes, Seth took a deep breath, trying to calm himself.

Charles stood at the opening of the cave, sniffing at the air. A malicious smile curled his lips as he swung around to look at Seth. "It seems the sheriff is almost here."

Charles disappeared through the mouth of the cave, and Seth wrenched at the bars again, almost ready to scream from the fear and frustration. A long loud howl sent a shiver of awareness down Seth's back, and he quivered in terror for his mate.

14

"KASEY!" Seth shouted the moment his mate appeared in the entrance. "Be careful!"

Kasey shifted on the run, racing to the cage that held his lover. "Seth, are you all right?" he demanded, grabbing at the bars.

"I'm fine. He didn't hurt me, but he injected me with something. My strength is gone. It's not Taggart, Kasey." Seth reached out and touched his mate's jaw.

Nick materialized next to Kasey. "It's not?"

Seth shook his head quickly. "No. It's Drakson."

Before Seth could explain further, the wolf in question, now in lupine form, snarled from behind them. Kasey and Nick whirled around to face their adversary. In seconds, the two men shifted, but the cave was too small for them to circle around Charles. Seth held his breath as he watched his mate and his best friend waiting for the crazy son of a bitch to attack. His fingers tightened on the bars until they turned white. He felt so damn helpless locked in the cage and unable to help.

When Kasey had seen Seth behind the bars of the cage,

his heart had nearly stopped, but the sheer joy on his mate's face when he'd seen Kasey jump-started it again. He gnashed his teeth together that someone had locked his lover in a cage again. The bastard would pay. When Seth told them it wasn't Taggart, he'd been surprised, but a regular wolf would be easier to face off against than a Created, especially with two on one. He snarled at the dark wolf before him.

Nick crouched slightly, waiting for Drakson to make a move first. Drakson's eyes flashed for a moment before he turned and darted back out of the cave.

Fat raindrops began to fall as Kasey and Nick gave chase. Mud snatched at their feet as they raced after the other wolf, reminding Kasey of just how dangerous the area really was. The rain over the last few weeks had really increased the flow of the river. It rushed past them at a menacing pace. Drakson stopped several yards ahead of them, turning abruptly. Kasey also halted, but Nick leapt straight for Drakson.

Drakson snapped at Nick's throat, missing it by centimeters as Nick danced around him, but his paw lashed out, catching Nick in the side. Nick let out a whine of pain, although he didn't stop moving. The rain became so thick it was hard to see. Nick's paws sank into the mud and water gathering around him. Kasey watched at the way Drakson kept to certain areas of the ground, places his feet wouldn't sink. He lowered his head and growled as he realized Drakson had an unfair advantage. Something hidden beneath the mud kept him from floundering the same as Nick.

Kasey launched himself onto Drakson's back, earning a loud yelp as his teeth sank into the other wolf's shoulder. Drakson struggled to dislodge him, stumbling around until his paws slipped from the object he stood on. He immediately sank several inches into the mud. Kasey bit deeper, wrenching his jaws to dig into the hard muscle to the bone. Drakson shrieked loudly and tossed around wildly. Memories of Seth's face upon entering the cave strengthened Kasey's desire to bring down the bastard who'd almost cost him his mate. But he didn't anticipate the dam ten miles upriver giving way and releasing a deluge of water that reached them in a matter of minutes, sweeping the three of them up in the rush.

The current tore Drakson away from Kasey, and Kasey flung his body at an outcropping of rocks to stop his momentum, scrabbling with his paws to hold on. He watched Drakson being swept further away until a huge log slammed into Drakson, knocking him unconscious and dragging him beneath the water. Nick had managed to shift and clung to a boulder in the center of the ravine. "Kasey!" Nick shouted. "Seth's still in the cage!"

Horror flooded Kasey as he realized how helpless his mate was and how the cave must be almost entirely under water. Seth would drown! Kasey shifted, knowing he had more control as a human than as a wolf, and struggled toward the cave entrance. They had been swept a couple hundred yards down from it.

His muscles were screaming by the time he reached it. He could just make out Seth's face pressed against the bars at the top of the cage as he tried to keep his head above water. "Seth!"

The water completely covered the cage, and Kasey let out a shout of denial as he dove beneath the swirling liquid. Seth yanked in vain against the bars, his strength still sapped from whatever Drakson had used on him.

Kasey grabbed at the door of the cage and pulled as hard as he could, but the door wouldn't budge. He swam to the bottom of the cave, searching for something to use on the overly large metal padlock. His hand grazed over a large, sharp rock, and he grasped it gratefully, pushing back to the surface of the water to breathe in. He dove beneath the water again.

Seth was beginning to run out of air; his eyes were almost wild with the knowledge. Kasey beckoned Seth to the front of the cage, where he pulled his mate's face to the bars, pressing his lips to Seth. He blew into Seth's mouth for a moment before kicking back to the surface for more.

Gasping, he broke the surface and dove under, gripping the rock tighter. He smashed at the padlock again and again, pulling on it at the same time, his arms straining to break the thick metal.

He saw Seth pointing at the surface, urging him to go back up, but Kasey shook his head. He would never leave his mate to die. His chest burned from the lack of oxygen, and he could only imagine how Seth felt. Seth's eyes were starting to close, and panic set in. Kasey couldn't lose Seth, not now. Just as Seth started to lose consciousness, Kasey felt the lock give way. He jerked the door open frantically and reached in, grabbing Seth by the wrist.

Kasey swam to the surface, hefting Seth above the water. Dread swamped Kasey when Seth didn't start breathing immediately. He pulled him toward the entrance and out into the ravine.

Nick helped wrestle Seth to an outcropping of rocks.

Kasey brushed the wet hair back from his mate's face. A tinge of blue colored Seth's lips. "Oh God," he said hoarsely.

Nick forced him out of the way, tilted Seth's head back, and began trying to resuscitate Seth. He breathed into Seth's mouth while counting mentally. Kasey initiated chest compressions. "One... two... three."

Sealing his lips to Seth's, Nick breathed into him again several more times before Seth started choking up water. They immediately rolled him to his side to help him dispel the water from his lungs. Kasey almost crushed Seth to him the moment he was able to breathe normally, his arms tight around his mate and his face buried in the strings of dark, wet hair clinging to Seth's nape. "I thought I lost you," he cried frantically.

Seth weakly linked his arms around Kasey's waist, trying to pull air into his abused lungs. Nick's hand rested on his shoulder as they all attempted to gather their strength for the swim to the other side of the ravine. "Where's Drakson?" Seth finally managed to ask.

"Gone," Nick replied. "Swept away in the water."

"Is he dead?"

When neither of them answered, Seth almost sobbed. Nick squeezed his shoulder. "We saw him go under, but he was unconscious. We figure he drowned, babe."

Seth clung to Kasey in remembered fear of the water rushing in while he remained locked in the cage with no way to escape. "I was so scared."

"I know, pup," Kasey murmured, nuzzling at Seth's throat. "I was terrified I wasn't going to be able to get you out of there."

Nick looked around them at the water rushing past. "Do you think you can swim across, Seth?"

Seth nodded, but Kasey stopped him. "No. I'll carry you across. Get on my back, Seth."

"I'm fine, Kasey. I can swim," Seth protested. Kasey glared at him, and he sighed. "Fine." He wrapped his arms around Kasey's back and his legs around Kasey's waist.

Kasey hefted him higher and shoved away from the rock, sinking further with Seth's weight on his back. Seth gripped at Kasey tighter as he felt the pull of the current. Swimming back to the trail leading out of the ravine would probably sap the last bit of energy Kasey still had.

Kasey glanced back at Nick and saw the other male struggling. He frowned as he remembered the swipe Drakson had taken at him. "Are you all right, Nick?"

Nick gave a sharp nod, but his face was extremely pale.

Seth looked at his friend with concern. "What's wrong?"

"It's nothing," Nick ground out, grabbing at the rocks as they neared the other side of the ravine.

"Drakson got him with his paw. I think he's hurt," Kasey ground out, all of his concentration on keeping both him and Seth above water while struggling to keep hold of the sheer rock face.

Seth glared at Nick while Nick glared at Kasey. "You're going to let me look at that when we get out of this damn ravine."

"No. You can't spare the energy," Nick snapped. "I'm fine."

"Shut up, Nick," Seth growled fiercely. "I'm not injured. You are. So you're going to let me look at your side whether you want me to or not."

Kasey would have chuckled at Seth's ferocity if he hadn't been so busy trying to keep them afloat. He almost breathed a sigh of relief when he saw the trail coming up in front of him. His fingers were raw and bleeding from gripping at the sharp rocks, and his arms trembled with exertion. He was strong, but the pull of the current and Seth's weight sapped his strength quickly.

The three of them dragged themselves up onto the path, slipping several times before they found their footing. Nick's hand pressed against his side as they reached the top, and Seth gasped when he saw the blood spilling out through his best friend's fingers. "Damn it, Nick. You are so stubborn," he shouted as he jumped from Kasey's back and rushed to his friend's side.

Nick collapsed to the ground as Seth reached him, and Seth sank to his knees next to Nick. He gently pushed the dark shirt Nick wore up to reveal a huge seeping gash in

Nick's side. Seth swore and placed his palms against the wound. Closing his eyes, he focused on pulling the negative energy inside of him. A shuddery breath left him as he felt the flow of energy reverse into his body and the dark fluid began to build up inside of him. Black spots danced across his vision within moments. Seth's breath wheezed from his throat as the gash in Nick's side started to knit together. Nick groaned in pain, his body stiffening as he attempted to hold still.

Kasey watched in fascination as his mate used the strange ability he possessed to heal his friend, but his heart tripped in his chest when he saw the strain it placed on his mate to use it. Anxiety spiked through him when he saw the sweat beading on Seth's brow and the way his fair skin paled even further. "Seth," Nick moaned. "Stop!"

Striding to his mate's side, Kasey gripped Seth's shoulders tightly. "Seth."

Seth jerked in surprise and fell back against Kasey's legs. Nick's side wasn't completely smooth—a pink scar ran the length of his ribs—but it no longer bled. Crawling a few feet away from the others, Seth retched to expel the foul liquid invading every inch of his innards. Kasey held his hair back and rubbed his shoulders soothingly. Seth would have slumped to the ground when he'd finished, but Kasey caught him up in his arms. "I've got you, pup," Kasey whispered gently.

Several wolves appeared in the clearing seconds later. When they saw Seth and Nick, they crouched low and growled menacingly. Kasey held up his hand. "No!"

They stopped snarling, but their stances didn't change as they waited to see if the threat still existed. Julian stepped in front of the four, and he trotted over to Nick and licked his cheek. Kasey shook his head, heaving a weary sigh. He wasn't ready to tell them. "You'll all receive an explanation later, but for now, just accept that these two are friends." Kasey stared at each wolf in turn, sincerity shining from his eyes. "Julian."

His deputy shifted, squatting next to Kasey. "What do you need, Kase?"

"Take them and search the ravine for any sign of a stranger. Gray wolf with black-tipped ears. He may have shifted back to human form if he's still alive. Go." He grabbed Julian's forearm before his friend could leave. "Be careful. He's not a Created one, but he's dangerous."

Julian clapped him on his shoulder with a cocky grin. "Don't worry, Kase. We got this. Just take care of your mate." He looked at the other four wolves. "You heard him. Let's head out." Shifting, Julian led the other four at a fast sprint along the edge of the ravine.

Nick ran a hand over his face as he sat up. "I think I need a vacation after this."

Kasey chuckled slightly, looking down at his mate. Seth's eyes were closed and his breathing shallow. Kasey trailed the tips of his fingers over Seth's cheek. "Let's go home, pup."

Two days later, Kasey's father, Jeremiah, the Alpha of the Senaka Pack, stood in the center of the village, all his wolves in a circle around him along with their mates and pups. "It's long been believed that we, as Native Americans, are the only ones with the gift of becoming the sacred wolf. We also believed any other aside from Cheyenne couldn't possibly have this ability without being one of the Created, a monstrous being. Recent events have shown us this is no longer our reality."

Furious whispers and gasps went up from the crowd. Jeremiah held up a hand, instantly silencing them. "This opens us to new opportunities as well as new dangers. It will give many of you a fresh chance at finding your mate, as my son has. We also must approach any newcomers with keen senses but without alarm."

Seth pressed closer to Kasey's side as the crowd's attention shifted to him for several moments. Kasey's arm crossed over his back, and his hand rested on Seth's hip. "Relax, pup. They're just curious as to who the mate of the Alpha heir is."

"In a week's time, the Alpha of my son's mate's pack will be arriving to discuss the possibilities of coming together at a summit every few months with the hopes some of you may find the mate destined for you. As your Alpha, I ask that you respect our visitors, but it is your choice to make if you wish to attend the summit. You will not be forced to do so." Jeremiah paused, looking around at his pack with pride before looking at his son. Curiosity shone from the eyes of most, while a handful still showed fear.

Kasey stepped forward, pulling Seth by his side. "Do not close yourself off from the other pack out of fear, my friends. I almost made the same mistake, and it would have cost me the one true mate destined to be mine. It is something I would have regretted for the rest of my life."

He dropped his gaze to look at his pup, smiling gently. "If you have the chance to meet the one that holds the other half of your soul, don't let it slip away. Don't let fear take them away from you."

Seth flushed and buried his face in Kasey's bicep, but he couldn't keep a wide grin from spreading over his lips. For the past two days, Kasey had treated him like spun glass. It frustrated him and annoyed the hell out of him, but it also made him feel cherished and loved. Kasey hadn't made love to him and had ignored all of his advances. His body ached to feel his mate inside of him. If Kasey didn't take him soon, he was going to tie the man to his bed and ravish him against his protests until he gave in and loved him.

After the pack meeting finished, many of the wolves with

their mates and children came up to greet Seth and welcome him to the pack. Seth was stunned at how many of them hugged him or kissed his cheek. It wasn't what he'd expected, as he wasn't Cheyenne.

Nick stood off from everyone else, and even though he tried to appear nonchalant, Seth could see the tension in his friend, his jawline tight as his eyes scanned the crowd. Seth's heart went out to his best friend. He wandered over to Nick's side, lightly touching his arm. "You okay?"

Scoffing, Nick shrugged. "Sure. Why wouldn't I be?"

A skeptical look came over Seth's features. "Come on, Nick. I've known you for a long time. I can see you aren't happy."

"I'm fine," Nick sighed, running a tired hand over his face. He forced a smile. "I'm glad you found your mate, babe. I always knew you would one day."

Seth wondered if he should mention what Drakson had told him in the cave before Kasey and Nick had shown up. He decided against it because he knew Nick cared about him, and he didn't want to cause him any further pain. If it was true, Nick was surely carrying enough guilt around to crush a lesser man.

There had been no sign of Drakson's body when the others finally returned from their search, but he could have been swept several hundred miles downriver. All they could do was hope to hear something on the news about a man or wolf found dead. Until then, they would always wonder if the rogue wolf had actually survived. "Let's go get something to eat," Seth said, smiling and reaching out to grab Nick's hand.

Kasey searched him out about a half an hour later, coming up behind his mate and dropping his hands on Seth's shoulders. Nick sat next to Seth, and they were talking about the pack Seth had come from. Leaning down, Kasey nuzzled Seth's neck. "I have a surprise for you, pup."

Humming in pleasure, Seth settled into his mate's body. "What is it?"

"If I told you, it wouldn't be a surprise, now would it?" Kasey winked at Nick, who laughed and shook his head.

"I need to get back to the pack. Your father and my Alpha are discussing the arrangement of the first summit meeting. Now that you no longer need me, Jack wants me to come home." Nick set his plate aside an instant before Seth punched him in the arm, hard. "Ow! What the fuck did you do that for?" Nick glared at him.

"No longer need you?" Seth growled. "You are my best friend, Nick. If you don't keep in touch, I'm going to come find you and kick your ass."

Kasey laughed loudly. It pleased him to see his mate so forceful and unafraid. "I think you should listen to him, Nick. Seems like he's serious."

Nick's disgruntled expression softened. "Of course I'm going to keep in touch, Seth. I just meant that now you have Kasey, you don't need me to protect you anymore."

"Oh." Seth grinned sheepishly. "Sorry."

Kasey reached down and picked up his mate's hand, tugging him out of his seat. "Come. I want to show you your surprise."

Seth hugged Nick briefly before following Kasey out of his parents' house. "What is it?"

"Nope. You have to see for yourself. Here." Once they were inside the truck, he handed Seth a blindfold, which Seth took with a lifted eyebrow. "Trust me," Kasey said.

A small smile twitched at the corner of Seth's lips. "I do trust you, Kasey."

Warmth spread through Kasey at the sheer trust and acceptance shining from Seth's eyes a second before they were covered by the blindfold. "No peeking," he ordered gruffly, hiding the way his voice thickened, tears prickling the corners of his eyes.

Seth huffed and crossed his arms. "I happen to have restraint."

"Oh? Is that right?" Kasey grinned as he pulled out onto the road leading from the reservation. "I guess we'll have to see how much restraint later, hmm?" Kasey's voice, husky with lust, sent a shaft of pure lust straight to Seth's groin.

Scowling, Seth shifted in his seat, but he didn't say anything. He knew Kasey had to smell his arousal. It was the jerk's fault he was so damn horny. They hadn't fucked in almost three days. Lying next to Kasey's hard body and feeling it pressed into his own had been exquisite torture the past two nights. "Where are we going?"

"Patience, pup. We'll be there in a few minutes." Kasey took Seth's hand in his and entwined their fingers. Excitement raced through him. He could hardly wait to see his mate's expression.

Sending a look at Seth to make sure he wasn't peeking, Kasey turned the truck into the clinic parking lot. He shut the engine off and climbed out of the driver's side, rushing around to the passenger side to help Seth out. "Are you ready, mate?"

The words sent a shiver of joy down Seth's spine. He was ready in more ways than one, but he just nodded. A gasp ripped from his throat the instant Kasey yanked the blindfold away. His heart beat against his ribs hard, fierce. Seth stumbled forward a few paces. "Why?"

"I told you, Seth. Our pack takes care of each other. My father knew you couldn't afford to fix it up on your own, and the pack members donated materials and time to fix it." Kasey lightly gripped Seth's elbow in case his mate fainted. He frowned. "Are you unhappy?"

Seth shook his head, his throat working to keep the tears at bay. "No," he whispered. "I… I just…."

"Let's go inside and take a look." The look on Seth's face told Kasey how overwhelmed his pup felt, and he smiled, gently guiding Seth forward. Kasey reached into his pocket for the key Chessie had handed to him a little bit ago. He unlocked the door and carefully pushed Seth inside.

Seth's hands shook as he looked around the lobby. Everything had been either repaired and painted or replaced. The furniture had been reupholstered with new fabric, the wooden chairs had been replaced completely, and the walls had a fresh coat of paint on them. He saw his license had been reframed and placed on the wall once more. Reaching out, he touched the edge reverently. Even though Nick had been there for him these past few years, Seth had never felt as loved as he did right then. "It's too much," he murmured softly. "I… I can't accept it."

"I called my friend Max," Kasey said, ignoring Seth's words. His mate would learn the pack took care of their own, and there was no way he could get around it. Besides, even if his father hadn't been able to provide the help, Kasey would have done whatever he needed to in order to help his mate. "He's due back in town for a visit in a couple weeks. He's agreed to paint a mural on your wall before he goes home."

"Kasey, stop!" Seth cried, covering his face. His shoulders shook with silent sobs. He felt warm arms come around him in a firm embrace.

"Shh, pup. No more tears, baby. You are my mate. Whether you understand fully what that means right now or not, you will come to understand as my mate I am here to take care of you just as you are here to take care of me. We belong to each other. Your troubles are mine to bear as well, Seth." Kasey ran his hands down Seth's back in a comforting gesture. "You don't have to go through anything alone ever again."

Seth sobbed harder as he threw his arms around Kasey's back and buried his face in his mate's neck. For a moment, he was airborne when Kasey picked him up and strode over to the waiting room couch. He clung to the big Cheyenne even harder, his slight frame shuddering with each gulp of air he took into his lungs. It took several long moments before Seth was able to calm down. It had been so long since he'd felt like he belonged somewhere.

"Better?" Kasey asked, his fingers sifting through the hair behind Seth's ear.

"I'm sorry," he muttered, embarrassed at how badly he'd broken down.

Kasey tilted Seth's head back far enough that he could look into his mate's red-rimmed eyes. "Don't be sorry, baby. You never have to be scared to show your emotions in front of me."

Wrinkling his nose at Kasey, Seth decided to look around his newly repaired clinic with a less overwhelmed view. He would find a way to repay the pack members for their kindness. He eagerly stood up and walked toward the examining rooms, then further still to the kennel in the back. Stopping at the door leading into his office, Seth let his hand hover over the doorknob for a moment at the memory of Ginger and the condition of his office the last time he'd seen her. He bit his lip and opened the door.

The only smells were of fresh paint and new carpet. Seth's eyes widened as he saw he even had a new desk and couch. "Kasey...."

His mate appeared beside him in an instant. "What's wrong, pup?"

"I don't know if I can go back to my house," he murmured in a rough voice. "The memory of B-Bullet and… and…."

Kasey stopped the flow of words by pressing two fingers across Seth's lips. "Baby, stop. You aren't going back to your house. I want you… I'd hoped you'd agree to move in with me."

A surprised breath escaped Seth. "Really?"

"Of course. We're mates, and I intend to sleep every night with that hot, sexy body of yours next to me." Kasey had a slightly guilty look on his face. "And I… ah… already had Nick bring your stuff to my house."

Seth's eyebrow arched. "Oh, is that right?"

Giving Seth a chagrinned look, Kasey replied, "I didn't think you'd mind."

"Taking advantage of the situation, wouldn't you say?" Seth started pushing Kasey backward to the leather couch. He shoved lightly once the backs of Kasey's knees hit the couch and watched in satisfaction as his mate had no choice but to sit down. Placing his knees on either side of Kasey's legs, Seth straddled his lover and ran his hands down Kasey's chest. "Am I going to have to beg you, Sheriff?"

Kasey gave Seth a confused look. "Beg me for what, pup?"

Grinning mischievously, Seth leaned in close to Kasey's ear. "To fuck me, Sheriff." He nipped at the lobe of Kasey's ear.

His mate's body responded at Seth's words, and Seth ground down into Kasey's lap. "Seth… pup."

"No," Seth growled lustily. "You've denied me for two long nights where I thought I would go insane with wanting you. No longer."

Surprised, Kasey stared at his lover. Seth had never taken the initiative, and Kasey bit back a groan when Seth rocked against his extremely hard cock. It might have been torture for Seth the past two nights, but it had been sheer agony for Kasey not to claim his mate again, marking him once more. He'd only wanted to ensure his mate had healed completely before he claimed him again. "Nngh, Seth," he moaned as Seth continued to dry hump him.

Seth made short work of the buttons on Kasey's shirt, spreading it open to greedily take in the sight of his mate's broad, tan chest and the hard, dusky nipples. He dove down and pulled one into his mouth while smoothing his palms across the dense muscles of his lover's body. The swift intake of breath sent a thrill through Seth. It made him feel powerful to know he affected his mate as much as Kasey affected him. He bit down gently, and Kasey's hips bucked up from the couch. Chuckling, Seth shifted to the other dark nub, sucking it wetly between his lips.

His hands expertly slid Kasey's belt through the buckle as Kasey watched him, desire glittering in his eyes. Seth unzipped his pants, slipped his hand inside, and lightly squeezed his mate's cock through his underwear. "Mmm, I think I found what I'd like for dessert," Seth said slyly, his lips twisting in a smirk.

A groan rattled in Kasey's throat at the feel of Seth's hand on him, but his words sent him up in flames. He reached out and abruptly pulled his mate's shirt over his head, baring his slim chest to his wandering hands. Seth grabbed at his wrists, pinning his hands to the couch. "Uh-uh. My turn, love."

It took every ounce of Kasey's strength not to ignore Seth's command and haul his mate against him. His cock jumped as Seth parted the front of his pants and lifted Kasey's hard length free. Slithering out of Kasey's lap to the floor, Seth looked up into Kasey's dark eyes as his light-pink tongue flicked out to taste his lover. "Shit, pup," Kasey swore, his hands gripping the cushions of the couch.

Seth chuckled quietly before dipping into the small slit at the tip to gather the pearl of fluid seeping freely. "You taste good," he murmured, sliding his tongue around the head slowly.

He leisurely, tenderly inched his lips down the shaft while his tongue wetly bathed the pulsing vein underneath. Seth lightly fondled Kasey's balls as he sucked gently, not enough to make Kasey come but just enough to make his sac tighten in preparation. Reaching down, he unbuttoned his own jeans and pulled his cock out, stroking himself at the same pace as his mouth slurped along his mate's shaft. Kasey's hand came to rest on the back of his head, sifting through his hair lovingly. "Fuck, Seth. Your mouth is so fucking hot."

Grinning around Kasey's dick, Seth hummed softly, causing Kasey to thrust upward at the vibrations running straight down to his balls. "Seth!"

He could sense Kasey wasn't too far away from the edge, and Seth stopped, sitting back on his heels. A disappointed look flashed over Kasey's features. Seth's cock bobbed in front of him, begging him to continue as he stood, stripping all of his clothing off. "I'm not done with you yet, Sheriff," Seth purred seductively, his blue eyes a stormy gray.

Seth offered two of his fingers to Kasey as he straddled his mate's lap, lovingly tracing the lines of his mate's mouth. "Wet them," he commanded huskily.

Kasey's fingers dug even deeper into the couch cushions as he realized what Seth's intentions were, and he eagerly sucked the digits between his lips, slathering them repeatedly with his tongue. His eyes never left Seth's during the bathing of his mate's fingers. A growl rattled in Kasey's chest at the sight of Seth sinking down onto the invading digits. A twinkle of mischief in Seth's eyes made Kasey snarl, "If you don't hurry up, pup, I'm going to finish that for you."

The only response Seth gave was a rough laugh, his breathing uneven. Using his free hand, he reached behind him and stroked Kasey's shaft, smearing the liquid gathering at the tip with his thumb. Guiding his mate's cock, Seth pressed downward, biting his lip as the flared head breached the tight muscle. A hiss whispered between Seth's lips as the shaft sank deep inside him. Kasey's hands came up to grip his hips in a hard grip.

Both of them released a loud moan the instant Seth sat fully on Kasey's cock. "You feel so good," Kasey said roughly, thrusting up into his mate.

Seth gripped Kasey's shoulders, tipping his head back in pleasure. He slowly began to ride Kasey, lifting himself up and dropping back down. Kasey's fingers dug into his flesh, but the pain only added to the song his body felt with his mate deep inside of him. He captured Kasey's lips in a searing kiss, darting his tongue in and out of his lover's mouth, imitating the actions of their bodies. Slow and intimate, there was no sense of urgency to their lovemaking, just the joy of being one together.

Sweat built on their flesh, searing their keen noses with the salty-scented fluid. Seth lapped at Kasey's throat, tasting his lover's skin, lust singing inside him. Kasey wrapped his arms around Seth, pulling him down for each plunge into his mate's snug passage. His fangs elongated as he neared the edge of his climax. His balls grew tight, the need to fill his mate's channel and claim him as his growing stronger. "Seth," Kasey ground out, "need you to come."

Pulling Kasey's mouth to his neck, Seth keened, "Please...."

Kasey bit down deeply, flooding his mouth with his pup's essence. Seth's inner muscles clamped down like a vice on Kasey's cock as his mate released between. He felt the hot seed splash across his stomach. The sweet tang of his pup's come and the feel of his tight hole fluttering around his hard shaft triggered Kasey's own orgasm. Letting out an almost yelping whine, Kasey shattered into a shuddering mess. His chest heaved with each shaking breath he took.

Seth collapsed onto Kasey's chest, moaning, his eyes

closed. The sweat cooled on their skin slowly, sending a shiver through Seth as the air-conditioning kicked on. Kasey reached out and pulled the blanket folded over the back of the couch around them to cover his mate's chilled flesh. "You're going to wear me out, pup," he said tiredly, pressing a kiss to Seth's temple.

Laughing breathlessly, Seth wrinkled his nose at Kasey without opening his eyes. "Me? Wear you out?"

"Uhm hmm," Kasey hummed. "You and that luscious body of yours I can't get enough of."

"Somehow I think you'll wear me out first." Seth finally gathered enough strength to look up into his mate's eyes. "Thank you for my clinic, Kasey."

Kasey smiled at Seth's words. "You're my mate and a part of my pack, pup. Of course I'm going to do whatever I can to help you out. You just need to learn to listen to your Alpha."

Seth's eyebrows went up at Kasey's words. "My Alpha? Who said you were my Alpha?"

A superior look crossed Kasey's features. "I did."

Indignation flared in Seth's eyes. He opened his mouth to argue, but Kasey cut him off with a deep kiss. Seth's lips were swollen and red by the time Kasey let him breathe, and whatever he'd been about to say was simply forgotten. "Love you, pup," Kasey whispered against Seth's mouth.

"Love you too, mate," Seth sighed as he snuggled closer to his sheriff.

***

Craving more urban fantasy or paranormal? Spell of the Werewolf is available now on Kindle & Kindle Unlimited!

A werewolf seeks to sever the curse. A hybrid hunter wants him dead. Will the next moonrise be his last?

Looking for something contemporary? Try Touch Me Gently! Available on Kindle and Kindle Unlimited.

A scarred young man jumping at shadows. A big-hearted, sexy cowboy providing him a safe haven. But is he able to trust his cowboy with his heart?

A NOTE FROM J.R.

Thank you for reading Chasing Seth. If you enjoyed it, I would truly appreciate if you could let your friends know so they can also enjoy the relationship between Seth and Kasey. If you leave a review for Chasing Seth on the site in which you purchased the book, Goodreads or your own blog, I would love to read it. Please email the link to jrloveless@gmail.com

ABOUT THE AUTHOR

J.R. Loveless began her adventure in writing at the young age of twelve. Her foray into creating her own worlds and telling her characters' life stories was triggered by her own love of reading. She currently resides in South Florida with her dog and two cats, and by day works as a manager for a financial lending institute.

Her journey into gay romance began in 2005 when she began posting her original fiction on a forum for feedback and readers' pleasure. In 2010, a good friend urged her to submit to a publishing company, and the day she received the acceptance and contract was the best day of her life. Since then, she has been noted to be one of the most purchased audio books after Fifty Shades of Grey on Audiobook.com and received best gay romantic fiction for Touch Me Gently in the 2011 TLA Gaybies.

J.R. adores her fans and loves hearing from them.

Never miss out on an update or sale by subscribing to J.R.'s Website. As a thank you, you'll receive a free short novelette called White Rain about two friends who become lovers!

J.R.'s Blog

J.R.'s Facebook Reader Group

facebook.com/authorjrloveless

twitter.com/J.R.%E2%80%99s%20Twitter

instagram.com/jrloveless

amazon.com/author/jrloveless

bookbub.com/profile/j-r-loveless

goodreads.com/jrloveless

Chapter One

I'm *from Texas, and one of the reasons I like Texas is because there's no one in control.*

It wouldn't be long before I found out how true that Willy Nelson quote was. But as my best friend Cassie and I navigated the steep rocky path down toward our destination on a sweltering Wednesday in the middle of August, trouble was very far from my mind.

We followed carefully behind my boyfriend, Ryan Iverson, and Cassie's boyfriend, Ty Clayburn, as we made our way to a little-known swimming hole about half an hour from Sugar Creek. The guys flew down the tricky path like it was another day in the park, but Cassie and I picked our way down the limestone and scrub-brush at a snail's pace, watching for snakes and cactus, and gabbing nonstop.

"Aunt Meg called last night," I said, adjusting my grip on the vintage picnic basket I carried. The pretty weave had caught my eye at an estate sale, but as I shuffled the heavy bulk of it back and forth between my hands, I regretted not packing our lunch into something more practical. "She's having a great time in Spoonbill

Bay with Bertie. They went jet skiing yesterday. Can you believe it?" I told her with a laugh.

My Aunt Meg, the spirited owner of Primrose House B&B, had taken an extended vacation to visit her cousin Roberta on the gulf coast after a traumatic incident where she was held hostage by a deranged woman. The experience had shaken her more than she'd let on, and after a lot of persuading, she finally agreed to take a break in Spoonbill Bay with Bertie.

Before leaving, she'd entrusted me with the responsibility of running the B&B, a decision that made both of us a bit uneasy. Aunt Meg's absence meant that I was juggling the B&B's daily operations along with my own small fledgling catering business. Thankfully, I wasn't alone in this endeavor. Aunt Meg's trusted helper, Maria, was a lifesaver. In fact, Maria was so capable that she practically managed the B&B by herself.

Cassie chuckled, brushing a strand of hair from her sweaty forehead. "That Bertie could talk a rattlesnake out of its own skin. Did they have fun? Or was Meg scared to death? I bet she was scared to death."

"A little of both, I'd say. It's been great for her. She keeps asking if she should come home, but I can tell she isn't quite ready, so I keep telling her no."

"And y'all are holding it together so far, right?" Cassie asked, eyeing the path ahead. "I'm sure it's hard for her to let loose on the reins after all these years. She's been the sole caretaker of Primrose House for a long time now."

I nodded. "Mostly holding it together," I said, huffing a bit as the weight of the picnic basket made my arms ache. "I don't know what I'd do without Maria. But I've got a couple of big catering jobs coming up and more guests this coming weekend. It's a lot to handle. But I'm sure we'll pull through like we always do."

Cassie gave me a sympathetic look. "You've got this, Abby. If anyone can juggle multiple businesses, it's you."

I smiled, appreciating her confidence. "Thanks, Cass. I just

hope I can keep juggling and not drop a ball." We were nearly at the end of the trek down and the guys were so far ahead of us that I could barely make them out. I took the opportunity of the distance to pry a little. "How was the trip to Dallas?"

Cassie blushed slightly, glancing at Ty, who was just coming to the end of the trail. "It was fun for the most part. But meeting his sisters was intimidating! It felt very serious. But they were all so nice. They'd fit right into our crowd."

I laughed softly. "Well, it sounds like things are moving in a good direction with you two."

We arrived at the end of the path and started the final climb down. It was rocky and took plenty of concentration not to slip. But once we finally passed through the last of the scrubby cedar trees and sharp rocks, the river opened up in front of us and I stopped and smiled, appreciating the scene. The river was wide and shallow, with an outcropping of rocks toward the east where small groups of sunbathers sprawled out and splashed.

Ryan set down the intertubes he'd been carrying at a shady spot under a big oak tree and turned back to me with a smile, holding out his hand to help me down the final difficult rock. With a grateful sigh, I finally set the picnic basket down and stretched, then pulled my coverup over my head. It was so hot I was already sweating through it and I couldn't wait to get into the cool river water.

Catching Ryan peeking at me in my bathing suit with undisguised interest, I blushed and looked away, suddenly not wanting to make eye contact. I appreciated his gaze, and I was happy that he was interested, but it still made me a little uncomfortable. Everything with him was still so new. It would take some getting used to, this whole being in a real relationship with him thing.

We made our way over to the sandy strip next to the water, and I sighed and closed my eyes as I stuck my feet in. Heavenly.

"Woo!" Cassie called as she hopped down onto the sand with us. "That was a workout!"

She laughed as Ty grabbed her and swung her around. "So worth it though!" he replied as he pulled her toward the water. "That river's gonna feel so good, honey!"

Laughing as they both ran toward the edge of the water like kids, I shaded my eyes and scanned the river. It was a weekday, so thankfully it wasn't overly crowded. Ryan came up behind me and wrapped his arms around me, his bare chest connecting with my bare shoulders. I sure could get used to this.

"You want to float, or should we eat something first?"

I grinned and turned to give him a sideways kiss. "Let's float. The water feels so good."

He grabbed two intertubes, and we awkwardly settled our bodies into them. The cool river water was a shock, but only for a second. I quickly grew accustomed as I splashed and floated my way toward where Cassie and Ty were wading.

We floated gently down the river, the cool water a refreshing contrast to the scorching August sun. Laughter and splashing filled the air as we drifted along, occasionally bumping into each other and playfully shoving off again. Cassie and Ty were in their own world, splashing each other and giggling like children, while Ryan and I floated side by side, our hands occasionally brushing as we maneuvered our tubes.

"Isn't this perfect?" Cassie called out, her face glowing with happiness. "I can't remember the last time I felt this relaxed."

"Me either," I admitted, letting the current carry me. "It's nice to just float and not think about anything for a while."

Ryan leaned back in his tube, closing his eyes and letting out a contented sigh. "This is the life. Good company, beautiful scenery, and no worries." It made me happy to see him so relaxed. With the safety of Sugar Creek always on his shoulders, he rarely had the chance to unwind. Ryan's dedication to his work as the town's sheriff often left him tense and preoccupied, but here, floating in the river with the three of us, he seemed to shed all those burdens. It was a side of him I cherished.

We floated in companionable silence for a while longer. The sun sparkled on the surface of the river. Every so often, a fish would dart by, a flash of silver in the clear water. Children jumped from a rock nearby, sending up sprays of water and shrieks as they hit the coolness. It was the height of relaxation and I soaked it up.

After a long while of floating in the river, I finally decided it was time for some grub. Heading toward the shore in my tube I called out, "I made something special for y'all if you're ready to eat!"

The group quickly followed me out of the water toward our spot and watched as I dug through the picnic basket to the very bottom and pulled out a large pie carrier. "This is for after lunch," I told them with a sly smile. "It's a blackberry pie. I made it just this morning."

Ryan groaned, and Ty licked his lips. Seemed I would have some takers. I'd gotten up early just for the pie, making the dough by hand and mixing the plump berries with sugar, cinnamon, nutmeg, and butter before sealing it with pretty crimping on the edges and baking it. Then I'd let it cool for as long as I could before I'd packed the rest of our picnic for the day's adventure. It had been a chore to make and an even bigger chore to lug down to the river, but the efforts were well worth it.

Cassie helped me spread out a picnic blanket, and we put out the cheese, meat, and cracker spread she'd made for the day. It looked delicious, with hard cheese, salami, dried fruit, and nuts. I added in an olive tapenade and baguette I'd picked up from the Sugar Creek Bakery and we tucked into our feast.

Midway through lunch, I realized that Ryan was giving Ty strange looks. I stopped chewing as my eyes bounced from one man to the other. "What's going on with you two?" I finally asked.

They both eyed one another but didn't answer me. "You got this, man. There's no slack in your rope. You'll be fine," Ryan told Ty with a solemn nod.

I glanced at Cassie and saw that she was nearly bouncing out of

her seat with excitement. Something was up, and I wasn't part of it.

Ty cleared his throat and got up on his knees in front of Cassie. He reached into a pocket of his swim trunks and pulled something out and my hands flew to my mouth. Finally, I knew what was going on. Ty was about to propose!

"Cassie, honey," Ty began. I watched as tears sprang to Cassie's eyes. "You know I'm over the moon for ya, don't ya?"

She nodded, and the tears began to fall. He took her hand and squeezed. "Well, I just know without a doubt that you and I were meant to be together. Like Desi and Lucy, right?" he said with a laugh. It warmed me all over. Cassie had always been a huge I Love Lucy fan. Ty did a good one, making that reference.

I giggled too, from nervous excitement and the joy I felt surrounding our little group. I leaned back into Ryan and he wrapped his arms around me, kissing the top of my head.

"I know, Ty. I feel the same," Cassie replied.

"Whew!" he cried with a laugh as he opened the box, revealing a beautiful antique engagement ring. "Cause if you didn't, I don't know what I would've done!"

"Ty, buddy. Get on with it," Ryan said, laughter in his voice.

He cleared his throat one last time. "Cassie Divine, you would make me the happiest man alive if you'd agree to be my bride. What do ya think?"

The tears were falling in buckets, both from Cassie's eyes and my own. She nodded wildly. "Of course I'll marry you, you silly man! I wouldn't have it any other way!" They kissed, and he slipped the ring on her finger. Ryan and I turned away, giving them a little privacy, and I busied myself pulling a few more things out of the basket.

"I think this calls for a toast!" I said, reaching for a bottle of white wine I'd snagged from Sheila Connoly at Wild Hare Winery the day before. Cassie beamed and grabbed the plastic cups out of the bag nearby.

"What a great idea!" she said, wiping her eyes. "How'd you know?"

I shrugged. "I had no clue! Just seemed like a good idea!"

I poured us all a glass, and we clinked our red solo cups together.

"To Ty and Cassie," Ryan said. "May you both have a wonderful life together."

"And to Abby, for making us such a delicious celebration pie!" Cassie added.

Our blanket was bubbling over with a happy energy. As I sliced up the pie and started serving it on paper plates, Cassie leaned over and squeezed my arm.

"Can you believe it? I had no idea!" She glanced down at the gorgeous oval shaped ring on her finger and giggled.

"Really? It seemed like you were in on the whole thing. I was fixing to be mad at you for leaving me out of it!"

Her eyes shot up. "I swear, I didn't know! But as soon as I saw Ty fidgeting, I started to guess," she told me with a laugh. She helped pass out the pie, and we all tucked in. It was delicious, tart and sweet, with a little crunch from the sugar-dusted crust.

I couldn't believe it. I knew it would probably come, eventually. Cassie and Ty had gotten closer and closer over the months that I'd been back in Sugar Creek. But I sure wasn't expecting it today. We would have to spend some time alone later going over every detail.

We spent another hour or so enjoying the river and each other's company. The men took turns racing each other down the shallow rapids, while Cassie and I sat with our feet in the cool water, already starting to dream up wedding plans.

As the afternoon wore on, I glanced at my watch and sighed. "I hate to be the party-pooper, but I should probably head back soon. I've got prep work to do for tomorrow's catering job."

Ryan nodded, pulling himself out of the water. "Yeah, I've got the evening shift starting in a couple of hours, too."

We packed up our picnic, still riding high on the excitement of the day. The climb back up was just as treacherous as the descent, but our spirits were so high we hardly noticed the effort. We were all caught up in the afternoon's magic—the proposal, the celebration, the simple joy of being together.

By the time we reached Ryan's truck, the sun was still high in the sky, but the day was winding down for us. It had been one of those perfect afternoons you wish would last forever.

CHAPTER TWO

But of course that kind of peace couldn't last. Not for me, at least. The trouble began as soon as we pulled into the parking lot of Primrose House late that afternoon.

We were only supposed to have one B&B guest until the following day, so the jam-packed tour bus of people descending with copious luggage was confusing, to say the least.

"Hey, Ed! What's going on?"

My old high school friend, Ed Morton, owned Two-Step through Texas Tours. He was a regular fixture around Primrose House.

"Oh, hey, Abby!" He replied as he unloaded an extremely bulky suitcase from the bottom of his bus. "This is the Waterstone group. Picked 'em up from the airport a while ago, got 'em fed, and now they're ready to check in."

My heart started to pound. Waterstone group? I had no idea what he was talking about.

He turned back to the bus to continue unloading, and I bounded up the stairs, deeply confused about why all these guests were being unloaded, not to mention frustrated that I was in a grimy bathing suit and cover up, my cheeks pink from sun and wine, rather

than in more professional attire. Pushing through the front door, I found Maria frantically typing into the computer at the checkout desk. A look of relief washed over her face when she saw me come in.

"Hey, what's going on?" I asked her. She frowned, glancing from the group coming in to the computer and back to me.

"I think there has been a reservation mixup. I talked to the woman in charge and she says that they made a reservation last month. But when I looked in our system, I saw that the date was for the fifteenth of September, not the fifteenth of August. I don't know if it was a mistake on our end, or on theirs. But they are here now, and they are requesting six rooms."

My eyebrows shot up. We only had eight rooms in the whole B&B and I knew we were expecting one more today and at least a couple of reservations tomorrow to stay for the weekend. "For how long?" I moved around behind the desk to look over her shoulder at the reservation screen and groaned. This group was also wanting to stay through the weekend. This was going to be a big fat problem.

"We should be good until tomorrow. We have one more reservation scheduled for today which will fill every room. But tomorrow we have two more bookings and that's going to push us over," she said, concern etched into her voice.

I nodded and then bit my lip and puzzled over it. "Okay, well, these people are here now, so let's go ahead and give them the rooms we have. I'm going to go shower and change real quick and then we can look over the schedule again and see what we can do for the guests coming tomorrow."

I patted her on the back and headed back toward Aunt Meg's bedroom, where I'd been staying for the last week since Aunt Meg had headed out of town.

Before I got far, though, I turned back to Maria, a smile back on my face despite the panic that was roiling inside. "Ty proposed to Cassie today!"

Her whole face brightened. "Oh, how exciting! Maybe we can have the wedding here!"

I nodded wildly. "Yes, I love that!" It was a great idea and I couldn't wait to propose it to Cassie. I could cater the wedding for free, whether she wanted me to or not. It would be a great way to pay my friend back for all she'd done for me since I'd moved back to Sugar Creek.

I flew through cleaning myself up, not wanting to dilly-dally when there was so much work to do. I rinsed the river water from my body quickly and threw on a shirtdress and sneakers, combing my wet hair quickly back into a ponytail. Taking a deep breath to steel myself for whatever lay ahead, I made my way back out to the front room that served as our check-in counter, lobby, and gathering room to help Maria out.

But when I got back to the main room, everything was calm and quiet. I frowned and stuck my head out on the front porch. Ed's bus was long gone and there was not a single guest in sight. Which wasn't very surprising, seeing as the porch was being hit with the blazing afternoon sun. Yuck.

I headed back to the kitchen and finally found Maria stirring honey into a mug of tea. "Oh, there you are," I said. "You sure got all that squared away fast!"

She nodded. "It was fine today, but it is going to be much worse tomorrow when the other two reservations arrive."

"Let's go look at the schedule again. Maybe there's something we can do," I told her. She followed me back to the front room, and we fired up the computer. "If I have to, I can give up Aunt Meg's room for a couple of nights."

"But where will you sleep?" she asked.

I shrugged. "The couch, I guess?" If worse came to worst, I could always sleep at Cassie's. But I really hated the idea of leaving the B&B to a bunch of guests without someone on site to help if needed. No, that wouldn't do.

"I think we'll just have to put them up elsewhere," Maria said as she sipped her tea. "I'm sure there is a hotel available."

But after she and I had called several local hotels, we were at our wits' end. It seemed there was a big archeology conference being hosted by the Sugar Creek Historical Society over the weekend, and everything was full.

"Let's put one of the reservations in Aunt Meg's room. I'll sleep on the couch. It's only for a few days, anyway," I said. It wasn't ideal, especially because I had a big weekend catering job, but I could endure it for a few nights.

"And the other reservation?"

Before we had a chance to talk anymore, the front door opened and an older man in khaki cargo pants, black t-shirt, and hiking boots stepped inside. He had an old army backpack slung over one shoulder and he gave us both a bright, toothy smile as he approached.

"Hello, ladies," he said as he set the pack down in front of the desk. "I have a reservation for this a room."

Ah, the other guest of the day. I gave him my warmest, welcoming smile. "Welcome to Primrose House. I'm Abby and this is Maria."

"Hello," he said, flashing another brilliant smile. "I'm Wade Harper. I have a reservation until Sunday. Here for the Archeological Association conference."

I nodded. "It must be a pretty popular conference. Most of Sugar Creek lodging is booked up through the weekend."

"Oh, I imagine it is. A famous archeologist, Dr. Ralph Stapleton, will be presenting some new artifacts he found on a trip to Papua New Guinea. Has everyone all abuzz," he told us with a laugh. He leaned on the desk and crossed his very tanned arms. Several beaded rope bracelets decorated both of his wrists.

Maria set about checking him in as I told him about some of the local restaurants and attractions, as well as our daily happy hour.

Maria handed him his room key. "You're all set, Mr. Harper. You're in room three, just up the stairs and to the right."

"Thank you, Maria. And please, call me Wade," he replied, giving her a charming nod and grabbing his bag. We watched him head up and my curiosity about him grew. He was ruggedly handsome and had a hint of a foreign accent that I couldn't place. It was clear that he was very different from our usual guests and I wondered what wild stories he had to tell and whether he was an archeologist himself or just a fan.

"Well, he seems interesting," Maria said quietly once he was out of earshot. "Quite the character."

I nodded and let my mind wander for a moment. I'd always loved the idea of adventure. Indiana Jones had been one of my favorite movie series when I was a child. I'd played adventurer or archeologist countless times over the years. But those were childish games that never seemed like a real possibility. Here, though, right in front of me, it seemed there was a real live adventurer. Someone who had made a life doing things I could only let my childhood self dream about. Jealousy mixed with a deep curiosity and I lost myself in daydreams for a moment.

But life doesn't stop for fantasy and so I went back to the reservation problem. Maria and I puzzled for a few more minutes, when suddenly I got a wild idea. "I wonder if Sheila and Mark might want to take that last reservation. They don't usually have stay-over guests at the winery, but who knows? They might be open to it. Might even spark a new side business for them."

I made a quick call to Sheila and spent a little time convincing her about having a guest at Wild Hare Winery over the weekend. She finally agreed, so then it was up to me to call the two reservations to see who might rather stay down the road at the winery. It didn't take much convincing on my part. The first couple I called were enthusiastic about the idea, so I gave them Sheila's contact information and wished them a pleasant trip to Sugar Creek. I hoped they would give us a chance on their next visit.

"It's too bad we have to turn people away," I told Maria after I got off the phone.

She shrugged. "Yes, and no. It wouldn't be so if we weren't completely booked for the weekend."

"Well, that's certainly true. I love how positive you always are, Maria," I replied.

She gave me a beautiful, gracious smile. "Well, thank you. I try, at least. It is not always easy."

Wasn't that the truth? But I tried to look on the bright side as she and I finished up with the reservation issue. We were booked solid and Aunt Meg's business was bringing in money, which was a great thing.

Once we had all the reservations sorted out, I left Maria to get to work in the kitchen. I had a small job catering a luncheon the following day, as well as a big buffet lunch on Saturday, and thanks to our trip to the river and the chaos with the guests, I hadn't even started to prepare. I brewed a pot of strong coffee and pulled out my notebook to try to re-orient myself about what I needed to do.

The luncheon job would be at Margie Belcase's house. It was a catered lunch for her book club. I would be setting up and serving, staying throughout and then cleaning up once they were finished. It should be an easy job, although the group was new to me, so I wasn't sure how demanding the five ladies would be. It could be a walk in the park or highly chaotic. Who knew? No matter what, though, I would be prepared.

Margie was also the one who'd booked me for the Saturday gig. Her volunteer organization was having a fundraising lunch at the Sugar Creek community center, and she'd booked me to serve a buffet for the group. Although most of the ticket money was going to their charity, the Friends of Sugar Creek Library, I would be paid well for the food, which I was grateful for. As much as I cared about the library, my little business was barely operational at present and I needed all the income I could get.

For the small lunch, I planned to do a mixture of finger foods

and small salads, things that could be nibbled and sampled during conversation. I would do a trio of mini sandwiches, curried chicken salad, ham and Swiss, and roasted red pepper and goat cheese. Deviled eggs were a no-brainer for this kind of event, but I planned to make them special by adding truffle salt. I also planned on serving a salad with Israeli couscous and roasted vegetables in a cumin vinaigrette. For dessert, I planned to make a new cookie recipe I'd been playing with lately—lemon lavender shortbread. As I thought through what I would be serving, I made two lists, one for shopping, and one for the timing of everything that needed to get done for the party.

Glancing at the clock a little while later, I realized it was nearly time to set up the B&B's happy hour. I'd planned to at least make the cookies for the luncheon today, but because of the chaos, I hadn't managed it yet. So much for getting any work done. At least I had a plan and a list, though. I was pretty confident that I could manage everything in the morning. I hoped so, at least. Between the sun, excitement, alcohol, and chaos at the B&B, I was plain old exhausted. Closing my notebook with a thud, I resolved to let the catering job wait for the morning and to get what little bit of peace I could for the rest of the day.

Chapter Three

Thursday morning dawned hot and humid, which was no change from any other day since I'd come back to Texas. I got up with the sun, hoping to get a handle on my catering work and still get breakfast out for the B&B crowd.

The first thing I wanted to tackle was the cookies. I could mix up the dough, roll them out and cut them, and then turn my attention to breakfast once they were in the oven. Tying my apron on, I set to work gathering my ingredients: flour, sugar, butter, fresh lemons, and a small jar of dried lavender I'd bought at the farmer's market a few weeks before. I loved the way the lavender added a subtle, floral note to the cookies, making them a little more special.

I creamed the butter and sugar together, watching as they blended into a smooth, pale yellow mixture. The rhythm of the mixer was soothing, a steady hum that matched the early morning quiet. I added the flour, a pinch of salt, and the finely grated zest of two lemons, filling the kitchen with their bright, citrusy scent. Finally, I sprinkled in the lavender, crushing it lightly between my fingers to release its fragrance.

Once the dough came together, I turned it out onto a floured

surface and rolled it into a smooth, even sheet. The familiar motions were comforting, and I let myself get lost in the joy of baking as I began to cut out the cookies, laying them carefully on the baking sheets.

Sliding the first batch into the oven, I set the timer and then turned my attention to preparing the simple breakfast we always offered at Primrose House. Maria had done a lot of the prep work the night before, and I unwrapped the plastic from a tray of danishes and muffins and started the coffee brewing. As the cookies baked, the kitchen filled with the delicate aroma of lemon and lavender, a scent that always made me think of summer mornings and fresh starts.

I glanced at the clock and sighed. It was only a little after six, but I already felt behind. Juggling the B&B and my catering business was proving to be more challenging than I'd anticipated. I missed having Aunt Meg around. It wasn't that we needed her to do the work so much as that I wanted to be near her, to have her steady presence to help me emotionally. I wondered, not for the first time, if I was in over my head.

The sound of footsteps on the stairs interrupted my thoughts. A few seconds later, an older guest came into the kitchen. He and his wife had checked in the day before the big group and I'd had a chance to get to know them both before the chaos had set into our little B&B.

"Good morning, Mr. Hoffman," I greeted him with a smile. "Heading out early today?"

He nodded. "Thought I'd get a bit of a hike in while Linda's sleeping. I've always been more of a morning person than she is. Mind if I grab a coffee to go?"

"Of course not! Help yourself! There are some muffins on the counter too, if you'd like one for the road."

As Mr. Hoffman left with a grateful nod, I turned back to my baking, my mind already racing back to the book club preparations. I started pulling trays and serving dishes from my makeshift

rack in the corner of the room that held catering supplies as I contemplated how I would get everything to and from Margie's house from my van as easily as possible.

The timer beeped, and I pulled the trays of cookies from the oven, setting them on a rack to cool. The cookies looked perfect, each one a little round of golden-brown goodness, speckled with tiny bits of lavender. I smiled as I took a hot bite and hoped the book club ladies would like them as much as I did.

My mind raced faster and faster as the morning slipped away. Guests came and went and I barely registered them as I arranged food on pretty plates and wrapped them in plastic wrap. Maria stopped in multiple times to offer help, but I knew she was busy enough herself running the B&B alone, so I shooed her away every time. Finally, a little before eleven, I packed up the last sandwich, zipped up the last cooler bag, and carried everything to my shiny new catering truck.

I decided to make a quick stop at Cassie's place on the way to Margie Belcase's house. I'd left some of my catering things at her place when I moved back into Primrose House, and I wanted to make sure I had everything I needed for the catering gig that day. It was one of the most frustrating parts of trying to take care of the B&B and my catering business—everything was spread all over the place. Normally I loved planning and organization, I loved my lists and my labeled pantry items. But right now, I would just have to resign myself to the chaos.

As I pulled up to the little bungalow behind Divine Finds, Cassie's antique shop, I heard an excited bark. My heart leapt at the sound. A moment later, a blur of shaggy brown and white fur came bounding around the corner of the house and barreled into me.

"Cocoa!" I cried, kneeling down to greet my energetic little terrier mix. He jumped into my arms, his whole body wiggling with joy as he licked my face. "Oh, I've missed you, buddy."

"Looks like someone's happy to see you," Cassie said,

appearing in the doorway with a grin. She was dressed in a sunny yellow summer dress, her curly hair pulled back in a messy bun.

I stood up, Cocoa still in my arms. "I've missed him, too. I wish I could have him at the B&B with me."

Cassie's smile softened. "I know. He misses you, too. But hey, at least this way, you have an excuse to visit more often, right?"

I laughed, setting Cocoa down and following Cassie into the house.

"Is the shop not open today?" I asked as I set my keys down and started to sort through my catering equipment, trying and failing to ignore Cocoa's little licks on my arm as I stooped to go through a cabinet.

"I let Mandy take over for a bit. I wanted to grab a quick bite and get some wedding plans started," she said with a blush.

I glanced up and raised my eyebrows. It hadn't even been twenty-four hours, but I imagined she must be champing at the bit with excitement to get the ball rolling on the wedding. I felt bad that I'd been so busy with the businesses that I hadn't had time to check in with her the night before and gab about the proposal. "I'm so sorry I didn't call you last night! Things got crazy..."

She cut off my apology with a laugh. "Don't worry about it, lady! I know what you're going through! And I know I'm getting to all this quick, but I am so excited!" She did a little hop and a squeal and it made me so happy to see her enthusiasm that I straightened from the floor and gave her a hug, squealing too. Cocoa bounced around us, wanting to share in the excitement.

"You're getting married! Isn't it exciting?"

"Exciting...and a little terrifying."

I pulled away and frowned. "Cold feet already?"

She laughed and swatted my shoulder. "No, not hardly. It's just strange to think about spending the rest of my life with Ty. I like him plenty and all, but it sure seems final."

I nodded. "It sure is. But it'll be great. You know it will." I glanced at the clock over her shoulder and cold terror spread down

my spine. "Shoot! I gotta get going if I'm going to make it to Margie's on time! Sorry I can't stay any longer."

Cassie nodded, understanding in her eyes. "Don't worry a bit about it! But hey, why don't I come over tonight? We can open a bottle of wine, and I can tell you all about my secret wedding binder," she added with a wink. "And if you think it's okay, I'll bring this little guy. He misses you and the B&B so much."

I nodded, a grin on my face. "That sounds perfect, and Cocoa can stay outside if anyone complains. With any luck, we'll have a few leftover cookies, too. I made lavender lemon shortbread today."

Cassie's eyes lit up, and I gave her a quick hug after I packed up the rest of the things I needed. Cocoa trotted over, looking up at me with those big, soulful eyes. I knelt down to give him one last cuddle. "Be a good boy for Cassie, okay? I'll see you soon, buddy."

Cassie walked me to the door, Cocoa at our heels. "Good luck today."

"Thanks, Cass. I'll see you tonight," I said, giving her a quick hug before heading to my van.

As I drove down Main Street, my mind was mostly on the job ahead of me and I barely paid attention to what was going on in our small downtown, although I slowed as I passed my friend Ellie's place, Sugar Creek Bakery, and smiled when I saw a line out the door. Ellie was pregnant and her business was booming—I was thrilled for her and made a mental note to go visit her soon and catch up on everything baby related.

As I turned onto Sycamore Street, where Margie Belcase lived, my mind shifted back to the task at hand. The neighborhood was on the nicer end for Sugar Creek, the street deeply shaded by old live oaks and large grassy yards spread out with pops of color from summer flowers. It felt peaceful and friendly, a place to settle down and raise a family. And thinking of that got me thinking about Cassie and Ellie and all the changes they were about to undergo. I wondered where Cassie and Ty might settle down once they were

married, which brought a brief hint of anxiety to mind about where *I* would go after their marriage. I'd been staying with Cassie since returning to Sugar Creek, but that couldn't last now, I supposed.

I saw Margie's white brick house on the right and I put all those thoughts about friends aside for the time being and focused on the job to be done. Something felt off as I parked my van in the driveway, although I couldn't place it until I made my way up the walk with the tray of cookies a few moments later.

The front door stood open as I walked up to the porch. I frowned. It was the height of summer, and Texans simply did not leave their doors open to the heat and the mosquitos. But maybe she'd left it open to make things easier for me?

I hesitated a second longer on the porch, listening for any sounds of activity inside. The house was eerily quiet. No voices, no TV, not even the hum of an air conditioner.

"Hello?" I called out, my voice sounding unnaturally loud in the stillness. "Margie? It's Abby from Deep in the Heart Catering!"

When no one answered, I touched the door lightly, and it swung open the rest of the way with a slow creak. I was about to call out again, but the words stuck in my throat as my eyes fell on a body lying sprawled face down in the hallway, one arm outstretched as if reaching for help that had never come. I cried out, the sound more of a strangled gasp than a scream. The tray of cookies I'd been carrying slipped from my grasp, clattering loudly on the tile floor.

For a moment, I stood frozen, my brain struggling to process what I was seeing. Then instinct kicked in and I rushed to the person's side. As I got closer, the metallic smell of blood hit me, making my stomach churn.

A pool of crimson spread around her head on the white tile floor and as I got closer, I realized it was Margie Belcase. With trembling fingers, I reached for her wrist, desperately hoping to

find a pulse. Her skin was clammy, and somehow I knew, even before I failed to find a heartbeat, that it was too late.

My own heart pounding in my ears, I stood and stumbled back, fumbling for my cell phone. My fingers shook as I dialed Ryan's number, leaving bloody fingerprints on the screen. I scanned the area around me as I waited for him to pick up. Right off the foyer was a library with floor to ceiling books and antiques in glass cases. Papers littered the floor of the space, as if someone had been looking for something. A few of them were soaked in Margie's blood.

I turned and went quickly back outside as Ryan picked up the dropped cookies crumbling beneath my steps.

"You aren't gonna believe this," I told him as soon as he picked up, cutting off the sweet nothings he was about to whisper. My voice sounded distant and shaky to my own ears. "I just got to Margie Belcase's for a catering job and... Ryan... I think she's dead."

He became very matter-of-fact then, and as I gave him the address, he told me to stay outside and not touch anything. He didn't have to ask me twice. The awful scene was almost too much for me to handle. The last thing I wanted was to go back through that door.

Chapter Four

Five minutes later, Ryan pulled up in his cruiser with a new deputy in the passenger seat. They'd recently hired someone to replace an officer who'd unfortunately passed away, and I hadn't had the pleasure of meeting him yet.

The new deputy was a tall, broad-shouldered man with a clean-shaven face and short, neatly trimmed blond hair. He had a serious, almost stern expression that softened slightly when he saw me. His uniform was crisp and well-fitted, and he moved with the kind of quiet confidence that suggested he'd been doing this for a while, even if he was new to our small town.

Now wasn't the time for introductions, however. There were more important things to attend to. I stood from the front stone step where I'd been since calling about Margie and tried to keep the tears from my eyes as Ryan approached.

"She's just inside," I told him, my voice trembling slightly despite my efforts to stay composed.

Ryan nodded and squeezed my shoulder, a gesture that was both comforting and grounding. "We'll take it from here, Abby. Just stay close, okay?"

I nodded, watching as Ryan and the new deputy stepped inside. The weight of the situation pressed down on me, making it hard to breathe. I glanced around Margie's front yard, taking in the neatly trimmed hedges and the flowerbeds she'd clearly taken pride in. Everything looked so normal, so peaceful, and yet inside was a scene of horror.

The sound of the front door closing behind them seemed to echo in the stillness of the late afternoon. I wrapped my arms around myself and sat on the cement step leading up to the porch. My mind raced, replaying the horrific scene I'd stumbled upon. Margie, lying there so still, surrounded by... I squeezed my eyes shut, trying to block out the image, but it was seared into my memory. How could this have happened? Just a couple of days before, I'd spoken to her on the phone, finalizing the menu for today's lunch. She'd been so full of life, excited about hosting her book club.

Part of me wanted to run, to get as far away from this place as possible, but I knew I couldn't. I had to stay, to help in whatever way I could. Ryan would need to ask me questions, and those poor book club ladies would be arriving soon, expecting a pleasant afternoon with their friend.

Friend. The word made me think of Cassie, and I longed for her comforting presence. What would she say if she were here? Probably some snark about how I couldn't even cater a simple lunch without stumbling into a murder investigation. The thought almost made me smile, despite everything.

I took a deep breath, trying to steady myself. I needed to pull it together. For Margie, for Ryan, for whoever else might need me in the coming hours. I'd been through difficult times before, I reminded myself. I'd found dead bodies before. I could get through this too.

Just then, the sound of an approaching car caught my attention. I looked up to see a Lincoln town car pulling up to the curb.

My heart sank as I realized it must be the book club members arriving. How on earth was I going to break this news to them?

With a heavy sigh, I pushed myself to my feet, brushing off my clothes. Whatever came next, I'd face it. For now, that meant greeting these women and somehow finding the words to shatter their world with the news that their friend was gone.

They were all laughing at something as they got out of the car, but their laughs caught in the air as they registered the police car in the drive. They made their way up the shaded walk slowly, all of them eyeing Ryan's cruiser and whispering to each other. As they approached, I realized that one of the women looked very familiar to me. She was tall and wore a navy dress and pearls. Finally, as they grew near enough to notice me, I realized who the woman was. It was Jane Henderson, my friend Georgie's mom.

Her eyes lit up when she saw me, too. "Well, Abby Hirsch! What a surprise! Georgie told me you came back to town, but what are you doing here?"

"I was going to cater for your book club today..." I trailed off, completely at a loss for what to say. "But I'm sorry, it isn't going to happen. Margie Belcase..." was she really dead? I didn't know for sure, and I didn't want to be the one to say it. I shrugged. "It doesn't look good."

"Is everything okay? Is Margie okay?" one of the women cried out. This woman had thin wire-frame glasses and a beautiful burgundy silk scarf tied at her neck.

I shook my head. "I'm afraid not. I don't know exactly..." Just then, the ambulance arrived, and a couple of EMTs jumped out, quickly pushing past us. We all watched as they met Ryan at the door and headed inside.

The third woman's hand went to her mouth when she caught a glimpse of Margie on the floor. "Oh, my goodness. Oh, no."

Tears sprung to the woman's eyes and immediately her two companions surrounded her and the three of them huddled

together as if to block out the horror of the day. We stood that way for a few minutes, an awkward, sad silence hanging over us all.

The air outside on the hot Texas day was stifling, and I tugged at my chef coat and glanced at the bag of sandwiches I'd set down on the stoop before going in earlier. Thankfully, I'd left them outside because if I'd taken them inside with me, they might have met the same fate as the cookies that now decorated Margie's entryway. They were in a cooler bag, but I wasn't sure how long it could stand up to this kind of heat. Should I take it back to the van? Would the women try to get in the house if I moved? And was it even my responsibility to keep them out of the house? Probably not.

The women finally parted and began to whisper and pace. Two of the women fanned themselves with their book club book. I noticed it was The Thursday Murder Club, a book that had been on my own list for quite a while. Now probably wasn't a good time to talk about a book, however. They all stood in a tight cluster, their faces a mix of shock and confusion and tears.

The third one, a woman who wore a floral dress and had silver hair pulled back into a severe bun, kept glancing towards the house, her lips pressed into a thin line. "This is terrible," she muttered, her voice trembling. "Margie was just fine yesterday. I saw her at the store."

"Do you think it was an accident?" Jane asked us all, her eyes wide with fear.

"I don't know," the woman with the glasses replied. "But it doesn't look good, does it? Not with the police and ambulance here."

The woman in the flowered dress lowered her voice and frowned, glancing over her shoulder. "You don't think... Is that nephew of hers involved? Hunter? He's been staying with her recently, right?"

The one with the glasses nodded. "Oh, Hunter. I wouldn't be

surprised if he had something to do with this. He's always had that look about him. Shifty, you know?"

Jane frowned. "We shouldn't speculate, Evelyn. You know Margie loved that boy."

The woman with the bun replied, "yes, but let's be honest. He's been in and out of trouble for years. Remember when he pawned Margie's silver last Christmas?"

Jane shook her head sadly. "Poor Margie. She was always trying to help him. Giving him money, letting him stay with her. I worried it would come to no good."

They all fell silent for a moment, the weight of their speculations hanging heavy in the air. I couldn't help but feel a twinge of unease. If even half of what they were saying was true, this Hunter character certainly sounded like he could be trouble. I would have to tell Ryan what I'd overheard.

Before they had time to speculate further, another car pulled up in front of the house, this one a sleek black Lexus. The book club women all perked up as another woman got out of the car and walked quickly toward us. Her hair was a very unnatural red in a saucy bob, and she wore a leopard print dress that clung to her body. She must have been sixty-five if she was a day, but the vibe she gave off was that of a much younger woman.

"Ladies, what's all this! What'd I miss!" she called in a sing-song voice as she got closer. She waved a copy of The Thursday Murder Club in the air as she said "all this" and the other women surrounded her and started talking at the same time.

The woman in the glasses, Evelyn, filled her in. "Linda, it's Margie. Something's happened. The police are inside."

Linda's eyes widened, and she pressed a hand to her chest. "Oh no, not Margie. What happened?"

"We don't know yet," I said, stepping forward. "I found her and called the police. They're trying to figure it out."

Linda's face paled, and she seemed genuinely shaken. She

glanced at the house, then back at us. "Poor Margie. She was such a dear. Always involved in everything."

I watched her closely, noticing the past tense she'd used. How did she know that Margie was dead? No one had come right out and said that. There was something else too, a flicker of something I couldn't quite identify. Was it guilt? Fear? I couldn't be sure, but it made me wonder what Linda knew about Margie's situation.

As we stood there, the awkwardness began to settle in again. I decided to make a move. "I need to get the sandwiches back into the van before they spoil. Would you ladies mind waiting here? The police might need to ask you some questions."

The women nodded, murmuring their agreement. I quickly grabbed the bag and loaded it back into the van, my mind racing with thoughts about what could have happened to Margie. As I closed the van door, I glanced back at the group. Linda was talking quietly with the other women, her expression serious. My mind raced, wondering what kind of relationships the women had with each other and with poor Margie. Would they know anything else that might be important? If they did, I was sure Ryan would figure it out. Warning myself about getting too involved in this thing, I walked slowly back to the group and stood just close enough to overhear their conversation without being too obvious.

But as I positioned myself to eavesdrop, the conversation was cut off by the EMTs opening the door and solemnly wheeling out a gurney with a body covered by a sheet. I moved quickly down to the path next to the other women to make way for them, and the five of us stood there in a state of shock as we watched them load Margie Belcase into the back of the ambulance. All the women began to cry softly at that moment and my heart went out to them. What a terrible thing to have happened to their little group.

Ryan stepped outside behind the EMTs with a frown and raised an eyebrow when he registered the women I stood next to. The air was thick with shock and unspoken questions. But just as

Ryan opened his mouth to speak to us, the sound of tires on gravel made us all turn.

An older model gold Mercedes sedan pulled up to the house slowly, as if the driver was unsure whether to stop. My heart raced. Who else could be arriving at this moment? And what new complications would they bring to this already overwhelming situation?

Chapter Five

The Mercedes finally came to a stop behind Linda's Lexus and we all watched and waited to see what this new arrival might bring. A moment later, a lanky red-headed man got out and awkwardly headed up the drive, a paper sack clutched under his arm. He moved with an unsure gait, his eyes darting around the scene, taking in the police car, the ambulance, and our group of shell-shocked women. He wore the most ridiculous outfit I'd ever seen. Bermuda shorts, a tank top, and Ugg boots. In the summer. I was stupefied.

I wondered if this was the nephew that the women had talked about. Despite the book club ladies' descriptions of a "shifty" character, what I saw was a man barely holding himself together. His red hair was unkempt, sticking up in places as if he'd been running his hands through it repeatedly. Dark circles under his eyes suggested sleepless nights, and his clothes hung loosely on his frame, as if he'd lost weight recently.

"What's going on here?" he asked as he reached us, his voice cracking slightly as he took in the scene. He shifted the paper sack from one arm to the other, his movements jerky and uncertain.

Ryan stepped forward, his expression neutral but firm. "Who are you?"

"I'm Margie's nephew, Hunter. I've been staying with her…" Hunter trailed off, his lower lip quivering, eyes filling with tears as they darted from Ryan to the ambulance and back again.

"I'm sorry, son, but your aunt has passed away," Ryan said, his tone softening slightly.

Hunter's reaction was immediate and visceral. He sank down to the concrete step, setting the bag beside him. As he put his head in his hands, his shoulders shaking with silent sobs, I felt a wave of sympathy wash over me. "This can't be happening. Not right now," he choked out.

I glanced into the paper sack he'd set down and saw a whiskey bottle and soda water. Glancing at Ryan, I noticed that he'd seen what was inside as well. I wondered what to make of it all. Despite the gossip I'd just heard from the book club ladies, it was hard to see this broken man as a potential murderer. An alcoholic, perhaps, or a man down on his luck. But a murderer? Then again, I reminded myself, appearances could be deceiving. I'd learned that lesson the hard way in my previous encounters with killers. I knew just how innocent they could appear.

Ryan cleared his throat gently. "I'm really sorry, but it would be a great help if you could come down to the station with me for a bit and have a chat."

I tensed, wondering how Hunter would react. Would this be the moment he revealed a guilty conscience?

Hunter lifted his head slowly, his eyes red and puffy. "I don't understand. Why do you need to talk to me? I didn't do anything."

His words sent a chill down my spine. Why would he immediately jump to defending himself? Was it just shock, or something more sinister?

"It's just routine," Ryan assured him, but I could see the slight tightening around his eyes. He was on alert, too. "We need to get

some information about your aunt and her recent activities. It will help us understand what happened here."

Suddenly, Hunter's demeanor changed. He shot to his feet so quickly he nearly lost his balance. "Are you arresting me? Am I under arrest?" His voice rose in panic. "You can't think I killed her!"

I sucked in a breath. Why would he leap to that conclusion? The book club ladies' whispers about his troubled past echoed in my mind. Maybe there was more truth to their gossip than I'd initially thought.

Ryan's frown deepened. "I never said anything about anyone killing her. Why would you think someone killed her?" He crossed his arms over his chest, waiting.

I watched Hunter closely, noting how the color drained from his face. His earlier grief seemed to evaporate, replaced by fear. "Oh, I don't know!" he backpedaled. "I just thought, you know because the police are here... You mean she wasn't killed?"

I glanced at Ryan, trying to read his expression. Was he seeing what I was seeing? A grieving nephew, or a man with something to hide?

Rather than answering the question, Ryan said, "would you rather we talked here in front of everyone? The house is being processed as a crime scene, so we can't talk in there. That leaves us with two options. We can talk here in front of everyone, and I am guessing there are some sensitive things you'd rather not discuss with the crowd..." he paused for effect and glanced at the book club women. They were all nearly salivating at the idea of being privy to so much juicy gossip. "Or we could go down to the station for a bit and have a nice private chat. I'm not arresting you, and you are welcome to drive yourself over to the station or ride with me. It's your choice. But I think it would be in your best interest if we spoke privately."

Hunter glanced longingly at the paper sack he'd set down on

the stoop, and then he nodded. "Okay, sure, Sheriff. I'll drive myself."

He grabbed his sack and headed back to the Mercedes without a second glance to the women, who were all eagerly watching the drama unfold. He settled into his seat and then slumped over his steering wheel a minute before starting the engine and heading downtown.

Ryan turned to the women. "Ladies, I'd love to have a chat with each of you as well when you have some time. No one is in trouble! I just want to pick y'all's brains and see if there's anything you know that might be helpful. If you'd be so kind as to write your names and numbers down for me, I'll be in touch." He handed Jane his opened notebook and a pen and when they were done, he gave me a quick nod. "I'll call you all later today." There was sympathy in his voice, and sadness too. Another murder in our tiny town...it was nearly unimaginable. It would be a difficult time for the Sugar Creek police force.

I gave him a small smile and nodded. He turned to the new deputy and spoke to him a minute, giving him directions about what to do with Margie's house, then returned to the cruiser.

As Hunter's Mercedes disappeared around the corner, followed by Ryan's car, I let out a breath I didn't realize I'd been holding.

"You see, I told you he had something to do with it!" the woman with the glasses said as we watched Ryan leave.

"Oh, Evelyn. We don't know any such thing. Poor Hunter seemed as broken up as any of us," the other woman replied.

Evelyn frowned, and Linda gave a sad smile. "Sarah's right. I'm sure they'll figure it all out soon enough. Poor Margie. What a way to go." She shook her head and stared down the road a moment, then turned back to the group with a mischievous grin. "Boy, that sheriff sure is a looker. Am I right, ladies?"

I blushed a deep crimson when the rest of them nodded. The

observation was oddly timed, given what everyone was clearly feeling, but pride swelled in me, knowing they were talking about my boyfriend.

"Alright, well, we better get going. I'm about to melt in this heat, y'all. See you ladies on Saturday?" Linda said.

"Wait, speaking of Saturday, shouldn't we say something at the luncheon? Some sort of tribute for Margie? Friends of the Sugar Creek Library was her baby, after all," Sarah said, her eyes welling with tears once again. "Oh, everyone is going to be so sad about this. Should we even have the event?"

"Of course we should! It's what Margie would have wanted. You all know that. We have to carry on. The library needs the money we'll be raising. A tribute to Margie is a great idea, though! Evelyn, you did such a moving tribute for Trevor last year. That slideshow you did of his archeology days was incredible. You should write Margie's, too. Maybe do a slideshow for her?" Jane said.

Evelyn put her hands up. "Oh, no. No, I couldn't. You know I don't like speaking. Sarah should do it, she is the best at speaking. And y'all know she has the most pictures. She'd be best for the slideshow."

The four of them debated for a moment, and then Sarah finally nodded. "Okay, I'll do it, but I want y'all to look over what I write before I get up there. Add whatever you want to."

The women were solemn as they said their goodbyes and made plans for the luncheon, none of them even realizing I was still standing there. The benefit of being a caterer, I supposed. I could blend in with the scenery and nobody ever noticed.

I glanced around the neighborhood as the women got in their cars and pulled away, and I was suddenly aware of the eerie quiet that had settled over Margie's street. The drama of the day had drawn an audience; curtains twitched in nearby windows, and a few curious neighbors stood on their porches, watching the scene

unfold. An elderly man across the street caught my eye, his weathered face creased with concern. I wondered briefly if he might have seen or heard something useful.

No, I scolded myself silently. *This isn't your mystery to solve, Abby. You promised yourself you'd stay out of these things.*

But even as I tried to push the thoughts away, questions bubbled up. Had any of these watchful neighbors noticed anything strange in the past few days? An unfamiliar car parked on the street, perhaps, or an unusual visitor to Margie's house?

I shook my head, trying to clear it. Ryan knew what he was doing. He'd ask all the right questions, follow all the proper procedures. My amateur sleuthing had caused enough trouble in the past. It was time to let the professionals handle this.

As I turned back to my van, I caught sight of my reflection in the window. I looked tired, disheveled, a far cry from the put-together caterer who had arrived just an hour ago, excited about a new job. Now, instead of serving a lively book club lunch, I was left with trays of food that would go uneaten and a head full of questions I had no business asking.

With a heavy sigh, I opened the van door. The smell of the sandwiches and cookies wafted out, a jarring reminder of how quickly life can change. One moment you're planning a pleasant afternoon, and the next, disaster. It wasn't something I could dwell on, though. I had a house full of B&B guests to care for and a huge lunch to cater in two days. Life continues, even when one of us departs.

I climbed into the driver's seat and cast one last glance at Margie's house. The new deputy was rolling out yellow crime scene tape around the porch and it fluttered in the breeze, a stark contrast to the cheerful flowerbeds and neatly trimmed lawn. My heart ached for Margie, for the life cut short, for the book club that would never again gather in her living room.

"I'm sorry, Margie," I whispered, starting the engine. As I

pulled away from the curb, I made a silent promise—to honor her memory by being the best neighbor and friend I could be to my own people. And that meant leaving the detective work to Ryan, no matter how tempting it might be to get involved.

Chapter Six

As shaken up as I was over finding Margie the way I did, I didn't have the luxury to wallow in sadness. I had a house full of people to care for. So as I returned to Primrose House with all the food I was supposed to have served Margie's book club, I went about the task of unloading my van as quickly as I could. Thanks to the afternoon sun, I was dripping wet and exhausted by the time I took everything back into the B&B's kitchen.

Frustration swirled up in me so much that I growled. Another senseless death! I hadn't known Margie more than a few phone conversations and one quick meeting, but I knew that she hadn't deserved to die in such a gruesome way. And now here I was, left with trays of food, an invoice that would never be paid even though I'd spent the money for supplies for the book club lunch... and a gnawing sense of guilt that I was even thinking about my business at a time like this.

I started to unpack the food from my portable bags and frowned. It was all such a waste. The sandwich tray looked very appetizing all of a sudden. I unwrapped the plastic and grabbed a chicken salad sandwich, the curry and golden raisins a bright spot

in this otherwise dark day. I frowned as I munched and threw containers of salad into the fridge. I really hated wasting food. And it really stank that I'd spent time and effort on a catering job and hadn't made anything from it. My little business was tipping toward the red more and more, especially now that I had the expense of a monthly payment for a fancy new catering van. Even this small event going south would make a dent in the meager savings I'd managed up to this point. How was I supposed to juggle running the B&B and keeping my catering business afloat if I kept stumbling into murder investigations?

As I chewed on the sandwich, an idea struck me. Instead of letting all this perfectly good food go to waste, why not set it out for the B&B guests? It would be a nice treat and might help brighten their day. If nothing else, it might get Aunt Meg's business a good review or two.

I started arranging the platters in the front room—the sandwiches, the couscous salad, and some artisanal cheeses I'd splurged on for the occasion. Then I remembered with a pang the beautiful lemon lavender cookies I'd left all over Margie's entryway in my haste to get out of there. Those were a total loss now, evidence in a crime scene.

I headed back to the kitchen for some lemon bars I'd stored in the freezer the week before. I'd made them for a different event and had a few left over. I hurried to pull them out, grateful for my habit of always having backup desserts on hand. As they thawed on the counter, filling the air with a citrusy aroma, I felt a small sense of accomplishment. It wasn't much, but at least I could salvage something from this awful day.

Wade Harper came down the stairs just as I set the tray of lemon bars out in the front room. His eyes lit up at the sight of food, reminding me of a kid on Christmas morning.

"Oh, food!" he exclaimed, setting his worn leather backpack down on a nearby chair. The bag looked like it had seen its fair share of adventures, covered in patches and stickers from places I

could only dream of visiting. "Is this up for grabs? I skipped breakfast this morning."

I smiled, gesturing towards the spread. "Help yourself, it's for B&B guests. My treat."

Wade rubbed his hands together with enthusiasm before selecting a curried chicken salad sandwich. As he took a bite, his eyebrows shot up in appreciation. "Ah, curry," he said, closing his eyes for a moment as if savoring a memory. "Always takes me back to India. I spent a year there once, trekking through the Himalayas."

My heart skipped a beat at the mention of such an exotic location. "India? The Himalayas? That sounds incredible," I said, trying not to sound too eager. "What was that like?"

Wade's eyes twinkled as he launched into his story. "Oh, it was something else. Picture this: snow-capped peaks stretching as far as the eye can see, prayer flags fluttering in the wind, and the most vibrant culture you could imagine."

I leaned against the table, completely engrossed. "What took you there? Was it for work or pleasure?"

"A bit of both, actually," Wade replied, reaching for another sandwich. "I was there with a colleague, we were looking for an artifact that nobody even believed existed. Can you imagine? Chasing a legend through some of the most remote places on Earth?"

My eyes widened, and I leaned in, hungry for stories of adventure. "That sounds like something out of an Indiana Jones movie. Did you find what you were looking for?"

Wade's expression turned wistful. "Not that first time. Or the second. We had to go back three times, actually." He paused, gazing out the front window, his mind clearly far away.

"Did you find it finally?" I asked quietly, almost afraid to break the spell of his reminiscence.

He turned back to me, a sad smile playing on his lips. "Yes, we did. But at great cost. And in the end, it didn't even matter." The

weight in his words hinted at a story far deeper than a simple treasure hunt, and I wondered what he meant by that last bit. Why didn't it matter?

I wanted to ask more, to unravel the mystery behind his words, but Wade glanced at his watch and his eyes widened. "Oh, would you look at the time? I'm late getting to the conference." He grabbed a third sandwich, this time opting for ham and Swiss. "I'll just take one for the road, if you don't mind. Not sure if I'll have time for lunch there."

"Of course, take as much as you want," I said, trying to mask my disappointment. There was so much more I wanted to know about his adventures, about the artifact, about the 'great cost' he mentioned.

He winked as he wrapped two more pieces of sandwich into a napkin, then slung his backpack over his shoulder. "Thanks a lot for the food! It really hits the spot."

I nodded. "Of course. Glad you like it. Hope you have a good day!" I tried hard to keep the disappointment from my voice. I wished we had more time to talk, more time for me to hear his stories, but it would have to wait.

Especially because, at that moment, I heard a loud pop and hiss come from somewhere upstairs and then seconds later guests running and rushing, talking and screeching, and a near stampede came down the stairwell all at once. Maria came around from the back of the house, her eyes wide, searching for me. When she found me, she rushed over and grabbed my hand, pulling me toward the stairs. "I know that sound. I think maybe it is a burst pipe."

Acid rumbled and rose in my throat as I followed her up. Sure enough, a river of water gushed out of one of the hallway bathrooms. "Oh, no!" I cried as I stuck my head inside.

Water was spewing from beneath the sink, soaking the floor and pooling around the baseboards. I quickly shut off the faucet handles, but it was clear the problem was deeper within the pipes.

The hallway carpet was already squishing underfoot and water continued to pour out of the sink and the wall.

"My suitcase is ruined!" cried an elderly woman, her face a mixture of anger and anxiety as she came out of the adjoining room with a dripping bag.

"What in tarnation is going on?" bellowed a portly man in a Hawaiian shirt who stuck his head out of one of the rooms down the hall. "I'm trying to sleep!"

The usually serene mood of Primrose House had transformed into chaos. As the air filled with the musty smell of wet carpet and the metallic tang of burst pipes, guests shuffled to and from their rooms, some of them going downstairs and others gawking nearby. The bathroom floor creaked ominously under our feet, and I silently prayed the water damage wouldn't be too extensive.

"Maria!" I yelled to her over the rush of water. "We need to find the main shutoff valve! Do you know where it is?"

"I think so," she called back and flew down the stairs, her footsteps splashing down the hallway.

Wade appeared at the top of the stairs as Maria went out the front door, his plans forgotten in the face of this new adventure. "Need a hand?" he asked, already rolling up his sleeves.

I nodded gratefully. "Grab any towels you can find. We need to try to stem this flood before it gets worse."

As Wade darted off to gather towels, I heard Maria's voice calling from downstairs.

"Abby! I found the main valve! The water should stop soon!"

Sure enough, the torrent from the pipes began to slow, finally reducing to a trickle. I let out a sigh of relief, but as I looked around at the sodden mess, I knew we were far from out of the woods.

Splashing my way back to the staircase, I saw a crowd of concerned and confused guests gathered in the front room below. Some were soaked, others clutched at their belongings, and all wore expressions ranging from worry to outright anger. Maria

went up to the bathroom with another handful of towels as I came down into the front room to address the group.

Taking a deep breath, I raised my voice. "Hey, y'all, I am so sorry for this inconvenience. We've had a pipe burst, but we've shut off the main water supply for now. We'll get this taken care of as quickly as possible, but we'll be out of water until it gets fixed."

A murmur of discontent rippled through the crowd. I held up my hands, trying to project calm I didn't feel. "I know this is frustrating. For now, if you need to use any water, I'm sure Sheila and Mark down the road at Wild Hare Winery would be happy to let you use their facilities if you need them. Just tell them I sent you."

Gradually, the guests began to shuffle out the door or back into their rooms, some grumbling, others looking shell-shocked. A few were distracted by my food spread and began to help themselves. I allowed myself a moment to slump against the banister as everyone's gaze turned from me, feeling the weight of the day and the great amount of responsibility pressing down on me. Tears began to well up. It was too much. I wasn't sure if I could keep going like this.

Maria came back down the stairs and as soon as she saw my face, she pulled me in for a hug. "Don't worry, Abby. We are going to fix this. Everything is fine."

I took a deep breath and felt the anxiety begin to recede as I hugged her back. What would I do without her?

"Thanks, Maria," I said as I pulled away and gave her a smile. Even that small moment of support really helped to clear my head. "I'll get on the phone and get us a plumber. Do you mind checking in with whatever guests are still here to see if they need anything?"

She nodded and turned to go back upstairs. As I walked toward the kitchen, I mentally began listing all the tasks ahead: calling someone to fix the pipe, prepping for tomorrow's catering job...

And then it hit me. If there wasn't water coming into the house, how in the world was I going to do the prep work for the

catering job? The anxiety whirled around again as I pulled out my phone and started to search for a local plumber who could get to our place fast.

I pushed open the kitchen door, the familiar scent of herbs and spices welcoming me like an old friend. The kitchen, where my love of cooking was born, would be the perfect place to take care of all the things that pushed down on me. The mountain of anxiety wasn't going anywhere, but at least I could deal with it in a comforting place.

Chapter Seven

It took me three calls, but finally I found a plumber who could make it over in the next two hours. After I made the appointment, I surveyed the kitchen and started to run through what prep work I needed to get done for the party. I grabbed my trusty notebook, poured myself a glass of sweet tea, and sat at the kitchen table to make a plan.

I would do two salads, a simple Caesar with homemade parmesan crusted croutons and a strawberry and goat cheese spinach salad. Two meats would make up the main entrée selection. For the first I would do a tender chicken meatball with a strawberry and ginger chutney. The second would be barbecue style baby back ribs, which I planned to cook in the oven, although I would enhance them with liquid smoke and barbecue sauce to give them a grilled taste.

I hoped there wouldn't be any die-hard grillers in the bunch. I knew from experience that Texans could get up in arms about anything called barbecue that hadn't spent time on a grill. And normally I would agree. There was nothing like a good smoke ring on a piece of meat. It had been my plan to smoke the ribs partway when I'd put the menu together for the group, but now with

everything else that was happening, there simply wasn't time for it, so oven ribs would have to do. I had already printed up labels for all the food, so I made a note to myself to create a new label, one that simply said "Baby-back Ribs" and leave off any claims of barbecue.

For the sides, I would do a classic mac and cheese and green beans almandine. And for dessert, a layered strawberry shortcake, a fruit bowl, and a tray of chocolate chip cookies. Enough for a crowd, and enough variety, I hoped, to satisfy every tastebud.

There were a lot of things I needed to do that required the water and would have to wait for the plumber—boiling pasta, washing the rest of the serving dishes from Margie's ill-fated party, washing fruits and vegetables—but there were plenty of things I could work on like sauces and croutons that didn't require the house water. I made a quick list of all those things and felt some of the anxiety fade. A plan always focused me and helped me through the anxiety that every event inevitably brought with it. I finished my glass of tea, took a few more deep breaths, and then went to the pantry and grabbed my apron to get started.

I got so lost in what I was doing that I didn't realize how much time had passed until Maria came in a while later. Looking up at the clock on the wall, I was shocked to see that it was nearly four. She glanced around the kitchen at all of my piles and dishes and frowned.

"It's time for me to leave," she told me. When our eyes met, I saw the concern in her gaze. "But do you want me to stay a little longer today? I can set up happy hour if you want me to, although most of the guests haven't yet returned, so I don't know how important it is to get done right away. Or do you need help with the catering prep? I could stay if you need me to."

I glanced at Maria's face, noticing the dark circles under her eyes and the slump of her shoulders. She was just as exhausted as I was, maybe more so. I felt a pang of guilt for even considering keeping her longer.

"No, no. You should go! I can manage," I said, forcing a smile. "You should go home and spend some time with Daniela. I'm sure she misses her mom. Besides, we'll be plenty busy this weekend. Speaking of which, I was wondering if you'd be able to come in a little early on Saturday? I wouldn't ask, except I'm going to be up to my eyeballs with this community center thing and I have to get out of here by ten."

Maria nodded. "Of course, it's no problem at all. I can be here at seven if that's early enough."

I gave her a grateful smile. "That's perfect. It would really help me a lot. I feel terrible about not being able to be here," I said, running a hand through my hair.

"Don't worry about it," she told me. "I'm comfortable taking over. And I can always call you if something goes wrong."

That was true, although with no one to help me with my catering job, I wasn't sure I would be able to do anything about it, even if Maria *did* call for my help. Not for the first time, the thought of hiring a part-time helper crossed my mind. But with my meager earnings, it just wasn't possible at present.

"Okay, then. Have a good night. And say hi to Daniela for me!" I told her.

She nodded and grabbed her purse from a shelf, then waved and headed out the door.

I sighed as I looked around at my messy kitchen. I'd brought the dishes back from the front room with Margie's leftovers a while earlier, glad to see that most everything had been eaten. Now the dishes piled around the sink, unable to be washed. I had pulled out the food processor and pans and sauce ingredients and the mess and chaos of it all overwhelmed me all of a sudden. I decided to focus on getting happy hour taken care of and get back to the catering work after that was done.

Moving back to the front room of Primrose House, I set out wine and beer and a cheese and veggie tray I'd thankfully made earlier in the morning. I cleaned up crumbs from the previous

food I'd set out and then took a minute to step out onto the front porch and catch my breath.

What a day it had been. I sat down on the porch swing and rocked back and forth a few times. Thankfully, I had the porch to myself. What I wanted more than anything was a few minutes of peace. The sun was still hot, but it was on the decline. I closed my eyes and tilted my head back, letting the rays hit my skin and warm me through. Still, I shivered when I thought about Margie's body. What had happened to her? She'd clearly been hit over the head rather than had some sort of accident because of the way she had been lying on the ground. Who had done it? And why? I pulled my phone out to check for anything from Ryan, but nothing had come yet. I knew he was in the thick of it investigating her murder, but I longed to hear his voice, to talk this all through with him. I wondered what he'd found out, and I wondered if he would tell me or if he would keep it all close to the chest this time around.

I tried to remind myself that this wasn't my concern, that I didn't need to get involved, and indeed, *shouldn't* get involved. But curiosity was a gnarly beast, one I'd never successfully controlled. I swung my legs a few more times and then stood and stretched, needing to get back to the kitchen and get my mind working on things it should be working on, rather than thinking about murder.

When I returned to the kitchen, I started with the barbecue sauce for the ribs, my favorite part of the menu. I could have used store-bought, but I liked to add my own touch to things and play with ingredients depending on what sides I planned to serve. Today I would slice up some strawberries and add them to the sauce and then use an immersion blender and a sieve to create a smooth consistency after it had all come together for a while on the stove. The sharp tang of apple cider vinegar made my nose tingle as I stirred it into a pot of ketchup, molasses, and sliced strawberries. A generous dash of Worcestershire added the umami that the sauce needed. As I added the spices—paprika, garlic

powder, mustard powder, and a touch of cayenne—the kitchen filled with a complex aroma that made my mouth water.

Once I set the sauce to simmer gently on the stove, I turned my attention to the salad dressings. The food processor whirred to life as I blended balsamic vinegar, Dijon mustard, a few more fresh strawberries, and olive oil together to make the vinaigrette for the spinach salad. After I finished, I grabbed a piece of mozzarella out of the fridge and slathered a bit of the sauce on to give it a taste. It was tangy and sweet, with a hint of complex salt at the same time —delicious.

I was just about to start on the croutons when I heard the doorbell ring and froze. I was so used to guests, neighbors, and friends coming and going whenever they wanted that the bell was a jolt to my system. Then I remembered the plumber, and I quickly wiped my hands on a towel, the lingering scent of garlic and spices clinging to my nostrils as I went to let him in.

Sure enough, when I opened the door, a tall man who looked to be in his thirties stood on the porch, a toolbox in hand and a grey work shirt with a logo of a wrench and three water drops that said "Stephenson Plumbing" below.

"Hi, I'm Brody Stephenson, Stephenson plumbing. You had a problem with your pipes?"

I beamed at him, grateful that he was about to take one of my problems off my plate. "Hi, yes. Come on in, I'll show you."

The logo on his work shirt caught my eye as he stepped inside and reminded me of something I couldn't place, something that felt important. I smiled and gestured for him to follow me up the stairs even as my mind started to churn. "Thanks for coming so soon. We have a house full of guests and I don't know what I would've done if we were out of water overnight."

"Oh, no problem, ma'am. Let's take a look."

"I'm not sure what happened," I told him as we climbed up together. "All of a sudden there was a loud pop and water started gushing out of the bathroom wall."

We made it to the bathroom, and I stepped aside to let him in.

Brody whistled low as he crouched down on his heels and pulled out a flashlight to survey the damage. "Yeah, you've got a real mess here."

Just then Wade came up the stairs with his pack slung over one shoulder. He gave me a smile and gestured with his head toward the bathroom. "Getting it sorted?"

I nodded. "I hope so."

Brody stood and wiped his hands on his pants, and as he did, he and Wade spotted each other. A strange look passed between them and I suddenly felt very uncomfortable. It was almost as if they knew each other. But the look passed quickly and Wade nodded to me and went on to his room without another word. Brody watched him go with a frown and I almost asked him if he knew Wade, but then he cleared his throat.

"Well, I've got good news and bad news," he said as he pulled a few things out of his toolbox. "Good news is, I can do a temporary fix to get your water back on tonight. Bad news is, I'll need to order a couple of parts to do a proper repair and this bathroom won't be useable until I get it fixed properly. I can come back in a day or two to finish the job, if that works for you?"

I nodded, relief washing over me. It wasn't a total fix, but we had three other bathrooms in the house and we would make do. "That would be perfect, thank you."

When I went back downstairs with Brody a few minutes later, I saw that several guests had gathered in the front room and were picking over the happy hour spread. I was glad to see they'd recovered from the plumbing incident. The last thing I wanted was for anyone to decide to leave after we'd gone through so much trouble to find everyone a room. I gave them all a thumbs up as I showed Brody to the door, letting them know that we were back in business as far as the water was concerned.

Brody stopped at the porch. "I'll get that main valve turned on

for you again before I leave. And I'll give you a call as soon as I get the right part to fix that bathroom, but it should be pretty quick."

I nodded. "Thanks so much. I appreciate it."

He headed out toward the street where the main water valve sat and I let out a breath I hadn't realized I was holding. Finally, things were starting to head in a better direction.

As I watched his truck pull away, it finally hit me where I'd seen that logo before. There had been a paper on the floor in Margie's messy library with that same logo. Was it a receipt? Had Brody Stephenson visited Margie recently? I doubted it mattered much. People had plumbers come to their home all the time. But I made a mental note to tell Ryan about it, anyway. You never knew what might be an important clue when it came to murder.

Chapter Eight

Ryan showed up ten minutes after Brody left. I'd just started cutting a boule of sourdough into cubes for croutons and I wiped my hands on my apron and pulled it off just in time for him to grab me and wrap his arms around me as he came into the kitchen. I sank into his embrace, not realizing until that moment how badly I'd needed to feel his strong arms around me. I'd been craving it all day long and now here it was, like plunging into deep water after a long desert stay.

"How's my favorite chef holding up?" he whispered into my neck. "It's been a tough day, huh?"

I closed my eyes and breathed in his manly scent. If only he knew the half of it. "It has, but I'm okay. For you too, I'm sure."

He pulled away and gave me a quick kiss as he nodded. "Not thrilled to be investigating another murder." He glanced longingly at the piles of bread on the counter and I smiled at him.

"I bet you could use something to eat. Want me to make you a sandwich?" I started to slice thick sourdough pieces and put them in the toaster before he could respond.

He nodded with a grateful smile and I turned to the fridge and pulled out some turkey breast and sliced cheese along with some

pickled onions I'd made the day before. With spicy mustard and a thick slice of tomato, it would all come together in a nice sandwich.

Ryan leaned against the counter as he watched me work and my heart pitter-pattered. I wanted desperately to know what he'd found out about Margie Belcase, but I also didn't want to ask. The last thing I needed was for him to think I was snooping again.

Luckily, he decided to fill me in all on his own. "We're almost done with Mrs. Belcase's house. We picked up an awful lot of fingerprints, but seeing as her nephew was staying with her and how often she entertained, it isn't very surprising. We're getting them all processed, but I doubt it'll lead to much. We won't know for sure what happened until we finish processing the house completely, but it looks like she was hit over the head with something heavy. She was murdered, Abby. We don't know exactly when she was hit yet either, but she probably died within minutes of you getting there."

My stomach dropped. If I'd only gotten to Margie's place a few minutes earlier, I might have saved her life. Or I might have ended up dead myself. The thought sent a shiver up my spine. I sat down slowly, needing a few minutes to process it all. Ryan put his firm hand gently on my shoulder and I leaned into his touch. "I'm sorry for all this. I'm sorry you were the one to find her."

It was all too much. Why was this happening again? It was starting to feel like groundhog day. I sighed and rubbed at my temples where a headache threatened to form. Couldn't things just be easy now and then?

Suddenly, I was overcome with the need to move. I stood quickly and grabbed the bread that had popped from the toaster and started to make Ryan's sandwich as I processed what he'd told me. He watched me silently, and I appreciated his ability to tell that I needed a minute of silence to turn it all over in my mind.

Margie Belcase had been murdered. There was no doubt now. And it happened close to when I found her. Who could have done

it? Was it the nephew? Someone else? I wouldn't even know where to start. I hoped Ryan did.

I set his sandwich down on the table and he pulled out a chair. "Do you have any idea *why* she was killed?"

He shook his head. "We aren't sure, although it looks like someone went through the library pretty thoroughly, so it might have been a robbery or someone looking for something. The nephew said that Margie's husband, who died a few months back, was a fairly well-known archeologist and had a lot of artifacts and things in his house from those days. Strangely, the lock on the back door had been picked but the front door, as you know, was left wide open as well. Not sure why someone would pick the lock on the back and then go out through the front. It doesn't necessarily mean anything, but it's a strange thing for someone to do if they were really there to steal things. You would think a thief would go in *and* out the back."

I frowned. Odd.

Ryan continued. "We talked to her nephew Hunter for a while, but he has an alibi for the morning, so we've pretty much ruled him out. He was seeing his therapist, and she confirmed that he was there."

Ryan took a bite of the sandwich and I poured us both some tea, then sat down at the table with him. "How sad, if it's true, that she was killed because someone wanted to rob her. I mean, it's sad no matter the reason, but it just seems so pointless, you know?"

He nodded and ate his sandwich for a few minutes in silence and I pondered what other reasons might lead someone to kill a defenseless older lady, but my mind wasn't ready to go there yet.

After a while we turned the conversation away from the investigation and I felt some of the sadness lift from my shoulders. I told Ryan all about the plumbing incident as he ate, probably making it more dramatic than was strictly necessary. "Oh, and I forgot until the plumber came, but I saw a paper, maybe a receipt or something? I don't know exactly, but it was on the floor near

Margie and it had the same logo on it from Brody's plumbing company. I'm sure you saw it already. Probably doesn't mean anything. But it was something I remembered from the scene, so I thought I should tell you."

He frowned. "Yes, we saw that as well. And you're right, it normally wouldn't be significant. He could have done plumbing work for Mrs. Belcase anytime. But we *did* get an interesting tip this afternoon from someone in Margie's neighborhood that he had seen Stephenson's truck nearby around the time of Mrs. Belcase's death. The neighbor thought it was suspicious because he saw someone get out of the truck and walk down the block and turn onto another street rather than go to the house he was parked in front of. Which, I agree, is mighty strange. We're looking into the company."

I frowned. That *was* a strange thing to do. "Did anyone see this person near Margie's place?"

Ryan shook his head, and we were both silent with our thoughts for a moment. Then Ryan asked, "when you got there this morning, was there anything else you saw that stood out? Anything at all?"

I thought back to the feeling I'd had as I'd arrived that something was amiss. What had triggered that thought? I couldn't figure it out. "Nothing I can remember offhand. Did Margie's nephew have anything else interesting to say?"

"Not other than the fact that he had an alibi and that he thought it might be related to his uncle's artifacts. We ran a background check on him and he's been in and out of jail a few times. There were two petty theft charges, and he's spent some time in jail. Which *is* interesting given what he said about his uncle's artifacts. But his alibi is solid enough that I don't think he had anything to do with this."

I wanted to know what he'd found out from the book club ladies also, but before I could pry further, he stood and took his

plate to the sink. "I hate to leave, I really do. But there's a lot to be done still and I need to get back to the station."

I stood, and he wrapped his arms around me again. I tried with all my might to hold on to the feeling of peace and safety I felt when he held me like this, knowing it would have to last me a while.

"Thanks, Abby. I love you."

The last words slipped out as if he'd said them a million times, but this was a first. I caught my breath, and he did too, both of us realizing just what had transpired. He seemed as surprised as I was. I had no idea how to respond.

He pulled away quickly and gave me a beautiful dimpled smile and grabbed his hat from the barstool he'd set it on earlier. "I'll call you later."

Just before he walked out of the kitchen, I shook myself out of my stupor. I went quickly to him and pulled him back in for a kiss. "I love you, too."

A massive shift had just taken place between us and I knew we both felt it. After a moment we let each other go, but I ached so much for him that it was hard to do. I smiled and held his hands as we walked out to the front door.

We were just about to kiss one last time when Cassie burst through the door, Cocoa right at her heels. "I heard what happened. This is craziness, sister! You are like a dead body magnet!" She immediately realized her enthusiasm was a little misplaced and toned it down, pulling me in for a hug. I leaned heavily on her, needing the embrace more than she knew. Between Margie's death, the botched catering job, and the pipe upstairs, I was just about all out of gas. Between her and Ryan, I felt like I would be okay for the rest of the day at least.

Cocoa danced around our feet until I stooped to pet him and I laughed as he covered my chin with kisses.

Ryan cleared his throat and gave her a look, a look that seemed to say *you two better stay out of this*. "I've got to go, but I'll call you

later, Abby. Let me know if you remember anything else or if you need anything."

I nodded, giving him a grateful smile and a quick kiss. Our eyes held one another a moment longer. "Thanks, Ryan. I will."

He smiled to us both before heading out the door, leaving me and Cassie alone in the quiet aftermath of the day's chaos.

I blew out a breath as I watched him go, wishing he could stay for a while longer, not ready for our big moment to be over yet. But I knew he had plenty on his plate, as did I. I turned back to Cassie, a crazy grin on my face.

"What? You look happy as a hog in mud! What's got you so satisfied?"

I leaned into her, still feeling off-kilter and dreamy. "Ryan told me he loved me just now."

"Eek!" she cried. I shushed her and leaned over to peek out the window, hoping Ryan hadn't heard. He was at his car and tipped his hat with a sly grin when he saw me in the window. No doubt he knew what we were making all the noise about.

"You want some tea?" I asked Cassie as we headed into the kitchen. She hopped up onto a barstool and nodded. Cocoa took up his normal roost under the kitchen table and promptly settled in for a nap.

"What a day, Cass," I told her as I poured us both a glass and sat down beside her. "I don't even know where to start."

She patted my leg. "Well, let's start with Ryan. So he said he loved you, huh?"

I nodded and sipped my tea slowly, remembering every detail of the moment. "It was kind of funny. It was almost like it just slipped out, like he'd been thinking it a while and just forgot that he hadn't said it out loud yet." I giggled. "It felt real good."

"Did you say it back?"

I nodded. "It took me a minute. He sure surprised me. But yeah, I said it back."

"Good."

My face turned down as I remembered the rest of my day. "I found Margie's body this morning when I got there to set up the lunch I was catering for her book club," I began, my voice wavering slightly. "Ryan says it looks like she was hit over the head with something heavy. She probably died just minutes before I got there."

"I'm so sorry, honey. I can't believe this is happening again. Does Ryan have any thoughts about who might have done it?"

"Not really, but they are processing her house, so maybe they'll know more soon. Have you heard anything from Ty?"

She shook her head and kicked her flip-flop on and off. "He didn't have much time to talk. Only told me what had happened and that you were there. Again." Her eyes lit up. "What do you think? Are we gonna help them solve this one?"

I vigorously shook my head. "No way, not happening." I'd had my fill of trouble three times over already. I wasn't about to get involved in this bit of things, not any more than was necessary at least.

We talked for a while about the wedding and the pipe bursting and all the little things we hadn't gotten a chance to catch up on since our river trip the day before. But as much as I wanted to sit and gab with Cassie, I had more work to do.

"Alright, I would love to hang out all night long, but I really have to get back to it. I didn't have any water this afternoon, so I'm way behind on the prep work. But if you want to come over tomorrow evening, I should have more time, assuming I get enough done tomorrow during the day."

Cassie stood with a smile and leaned over for a quick hug. "No problem, lady. Do you need help tomorrow? I was planning to hit some sales in Fredericksburg, but I could come over for a few hours in the morning and chop vegetables or grate cheese, or whatever easy things you have left."

"No, no. I've got it. At least I think I do. Now that the water's

back on, things should be okay. But come over for a drink tomorrow night and let's talk more about wedding plans."

"And Margie Belcase," she said as she waggled her eyebrows and gestured for Cocoa to follow her.

"We'll see," I said with a laugh. I really didn't want to get involved, and yet my mind was already churning with the puzzle of it all. I doubted we could stay out of it if we tried. We headed back out to the front of the house and I gave Cocoa a good hug and a pat before they took off.

Cassie pulled out of the driveway a few moments later with a wave out the window. Cocoa hung his head out and watched me, his tongue lolling. Boy, I loved those two. And I wished tonight, at least, that I could go back to Cassie's place with them and spend the night gabbing and forgetting my worries.

But there was too much to do, and a houseful of guests that were my responsibility and so with a deep breath and a stretch I headed back inside.

Chapter Nine

Friday morning I woke with a stiff neck. I'd had a fitful night on the couch. Giving my room up to the guests who'd arrived yesterday had seemed like a good idea at the time, but I'd barely slept between the constant house noises, the worries about the event ahead of me, and the memory of finding Margie in such a terrible way.

I sighed as I willed my body to move and instead sank lower into the lumps of the decades-old couch. I still had plenty of time to deal with the catering, although I had a mountain of physical labor ahead of me and knew my poor sleep wouldn't help things one bit. But what really weighed me down was the thought of Margie Belcase.

I felt the anxiety rising, and I was tempted to give in to the stress. My mind began to spin with negative thoughts and emotions. I even had the fleeting thought that I wanted to just give up and go back to working for someone else. But as I started to descend, I caught myself. I took a few deep breaths and remembered Aunt Meg's support and enthusiasm when I'd returned with my catering business, Cassie's compassion when she took me in, Ryan's strong embrace as we'd grown closer. I closed my eyes and

smiled, leaning into the gratefulness I felt wash over me for the people I had in my life. I was so blessed, and it bolstered me. I knew that no matter what happened with the catering jobs and the B&B and the murder investigations that I had good people who cared deeply about me on my side.

It was enough to push through the darkness. And it was even enough to turn my mood around. As I grabbed my things and headed to the kitchen to get the day started, I felt excitement more than anxiety for what was ahead of me.

I ran quickly through the morning B&B tasks, champing at the bit to get started on all the prep work I'd neglected the day before because of the water issue and the chaos. There would easily be enough to keep me busy all day long, and that was barring any new surprises.

After I got the breakfast and coffee set up, I pulled out all the ingredients for the chicken meatballs I would serve at the party. Because ground chicken could be dry, I liked to add plenty of freshly grated parmesan, eggs, and panko breadcrumbs to my meatballs to help hold the moisture in. Starting with that base, the meatballs could be made with all sorts of flavors. I'd done Mediterranean meatballs with Za'atar seasoning, parsley, and garlic, I'd done Mexican inspired meatballs with cumin, cilantro, and poblano, and of course an Italian version with basil and mozzarella. For this party, I would be making a simple meatball with garlic and thyme, which I hoped would pair well with the ribs and sides. To make it special and to tie it in with the strawberry salad and barbecue sauce, I planned to make a sweet and tangy strawberry chutney to go on top.

The bowlful of ground meat was freezing cold as I started to mix it all together, but I gritted my teeth and pushed through the discomfort of it. A few minutes later, after I'd thoroughly mixed it all together, I heated up a frying pan and added a small patty of the meatball mixture and cooked it so I could check the seasoning. As I waited for it to cook through, I turned my attention to cleaning

and chopping a mountain of strawberries. I'd need them for several of the dishes I planned to prepare, so I sliced several pints and packed most of them into containers, reserving a bowl of them to make the chutney. These I dusted with a bit of caster sugar so the juices would start to release and then pulled my meatball sampler off the stove and let it cool a moment before popping it in my mouth.

It needed a bit of salt, but the flavors were already starting to meld and I nodded my head as I imagined how it would taste with the tangy sweet sauce. Sprinkling the mixture with a little more salt, I dove back in and massaged it until combined, then rolled them out and put them on parchment lined baking trays and popped them into the oven.

Maria came in as I placed the final tray to bake. She carried dishes she'd cleaned from some of the rooms in a bus tub and puffed out a breath as she put it on the counter near the dishwasher. "This group is certainly a messy one. This is only from three of the rooms." She opened the dishwasher and began putting dishes away. Between the catering work, the happy hour dishes, the room messes, and yesterday's water issue, we were in over our heads in the dish department.

"How was your night on the couch?" she asked as she scraped dishes and loaded them.

I rolled my shoulders. "Okay," I lied. "Glad it's not for too long, though."

"Do you need any help this morning?" she offered.

"I'll let you know, but right now, it's looking good."

She nodded and finished up the load of dishes and turned the washer on, then headed back out to continue cleaning rooms.

After about an hour of prep work, I hit a lull and decided to sit on the porch steps, have a much needed cup of coffee, and call Aunt Meg.

"Abby, girl! I was just about to call you! What a coincidence," Aunt Meg said when she picked up a moment later.

"Well, look at that, two great minds," I said with a laugh.

"How's my favorite niece?"

I shrugged even though she couldn't see it and leaned against the step. "I'm not too bad. Things have been a little crazy, but we've got it under control."

"Oh, no! What's going on? Should I come back?"

"No, not at all! Maria and I have everything under control. It's all good. Forget I said anything. Mostly, I just called to hear your voice and see how things were going with you."

"You can't fool me, girlie. What's going on?"

I sighed. There was no hiding things from Aunt Meg. I should've just waited to call when I had things all back to normal. But then the thought of Margie's body popped into my mind and I sighed. I wouldn't tell her about the burst pipe because it might make her come home, but I *could* tell her about Margie.

"I went to do the lunch for Margie Belcase's book club yesterday and I found her dead. Aunt Meg, somebody murdered her."

"Oh, Abby! Not again! How terrible!"

"I know. It was a shock. Ryan thinks someone hit her over the head and might have been trying to steal something."

"That's awful. She'll certainly be missed. I know she was very active in the community."

"Did you know her well?" I asked, realizing I didn't know much about Margie's history in Sugar Creek.

"I knew her in passing. We had a lot of the same friends, although she seemed to be friends with the whole town, so that isn't surprising. She and her husband were very popular."

I recalled the book club women talking about Margie's husband's funeral the day before. "Her husband? The one who passed away recently?"

"That's right, Trevor. He was quite the character, an archae-ology professor. Margie met him on some cruise she took after divorcing her husband a few years ago. There was a little hubbub

when she brought him back home only two months after her divorce was finalized, but everybody liked him so much they forgot quick enough. He died of cancer a few months back."

I wondered briefly if anyone at this big archeology conference that Wade was attending had known Trevor. And that led me to question the timing of Margie's death. Would one of the people in town for the conference have a reason to kill Margie? It was an interesting possibility, but probably nothing more than that.

"And how's everything else there at Primrose House?" Aunt Meg asked. "Maria texted me about the unscheduled guests. You got all that figured out?"

"Yep, everything's taken care of." I filled her in on how we solved the problem and we chatted a few more minutes about small things.

"Say hi to Bertie for me," I finally said as I drained my cup of coffee. It was time to get back to work.

"Will do. Keep your head up, girl. You've got this. I'll be home soon."

"No, you stay as long as you want to! Things are fine over here." I felt bad for giving her any reason at all to cut her trip short.

She laughed. "To tell you the truth, Bertie is wearing me out! That woman is like a train engine. I might need a vacation from my vacation soon. Good luck tomorrow, you'll do great as always. Love you, girl."

"Love you too, Aunt Meg." I hung up the phone and stretched in the sun for a minute before heading inside to get back to work.

Midmorning, after I pulled and cooled and packed up the meatballs and had the salad and rib prep all done, I decided to take a break and head over to visit my friend Georgie. Her gourmet food shop, Henderson's Fine Foods, was located on Main Street in the heart of downtown Sugar Creek. I needed to pick up some special goat cheese for a salad, but I also wanted to see what kind of gossip was floating around town about Margie's death and Georgie had a good pulse on the happenings around town, having grown

up in Sugar Creek and owning one of the most popular local stores.

Henderson's Fine Foods was a small, cozy shop with polished wooden floors and neatly arranged shelves lined with an array of gourmet items. The walls were painted a warm, inviting yellow, framed pictures of Sugar Creek's history hanging here and there. The scent of exotic spices greeted me as I walked in, and a display case near the cash register held an impressive selection of cheeses and cured meats.

Georgie had her long blonde hair pulled back in a ponytail and cutoff shorts and a t-shirt showed off her long lean runner's body. She grinned when I came through the door. "Well, look what the cat dragged in!"

"Hey, Georgie! I saw your mom yesterday!" I told her as she came around the counter and gave me a quick hug. My face turned down as I remembered the sad circumstances. "It was at Margie Belcase's house."

Georgie nodded, sadness collecting in her eyes as well. "It's such a shame. She and mom were real close. The whole group is broken up about what happened. Those women spent an awful lot of time together, have for as long as I've been around, at least."

I nodded. "I could tell yesterday. They were all pretty upset."

"They were," Georgie agreed. "Although they've been fighting a lot lately," she said as she straightened jars of fig jam on a shelf. "Mom's been complaining about it for months now. And I'm sure they're all feeling mighty bad about it now."

"Who's been fighting? With Margie, you mean?"

Georgie nodded. "That tight group of 'em, the ones in the book club. I guess Linda has been pulling away, and it's causing some tension. And I know Margie's husband dying put everyone in a state, too. Everyone really loved him."

That seemed like an odd thing for a tight group to get into a huff with each other about. "That's strange, don't you think?"

She shrugged. "Who knows with them? Mom said their last book club meeting kind of exploded because Margie was trying to sell some artifacts that her husband had collected over the years to make ends meet and Evelyn was all up in arms about it. I guess Evelyn was in favor of donating the stuff to the museum, where they do a lot of their charity work. The two of them went at it right there in front of everybody. Margie'd gotten an appraisal and was sure she could get some good cash and when she mentioned it, Evelyn got all in a huff and left."

I folded my arms over my chest and frowned. "Well, she must have let the beef go, because she was there with the group yesterday." I remembered the older woman, the one with glasses. She seemed mousy to me and I had a hard time imagining her fighting with anyone. But people were never as clear-cut as they seemed at first glance. I knew that the hard way. Maybe Evelyn had a mean streak.

Could that have led to her killing her friend? It was a stretch, especially for something as slight as an argument over some artifacts, and I felt bad for thinking poorly of an innocent woman. Still, Ryan might like to know what Georgie had told me.

"I don't know how serious it all was. The whole thing probably blew over a long time ago and I just didn't hear about it. Mama likes to tell me the exciting bits but isn't much on sharing the resolutions," she said with a laugh. "Anyway, let me get you what you came here for. I'm sure you've got your hands full. I heard that your aunt left for a while and you're taking care of the B&B, too. That must be a chore and a half."

I nodded, but decided to spare her the details. "We're making it work. But I have an event tomorrow and I was hoping to get some goat cheese for a strawberry spinach salad."

Georgie nodded and moved towards the cheese display. "I've got just the thing for you. This local goat cheese will pair perfectly with your strawberries." As she wrapped up my purchase, I mulled over the information she'd shared about the book club ladies.

What had seemed like a tight-knit group of friends was apparently more complex than I'd realized.

I paid and gave her a hug before saying goodbye. We promised to catch up more sometime soon, and I immediately had the idea to put together a little get-together with Cassie, Georgie, and Ellie from the bakery when things settled down some. We needed a good girlfriend catch up night.

Walking out of Georgie's shop, I shifted back toward catering plans. But as I made my way back to Primrose House, my mind kept circling back to the book club dynamics. The tension between the women, Margie's financial troubles, and her husband's recent passing all painted a picture more complicated than I'd initially thought, one that made little sense in my mind.

Chapter Ten

Unfortunately, I didn't have the luxury of free time to think about the women and their problems, so when I returned to the B&B I got straight back to work washing vegetables and trimming the racks of ribs I planned to serve, and tried to turn my mind toward the task at hand.

Later, as I was working through the mountain of dishes left over from my prep work, my phone rang. I wiped my hands and fumbled for the phone in my pocket, hoping it might be Ryan. I was only slightly disappointed when I saw that it was Brody Stephenson instead.

"Hello?" I answered. Hopefully, he was calling with good news.

"Hi, this is Brody, with Stephenson plumbing? I wanted to let you know I have the part for your sink and I can come by and fix it, if now is good."

"Sure! That would be great!"

"Oh, good. I'm actually right down the street. I can be there in about five minutes if that works for you."

I was thrilled to hear it. One more problem taken care of, and this time all the way. "That would be perfect, thank you!"

Brody arrived only a couple of minutes later. I opened the door for him with a smile. "Need me to show you where it is again?" I asked as he stepped inside.

"No, ma'am. I'm just fine on my own. Shouldn't take more than half an hour or so. I'll let you know when I'm finished."

Nodding, I watched him head upstairs and saw the Two-Step through Texas Tours bus pull into the parking lot a minute later. I waited to greet the guests as they came inside after a day of sightseeing. Most of the group looked exhausted and hot, and they headed up to their rooms. A few grabbed water bottles and sat on the couches, ready to chat with one another. After a few minutes, I left them to it and got back to my dishes.

I unloaded and then loaded the dishwasher yet again and then pulled out a couple of pineapples and started slicing them up for a fruit bowl I would serve at happy hour. I gazed out the kitchen window a few times as I did. The day had been another hot and sunny one and I noticed Aunt Meg's flowers near the side of the house had started to wilt in the late afternoon sun. I would have to take a break later and give them some water.

Once I was done with the pineapple, I turned to a cantaloupe, which I quickly peeled and diced and added to the pineapple in a massive crystal bowl I'd picked up at an estate sale with Cassie. Next was half of a large watermelon, which mostly made it into the bowl, although I snagged a couple of large juicy chunks for myself as I worked.

The fruit finally cut up and put away, I checked the clock and was surprised to see that nearly an hour had passed and I still hadn't seen hide nor hair of Brody. Frowning, I headed upstairs to check in with him, but when I got to the bathroom, it was empty. I frowned even deeper. Had he left without telling me? No, his tools were still pushed into the corner on the other side of the toilet. Where had he gone?

Peering back down the stairwell, I saw nothing out of the ordinary. Maybe he needed something from his truck and he'd gone

out front? I was about to go down the stairs to look when I heard something crash from Wade's room. I'd seen Wade leave not too long ago, so I knew he wasn't inside, but when I looked down the hall again, I realized the door to his room was slightly cracked. My heart raced, and I hesitated before peeking in. Sure enough, Brody was inside, rummaging through Wade's bag.

I pulled quickly away from the door and debated what to do. Should I confront him? I was in charge of the B&B after all, and from all signs, it looked like he was trying to rob a guest. But he was a large man and I am not ashamed to admit that I was plain old scared of him. Instead of any kind of confrontation, I flew down the stairs and pulled out my cell phone and dialed Ryan's number. Thankfully, this time, he picked up.

"Hey, can you get to Primrose House fast?" I whispered into the phone without bothering with a greeting. "Brody Stephenson, that plumber, is here, and he's broken into someone's room. I'm scared, Ryan. I don't want to confront him, but I don't want him to get away, either. What if he steals something?"

"I'll be right there, and Abby, whatever you do, do not confront him! That's the last thing I want you to do. You hear me? Let him go if he tries. We'll pick him up no matter what."

I hung up the phone and bit my lip as I waited for Ryan. To say I was a bundle of nerves was a major understatement. Glancing up the stairs and then back out to the parking lot, I willed myself not to pace in case Brody came back down. I didn't want to let him know anything unusual was happening. I didn't want him to know that I knew he'd been in Wade's room. What if he turned violent?

A new thought struck me. What if he was the one who'd killed Margie? I thought back to that paper on her floor and what Ryan had said about a neighbor reporting someone from Stephenson Plumbing acting suspicious nearby the day Margie was murdered. Maybe he'd done the same thing as he seemed to be doing now. Maybe he'd told her he would be back in a couple of days with

parts and then tried to break in and steal something from her and she'd caught him in the act and he killed her. It was totally possible, given what I'd seen upstairs. Brody was a big man. He would have no trouble whatsoever hitting Margie over the head with enough force to kill her. Or to kill me, for that matter.

My heart raced as boots clomped toward me. Frantically I looked out the window for Ryan, but he still hadn't come. Brody came down the steps, and I nearly jumped out of my skin. What should I do? Should I try to stop him? Ryan had told me not to, but I really didn't want him to get away, especially if it turned out he was a murderer. I would never forgive myself. So despite the terror that was bubbling up inside, I pasted on my best caterer smile and tried to hide my fear.

"Alright, ma'am. You should be good to go. I'll email a receipt to you, but you aren't looking at too much. It was a straightforward replacement other than the older fixtures that needed to be ordered."

I nodded and glanced quickly out the window again. Still no Ryan. "That sounds good. Thank you for your work."

He nodded and started to head out the door. "Wait!" I called, my mind racing. "Do you want a couple of lemon bars? I have some left over from yesterday."

He hesitated and, to my chagrin, also looked out at the parking lot. If he saw Ryan pull up, what would he do? Would he run? Would he confront him? Or, like Aunt Meg with our last brush with a murderer, would I become a hostage?

But he didn't see Ryan because Ryan still hadn't arrived. Brody glanced up the stairs and hitched the tool bag up on his shoulder. "That's very nice of you to offer, ma'am. But I really should get going. I have another job still I have to get to. Thank you, though."

I shrugged, and he smiled and then turned to leave, and I resolved to let him. He was big and imposing and terrifying. Thinking about him being the murderer, thinking about the possi-

bility of him seeing Ryan and turning on me was too much to bear. As he walked out the front door, relief came, but it was quickly followed by a wave of anxiety. Would Ryan find him if he left? I tried to console myself with the fact that it was a small town and he had a work truck with his logo clearly on the side. He couldn't go too far. But still. He needed to be stopped.

Where was Ryan?

Leaning into the window, I breathed hard and bit my lip as I watched Brody make his way to his truck, wishing with all my might that Ryan would arrive. And it must have worked, because just as Brody opened the side door and threw the tools inside, Ryan raced into the parking lot, his lights flashing, and skidded to a stop right in front of Brody's truck.

Chapter Eleven

I held my breath and stared out the window, watching the scene unfold. The guests who had returned came down the stairs and moved over to the window to watch with me when they heard the commotion.

"Oh, my goodness!" a pretty, petite woman with a foreign accent said. "What is happening? Is that the police?"

"It's okay," I told her. And then I didn't know what else to say. The last thing I wanted the guests to know was that someone had been inside Primrose House burglarizing rooms. People might panic. What else could I tell them, though? I improvised and hoped it was enough. "It's a city matter, I'm sure. No need to worry."

It must have been good enough because I didn't get any more questions. We all watched as Ryan and Ty argued a moment with Brody and then cuffed him and put him into the cruiser. Ty got into the driver's seat and Ryan leaned over to talk to him a few minutes before Ty pulled out of the parking lot and Ryan headed back toward the house. I moved quickly to the door and outside, hoping the guests wouldn't follow and that I would have a few minutes to speak with Ryan alone. He bounded up the steps, and I

wanted so badly to lean in for a hug, but we had an audience. He eyed the guests, who all stared out the big front window at us and motioned for me to follow him down to the side of the house where a path snaked around some rose bushes.

"Hey, honey. Ty is taking Mr. Stephenson down to the station, and I need to process the room that was broken into as a crime scene."

My face fell. This was going to upset the guests and create yet more havoc. Friday evening was a time when people should be relaxing and enjoying their vacations, but now there would be a police presence and tension over everything. I sighed and tears sprang to my eyes. What would Aunt Meg do in this situation? I was sure that she would have some clever way to diffuse the tension, but I was not nearly as skilled at running the B&B as she was.

He saw my tailspin and grabbed my hand, pulling me toward the front door. "I need to get up there and secure the room before anyone else gets in there. Come with me and tell me what you know." He gestured toward the porch and I led the way as we brushed through the crowd of guests and headed upstairs.

I spoke as we climbed up. "Brody called a while ago to finish the plumbing repair. He didn't need me to come up with him, so I went back to work in the kitchen. Eventually I noticed he'd been up there a long time, so I went to check on him and when I did, I found him in Wade Harper's room. That archeologist who's staying here, you know? The door was open a little, and it seemed like he was going through Wade's things. I don't know if he took anything, though."

"Do you know if he was in any of the other rooms?"

I shook my head. I had no idea. "The big group that's staying with us came back right after he arrived, so I doubt it. But I don't know for sure."

Ryan nodded. "And I take it Mr. Harper isn't here right now?"

We stopped in front of Wade's room and I pulled out my

master key and knocked first, then opened it for Ryan, shaking my head as I did.

"Alright," he said as he pulled a pair of gloves and several baggies out of his back pocket. "Morgan, that new deputy who just joined the force, should be along any minute to help me out. Do you mind showing him up when he gets here?"

I nodded and bit my lip as I peered inside, not sure what I was looking for, but curious anyway. From the little I saw, the room looked absolutely normal.

He gave me a reassuring look. "I'll be quick, don't worry. I know Friday night is no time for a police presence here. Try to keep everyone calm and busy as best you can. I know you know what to do. And if you don't mind, can you get this guest's contact information for me? If he doesn't show up before I'm finished, I'd like to try to track him down."

I nodded and tried to think through how I might diffuse the tension downstairs. As Ryan disappeared into Wade's room, he gave me a tight smile. I took a deep breath and then headed slowly back downstairs to assuage the curious guests. Their faces were a mix of concern and excitement as I approached.

"Hey, y'all," I began, trying to channel Aunt Meg's calm demeanor. "I apologize for the disturbance. We've had a small incident that the police are looking into, but I assure you, there's no cause for alarm. Your rooms and belongings are perfectly safe."

There were a few grumbles, but I was pleasantly surprised when most of the group nodded and headed out the door or back up to their rooms.

That having went better than I expected. I took a deep breath and headed back to the kitchen to concentrate on getting things finished for happy hour. I wanted to get it out quickly to distract everyone. And I knew the work would calm me better than anything else.

Back in the kitchen I went about happy hour prep in a daze. I couldn't believe that this was all happening. What had happened

with Brody wasn't my fault, but I couldn't help but feel like I wasn't doing my best at taking care of Primrose House. I wished more and more that I didn't have the catering job the next day. It felt like I would be a lot better off focusing on making the guests happy.

But it was too close to the event, and I was too far into the prep to cancel, not that I ever would, anyway. I would just have to be okay with being tugged in every direction possible and the anxiety that came with that. After tomorrow's lunchtime event, I could put all of my attention toward doing better at the B&B.

Setting out a few extra bottles of wine and beer to distract the guests away from Ryan's presence, I glanced around to take stock of what else I needed to set out. A few more plates and napkins would be good, and the rest of the food. As I added a serving spoon to the bowl of fruit, I noticed the new deputy at the door and moved quickly to let him in.

"He's upstairs," I told him. The man nodded and headed up, and I heard Ryan talking to him a minute later.

That chore taken care of, I finished setting everything else out for the happy hour and then wandered around the front room, lost in thought and trying to keep an eye out for Wade, who still hadn't returned. I was anxious about how he would react to his room being broken into.

Groups of guests ate and drank and talked excitedly about the things they'd done that day and all the excitement with Brody and the police. I tried to keep the happy hour stocked and cleaned up until things wound down, but as evening finally began to approach, I found myself slowing down and after a while I realized I'd been standing at the window looking out on the overgrown field next door for a very long time.

The field had been popping with wildflowers when I'd arrived in the spring to help Aunt Meg cater a wedding, a weekend that had changed the course of my life. It was strange to think that only a season had passed since I'd made my deci-

sion to come back to Sugar Creek. Some days, it felt like a lifetime ago.

A minute later, I was pulled from my thoughts by Ryan and Morgan coming down the stairs. Everyone grew quiet and watched, hoping for some tidbit of information.

"Good evening, folks," Ryan said, addressing the crowd. "Sorry for the disturbance. Nothing to worry about." He motioned with his head for me to follow him outside and we stepped out onto the porch, the wall of early evening heat hitting us as we did. Ryan turned to me as Morgan headed down to his patrol car.

"Unfortunately, without Mr. Harper here, it's hard to say what, if anything, that Mr. Stephenson took from the room. I had Morgan take plenty of pictures and I'll take Mr. Harper's statement as soon as he's available, but until then I won't know much. Sorry this happened. You've been through a lot already, I know."

I nodded and handed him a slip of paper with Wade's information on it. "It's okay. It's not your fault."

He blew out a breath with his hands on his hips and looked out at Morgan in the patrol car. It seemed like he wanted to say something else, but he paused. And then his eyes met mine, and he gave me a sweet, genuine smile. "Alright, I'm going to get back to the station and see what's up with Stephenson. As soon as Mr. Harper returns, can you have him call me?" His eyes darted to the people once again watching us in the window and he gave my hand a quick squeeze despite the stares. "Sorry I haven't had a chance to talk lately. This whole thing is probably going to make it even worse. But I'll call you as soon as I have a little time, I promise."

He gave me a dimpled smile and my heart flip-flopped as I watched him walk back to his car. His uniform fit him just right, and I didn't mind the view. I tried to wipe the silly grin off my face as I went back inside a minute later, but I didn't do it well. That man made me giddy.

"Oh, you are with the sheriff romantically, yes?" the European

woman asked as I came back inside. She waggled her eyebrows up and down. She leaned in. "He is quite the looker. Good job."

I blushed and tried to ignore the stares as I made my way back to the kitchen to get some more catering work done while the guests were distracted with happy hour.

An hour later, I put a few more containers into the fridge and wiped the counters. I'd wanted to get more done before tomorrow, but with all the excitement and craziness, I was downright exhausted and decided to be done for the day. I could get up very early in the morning and finish the rest of it.

I sighed and glanced around the front room as I walked back in, taking stock of what else I had to do before I could go to sleep for the night. The guests had moved on to do their own things. It was way too early for bed. The sun was still lighting up the sky, but my eyes drooped regardless. What I needed to do was to clean up the happy hour mess and load the dishwasher again. But I couldn't muster the energy and so instead I plopped down on the sofa.

Which is exactly where Sheila Connoly found me when she arrived a little while later. She wore a red tank top and capris and had her gray hair pulled back in a ponytail. "Hey, there, Abby! Mind if I interrupt for a bit?" She held up a bottle of Wild Hare wine with a smile.

I beamed at her as I pushed myself off the couch. "Not at all!"

I headed into the kitchen and grabbed two wine glasses. "Let's go out on the porch and see the sunset," I told her. A nice sit with a good friend was exactly what I needed to restore my energy.

Chapter Twelve

Sheila followed me through the house, nodding to the few guests who still lingered. Several of them had gathered in the front room for a chat and a few more sat at one end of the porch as we headed out, but there was a nice private space on the other side and we each grabbed a rocker. It was still warm out, but the sun setting put a beautiful golden glow on the world. I leaned my head back and breathed in deep, happy to be sitting for a few minutes.

Sheila poured us each a generous glass of her latest vintage, a crisp white that sparkled in the fading sunlight. "So, how are you holding up, honey? Between caring for this place and your catering business, I bet you're running ragged."

I sighed and took a sip of the wine. It tickled my nose and had a cool refreshing feel going down. "You're not wrong. It's been a whirlwind, that's for sure. But I'm managing, thanks to Maria's help." I thought about Brody and Margie and my face fell. "Mostly, anyway."

I took another sip of my wine before telling her about the commotion with Brody breaking into Wade's room and being arrested. As I told her the details, my mind turned it all around and

around and spun it together with Margie's death and I started to wonder again... did Brody have something to do with that, too?

"Oh, that's terrible. That's the last thing y'all need," Sheila responded and reached over to squeeze my hand. "But from the look of it the guests didn't mind too much."

I nodded. "Ryan helped me diffuse the situation some. I think a few of them like the excitement. But all things being equal I'd much rather have it quiet around here."

"And how's your Aunt Meg doing? Have you talked to her recently?" Sheila asked, taking a sip of her wine.

I nodded, feeling a pang of guilt that I hadn't called Aunt Meg more often. "We talked a bit this morning. She's having a wonderful time with Bertie. You know how those two are when they get together—thick as thieves and twice as guilty."

Sheila laughed. "Oh, I can just imagine. Those ladies probably have half of Spoonbill Bay wrapped around their little fingers by now."

"Probably," I agreed with a smile. "Aunt Meg sounded so relaxed, it made me glad she's taking this break. Though I have to admit, running this place has given me a whole new appreciation for how much work she puts in."

"I bet," Sheila said sympathetically as she pushed her rocker back and forth. "Can you believe all this stuff going on with Margie Belcase?"

I shook my head. "It's tragic. I don't know if you'd heard, but I was the one who found her."

Her eyebrows shot up. "I had no idea! I'm so sorry, Abby!"

"It's okay. I'm trying hard to keep my head down and focus on the work, but her death really has me shaken up. I can't stop thinking about it."

"Margie and I knew each other some. We went to church together and all that, but I never was very close with her. We run in different circles. She seemed like a nice enough woman, though. Not sure why anyone would want to kill her."

"Ryan thinks it might have been a robbery gone wrong."

"Oh, that's horrible! Another robbery!" Her eyebrows shot up. "You don't think it was that same plumber fellow that Ryan just arrested, do you?"

I shrugged. "It makes you wonder, right? I mean, how often do robberies occur in Sugar Creek?"

"I don't know the statistics," Sheila replied. "But two in one week sounds way out of the ordinary."

We both processed this for a minute as we watched the bees buzzing in Aunt Meg's salvia. "Thank you again for taking on a house guest to help us out. I hated to turn them away, but I couldn't split this group up," I told her.

"No problem, sugar! It's good for our business too, so no harm no foul. It takes a little getting used to, though, if I'm honest. Can't walk around in my nightgown all morning long." She tilted her head back and laughed and I laughed with her, knowing exactly what she meant. I was happy to be helping Aunt Meg out, but when it was all said and done I was looking forward to having my own place again, one where I could kick my feet up and be comfortable. My mind wandered to the predicament of where I would live after this. With Cassie engaged now, I would definitely need to find a new place to live. Newlyweds would not want an extended house guest, no matter how close Cassie and I were and no matter how much she might say otherwise.

Just as I was thinking of Cassie, the familiar rumble of her old pickup truck filled the air, along with the thumping whine and twang of a Shania Twain song. She pulled into the parking lot, kicking up a small cloud of dust, and I grinned. Cocoa's furry head was hanging out the passenger window, his tongue lolling out in a doggy smile.

"Well, look who's here!" Sheila exclaimed, raising her wineglass in greeting.

Cassie cut the engine, and before she could even get out, Cocoa had already scrambled over to her side, pawing at the

window in excitement. The moment Cassie cracked open the door, he shot out like a furry bullet, nearly knocking her off balance in his rush to get to the porch.

"Cocoa! Hold your horses!" Cassie called after him, laughing as she climbed out of the truck.

She was dressed for the warm Texas evening in denim shorts and a faded Sugar Creek Wildcats t-shirt, her curly hair pulled back in a messy ponytail. I bent down to greet the enthusiastic pup, and he nearly made me drop my wineglass as he hopped up and covered my face with wet doggy kisses. "Okay, okay, I missed you too, buddy," I laughed, scratching behind his ears as he settled at my feet.

Cassie finally made it up the steps, slightly out of breath but grinning from ear to ear. "Howdy, ladies! What's goin' on?"

Cassie plopped down in one of the rocking chairs, kicking off her tennis shoes with a contented sigh. Cocoa moved between the three of us, hungry for pets.

"You want some wine? Let me go get you a glass!" I said and started to stand, but she waved me away. "I'll go get a glass. You stay put." She went into the house and came back a minute later with a glass and handed it to me as she pulled over another chair. I poured her a glass and handed it back.

"Ty texted me that you had some commotion over here," she said as she settled in. "Something about a robbery and an arrest? He didn't have time to give me the details but told me I should come check in on y'all."

It warmed me all over to know that people cared about me enough to check in. I nodded and poured myself another glass of wine as I told the story of Brody breaking into Wade's room yet again.

"Woo!" Cassie said after she'd heard the whole tale. "You know how to keep things lively around here!"

"I try," I replied.

She laughed. "It's strange that this is happening so soon after Margie got killed because of a robbery."

"My thoughts exactly!" Sheila cried, and she too poured herself another glass.

"Hey, speaking of Margie, Ty told me some interesting things about what was taken from her house," Cassie said.

Sheila and I both perked up, our attention fully on Cassie now.

Cassie glanced around, as if to make sure no one else was listening, before continuing in a lowered voice. "You know Margie's nephew, Hunter? Apparently, he went back to Margie's house after the police were done processing it as a crime scene."

"And?" Sheila prompted, leaning in closer.

"Well, according to Ty, Hunter found several unusual things missing. Someone had taken two of the artifacts that belonged to his Uncle Trevor and two pictures that were on the bookshelves nearby. Not Margie's jewelry, which was worth quite a bit, or her cash or the electronics. Old dusty artifacts and pictures."

She leaned back and let us process this.

"Oh my," Sheila said and put a hand to her throat. "So it wasn't just a random burglary, then?"

"Doesn't sound like it," I mused, my mind racing. "Whoever took those items was looking for something very specific. Why take photographs? Unless the murder and robbery was something personal? Or unless it was to throw the investigation off somehow?"

Cassie took another sip of wine. "Ty says they're looking into it, but it definitely complicates things. Makes you wonder. Hunter doesn't remember what the pictures were of, just that they were there before Margie's death and aren't there now."

As we sat there, pondering this new information, I realized that the mystery surrounding Margie's death had once again gotten more complicated. What was the significance of the artifacts and the photographs? It made me wonder, too, just what Brody

had been searching for in Wade's things. I'd assumed it was a garden variety robbery but now I started to wonder. It clicked as I thought about it that Wade, too, was somehow involved in the archeology field. Yet another strange coincidence.

"Do they know what the two artifacts were?"

Cassie nodded. "One was some sort of ceremonial dagger that had some jewels in the handle. The other was an old jade carving that Hunter thought was very old. He said his aunt was trying to sell the carving before she died and had gotten an appraisal of it just a couple of weeks before. He and Ryan are looking into the company who did the appraisal to see if there's anything shady there."

I pondered all this for a bit as the sun finally sank below the horizon. It was interesting timing that Margie was killed after getting an artifact appraised. It added yet another complication to the puzzle.

"You know what we should do?" Cassie asked after we all fell silent a moment. I frowned. I didn't like the excitement in her voice.

I raised an eyebrow. "What?"

"We should go crash that archeology conference. See if any of them know anything about Trevor."

I shook my head even as I contemplated this idea. Would we even be allowed in? I wondered if Wade would be any help or if he might even know something himself about Trevor. I would ask him the next time I saw him. And as I had the thought, I realized he still hadn't returned. I wondered if Ryan had gotten hold of him yet.

Turning back to Cassie, I said, "that's a bad idea. You know Ryan and Ty don't want us to get involved."

"We aren't getting involved," she protested. "We're just exploring some avenues. Ryan and Ty are so busy as it is. This will help them, I'm positive."

I wasn't so sure, and I certainly wasn't willing to commit to

anything at the moment. Shrugging, I said, "I don't know. We'll see."

My eyebrows shot up as I realized Sheila hadn't heard the big news. It was the perfect thing to get us all focused on something more positive. "Sheila! Guess what happened on Wednesday?"

Cassie got a big grin on her face.

"What?" Sheila asked, leaning in for the juicy gossip.

"Cassie got engaged! Ty asked her to marry him!"

Sheila slapped her thigh. "Oh, that's fantastic! Congratulations, honey!"

"Thank you. I'm mighty excited," Cassie replied. "It's going to be a lot of work, but I'm ready for it. I'm thinking we'll have the wedding next spring."

"Such a beautiful time for a wedding, especially around here," Sheila said. "You are planning to have it in Sugar Creek, right?"

Cassie shrugged. "I hope so, although most of Ty's family is in the Dallas area. We haven't had much time to make plans yet."

"I know Dallas is big and fancy and has plenty in the way of wedding venues, but we've got several lovely choices here too," she said with a grin.

"You are so right," Cassie replied. "It might take some convincing on the part of his family, but I'm the bride, right?"

"You most certainly are!" I said, and we all laughed. After a while, the conversation lulled and the gentle creak of our rocking chairs filled the air. A couple of guests strolled past, nodding politely as they headed inside. The sky had turned a deep orange and then pink, casting a warm glow over the porch.

The three of us finished the bottle of wine and continued to talk as the sun gave up its fight for the day. Cocoa laid at our feet and pretended to sleep, although he wagged furiously every time a guest passed us. What he wanted most in life was for everyone to love him, and thankfully for him, he mostly got his wish.

I missed Aunt Meg horribly all of a sudden. She would have loved being with us all like this. I hoped she was still enjoying her

time away, although I had a sneaking suspicion that she wouldn't be able to hold off from returning to Sugar Creek for much longer.

After a while, we said our goodbyes with hugs all around. I checked the parking lot again for Wade's jeep but still didn't see it. Heading back to the kitchen, I tried to clear my head of thoughts about murder and robberies, artifacts and archeologists, but everything Cassie said swirled around and mixed with the things Georgie had told me earlier about Margie and her book club and it all made me mighty confused. My mind was full to the brim, but I tried to push it all to the side as I sat down with a glass of water and went over my catering lists for the morning one last time before going to bed. Tomorrow would be a big day, but at least I would be prepared.

Chapter Thirteen

I woke up early on Saturday with a deep feeling of dread pressing down on me. While I didn't regret hanging out with Sheila and Cassie the night before, I had a huge pile of work to do and not much time to do it. I didn't dilly-dally but got right up and changed into my cooking clothes before heading to the kitchen to get to the cooking.

I hadn't heard any more from Ryan the night before except for a quick goodnight text, and I was dying to know what was happening with Brody. Had they found out he had something to do with Margie's murder? Or was the attempted burglary all he was guilty of? As much as I wanted to know, I was determined to give Ryan some distance until he was ready to talk to me.

I'd missed Wade coming in as well. He hadn't arrived back by the time I'd zonked out on the couch, so he must have come in late.

Most of what I had to do was putting together all the pieces I'd prepped over the last two days. I pulled out my biggest stock pot right away and filled it with water and salt so I could get the macaroni and cheese going. Next, I whipped heavy cream with powdered sugar to make a topping for the desserts. Then I mixed a

massive bowl of sweet biscuit dough and started to form biscuits for the strawberry shortcake. As I formed the biscuits, sunlight began peeking through the kitchen window. I kept my mind on my work and barely noticed when Maria came in a little while later to get breakfast for the B&B guests set up.

"Good morning, Abby! Looks like you've been at it a while!"

I laughed and brushed a strand of hair out of my face, getting flour all over myself in the process. "You know it. Thanks for coming in so early today. I really appreciate it."

She smiled. "It's no problem at all. We're a team, right?"

I grinned and nodded and popped a big sheet pan of biscuits into the oven. "That's right, sister!"

We caught up for a few minutes and went over what needed to be done for the B&B that day and my plans for the catering job and then Maria headed out to the front room to get started on the mountain of things she would need to do for Primrose House.

Guests had started to come into the kitchen for breakfast and I decided to add a small basket of the biscuits to their breakfast spread, thinking it probably wasn't fair for them to smell the deliciousness but not get a taste. Just after I pulled the biscuits out of the oven, and popped a few in a basket lined with a cloth, my phone rang. I scrambled to find it then smiled when I saw that Ryan was calling me.

"Hey there, mister," I began with a grin on my face. I sat on one of the barstools and grabbed my coffee, ready to get comfy for our conversation, which was a mistake.

"Hey, Abby. Is Wade Harper there at the B&B right now?" I sat up straighter at the tone in his voice. He was all business.

I stood up and moved to the front room quickly and looked out the window at the parking lot. Sure enough, his Jeep was sitting there. "I think so. His car is here. Why?"

"I need to talk with him right away. I'm on my way over..." He hesitated and I could feel that there was something more he wanted to say.

"What?" I asked, and he growled. I raised an eyebrow and waited.

He cleared his throat finally. "I hate to say this, given your history. But it's important that I talk to him immediately. Try to keep him there if he gets a notion to leave before we get over there, okay? But Abby, honey..." he growled into the phone. "Harper may be dangerous. I know how flippant you are about danger, but this is important. I don't want you to get hurt. So try to keep him there, but not in any way that would be dangerous. Ty and I are on our way now. We'll be there in less than five."

I frowned. I wasn't flippant about danger! How dare he!

But before I had the chance to state my case, the line went dead. It was my turn to growl.

I put my phone down and gazed out at the parking lot where a few guest cars sat in the early morning sun. Why would Ryan say that Wade might be dangerous? It made me nervous suddenly, and I began to pace.

Glancing up the stairway, my heart raced as I tried to come up with ways I might stop him if he tried to leave, but hoping that he was still asleep. He had come in late last night, so there was a good chance of it. I continued to pace the front room, stealing glances at the parking lot every few turns, hoping to see Ryan's cruiser. If Wade did come down, what could I possibly say to keep him here without arousing suspicion?

Every creak of a floorboard had me on edge. When a middle-aged woman came down, one from the tour group, I nearly jumped out of my skin.

"Are you alright, ma'am?" she asked, concern etching her face. "You look as if you've seen a ghost."

I forced a smile. "Too much coffee, probably," I mumbled and turned away so she couldn't see the anxiety collecting in my brows.

As the minutes ticked by, my concern grew. Where was Ryan? What if Wade had already slipped out without me noticing? This felt way too similar to what had happened the day before with

Brody. I was not okay with this much stress! My body was going to mutiny, I was sure of it. Acid gurgled in my belly to prove it.

Just as I was about to crack under the pressure, I heard the familiar sound of tires on gravel. I rushed to the window, relief flooding through me as Ryan's cruiser pulled into the parking lot.

I let out a long breath I hadn't realized I'd been holding. Whatever was going on with Wade, it was out of my hands now. Ryan would handle it. I watched him and Ty approach the B&B and opened the door for them as they came up the porch steps. "What's going on?" I asked as they stepped inside.

"I'll tell you later," Ryan said with a quick squeeze of my hand. "Where is he?"

I shrugged. "Upstairs, probably. I haven't seen him yet today."

"Do you mind giving me the master key?"

What the heck was going on? This was getting ridiculous! Still, I nodded and grabbed the key ring from the check-in desk. "He's in room four still," I told him.

I bit my lip as I tried to decide what to do. I desperately wanted to go upstairs and see what was happening. But I didn't want to add to any commotion, and I didn't want to be in danger. Ryan's knock and voice trailed through all of Primrose House and my pulse raced. What would the guests think of this on a Saturday morning? How could I explain this new intrusion away?

"Mr. Harper. It's Sheriff Iverson with the Sugar Creek Police Department. Open the door, please."

A commotion began, and I stuck my head up the stairs to get a better look. Wade's door was open and Ryan and Ty were in the entry to it. Guests shuffled out of their rooms and gathered in the hallway. I heard a lot of muffled talking, but not much else happened until after a while, Wade came down the stairs in front of Ryan, handcuffed and looking as confused as I was. His hair was disheveled and his face wide and creased like he'd been in the middle of a dream when they'd surprised him. I heard Ty upstairs saying, "please everyone, y'all need to back up.

This is a crime scene. Under no circumstances is anyone allowed in." And then the ripping sound of crime scene tape being portioned out.

I tried not to get in the way, to let them do their work. But I was desperate for answers. "What's going on?" I asked Ryan as I followed him through the front room. "Are you arresting him? Is this about Margie?"

Ryan nodded quickly and brushed past me. He was distracted, giving a couple of other officers at the front door directions to search Wade's room...again. Ryan was in hardcore investigation mode at this point. I could tell he barely noticed me. I tried hard not to let it hurt my feelings how he'd brushed me off. Logically, I knew he had a job to do, and he didn't have time or mental energy to be my boyfriend, fill me in, or comfort me. But it hurt nonetheless.

I stayed by the window and chewed my lip as I watched Ryan walk Wade out to the cruiser. They pulled away a minute later.

"Boy, this place is nonstop action!" one of the older male guests said as he glanced out the window with me. "We live in New York City and don't normally see so much police activity at home."

Turning to him, I said, "I'm really sorry about the chaos. I promise you, it's not usually like this here..." my voice trailed off as I thought about all the other chaos and murder that had come and gone through Primrose House lately. I pasted on a friendly smile. "You should give us another try if you're ever in the area again. I'm sure it'll be quite a bit more peaceful."

"Oh, I don't mind the excitement. It's kept things a little interesting. I might've gotten sick of all the wine and the shopping otherwise. It's fun to speculate with the others about what all was going on."

I let him stand there and ponder and turned back to the kitchen. There was nothing I could do about the situation with Wade. Ryan knew where to find me if he needed me. And the

clock was not going to stop moving forward for drama. I needed to get back to the catering work.

I took a few minutes to pull my catering truck around closer to the kitchen door and loaded it up with all the chafing dishes, serving utensils, cooler bags, and other odds and ends I would need throughout the day. Luckily the community center had plates and silver and such already, so I didn't need to transport those, although it would mean a lot more cleanup at the event space than I was used to.

Once I finished with that task, I quickly mixed the pasta I'd cooked with a creamy rich four cheese sauce I'd made the day before and loaded three pans full, sprinkling the top with shredded cheddar and parmesan before covering them all with plastic wrap and popping them into travel bags. The work helped me to pull my mind away from what was happening in the front of the house and I focused as much as I could on getting the food done right. It was getting close to time for me to head out, so I started to transfer the rest of the food from the fridge to the bags as well and carried them all out to the truck.

The tangy smell of barbecue sauce wafted over me as I pulled the par-cooked ribs out of the fridge. I would finish cooking them and the meatballs over in the community center oven right before the event began, but for now I double-checked that they were wrapped tight and added them to the growing piles of food in the truck.

Between packing things in the truck and trying to clean up some of my mess, I was hot and sweaty within minutes. *Blessed air conditioning*, I thought when I finally came back inside to finish the last of my kitchen work. Wiping my hands on my apron, I took a moment to run through my mental checklist. Food? Check. Serving equipment? Check. My catering emergency kit with extra utensils, aprons, and first-aid supplies? Check. I patted my pocket, feeling the reassuring bump of my phone. I moved into the front part of the house to check on what was happening with the police.

Maria busily cleaned up the breakfast mess and, when she turned to me, I could tell she was frazzled. The officers were still upstairs, although Ryan had left with Wade some time ago.

"I've got to leave soon. Are you going to be okay here? You sure you don't want me to call Cassie?"

She shook her head and loaded a pile of coffee cups into a bus tub. "No, Abby. Thank you. Everything is fine. I'll call you if anything changes."

I hated leaving her with everything that was happening, but I really had very little choice. It was already ten by the time I hopped into the catering truck. Time to get the show on the road.

Chapter Fourteen

I tried to put Ryan and Wade out of my mind as I headed downtown. What I needed to do was concentrate on the catering job. There would be time to figure out what was going on later. The streets were mostly quiet, other than a few kids on bikes and some early shoppers strolling Main Street. It still gave me a little thrill every time I drove my new catering truck, and I turned the radio up when Fleetwood Mac came on and sang at the top of my lungs as I headed toward the community center.

Pulling up a few minutes later, I parked near the back and took a few deep breaths, trying to calm the nerves that had started to get to me. It wasn't just the catering job that had me jittery, I realized, but the idea of seeing Margie's friends again. The last time we'd seen each other had been a sad day, and I didn't want my presence to remind them of that. But there was little I could do other than try to be as cheerful as possible and get everyone focused in on the food.

Jane and Evelyn were waiting for me when I pushed through the front door of the community center a few minutes later, loaded down with food bags. The looks on their faces immediately had my heart racing. What now?

"Hey, ladies. How are you? I'm just here for the catering," I told them with a small laugh. Maybe my fears were well founded and the sight of me again so soon after what happened at Margie's house had them spooked . Maybe I needed to put them at ease.

Hi, just here to cook, not the grim reaper...

They glanced at each other and I really started to get nervous. "Abby, hi. Thanks for coming," Jane began as they motioned for me to follow them back to the kitchen area.

As we approached the back of the building, the temperature noticeably rose. Jane hesitated as we reached the kitchen door. "I'm afraid we have a bit of a situation, Abby. The air conditioning unit for this part of the building went out last night. We've got someone coming to fix it, but..."

"They won't be here until this afternoon," Evelyn finished, her lips pressed into a thin line.

My heart sank as I pushed open the kitchen door. A wave of heat hit me, and I could already feel sweat beginning to form on my brow. The kitchen, usually a place of comfort for me, suddenly felt oppressive.

"We've set up some fans," Jane said apologetically, gesturing to a couple of industrial fans in the corners. "And we'll make sure you have plenty of water."

I nodded, trying to keep my expression neutral. "I'll make it work," I assured them, even as I wondered how I was going to manage in this sweltering heat. The fans weren't doing much more than pushing the hot air around. I knew the ovens would only make it worse.

"We'll be out in the main room setting up if you need anything," Jane told me as she patted my arm, then the two women left me to my sauna and my chores.

I started up the ovens so I could warm the food and finish up cooking the ribs and then I grabbed a cart and headed out to the car for the rest of the supplies and food. Ten minutes later, I put the last of the salads and desserts in the fridge and had a hard time

pulling myself away from the open door when I was done. The heat was already getting to me and the blast of cool air was heavenly. What I really wanted to do was get out of this kitchen. Between the oppressive heat and my desire to snoop, I was determined to spend as little of this day in the kitchen as possible. I only hoped I would be able to make it work.

Filling the cart again, this time with chafing dishes, burners, and utensils, I moved back out to the main dining area where the banquet was to be held. Jane and Evelyn were there setting flower arrangements out on each of the round tables. I smiled at them but they barely acknowledged me, so I headed over to the side of the room to the set up the buffet line.

"She isn't coming? Are you sure? What about the tribute to Margie?" I heard Jane say to Evelyn a few minutes later. I tried to look like I was busy, but all my attention laser-focused on the women.

Evelyn shrugged. "I guess that man of hers is more important."

"What man? What are you talking about?" Jane replied as she straightened a dark blue tablecloth.

Evelyn's face looked contrite, as if she'd let a secret slip that she shouldn't have, but there was something I didn't trust about the way her eyes narrowed. It looked like she was about to offload some juicy gossip. I leaned in even more and pretended to mess with a burner on one of my chafing dishes, but I was desperate to hear about Linda's man.

"Oh, I shouldn't say anything..." she fiddled with a flower arrangement and looked very much like she wanted Jane to ask more.

"Come on, Evelyn. Spill it."

Evelyn leaned in and dropped her voice, but I still heard most of what she said. "...she's been seeing somebody who isn't her husband...told me all about a night they spent together...thinking about leaving her husband..."

Jane reared back like she'd been slapped. "What? Are you sure? I can't believe it. No way Linda would do something like that!"

"It's true. I saw them together over in Kerrville one day and asked her point blank. She didn't deny it."

"That doesn't mean she admitted it, though," Jane shot back.

"Margie knew," was Evelyn's cool response.

Jane went very still. "Margie knew what? About Linda, you mean?"

Evelyn nodded and replied, "I heard them talking about it. She told Linda she was gonna tell her husband if she didn't stop seeing him. It made Linda mad as a hornet. As you can imagine. You know how Linda hates anyone telling her what to do..."

The two of them walked out of the room deep in conversation and it took everything I had not to follow. I wanted to know the rest of the story, but I didn't want them to know I was listening. With a frown I let it go and went back to my catering work, but my curiosity was really eating me alive at this point.

An hour later, I was sweating profusely, but all the food was finally out for the banquet and looked delicious. I fiddled with the sauces and put a few garnishes on the platters and dishes of food as I waited for the event to get started. People had begun to stream in a few minutes before, and several of them mingled, chatted, hugged, and found their places at the tables around the room. A few of them perused my buffet line, waggling their eyebrows at me and patting their stomachs. Finally, the main presenter made a quick announcement that the buffet was open and people started to grab plates and tuck in.

I scurried around replenishing food and answering questions as the people loaded their plates. I was proud of what I'd pulled off and watched closely what everyone gravitated to and stayed away from so I could adjust things for the next buffet I catered. No matter what, I always wanted to keep learning and improving my craft and my business and the feedback of hungry people was like gold as far as improving my catering business was concerned.

When the group had finally settled in their seats, Sarah from the book group took the stage, papers in a shaky hand, and settled behind the podium. "Good afternoon, everyone. We were originally holding this fundraiser to raise money for the library expansion, as y'all know, and that is still happening! But as many of you also know, we lost one of our most cherished members of our group this week under terrible circumstances. Margie Belcase was murdered..." Her voice hitched, and she put her head down to collect herself. The room was totally silent, waiting for her to continue.

"It is such a terrible loss to our community, and especially painful after having lost her husband Trevor just a few months ago."

Out of the corner of my eye, I noticed Evelyn, who had been standing near the back of the room, turn and head out the door.

Sarah took a deep breath and continued, her voice growing stronger. "Margie was more than just a member of our community. She was its heart. For years, she poured her energy into every fundraiser, every charity drive, and every community event of the Friends of Sugar Creek Library as well as several other town causes. Her passion for helping the town was infectious, and her ability to bring people together was unmatched."

A few people in the crowd nodded their heads. Many of them were crying. "What I'll remember most, though, is her kindness. And that mischievous twinkle in her eye whenever she had a new idea to make Sugar Creek a better place.

"Margie believed in the power of community, and she lived that belief every day. She saw the best in people and brought out the good in all of us. Her loss leaves a void that won't easily be filled, but I know she would want us to carry on her legacy of compassion and service."

"So today, as we gather for this fundraiser, let's do it in Margie's honor. Let's channel her spirit of generosity and her

commitment to making a difference. Because that's what Margie would want us to do."

Sarah paused, her eyes glistening with unshed tears. "Margie, wherever you are, we miss you. We love you. And we promise to keep your spirit alive in everything we do for this community. Thank you."

As Sarah stepped down from the podium, a soft murmur of sniffles, quiet conversations, and shared memories of Margie filled the room. I noticed several people dabbing at their eyes with napkins, and even I felt a lump in my throat, despite not having known Margie well. I hoped more than ever that Ryan and his crew would figure out who'd killed Margie soon. The whole town needed closure after this senseless and sad murder.

After another minute, I turned back to inspect the buffet line and see what needed to be replenished. I wondered about Evelyn's disappearance during Sarah's speech. Why hadn't she stayed? Was it because of something Sarah had said? Or had Evelyn simply needed to leave for some innocent reason? What was going on with these women that I didn't see? I puzzled over it as I headed back to the kitchen to get a backup bowl of the strawberry chutney. Clearly, there was a lot going on under the surface. I just wondered how much of it had to do with Margie's death.

Chapter Fifteen

An hour later, the fundraising banquet had nearly come to a close, and I was hustling to keep food out for everyone who returned again and again to refill their plates. I loved that people were enjoying my food, but I also could not wait until this thing wrapped up. What I wanted most in the world was to finish this gig and get myself back to Primrose House, where I planned to take a nice cool shower and rinse the grime from my body and then have multiple cold beverages.

But for now I wiped the sweat from my brow and dug deep as I tidied the dessert station that had become a serious mess. A stooped man with a very thick middle came up to me as I was trying to stack what was left of the cookies and pointed down at his plate, which was littered with rib bones. "These ribs are out of this world, miss. Tell me, did you grill them? Or did you cook them in the oven?" His eyebrow raised at the mention of the oven and I froze.

I blushed a deep crimson, my eyes darting around. The last thing I wanted to do was get into a conversation about barbecue with this man. Thankfully, I was saved by his wife.

"Don't talk to her, Ellis! She's dating the sheriff!" the woman hissed as she grabbed his arm and tried to drag him away.

I rolled my eyes. That seemed a little overly dramatic. What did it matter if I was dating the sheriff? Evidently, my relationship status was making its way through town. Whether that was a good thing or a bad thing was yet to be determined.

He frowned. "What does that have to do with ribs?"

My thoughts exactly.

"She's probably snooping about Margie," the woman said under her breath as she shot me a dirty look and pulled her husband away. "Tina said she was snooping on Trisha's murder. You remember that? I bet she's one of his *spies*." She hissed out the last word and I shrugged. It was true, to a point, but at least I hadn't had to answer his question about the ribs.

Finally, things started to die down, and I took it as my cue to begin packing up the leftover food and cleaning the dirty dishes that would stay here at the community center. I pulled half finished trays of food out of the chafing dishes and combined what I could, then wrapped the leftovers in plastic wrap. As I was putting the chafing dishes onto the cart, I saw Evelyn, Jane, and Sarah huddled nearby in deep discussion. Slowly, I pulled my cart over closer to them, hoping I could eavesdrop on the trio a little more before the event came to a close.

"You know, now that you mention it, isn't it funny that Linda showed up late to book club on Thursday? Anyone else notice that?" Evelyn whispered with a frown.

It seemed like they were back on the subject of Linda. I got even closer, pretending to scrape two bowls of salad together.

Jane nodded, her eyes growing wide. "That's right, I forgot about that. What was it, maybe ten minutes, fifteen even after she was supposed to have arrived? That ain't like her, now is it?"

Sarah interrupted. "Oh, that don't mean anything. Are we really going to do this again?" She crossed her arms over her chest

and frowned at her friends. "She said her hair appointment went long."

Evelyn harrumphed. "Sounds slicker than a slop jar, you ask me. She wouldn't have scheduled a hair appointment so close to the book club. Uh uh, I ain't buying it."

I looked back and forth between the women, trying to gauge their feelings by their expressions, and then when I felt like I'd lingered too long, moved slowly down the buffet line so I wouldn't be noticed.

"All I'm saying is, Linda's *never* late. If anything, she's too early to everything. So why was she late getting to Margie's house on the day she died? Unless she wanted us to think that she had an alibi. I don't know. It makes me wonder if she had something to do with Margie's death," Evelyn continued.

"Oh, please!" Sarah cried. "Not a chance."

"What about that thing you told me earlier, about how she was having an affair? What if she was late because of that?" Jane asked.

"What? What affair?" Sarah cried. Just as she did, Evelyn noticed me nearby and frowned. She motioned for the other two to follow her and the three of them walked out of the dining hall. So much for my snooping going unnoticed.

I sighed and angled my cart toward the front doors of the community center and headed out to my truck. After I unloaded the things from the cart, I headed back to the overheated kitchen. The macaroni and cheese, stale bread, and smears of sauce all over the countertops stared back at me when I looked around the room. It was going to take all my energy and then some to get this job finally over with. My goal was to get the cleanup done as fast as humanly possible and get out of this inferno. I ripped off my chef coat and fixed my ponytail, then dove into the dishes with every-thing I could muster.

As I scrubbed at a particularly stubborn spot of barbecue sauce, my mind whirled with everything I'd overheard. Linda's potential affair, her tardiness to the book club meeting, Evelyn's

suspicions—it all seemed to point in Linda's direction. But maybe that was just want Evelyn wanted everyone to think. Why was she so quick to throw Linda under the bus? I wondered what the friendship between the two of them was really like. Although I doubted the women had anything to do with Margie's death, I wanted to know more about their relationships so I could understand better what was really going on.

I thought back to what Ryan had told me about Hunter's alibi, too. He'd been in therapy at the time they thought Margie had been killed. But what if the time of death was wrong? I made a mental note to ask Ryan if there had been any updates on that front. If Margie had been killed earlier or later than they initially thought, it could change everything and put Hunter back in the hot seat. Hunter as the killer made an awful lot of sense to me. Someone close to the family who was down on his luck. He would likely know his aunt and uncle well enough to know which of the artifacts would be the most valuable, too.

And then there was Evelyn herself. Why had she left during Sarah's speech about Margie? It seemed odd for someone who was supposedly Margie's close friend. And she seemed awfully eager to point the finger at Linda. Jane and Sarah were possibilities too, I supposed, if I was going to start suspecting the book group. But I'd known Jane Henderson forever and I couldn't imagine her doing a thing to hurt a soul. Although I didn't know Sarah, she seemed as mild tempered as Jane. Evelyn, though, had something brewing down deep. And Linda was a wild card that I didn't know well enough to form any kind of opinion of.

I sighed as I rinsed off a serving spoon. I was probably reading too much into things. After all, I didn't really know these women or their relationships. For all I knew, Evelyn could have been upset by the speech and needed some air. And Linda's lateness could have been exactly what she said—a hair appointment running long.

Just as I was sealing a container of ribs and piling it onto a cart

to take to the truck, a little girl ran into the kitchen. She wore a pink dress covered with tiny beads that caught the light. Her hair was in two messy pigtails, and she looked around with wide, curious eyes.

I gave her a tired smile and glanced around for my cookie stash. Grabbing a chocolate chip cookie, I bent down to her level. "Did you like the food today?" I asked her.

She stuffed half the cookie into her mouth and talked around it, dropping crumbs all over the floor as she did. "It was okay," she informed me with a frown. "The mac & cheese was way too lumpy, though. My mom says you're a big fat snoop."

I blinked, taken aback by her bluntness. She turned and ran out of the kitchen with my cookie before I could respond, which was probably a good thing, because I was sorely tempted to grab the rest of my cookie from her and throw it in the trash.

It seemed my reputation was really starting to get around. I wondered if I should try to combat it or if I was better off leaning in and being known as the town snoop. I knew Cassie would choose the latter in a heartbeat but I was still so newly back to Sugar Creek and my business was at least partially hanging on my reputation and good standing in town. What I wanted to be known for was my food, not for being a busybody.

Shaking my head, I decided to deal with that problem another day. I finished packing up the food and headed out to my van. The parking lot was mostly empty, but a few cars stilled dotted the space. I began moving the food in bags to the back of the van, huffing and sweating in the afternoon sun as I went.

As I lifted a heavy bag of utensils and threw them into the front seat, I suddenly got the eerie feeling that someone was watching me. I paused, glancing around the lot, but saw nothing out of the ordinary. The hairs on the back of my neck stood up, though, and I felt a chill despite the sweat that covered my face.

I continued loading the van. As I bent down to place a cooler on the floor of the backseat, I heard a faint rustling sound behind

me. My heart skipped a beat, and I spun around, my eyes scanning the lot.

For a moment, I thought I saw a shadowy figure at the edge of the building, but it disappeared so quickly I couldn't be sure if it was real or just my imagination. My pulse raced, and I felt a knot of anxiety tighten in my stomach. I hastily closed the van doors and locked them, casting another nervous glance around the lot, and headed back to get the rest of my things.

Halfway back to the community center, I noticed a gold Mercedes in the parking lot and my blood ran cold. It was the same car Hunter had been driving the day I'd found Margie's body.

A figure suddenly stepped out from behind a nearby truck. My heart leapt into my throat as I recognized Hunter. He looked even more disheveled than before—his red hair was wild and unkempt and dark circles hung under his bloodshot eyes. The smell of stale sweat and something stronger—whiskey, maybe?—wafted towards me on the hot afternoon breeze.

Time seemed to slow down. I became acutely aware of my surroundings—the harsh glare of sunlight on the asphalt, the distant hum of traffic on the main road, the oppressive weight of the humid air. Sweat trickled down my back, and I could hear my own rapid breathing.

Hunter's face twisted with anger and desperation as his eyes locked onto mine. The world narrowed to just the two of us in that moment, the rest of the parking lot fading away.

"You!" he snarled, pointing an accusing finger at me. "You're the one who found her, aren't you?"

I backed up into a nearby car, but he had me cornered. Frantically, I looked around the parking lot for help, but the two of us were alone.

Chapter Sixteen

Hunter took a step closer, his eyes wild, and I started to really get scared. I reached slowly for the keys in my pocket, thinking that I could at least hit him with them in my hand if I had to.

"Where is it? The carving?" he demanded. "I know you took it!"

I opened my mouth to respond, but my mind went blank and for the life of me, I could not figure out what to say. Hunter's face darkened.

"Listen," he growled, his voice low and threatening. "That carving is rightfully mine. My aunt and uncle would have left it to me. I need that money more than anybody else. I know you took it."

"I don't know what you're talking about," I told him. "I don't have any carving! When I got to Margie's house, she was already dead and whatever was taken was already gone. As soon as I found her body, I called Sheriff Iverson and no one else went into the house until he arrived. Why would I take anything if I was the one to call the sheriff?"

He frowned and took a small step back, seemingly trying to

piece together what I was saying, and I breathed deep, praying that he would believe me, would see the reason in what I was saying, and would not do anything crazy.

After a moment, he let a long breath out and ran his hand through his wild red hair. "Okay, maybe. But if you don't have it, who does?"

I glanced around, hoping someone would come outside and save me from any further threats or accusations, but the place might as well have been a ghost town. "I don't know. But I'm sure the sheriff will figure it out. I know him well and I know he's working hard. You should let him do his job."

Before he could respond, the community center doors burst open and two children ran out, chasing a third. It spooked Hunter and after one last menacing glare at me he turned and jogged back to the Mercedes. I let out a huge breath as I watched him pull out of the parking lot and fought the urge to call Ryan immediately. As much as I wanted to tell him about Hunter, I knew he had plenty on his plate already, and the truth was, Hunter hadn't really done anything more than frighten me.

No. What I needed to do was to get home, get the leftover food taken care of, take a shower, and sit down for a while. My stress level was at an all-time high, made worse by physical exhaustion. The things that I'd overheard and witnessed over the last few hours were important, and I wanted to tell Ryan everything about Hunter surprising me. But it could all wait until I didn't feel like I was about to have a heart attack.

I leaned over the steering wheel as I climbed into the truck, suddenly all out of gas. I didn't know how much more of this I could take. Who would have thought that running a catering business in a small town would be more stressful than working in an upscale Los Angeles restaurant? For the first time in a while, I found myself craving my culinary school days back in California. I'd worked my butt off then, but it had only been physically exhausting, not mentally and emotionally so much.

But I wasn't going to let myself sink into that kind of thinking. Things were better in Sugar Creek. I knew they were. I rolled my shoulders and started my truck, reminding myself once again of all the good things that had come when I'd moved home. It was enough to push through, at least. The rest of the drive home passed in a fog of exhaustion and adrenaline, and I swore to myself that after I was done with the work that had to be done, I would find a quiet corner to myself and decompress.

A while later, after I'd unloaded everything from the catering truck and gotten the leftover food put away, I checked in with Maria, but she had all the B&B business under control so I took the time to have a nice long hot shower. The warm water soothed my aching muscles, but my mind raced with everything that had happened. I couldn't stop thinking about how terrifying my encounter with Hunter had been. If he wanted to hurt me, I doubted I could do anything about it. He was so much bigger... and unhinged. There was no telling how much of a threat he really was.

I got dressed quickly and tried to call Ryan. I was dying to know what was going on with Wade and Brody. The not knowing was excruciating. And not only that, but I wanted to tell him everything I'd learned about Linda and give him the rundown of what had happened with Hunter as well. Really, what I wanted was for him to comfort me, to make me feel safe, or maybe promise to go rough Hunter up some for me. But Ryan didn't answer the phone and after leaving him a quick message, I went back to the kitchen to start on all the work I still had to do to wrap up the catering job.

The first thing I did, though, was to get a massive glass of ice water and sit at the kitchen table with my notebook. I liked to record everything about events I completed so I could look the notes over when I was planning new ones. I added details like how many pans of a given food item I'd made versus how much was consumed, added up receipts to know how much I'd spent, and

any compliments or complaints that stood out. I'd made too many ribs this time, although they wouldn't go to waste. No doubt I could find takers if I tried. The strawberry shortcake had evaporated immediately, along with two-thirds of the cookies and most of the fruit. People sure liked their desserts, and I made a note to make more for big buffet style events in the future.

After I finished making notes, I stood and stretched, then started in on the dishes. Maria came in a little while afterward. "I'm finished with my work for the day," she told me as she eyed my piles of dirty dishes. "Do you need help?"

I smiled and shook my head. "You are so nice to offer, but I'm sure you did plenty already today. Why don't you take off, go home and spend some time with Daniela? I've got things around here for the rest of the night."

"Are you sure? I won't be here tomorrow, and it looks like you have a lot to do."

I waved her away with a soapy hand. "I'm sure. I can manage this. I want you to go get off your feet and enjoy the rest of your weekend. Who knows what fresh craziness the universe will throw at us next week, am I right?"

She nodded and smiled and went to the closet to grab her purse. "Have you heard from your aunt? Do you know when she plans to come home?"

I wasn't the only one missing Aunt Meg, I realized. "No, I haven't talked to her since yesterday, but I'll let you know as soon as she tells me. Sorry she's gone and you have so much on your plate right now."

"It's okay. The overtime pay is needed and I don't mind. But it isn't quite the same around here without her, is it?"

I shook my head. "No, it isn't."

"Have a good night. Don't work too hard, Abby. The dishes will wait until tomorrow."

I laughed and nodded. "Okay. I'll see you on Monday."

Drying my hands on a dish towel, I moved to the window and

glanced out at the fading light. I'd finished yet another event and hadn't even had time to process or celebrate properly. It was a big one, and it seemed that people had been happy with my food for the most part, other than the little girl. I brushed the thought of her away quickly, knowing that my mac and cheese was nowhere near lumpy. She was probably just used to the fake boxed stuff.

Moving into the front room to check on the remains of yet another happy hour, I puzzled over my day. Wade's arrest, the catering job, and Hunter all swirled around, and I had trouble concentrating on the present. A few guests nodded and smiled at me, and I tidied and made small talk for a minute before heading back into the kitchen. The truth was, I was all out of energy and had very little left in me for small talk with strangers. Aunt Meg would have been more friendly with them all, I knew. But there was only so much I could do.

I glanced at the dishes and decided that Maria was right. They could wait. The dishwasher was running at full speed and I could load it again when it was done. But for now, I could sit down and take a nice, long breather. I poured a glass of tea, then headed for one of the kitchen barstools and plopped down with a small bowl of fruit to munch on.

A few minutes later, my phone rang, and I smiled as I saw Cassie's number.

"You would not believe the day I had, Cass," I said when I answered the phone. Leaning back into the barstool, I closed my eyes. "Ryan came and arrested that archeologist this morning and didn't tell me why, I busted my butt at that event and they didn't have A/C in the kitchen, and then Hunter, Margie's nephew, threatened me in the parking lot..."

"Whoa, sister! Slow your roll. You're makin' me dizzy! This is too much information for a phone call," she said with a laugh.

I lifted my eyes to the ceiling and gazed at a cobweb hanging there. I should have gone to get a duster and take care of it but for the life of me I could not get off my butt.

"Hey, Georgie and me were talking about going down to the Salty Dog to get a drink or two. Wanna join? Then you can tell us all about this crazy day you had."

"As much fun as that sounds, I have to stay here and mind the B&B. Maybe next time," I told her. I was a little sad I couldn't meet them out, but I was also so exhausted from my day that there was no way I wanted to go to a noisy bar and watch a bunch of goofy people try to dance and drink.

"Oh, shoot. Yeah. I forgot about that, sorry." She was quiet a moment, and I was just about to say goodnight when she perked back up. "Why don't we bring the party over to you, then? We don't need to go out. All we wanted to do was gab, anyway!"

I hesitated. As much fun as all that sounded, I really did want to check out and have a little peace and quiet, maybe read a novel in my makeshift couch-bed.

"Come on, you know you want to! We need to figure out what's going on with the arrests and the murder!"

She got me. "Okay, come on over. Bring Georgie if she wants to come. I have a pile of leftovers from the party today, ribs and such. Hope y'all are hungry!"

I hung up the phone and smiled despite the exhaustion that threatened to topple me. I figured I could sit in the kitchen with my girlfriends and gab for a couple of hours, maybe see that pooch of ours for some good furry love. When I thought of Cocoa, I texted Cassie to tell her to bring him along, too.

The B&B guests were mostly out and about enjoying their Saturday evening or already in their rooms, so we would have Primrose House to ourselves for the most part, and I didn't feel bad having some girlfriends over. We would keep things quiet... probably. And I was sure they'd leave whenever I needed them to. I found a new reserve of energy and busied myself with one more load of dishes and pulling out a couple of tubs of salad and ribs for us to snack on while I waited.

Finally, my day was turning around.

CHAPTER SEVENTEEN

Twenty minutes later, just as the night was fading into blackness, I heard a sharp rap on the glass of the kitchen door and saw Cassie and Georgie standing there beaming, Cassie holding a pitcher of what I could only guess were her famous margaritas. I grinned and let them in, and Cocoa charged me once again. I patted him, then distracted him with a meatball so I could hug Georgie and Cassie. "Thanks for changing plans for me," I told them. "Sorry I'm an old fuddy duddy tonight."

"It's no problem, honey. I didn't feel like dancin' anyhow," Georgie said with a laugh. I grabbed three glasses and handed out plates and after we piled them with salad and ribs and green beans, the three of us settled in at the kitchen table with our food and Cassie's pitcher for some much needed chitchat.

"That goat cheese was perfect, by the way, Georgie," I said before taking a big bite of the spinach and strawberry salad dotted with tangy goat cheese and rich pecans.

Georgie nodded in agreement as she tried the salad, too. "That reminds me, I had an idea that might be good for both of our businesses. What if I bring you some samples of foods I'm trying to promote and you come up with recipes and then we can either do

some tastings at my shop or I can print recipe cards with your catering business info to share with customers?"

"I love that idea! And I get the perk of getting to try your delicious ingredients!"

My mind immediately began brainstorming possibilities, and it took me a moment to switch topics when Cassie said, "okay, catch us up on the archeologist being arrested. Ty told me about Brody Stephenson yesterday, but I haven't been able to get hold of him today. Which makes sense now that I'm hearing they arrested someone else this morning. I bet they're all mighty busy right now over at the station with two arrests so close together."

"I wish I had more to tell y'all, but Ryan hasn't called me either. All I know is that they arrested Brody yesterday after he was breaking into Wade Harper's room, and then this morning they came and arrested Wade Harper too. Which is mind-boggling to me. What's the connection? But there must have been one, right? Too much of a coincidence. I'm wondering if they found something in Wade's room that implicated him in something. Maybe even Margie's death."

"Whoa," Cassie said and sipped her drink. "That's an interesting idea, especially since we're talking about someone who's involved in the archeology world like Margie's husband was. Do you have any idea yet if they knew each other?"

"No. I didn't get a chance to talk to him when he came back last night and this morning Ryan came and arrested him while he was still in bed."

"*I* want to know more about Brody Stephenson," Georgie said as she chomped down on a rib. "Cassie told me some of it on the way over, but I just can't imagine. I knew him in high school. He was always kind of a wimp but robbing his own clients?" She rolled her eyes.

"I don't have a whole lot to tell, unfortunately. He came by to fix the broken pipe upstairs and I let him go up on his own, thinking I could trust him." I blew out a breath and took a big sip

of salty and tangy margarita. "And then a while later, I realized he'd been up there for a real long time, you know? So I went up to check on him and found him rifling around in Wade's room."

"Wow, that's a pretty brazen thing to do. What if someone had walked in on him? What was he looking for, I wonder?" Georgie asked.

"I have no idea. It was strange, the other day when Brody was here for the first time, Wade came up and the two of them looked at each other real funny, like they recognized each other, but neither of them said a word so I almost thought I'd imagined it. I wonder if they did know each other or if he was just trying to steal things from whatever room, he was able to get into."

"What's the story there, I wonder, if they did recognize each other?" Cassie asked with a frown. "Why would some out-of-towner archeologist know a plumber from Sugar Creek?"

We were all silent a moment, thinking it through. "Maybe they ran into each other somewhere else? Maybe Brody has been at the conference for some reason, or around there? Or maybe all of this is totally meaningless and the look between them was nothing more than Brody assessing him as a robbery target."

It sounded as good a theory as any of the other things we'd come up with.

"Ryan said that one of Margie's neighbors saw someone from his plumbing company acting suspicious in the neighborhood the day she died, too. It's a stretch, and just because he broke into someone's room doesn't mean he broke into Margie's place or killed anyone, but part of me is wondering if he had anything to do with all that business, too."

"Oh, that's no good. You think Brody might have killed Margie?"

I shrugged and sipped, letting my thoughts wander. "It's hard to say, right? Well, Ryan has him in custody now and he knows all about this suspicious stuff that happened in Margie's neighborhood, so I'm sure he'll get to the bottom of it."

After we talked through Brody's burglary and Wade's arrest enough to satisfy us all, we switched to the topic of Hunter and I filled them in on him, surprising me at the community center. "I was so scared, y'all! He came out of nowhere and got right in my face."

"What about *him* as a suspect? You don't think he killed Margie, do you? I mean, he's the one who was closest to her from the sound of it. And he seems a little...nutso," Cassie said.

"I thought so at first, but Ryan told me he had a solid alibi, so no. I kind of wish it was. It would make more sense to me. Also, why would he accuse me of taking the carving if he was the one who killed her?"

"That's true. Well, it could still be one of the book club ladies, too, though, right?" Cassie shot a glance at Georgie. "Sorry, Georgie. Not talking about your mama, but the rest of them."

Georgie patted Cassie's leg. "It's alright, I know. And you're right, those women are up to something. They've always been a little too much, if you ask me. But I'm not sure which of them would have sunk so low as to kill her own friend, other than my mama, of course. There's no way," she said and Cassie and I both shook our heads in agreement.

"At the event today, I overheard some things about Linda. She didn't show up to the fundraiser, and it seemed like they were all bent out of shape about it. Evelyn spread some news that Linda was seeing some man on the side, and all but accused her of murdering Margie. I guess Margie knew about the affair and threatened to expose Linda if she didn't stop."

Georgie frowned. "I didn't know about this, but I'm not surprised either. Linda's always been one of those people who just seem to want more out of everything, you know what I mean? Would she be worried enough about the secret getting out to kill Margie though? That's hard to believe."

"Maybe we should go have a chat with her, see what she has to

say for herself," Cassie chimed in as she gave a piece of rib meat to Cocoa under the table.

"No way, not happening. I'm not confronting anyone else about secret affairs. Remember how that turned out last time?" I reminded her, thinking of our very first brush with a murderer. I turned back to Georgie. "What else do you know about their group? Did they all grow up here in Sugar Creek?"

Georgie frowned. "Mama grew up here and I know Margie and Evelyn did, too. Not sure about Sarah and Linda, though."

"Were they as close growing up as they are now?" Cassie asked.

"I think they had their ups and downs like any group of women. But yes, I think they were always close. I remember Margie getting divorced when I was a teenager and coming back with Trevor. It was all they could talk about for a while. I think sometimes people get so settled and so comfortable with everything being the same day after day that when someone goes and bucks the trend, it really upsets the whole thing."

I nodded, knowing what she meant. I'd seen the same plenty myself and not just in our small town. People everywhere liked to keep things a certain way once they got themselves into a groove. I wonder if Margie's bucking of the trend had anything to do with her death, although I doubted it. All that seemed very far in the past.

Finally, as the food and the drinks settled in my belly and the darkness crept into the kitchen window, the day caught up with me. I felt my eyelids begin to droop and Cassie noticed it, too. "Looks like our girl could use some rest," she told Georgie and gave her a look.

Georgie nodded, and the two of them stood and cleared the dishes away. "Thanks for the food, Abby. It was delicious as always! Don't forget about my idea about working together. I think it could be fun."

"Yes!" I replied as I stood and hugged her and then Cassie. "I'll come by next week and we can brainstorm."

I bent and wrapped Cocoa up in my arms, wishing he could stay with me for the night. I missed him so much and couldn't wait until we could be under the same roof again for more than a couple of hours. The licks he gave my chin and the wag of his tail told me he felt the same.

Walking them out to the front porch, I stood there and watched them go, contemplating the yard lit up in the moonlight. It was nearly full tonight, and bright as could be. I wished that Ryan was making progress and that he would get in touch with me. And I wished, too, selfishly, that Aunt Meg would come back soon. I was ready to be done with running both businesses. But also I simply missed my aunt and wanted her home.

Tonight, though, I was on my own, and the B&B was my responsibility. I watched until Cassie pulled onto the main road and then went back inside to finish the work that needed to be done before I could climb into my couch bed for some much-needed sleep.

Chapter Eighteen

Even though I woke up on the lumpy couch again Sunday morning, everything felt bright and fresh and peaceful. It had done me a world of good to spend some time with Cassie and Georgie the night before. I smiled as I sat up, even though I didn't have time to lie around since we still had guests in the house who needed breakfast. With no other catering job on the books until the following weekend and almost all the guests planned to check out today, I would have plenty of time to recuperate and get ahead of the game for the for what came next and that was a delicious thought. I was also mighty proud of myself that I'd made it through all the craziness without needing to call Aunt Meg home.

I was still worried about what was happening to Wade and I was even more worried that I still hadn't heard much other than a quick text check in from Ryan. It wasn't like him to be so quiet. I knew they were up to their eyeballs in police business, so I tried hard to push my frustration back and wait until he was ready to talk, but I didn't like it.

Instead of dwelling on that, I went to the guest bathroom and put myself together for the morning in a simple sundress and ballet

flats, then headed into the kitchen to get the morning chores started.

We normally served a very simple breakfast to the guests—pastries and muffins and fruit with coffee and tea—but I felt so refreshed and full of energy that I decided to do a little more, so after I got the coffeemaker going I pulled out ingredients to make a big veggie frittata.

The kitchen soon filled with the aroma of freshly brewed coffee and sizzling bacon, and I whisked eggs together with a little cream then cut up a mountain of onions, peppers, mushrooms, and zucchini. The early morning sunlight streamed through the windows, casting a warm glow on the polished countertops and when I popped my head out of the kitchen door to grab some fresh basil from Aunt Meg's garden, I was pleasantly surprised to find a cool breeze blowing. I knew it wouldn't last, but I took my time gathering herbs and pulling a few weeds in the early morning light.

I went back inside a few minutes later and started to sauté the veggies and check on the bacon in the oven. Guests trickled in and I fell into a comfortable rhythm as I refilled coffee cups, made small talk, finished up the frittata and put everything out on the sideboard for people to help themselves.

The gentle clink of cutlery and murmur of conversation filled the air as guests enjoyed their breakfast. The satisfied faces and quickly disappearing food energized me. Despite everything else going on, at least I could still provide a good meal and a welcoming atmosphere for our guests. I knew I was doing my part in helping make the B&B a success, and that really made me feel good.

After the breakfast rush was finished, I grabbed myself a cup of coffee, whisked in a little half and half, and headed out to the porch to do some quiet thinking. Ryan still hadn't called, although I'd checked my phone about a dozen times. As much as I wanted to call him, I refrained and decided to turn my thoughts to

Margie's murder now that I didn't have the catering job to distract me anymore.

But before I had time to dig into the puzzle of it all, Ed's tour bus pulled into the parking lot and I went inside to check everyone out. The group of guests that had graced us with their presence for the last several days began to descend the staircase and form a line. I turned on a smile and tried my best to work through the checkout process that was still new to me. I asked them if they enjoyed their time with us, and told them about the QR code at the bottom of their receipt where they could review the B&B for a discount on their next stay.

"It was beautiful out here. You all sure know how to keep things lively, though! Boy, I wasn't expecting so much police activity," one of the ladies told me as I handed her the receipt.

"I'm so sorry for all the commotion. It normally isn't like that around here..." I wondered just how long I could keep saying this with a straight face... "and I hope your next stay with us is much more peaceful."

After I checked them all out, the front room grew very quiet as the group went out to the bus to load up. We still had one more couple staying with us through the next week, so the place wasn't totally deserted, but after the constant commotion of a big group, it felt very quiet indeed. I took my coffee to the kitchen and warmed it in the microwave, then tidied a few things in the front room as I tried to re-acclimate to the quiet of an empty house. As much as I'd wanted a break, the silence was strange. I moved to the window, watching the last of the tour group load their luggage onto Ed's bus.

But just as the bus pulled out of the parking lot, Ryan's truck pulled in and my heart went crazy. Finally! I wasn't sure if I was angry at him for the silence, thrilled to see him, or excited to finally learn what the heck was going on, but I rushed out the door and met him at the truck as he parked.

"Well, hey there, pretty lady," he said as he opened the door

and I pulled him in for a kiss. I was mad, but that could wait. Right now, I just wanted to hold him.

He looked exhausted, dark circles under his eyes, and my heart ached for him, knowing he must have been through a lot in the last few days. His hair was damp from the shower and he wore a clean uniform, but his shoulders sagged.

"Did you get any sleep last night?" I asked, pulling him back into me for another hug, which we both needed. He leaned heavily into me another minute and then pulled away.

He sighed, running a hand through his hair. "Not much. Not enough. I'm really sorry I haven't called, honey. I know you tried to call a couple of times. I figured you'd call into the station if it was really important. It's been non-stop over there since we brought Brody in and then Wade. But I wanted to come by and update you in person before heading back to the station."

I waited, trying to keep my impatience in check.

"Brody confessed to breaking into several houses around town," Ryan began. "He's got some serious gambling debts and started stealing from his clients to cover them."

My eyes widened. "And Margie?"

Ryan nodded grimly. "He went to her house that day to steal the artifacts. He thought she was gone because her car wasn't in the drive, but *we* know that Hunter had taken the car to therapy. Brody had seen an appraisal document when he was at Margie's place for a job a couple of weeks back and knew that carving was valuable."

"But something went wrong," I guessed.

"Yeah," Ryan confirmed. "When he got there, he says he found Wade in the library with Margie's body. Brody panicked, thinking Wade had killed her and taken the carving. He says he was afraid that Wade would kill him too, and he skedaddled. But that's why he broke into Wade's room here—he was trying to steal back the carving. He said he'd waited until he saw Wade leaving the B&B to come fix the pipes."

I felt my head spinning. "So Wade...?"

"We had to bring him in too," Ryan said. "Brody's accusation is serious, and there's evidence placing Wade at the scene. But," he added, seeing my dejected expression, "we're still investigating. Nothing's certain yet. He has a story that seems to make sense, but we won't know for sure until we hear back about some things."

I nodded, trying to process it all, trying not to be frustrated by the vagueness of 'some things.' He seemed to register my frustration because he gave me a half smile. "We *did* hear back about the time of death," he said, grabbing my hand. "She died a little earlier than we originally thought, about an hour before you got there, so there was no way you would have been able to save her. I know you were feeling bad about that."

My eyes lit up. "So, does that mean Hunter could have been responsible?"

"No, he's still covered by his therapy session. But it widens the possibility of who killed her somewhat." I supposed that meant one of the book club women, Linda perhaps, could have been responsible, too. It wouldn't take much in our small town to go to Margie's place, kill her, and then get back home in time to leave again for the book club. I blew out a frustrated breath.

Ryan reached out and pulled me into him, nuzzling my neck. "I know it's not easy being kept in the dark. I wish I could tell you everything, I do. But I've got to balance keeping you informed and maintaining the integrity of the investigation. It's my job."

I nodded and put my cheek on his chest. He stroked my hair. "Hunter surprised me in the parking lot yesterday, accused me of stealing the carving," I told him.

He pulled away and looked at me with alarm. "Did he hurt you? Did he threaten you?"

As much as I would have loved to have Hunter arrested too, I shook my head. "I think he just wants the carving back. He didn't do anything much other than accuse me."

Ryan put his hands on his hips and looked off into the

distance. "I'm sorry I didn't answer your calls yesterday. That must've been scary for you. I want you to call me if you so much as see him again, okay? I don't want him anywhere near you. I'll pick up if I'm able, I promise."

I nodded, and he pulled me back into him. "I hate that I haven't been here for you."

"It's okay. I know you're doing your job." All of my frustration and anger at him melted away as he kissed me. This was simply the way it was going to be with him. I knew that now. His job was important, and it would very often have to come first. It was a fact, whether I liked it or not.

"I've got to get back," he whispered. "But I'll call you later, I promise."

I nodded and gave him a kiss. "I love you," I told him, blushing. It still felt strange to say.

He grinned and kissed me once more before climbing into his truck. "I love you too, Abby. Be careful, alright? I'll be in touch again as soon as I can."

I went back inside where it was nice and cool and wandered through the house thinking about what Ryan had told me. Brody and Wade had both been at Margie's house the day she was murdered. And Brody said he'd seen Wade with Margie's body. So this had to have been after she was killed. It was fairly obvious that Wade was guilty. What other explanation could there be? Brody was a petty thief, but Wade could be much more than that. He could be a murderer.

It made my heart hurt to think about. There was something about Wade from the very beginning that I'd liked. Maybe it was my own desire for adventure, how much I'd enjoyed his stories, or the way his eyes twinkled with excitement when he'd told me about the Himalayas. He had such passion and bravery to go out and make that kind of life happen, a life that I could only dream about. How could that same man be responsible for killing

Margie? Why would he risk throwing all of that away for some artifacts?

My mind went back to Hunter and what he'd said. He had accused me of taking the carving, but not the other things. And I thought too about what Cassie had said, that there were multiple things stolen, not just the carving. Did that mean something?

Another question played on my mind suddenly. Could it be that the killer was not the same person as the thief? We'd assumed that the killer had also been the one to take the things from Margie's house, but now that I'd had the run-in with Hunter it got me thinking about other possibilities. But no, it sounded way too complicated.

Keep it simple, Abby.

They were all interesting theories, but the truth was, I didn't have any idea which one of them was right, and I probably wouldn't know until Ryan and his crew figured it all out.

What I *could* have some control over was my catering business. Now that the community center job was finished, it was time to get back to work looking for new gigs. I had a couple of small things over the next few weeks, but not enough to keep the money flowing, especially after losing the money for Margie's gig on Thursday. I'd need to go pound the pavement again, see if it was possible to drum up some more business.

I thought again about the technical school I'd visited a while back. I still hadn't heard from them and made a note to give them a call and check in. Summer was always tough for caterers and I needed to go the extra mile if I was going to make it through to the holiday season.

I sighed, resting my forehead against the warm glass as my mind wandered back to Margie and Wade and I stood like that a good long while without getting any closer to understanding what had happened.

Doing my best to put it all out of my mind, I went into the kitchen and poured myself a glass of tea then grabbed a fat stack of

Food and Wine and *Southern Living* magazines I hadn't had a chance to read and headed out to the cozy blue armchairs in the front room. What I really wanted to do was lose myself in new recipe ideas. But my mind kept circling back to Wade, to Margie, to the web of connections I couldn't quite unravel.

Just as I started to finally dig into a delicious article on smash burgers, I heard the familiar rumble of Cassie's old pickup truck pulling into the driveway. So much for a quiet afternoon of recipe browsing. I put the magazine down and headed to the porch to wait for her, eager to tell her all about Brody and Wade and see what she knew that I didn't. But I could tell by the look in Cassie's eye as she bounded up the porch steps that she was on a mission and I was equal parts worried and excited.

"Abby, I've got an idea!" she told me as I opened the door for her. I could tell by the excitement on her face that I was in for trouble. I grinned and let her in.

Chapter Nineteen

"The archeology conference!" Cassie said as she came inside and fanned herself. "Boy, it's hot. You got any tea?"

"What about the conference?" I asked, as we headed to the kitchen.

"We should go over there and see if we can find anybody to talk to who knows Wade or might have known Trevor."

I frowned and pulled out a pitcher of tea and poured us each a glass. I doubted we would learn very much that we didn't already know. But it wasn't like I had much to do. "I don't think so..."

Cassie cut off my protests. "Now is the perfect time! Let's go over to the Bluebonnet Hotel and poke around, ask a few questions. If anyone knows about Wade's connection to Margie and Trevor, it'll be those folks."

"I can't just leave, Cass. I'm the only one here. I have to take care of the B&B."

"Oh, do y'all still have guests? Sorry, I didn't realize." She listened for a minute and I sighed.

"No, the last of them other than Wade checked out today. But

we could get someone in off the road or a last-minute reservation any time. I don't feel comfortable leaving the place empty."

"What about Maria?"

"It's her day off and she's worked so hard lately. I couldn't possibly ask her."

"I could see if Mandy would come and watch the place for a while." It felt a little reckless leaving a teenager in charge of an entire B&B, but it wasn't like I was going to Bermuda and technically, since Wade was still in jail, we didn't have any guests at the moment.

"Okay, but I don't want to be gone for long." She'd already started texting before I even finished my sentence. Fifteen minutes later, Mandy arrived, and I walked her through what to do while I was gone, which was mostly just to call me if anyone at all showed up.

"Alright! Woo! Let's shake a leg, sister!" Cassie said as she headed toward the door, talking a mile a minute. "Who knows? We might uncover something crucial. At the very least, we'll learn more about Wade and Trevor's history."

She was right. There might be something interesting to learn and I knew Ryan and Ty were probably too busy to work this angle. At least it helped me justify what we were about to do. "Alright, alright. Let me grab my purse."

As we cruised down Main Street in Cassie's old pickup, the charm of Sugar Creek on a lazy Sunday afternoon enveloped us. The sun-dappled sidewalks were dotted with couples strolling hand in hand, and the sweet scent of jasmine vines wafted through the open windows. I kicked off my sandals and propped my feet up on the dash, feeling the warmth of the day seep into my bones. For the first time in days, I started to relax.

"So, have you thought any more about your wedding dress?" I asked, glancing over at Cassie.

She grinned, her eyes sparkling with excitement. "Actually, I

was thinking we could take a trip to Austin soon. Maybe make a whole weekend of it?"

"Ooh, that sounds fun!" I replied, already imagining the adventures we'd have. "We could hit up some of those fancy boutiques, maybe grab dinner at a new farm-to-table place I keep hearing about. Once Aunt Meg gets back, I should be able to take some time off."

"Speaking of which, any word on when she plans to grace us with her presence again?"

I shook my head. "Last time I talked to her, she was starting to sound homesick though, so I'm guessing it won't be too much longer."

On the other side of town, we hit the highway and crossed over it to the Bluebonnet Hotel, which had been around for as long as I could remember. It was a two story stucco affair and had bright turquoise shutters and trim and plenty of Esperanza and salvia out front to accent the antiquated hotel.

"You sure this is where the conference is?" I asked as we pulled into the parking lot. There were only a couple of cars parked there and the place felt like a ghost town, not what I would expect of a hotel that was hosting a conference.

"I'm sure," Cassie said as she leaned over the steering wheel and squinted out at the empty parking lot. "Shoot, I think we're too late."

"Well, we're here. We might as well go check it out."

We pushed through the glass doors into a lobby that looked like it hadn't changed since the Nixon administration. The place smelled faintly of cigarette smoke and furniture polish, with a hint of musty carpet underneath. We looked around, but the lobby was totally deserted and then Cassie pointed to a sign hanging on the wall.

"There it is," she said, and we headed back toward some conference rooms. The place was as deserted as Primrose House had been, and I doubted we were going to be successful.

"What you gals lookin' for?" a grizzled older man wearing a leather vest over a denim long-sleeved shirt asked us a minute later when we stuck our head into a small conference room.

Cassie and I glanced at each other. "We heard there was an archeology conference being held here."

"Yep, you're too late by a mile. Conference was over an hour ago. Everybody's left."

"Shoot," Cassie said. "We were hoping to…"

What were we hoping to do, exactly? I wasn't totally sure, but I decided to improvise and see where it got us.

I stepped all the way into the room and gave the man a friendly smile. "I had the pleasure of meeting Wade Harper recently and I wanted to come over and see if I could learn more about him and his work from people who might know him better."

"Oh, did you now? Quite the character, huh? Yeah, Wade was here, but I heard he got himself arrested over that bit with Trevor's wife." He trailed off and sadly shook his head and then he leaned in and gave me a good stare, then pulled back and looked at me again. "Oh, you're that gal who's dating the sheriff, right? The one with the food?"

I blushed and nodded, not sure if he saw this as a good thing or a bad thing.

"That sheriff of yours done hung the wrong horse thief. Wade and Trevor were like brothers, even when they were fighting. *Especially* when they were fighting. He loved Margie too. I know the three of them were as close as they come. There's no way he killed her to get to Trevor's stuff. I won't believe it."

I nodded and frowned. "That's what we thought too, after meeting him. But you know, it isn't much to go on. We were hoping we could learn more about Wade…and Trevor… anything that might help Sheriff Iverson and his team figure out the truth."

"Well, there isn't anything to learn here," he said and waved to the empty room. "But if you want, we can head back over to the museum. I can show you a few things. Those two collected quite a

bit over the years. We even have a whole display dedicated to Trevor's work."

Cassie and I looked at each other. Would this lead to information we wanted, or an afternoon at the mercy of an obsessive old history buff who had to show us every coin and bullet from his civil war collection?

Cassie shrugged. "Sure, sounds like fun."

His face lit up, and I got a bad feeling about the rest of my Sunday.

"You can follow me if you don't know the way. It's just west of Main Street," he told us as we headed out the doors of the old hotel.

Of course, we already knew where the museum was, both of us having grown up in Sugar Creek. But we nodded and followed his dusty old blue pickup truck to the other side of town and pulled into a spot next to him when we reached the single story sprawling building. The heat beat down on us as we all made our way to the entrance.

"Normally we're closed on Sundays. But since I'm the director, I can do whatever I please," he said with a great deal of satisfaction as he pulled a key ring out of the pocket of his jeans. I could tell it was a position he cherished.

Before we headed inside, he stuck out his hand, which Cassie and I took turns shaking. His grip was strong and sure. "I'm Artie Lancaster, by the way. Curator here at the museum, have been for nearly thirty years."

"Nice to meet you, Mr. Lancaster. I'm Cassie Divine, and this is Abby Hirsch."

Artie waved a hand dismissively. "Just Artie, please. Mr. Lancaster was my father, and he was a stuffy old coot." He winked at us and then turned on the lights near the door. The shadowy darkness was lit up by display lights, illuminating glass cases filled with an eclectic mix of local history and archaeological finds.

"Now, let me show you ladies around. We might not have the

Smithsonian's budget, but we've got some real treasures here in Sugar Creek."

As we stepped further inside, the cool air and musty smell of old books and artifacts surrounded us. "This museum's been here since 1952," Artie said, his voice taking on a reverent tone. "Started as just a single room in the old library. Now look at us—three whole galleries and a research center to boot."

As we moved through the museum, Cassie's eyes widened at a particularly ornate Native American headdress. "Wow, all these artifacts must be worth a fortune," she mused, leaning in for a closer look.

Artie let out a hearty chuckle. "Oh, you'd think so, wouldn't you? But here's a little museum secret for you." He glanced around conspiratorially, as if checking for eavesdroppers in the empty museum. "Most of what you see here? They're replicas."

I raised an eyebrow, surprised. "Really? But they look so authentic."

"That's the idea," Artie said with a wink. "We've got some talented artisans who make these replicas. The real McCoys are tucked away in our climate-controlled storage unit. Can't risk damaging the originals, you know. Plus, it's a great deterrent for would-be thieves."

Cassie nodded, impressed. "That's pretty smart. I guess you can't be too careful with historical artifacts."

"Exactly," Artie agreed. "Now, Trevor's donations are a different story. Those are all authentic—he insisted on it. Said the public deserved to see the real thing. But we take extra precautions with those, as you can imagine. I'll show you his things in a minute."

Artie led us through the galleries with the enthusiasm of a kid showing off his favorite toys. We passed cases filled with arrowheads and pottery shards, old photographs of Sugar Creek's founding families, and even a restored Model T Ford that had apparently been the town's first taxi.

"And here," Artie said, gesturing grandly to a wall covered in black and white photos, "is our Wall of Fame. Every notable person who's ever set foot in Sugar Creek."

I scanned the faces, recognizing a few local legends and even a movie star or two. But my eyes were drawn to a familiar face near the center—Trevor Belcase, grinning widely as he held up what looked like an ancient piece of pottery.

"Ah, I see you've spotted our local Indiana Jones," Artie said with a knowing smile. "That's where our real adventure begins."

Artie's eyes lit up as he began to speak about Trevor. "Trevor Belcase blew into town a while back with Margie. She'd been away and returned with this dashing archaeologist on her arm. Caused quite a stir, if you can imagine."

He led us to a display case filled with various artifacts. "Trevor was a godsend for our museum. Donated dozens of pieces over the years, always had a story to tell about each one."

Pointing to a weathered ornamental box in the case, Artie continued, "This here? Trevor and Wade Harper found it on their first expedition together in the Himalayas. Those two were as close as two men could get, I reckon. Trevor told me that they'd been digging together for nearly forty years. Wade comes to Sugar Creek from time to time to visit Trevor. Although not anymore, I suppose." A sadness crept into the old man's face. "He wasn't here for the funeral, which was a surprise. But I suppose he was off doing something in some far corner of the world."

Artie's expression brightened suddenly. "You know, we were supposed to get more of Trevor's collection. Evelyn Brooks, you know, the one who's in that book club with Margie? She's a regular volunteer here at the museum. She was trying to convince Margie to donate more of Trevor's things to us. Evelyn was very passionate about preserving Trevor's legacy. I think she was a bit of a fan girl, if I'm being honest."

I exchanged a quick glance with Cassie. "Oh? Did she say which things of Trevor's specifically?"

Artie frowned and shook his head. "No, but from the way she talked, I expected it to be a big donation. But I know Margie was coming on hard times after Trevor passed, so it surprised me that she wouldn't try to sell his things. As much as we would love to have more of Trevor's artifacts, I wanted Margie to be okay financially, too. I'd planned to go over and talk to Margie about the whole thing myself, but I never got a chance."

His voice trailed off, and I nodded sadly.

"Anywho... I'd better be getting home. The missus is going to start to think I'm doing something I shouldn't." He laughed as he started walking us back toward the front. "I'm glad you ladies took the time to see some of our local history! Come on back anytime and bring your friends!"

CHAPTER TWENTY

"Well, that was informative," Cassie said as she pulled on her sunglasses when we stepped out into the afternoon sun a few minutes later. I nodded and slid my own shades on. Boy, was it hot.

We were silent as we climbed in the truck and backed out of the museum parking lot, each of us lost in our own thoughts. I replayed everything Artie had said about Trevor and Wade and Margie. Why was Evelyn so obsessed with Trevor? I felt like I needed to understand that story more. Maybe talking to Georgie's mom, Jane, would help.

Cassie veered over two lanes and turned sharply toward the store as we passed, pulling me out of my thoughts and causing me to nearly topple in the truck seat. "Cassie! Jeez, you nut! What are you doing?"

She grinned at me as she pulled into a parking spot. "I got an idea. I think we should go visit Margie's nephew. Maybe he knows something about Evelyn wanting to donate Trevor's things. Come on, lady, light a shuck!"

I sighed as I climbed out of the truck and followed her inside. She was on a mission, and it was tough to keep up with her. "What

are we going to do that for? I don't ever want to see that crazy guy again! He terrified me yesterday!" I slowed to a stop. "And why are we at the store if we're going to visit Hunter?"

She turned back and grabbed my hand, pulling me toward the section of premade meals near the produce aisle. "We're going to take him some food. He's grieving, right? So let's bring him some food and then when he's off his guard, maybe we can do a little snooping. And I can ask him point blank why he threatened you yesterday."

"Ugh," I replied as I slowed down. This was not at all what I wanted to be doing with my day off. "I don't want to confront him!"

"I didn't say *you* would confront him. I said *I* would confront him."

"I don't want that either."

People in the store were watching us and I realized our argument was getting a little too loud. "I don't want to do this, Cassie!" I said under my breath.

"Come on, Abby! We need to figure things out. I want to know why he threatened my best friend. And I want to know what he knows about Wade and Trevor and Evelyn. If he's looking for the artifact and blaming you for taking it, he probably isn't the one who killed Margie and stole the stuff, right?"

"Unless he only did the killing part and somebody else took the stuff." Now that the theory was out of my mouth, I started to think more seriously about it. If Hunter didn't steal the carving and Brody got to the house too late to steal it, as he said, then there were two major candidates in my mind—Wade and Evelyn. I doubted any of the other women in the book club would want Trevor's things, either to donate or to sell. But Wade had a good reason, and Brody had seen him at the crime scene. And Evelyn clearly had an obsession with Trevor and his things.

But then who killed Margie? Could it have been Linda trying to keep the secret of the affair? This seemed doubtful. Besides, it

felt like too much of a coincidence that Margie would be killed and then, on the same day, probably around the same time, someone *else* would steal artifacts from her. No, this theory wasn't feeling right either. I blew out a frustrated breath and followed Cassie slowly as I continued to think.

Cassie ignored my lost-in-thought expression and picked through the oven ready meals. "What do you think he would like?"

"I don't know, whiskey or gin?" I deadpanned and then sighed and pulled out my ponytail and ran a hand through my hair. "Get him the King Ranch Casserole. Everybody likes that."

Cassie nodded and grabbed a family pack of the cheesy tortilla laden casserole and headed to the checkout so fast I almost had to run to keep up with her. "Why are you moving so fast, woman? It's Sunday morning, for crying out loud and I'm still sore from yesterday," I complained as I caught up to her at the checkout. She grabbed a pack of gum and two Dr. Peppers and threw them on the conveyor with the casserole.

"I want to get over there before he skips town."

I rolled my eyes. "If he hasn't skipped town by now, why would he at all?"

"You never know," she said as she smiled at the clerk, thanked her, and grabbed her bag.

Back in the truck, she popped a Dr. Pepper and handed me one too. I wasn't big on sodas, but after all the running around we'd done in the summer heat, it was mighty refreshing. I guzzled it down as Cassie screeched out of the parking lot and I tried my best to keep my balance and catch my breath.

"Now...where am I going?"

I knitted my brow and pointed her in the direction of Margie's place. Ten minutes later, she pulled to a very abrupt halt as I pointed to Margie's house. The grass was long and weedy and several newspapers littered the drive. Clearly, Hunter wasn't big on maintenance.

Cassie bounded up the walk, casserole in hand, while I hung

back, suddenly fascinated by a crack in the sidewalk. My heart raced as she rang the doorbell, her face set in a determined grin.

After what seemed like an eternity, the door swung open violently, revealing a disheveled and angry-looking Hunter. His eyes landed on me, and I swear I could see steam coming out of his ears.

"You!" he snarled, pointing an accusing finger. "What are you doing here?"

Why was he so mad at me? He couldn't think I had anything to do with what had happened to Margie, still, could he?

Before I could stammer out a response, Cassie thrust the casserole forward like a shield. "We just want to talk to you for a few minutes," she said, her voice sticky sweet. "Mind if we come in?"

Hunter's nostrils flared and his eyes narrowed as he looked from Cassie to me and back to the casserole. I could almost see the gears turning in his head as he weighed his options: slam the door in our faces or accept the peace offering of cheesy chickeny goodness.

Finally, he stepped back with a grunt. "Fine. But make it quick."

The place had been transformed from the tidy home where I'd found Margie only a few days before. Empty beer bottles littered the coffee table, and takeout containers were strewn across the kitchen counter. The library was still in disarray from the police search, papers scattered across the floor just like they'd been when I found her body.

Hunter led us into the living room, clearing a spot on the couch by sweeping a pile of crumpled newspapers onto the floor, and then he plopped down and crossed his arms with a frown. Cassie set the casserole on the coffee table, deftly moving aside a half-empty bottle of whiskey.

"You really scared her, you know," Cassie said, her voice firm as she gestured towards me. "It's not cool to scare my best friend like that."

His whole demeanor changed suddenly, like a little kid who was being scolded. His eyes darted around the room, not meeting either of our gazes. "Sorry," he mumbled. "I didn't mean to do that. I thought you took the stuff. I thought maybe you killed her."

"Why would you think that?"

"Well, you were here! You were the one who was alone with her. Everybody else showed up after."

"I was here to cater her book club meeting. I never even met Margie in person, only talked to her a few times over the phone and I certainly had no idea about any artifacts, valuable or not. I'm the one who called the sheriff. I'm *dating* the sheriff. Why on earth would I steal from her?" My fear had turned to anger. How dare he intimidate and accuse me!

Hunter's shoulders slumped suddenly, and he looked much more vulnerable than he had at the door. "I just... I loved my aunt. She was the only one who ever believed in me, you know?" His voice cracked slightly as he continued. "I've had a hard life. Made a lot of mistakes, got in with the wrong crowd. But Aunt Margie, she saw something in me that nobody else did."

Hunter's eyes glazed over, lost in memory. "When I hit rock bottom, she took me in. Gave me a place to stay, helped me get into therapy. She was helping me turn my life around, one day at a time." He looked up at us, his eyes brimming with unshed tears. "And now she's gone. I feel like I've lost my anchor."

He ran a hand through his disheveled hair. "All these things are missing, including that artifact she was planning to sell. I thought... I thought if I could find it, maybe I could use the money to start over somewhere else. Do something with my life that would make Aunt Margie proud." He shook his head, a bitter laugh escaping his lips. "Instead, I've just made a mess of things. Again."

Hunter looked directly at me, his expression a mix of shame and desperation. "I'm sorry I scared you. I just... I don't know

what to think or who to trust anymore. Without Aunt Margie, I feel lost."

My anger gave way to sympathy as I started to see how much mental anguish this man was in. This wasn't a hardened criminal, this was a lost soul grasping at straws.

"We understand," I said softly. "That's actually why we're here. We want to help figure out what happened to Margie. And we thought maybe you could help us understand a few things."

He glanced out the window a minute and then nodded, standing up and heading back toward the library at the front of the house.

"Can you tell us about Wade and Trevor? Do you know much about their relationship?"

He shook his head. "I didn't know my uncle Trevor all that well, honestly. He and my aunt married after I was already an adult and I wasn't around much..." his voice trailed off and his face turned down. I worried we were going to lose him in nostalgia, but after a minute, he looked back at us. "I didn't even know much about the Wade guy until the police asked me about him yesterday."

So he wouldn't be able to add anything to the Wade angle.

"What can you tell us about the things that were stolen?" Cassie asked.

He moved to the bookcase in the center of the room, where an empty shelf caught my eye. "I noticed right away that things were missing," he replied, gesturing to the empty spot. "Uncle Trevor had a lot of stuff, so I don't know what all exactly was stolen, but I know this spot here was dedicated to some trip he took to the Himalayas. That's where that carving and the dagger were. And two pictures too."

"Do you know what the pictures were of?" Cassie asked.

"One of my uncle in the Himalayas with his friends. Another one of just Uncle Trevor on some hiking trip. And I don't know why someone would take the pictures! It doesn't make sense. But

who knows with people? Maybe the murderer wanted a memento or something?" He shuddered as he said it and I did the same. What a terrible thought.

"Other things could have been taken too, I don't know. But those things stood out because they were always so prominent in here, you know? I think they were Uncle Trevor's prized collection, his favorite memories."

He ran a hand through his hair. "I wish I had more to tell you, but that's all I know. I really have no clue what happened to it all. I thought it was you." he pointed at me and laughed. "But I guess I'm no detective."

I shook my head, and then after a minute, I raised my eyebrows at Cassie and she nodded. "Thanks for your time, Hunter. We'll let you get back to your day. I'm sorry about your aunt."

He cleared his throat. "I'm sorry I scared you yesterday."

I nodded, and we headed toward the door. "Thanks for stopping by," he said as he let us out. "I hope you all figure things out soon. This town is too crazy for me. Can't wait to get out of here."

Cassie and I grinned at each other. Sugar Creek *was* crazy, in a way. But it was just our kind of crazy. As we headed down the path to the truck, I was surprised to see Evelyn coming up it to the house.

"Who's this?" Cassie whispered as we got closer.

"That's Evelyn, one of the book club ladies."

"The one who keeps trying to finger the nephew and the cheater? Weird that she's here." I swatted her side so she would shut her trap before Evelyn heard us.

"Oh, hi, Evelyn! What are you doing here?" I asked as we got closer. Evelyn's eyes darted around the neighborhood before coming back to us.

She patted the casserole dish. "I thought I'd bring Hunter something. He just lost his aunt, after all. It's the right thing to do."

"That's thoughtful of you," I told her. Seemed we weren't the

only one with good ideas. I wondered if, unlike us, she was there out of the goodness of her heart, or if she too had ulterior motives.

"What are *y'all* doing here?" she asked, clearly suspicious of us.

"Same as you, bringing sustenance to the grieved," Cassie replied. I could feel her getting riled up beside me, and I grabbed her arm and hustled her to the truck before she could start anything. The last thing we needed was to raise suspicions with the book club crowd. If they thought we were snooping, our ability to pry into their problems would go up in smoke.

"Have a good day!" I called back to her as we got to the truck.

CHAPTER 21

"I don't know what you thought about that," I said as we got back into the hot truck, "but it seems like we can cross Hunter off as a suspect for sure."

I watched as Evelyn rang the doorbell and then Hunter let her in. *What was she up to?*

Cassie nodded as she turned the key in the engine and pulled away from the curb. "That poor man is just a mess. I hope he is able to find his way, eventually."

We were silent on the way back to Primrose House, both of us thinking through all we'd learned. I knew Ryan was still working on things with Wade, but after talking to Artie, I highly doubted Wade had killed Margie. He might have taken the artifacts, but I had a hard time believing that he would have killed Margie for them.

With Hunter and Wade largely off the list of suspects, it seemed suddenly that the most likely possibilities for who killed Margie were the women in her book group. It was an ugly thought that Margie had been killed by one of her own close friends, but more and more it felt like truth to me. But which one? And why?

Cassie pulled up to the front porch and let me out. "I have

some stuff to do back at the shop, but let's powwow again tomorrow," she said with a grin. "I don't know how you're feeling, but I think we're on a pretty good roll."

I nodded my head, glad we'd gone out and talked to a few people. I felt like our adventures had led to a lot more clarity. The only question was how to make Ryan see it all, too. "Bring Cocoa by tomorrow. We don't have any guests planned for a couple of days, so it should be fine to let him roam."

She nodded and waved as she pulled away. I went inside and after briefly confirming with Mandy that no, nothing at all had happened at Primrose House since I'd left, I paid her for her time babysitting the empty house and let her go.

The house was incredibly quiet after she left, and I was brimming with energy after our outings. I went quickly up to the rooms and started stripping beds and gathering towels. The whole place didn't need to be spotless, but I wanted to see how much I could get done before Maria came back. She'd worked so hard lately, I hoped to lighten her load.

Once the washing machine was running, I headed into the kitchen and pulled out my catering notebook, wanting to see what I had to work on. Unfortunately, my catering calendar was mighty sparse. I sighed and looked over my notes again, and tried to decide what to do next.

I'd wanted to expand into sweets more for my business, especially after nearly running out of desserts at the event over the weekend, but pastry had never been a strong point for me. So I decided to use the downtime to work on a few recipes with Ellie's baby shower in mind.

Directionless recipe testing could be fun, but it always helped to have some event to point my experiments toward. I also wanted to create some things that would photograph well for my website. The current state of my site was minimalist at best, just a couple of sample menus, a short about page, and ways to contact me. I knew

that pictures, and maybe even a social media account, would get me more business.

I wandered around a while, looking at the ingredients we had in the fridge and the pantry, and then started to get some ideas. Poking around on the internet I found a couple of interesting recipes I liked and thought about ways of changing them or combining them to make something unique for my own business.

An hour later, I threw a couple of round cakes into the oven. They were a simple butter cake that I'd added orange blossom water to. I planned to fill the center with a citrus cream made from a cream cheese type frosting dotted with lemon, orange, and grapefruit zest. The citrus brightened the whole place and lifted my mood. It would be the perfect cake for Ellie's baby shower.

Late in the afternoon, as I was folding towels, I got a text from Ryan. "I have a little time tonight. Want to come over for dinner? We could get takeout."

"Yes! But I have to stay here to watch the B&B. Do you mind coming over here? I'll order a pizza," I responded immediately, my heart thumping wildly. I was absolutely giddy about the idea of actually sitting down with my man for an extended period, hugging him, catching up with him... and catching up with his investigation. I wanted to know exactly what they had on Wade, what the "things" were they were looking into, and run some of my theories by him. I only hoped he would cooperate with my plan.

He agreed and said he'd be over a little after seven. I went back to the kitchen to do a little more work on the cake, and then I hopped into the shower and spent a good amount of time making myself pretty. I even curled my hair a little, luxuriating in the fact that I had enough free time to do it.

I was so glad Ryan and I would be able to spend some time together in person. I felt like we'd barely seen each other lately and I needed to see him, feel his arms around me, even if only for a few

minutes. That big L word hovered between us, but I hadn't had a chance to enjoy our new relationship development.

Not only that, I wanted to know what was happening with the investigation and Wade Harper. I couldn't imagine him having killed Margie. He was so interesting and had seemed so kind. I hated to think that he may be responsible. And I wanted to talk it through with Ryan and try to convince him of what was so clear to me.

I ordered the pizza and put a few more touches on the cake and iced it, then tried to arrange a few curls of zest on top and took a few photographs. I was no camera whiz, and I knew my pictures probably weren't anywhere near internet worthy, but I tried my best. Once I started making more money, I would hire a photographer to get some better pictures, but for now, this was as good as it got.

Ryan walked in as I was readjusting a few tiny bead shaped sprinkles on top of the cake. "Whoa, looks serious," he said with a grin. "Seriously delicious, that is."

I put my tweezers down and went over to give him a hug. He wrapped me in his arms and I nearly melted into him. "Thanks for coming over. I've been missing you."

"I've been missing you too," he said as he nuzzled my neck.

The pizza arrived a few minutes later, and we loaded our plates and sat at the kitchen table. Our local pizza place was incredible. Whatever they did with the crust was out of this world—it was chewy and crisp in all the right ways and the freshly made sauce was tangy and full of herby flavor. I realized as I tucked into a slice that I'd forgotten to eat for most of the day. We'd been so busy traipsing through town that other than the Dr. Pepper, I'd barely had anything. I sighed as the food started to go down, and Ryan grinned.

"Good stuff, huh?"

I nodded and took another bite.

"This is better than anything I ever had in Dallas. Sugar Creek is constantly surprising," he told me.

We ate for a few more minutes and I wondered how I should broach the topic of the investigation. Ryan seemed content to keep it personal and enjoy my company. But I wanted to talk about murder. After we finished, we cleaned up our plates, and I put the pizza box in the fridge, then we headed into the front room to sit on the couch and look out the big front window at the setting sun.

"Any new developments with the case?" I asked him finally, as casually as I could.

We held hands, and he rubbed his thumb along my wrist and sighed a deep, exhausted sigh. "Well, it looks like most of the ideas we had are wrong. Brody was there that day, but I'm positive it was only to rob Mrs. Belcase, which he didn't even do because Wade was already there. Wade confessed to being there and to seeing Mrs. Belcase dead and not reporting her. He's saying that they were supposed to meet and when he got to her house, the door was unlocked, so he'd gone in and found her dead. And he admitted he took a couple of insignificant things from the library, wanting to have something from Trevor, but not out of malice. He's saying, and I believe him, that it was purely out of nostalgia."

"He took the pictures?"

Ryan nodded. "And another artifact, some tourist thing that I guess was an inside joke between him and Trevor. I don't know why he didn't wait to take the things or why he didn't report the murder right away. He doesn't have a clear explanation for that, which worries me. But for the most part, we think he's telling the truth. We've been looking into his background and trying to find out about his past with Trevor Belcase, but there isn't anything there to suggest he would have killed Mrs. Belcase."

"So, are you going to release him, then?"

He nodded. "We're waiting to hear back from the police in Pennsylvania, where Wade lives. I guess he shipped the things he

took back to Philadelphia the day he took them. And so once they open that package and confirm that it's just nonvaluable things he took, it should be good enough to show he didn't have a motive to kill her. But I want to wait until we have that before we release him."

I nodded and leaned into his shoulder. It was so good to be near him finally. I didn't want to break physical contact.

"We went over to Margie's house this afternoon to talk to Hunter again," he said after a while. "I wanted to see if he had any information in regards to the relationship between Wade and Trevor and Margie, or whether *he* knew about Wade and Margie meeting that day. But he wasn't there. One of the neighbors told me she saw him packing up his car and pulling out, so he might have left Sugar Creek for good."

I frowned. "Really? Cassie and I just saw him a while ago!" Ryan must have gone over not much longer after Cassie and I had left. I was glad he hadn't caught us there.

He frowned and pulled back to look at me. "When did you see him? *Why* did you see him?"

Uh oh. Maybe I shouldn't have said anything. How was I going to explain to Ryan that Cassie and I were snooping into Margie's murder?

"Y'all are snooping again, aren't you?" He slapped his leg. "Dang it, Abby! I thought you were gonna leave this one to us! It's too dangerous for you girls to be poking around, you know it is! Or you *should*, from past experience."

"Women. We are *women*, not girls," I said, suddenly in a serious huff. *We* could call *ourselves* girls, but I was in the mood to take offense at being talked down to by a man at the moment. Especially one who was treating me like a child. "And last I checked, it's a free country and Cassie and I can talk to anyone we want."

Of course, as soon as I said the free country bit I felt exactly like a girl. I looked away so he wouldn't notice my conviction falter.

"Okay, I'm sorry. You're right, y'all are women. But I don't like you getting involved in murder, you know that! It's too dangerous. And you and Cassie have been too much trouble. Please promise me you'll leave it be."

I wasn't about to do any such thing. But I sort of nodded and didn't meet his eye and called it good enough. I guess it was good enough for him too, because he pulled me closer and we snuggled for a while. But as we sat there, I started to think about Ryan and how he was in danger all the time and how that didn't seem so fair. I knew it was his job, but it didn't mean I liked it. My mind started to process all of this in a way it hadn't before, especially now that we'd said we loved each other. I thought about Ryan being the sheriff of our town, and how much danger that job would involve, even in a mostly quiet, cozy place like ours. Suddenly, it all condensed in my mind that I was in love with a man who was constantly in harm's way. Anxiety roiled my stomach.

I'd refrained from asking him too many questions about his work before now. Whether my hesitation came from the newness of our relationship or embarrassment around all of my own run-ins with the Sugar Creek police force while sleuthing, I wasn't sure, but up to now, I hadn't pried. Things had changed, though, and my curiosity and worry wouldn't be assuaged.

Finally, I broke our embrace and leaned back to look him in the eye. "I bet it's crazy to pull someone over. I can't imagine having to deal with that kind of conflict on a regular basis."

He laughed and pulled me back into him. I rested my head on his shoulder and waited for him to respond.

"It's crazy every time. You never know who's on the other side of that window. Most of the time, it's simple and routine. Most of the time it's someone in a hurry to get to work, or not paying attention as they run a red light."

"Do they confess to their crimes?"

He laughed again, a deep chuckle shaking both of our bodies. "Almost never. More often than not, there's a story. People can't

help themselves. They lie to me all the time. You wouldn't believe some of the whoppers I've heard, people trying to justify their actions."

"But they aren't usually dangerous, right? Just making things up?"

"No. They aren't usually dangerous." He kissed the top of my head and we were both quiet a moment. I tried hard not to dwell on that *usually*.

He broke the silence with another chuckle and pulled me in closer. "But every now and then I get one heck of a surprise. Back in Dallas, there was a neighborhood I patrolled pretty regularly. An old woman insisted on driving this junker of a Buick around. She'd lost her license years before and veered all over, ran red lights. I had to pull her over often." He laughed again, deeper this time. "Every single time, without fail, I was greeted with a civil war era revolver pointed in my face. Mrs. Dellacorte. She was quite the character."

His voice soothed me even as his words made me nervous. I hated to think about him out in the world, facing danger every single day. Even in a town as small and quaint as Sugar Creek, anything could happen. But what could I say or do? I was in love with this man and he was the sheriff.

I closed my eyes and tried not to give in to the anxiety, but I knew that it would very likely be a constant part of my life going forward. For Ryan, I would stomach it.

Chapter 22

Tuesday morning I was out watering Aunt Meg's copious flowers when Ryan's cruiser pulled into the parking lot. The early morning sun cast long shadows across the B&B's porch as he and Wade stepped out. I broke into a grin, happy to see the old adventurer out of jail.

I turned off the hose and waited for them to approach me. Ryan gave me a smile but stayed behind Wade, clearly in police business mode. "Mr. Harper is free to go. We got the all clear this morning from the Philadelphia PD."

"I'm so happy to hear it," I told them.

Wade gave me a friendly smile, and his eyes crinkled in the corners. "You and me both," he replied.

"We left your things the way they were after the police searched your room. I wasn't sure if we should clean it up or leave it be, so I decided it would be better to protect your privacy and left it all. I hope that's okay," I told him.

He gave me a sad smile. "Of course, that's fine. Under the circumstances, I feel like you had every right to throw my things out. I'm sorry I took up an extra room for nothing all this time."

"Oh, it's no big deal. We don't have any other guests right now, anyway."

"Well, thank you for leaving it. As much as I'm ready to put all of this behind me and get back home, I was hoping you'd let me stay one more night. I'm downright exhausted and could use a day to recuperate and rest before I drive back to the east coast. I'm not as young and chipper as I once was and I tell you, a stint in jail is not great for one's physical and mental condition."

I nodded. "Of course, you're welcome to stay as long as you like. I'm sorry everything happened the way it did."

Wade shrugged. "It's my own fault. I should have told the authorities as soon as I found Margie's body," he said, glancing back at Ryan. "But I was selfish. And slightly delusional. I thought if I kept my mouth shut that I would be able to give my talk, finish the conference, and be on my way without getting involved. And, yes, I was able to give my talk, but now everyone who was here knows that I was arrested and I'm afraid my reputation has been seriously tarnished."

My cheeks flared as I remembered Ryan arresting me as well after I'd first arrived back in Sugar Creek and gotten mixed up in the death of a local councilman. That was a sting that was still fresh, and I knew exactly what Wade was talking about. "Don't worry," I told him, only slightly sure I was telling the truth, "people forget quickly. You'll move past all this soon enough."

He nodded. "Let's hope so. Take care, Sheriff," he said to Ryan with a wave before he headed inside.

After Wade left, Ryan pulled me aside.

"Although we're letting him go for Margie's murder," Ryan said in a low voice, glancing towards the B&B. "technically, Wade could be charged with theft and failure to report a crime."

I frowned. "But you're not going to, are you?"

Ryan shook his head. "No, we're not. Given the circumstances and Wade's cooperation, I've decided to use my discretion here.

His information was crucial, and pressing charges wouldn't serve justice in any meaningful way."

"That makes sense," I nodded, feeling relieved. "But won't you get in trouble for that?"

"It's within my authority," Ryan assured me. "Plus, the DA agrees that pursuing charges against Wade would be a waste of resources when we have a much bigger case to focus on."

"I'm glad you're letting him off. I don't think he meant any harm."

Ryan nodded. "Same here. Alright, I better get back to the station. Now that Wade isn't a suspect, we've got to go back to the beginning."

"Actually, Ryan, before you go, I had an idea," I said, and he turned back to me. I blushed, thinking of how to propose what I was about to propose without sounding silly. But I felt so bad that Wade's trip had ended the way it had, and I wanted to spend a little more time. "What if we do a dinner tonight? With Wade and you and me. We could have Cassie and Ty too, make a party out of it. I know y'all are busy, but you have to eat, right? It might be fun to hang out a bit. Maybe he'll tell us some of his adventuring stories."

I wasn't sure Ryan would want to hang out with a man he'd just had in jail for several days. Or if Wade would want to hang out with *us*. But it was worth a try, and if Wade said no, the four of us could enjoy a meal together and catch up at least.

He frowned and glanced up at the house, clearly thinking through the same problems.

"If Wade agrees and if Ty and I aren't too wrapped up in this murder thing, then sure, why not? But I don't want you to go to a lot of trouble and then have us get wrapped up with work and not be able to make it."

I waved that off. "It's fine. You know I like to cook. And Cassie and I can enjoy the food if you two aren't able to make it or if Wade decides he'd rather do something else."

He pulled me into him for a quick kiss. "You're always willing to solve everything with food, aren't you?"

I pulled back, offended, and he laughed. "I meant that as a compliment. So many people want to make conflicts worse, want to cause trouble. But you and your delicious cooking are always ready to smooth out the edges and bring people together. I like that about you."

After a quick kiss, he pulled away. "I'll let you know about tonight. Barring anything new, it should be okay. We might not be able to stay too long, though."

"Great! I'll call Cassie and let her know." I was already thinking of what food I wanted to cook. Whatever it was, I wanted it to be a warm send-off for Wade to remember us by.

After Ryan left, I stood on the porch for a moment, letting the morning sun warm my face as I considered the dinner plans. It felt good to have something positive to focus on after all the tension of the past few days. With a renewed sense of purpose, I headed back inside to update Maria on Wade's situation and the potential dinner plans.

After I told her about Wade's release and him staying with us another night, I got another idea. "I'm thinking of having a little dinner party tonight with Wade and Cassie and the guys. Would you and Daniela like to join us?"

Maria's face lit up with a warm smile. "Oh, that sounds lovely! Daniela and I would be delighted to come. Are you sure you don't need any help with the preparations?"

"That's sweet of you to offer," I said, touched by her thoughtfulness. "I might take you up on that. Let's touch base this afternoon and see where we're at."

"Perfect," Maria nodded, her smile widening. "It'll be nice to enjoy each other's company for a while."

I figured I should probably at least invite the guest of honor, but I didn't want to bother Wade after he'd just gotten back to his

room so I wrote him a note on some pretty cream stationary I found in the front desk inviting him to dinner with us if he wanted and gave it to Maria to pass along when she saw him next.

Back on the porch, I pulled out my phone to call Cassie. As I dialed, I felt giddy, thinking about how she'd react to the news about Wade being released and the potential for a dinner party. Sure enough, her enthusiasm was infectious.

"A dinner party? Count me in!" Cassie exclaimed after I filled her in on the latest developments. "It'll be nice to have something to celebrate for a change."

"I thought you'd be up for it," I laughed.

"Well, of course I am. You know me!" Cassie replied. Then her voice took on that tone I knew all too well—the one that meant she was brewing up trouble. "Are you busy right now? Because I've got an idea."

I stopped pacing and gazed out at the parking lot. I could almost see the heat rising from it. "Please, don't say anything crazy, Cassie. I'm all full up on crazy."

"Not crazy at all, trust me!" This worried me even more. "We have to go talk to this Linda person. Confront her about the affair. See what she has to say for herself."

I sighed and paced the front porch. "I was thinking we should start with Georgie's mom, actually. Jane is close with everyone and we know her a lot better."

"Okay, Jane it is. But then I want to talk to Linda."

"Alright, but I want to get back here before three to get this dinner thing set up."

"No problem! We can swing by the store if you need to," she told me. "I'll be over in five to pick you up."

"Hey Cassie, Bring Cocoa," I told her before she hung up. "Maria wants to see him and he can hang out here until we get back."

"Got it. See you soon."

Never a dull moment, I thought as I went inside to get my tennis shoes and purse and tell Maria I'd be out for a while.

Never a dull moment.

CHAPTER 23

While I waited for Cassie to pick me up, I gave Georgie a call to talk about her mom and see if Jane would be willing to chat with us. Georgie, always quick to help, said she'd call Jane and see if she could stop by the shop. It was the perfect plan—having Georgie there might make Jane more comfortable opening up to us.

A few minutes later, my phone buzzed with a text from Georgie: "Mom says yes! We'll be waiting at the shop. See you soon!"

Cassie picked me up a while later, Cocoa's happy face poking out the passenger window as she pulled up to the porch where I waited. I opened the door and loved on Cocoa a minute before I let him inside to visit Maria and jumped into Cassie's truck. I told her about Jane agreeing to help as we pulled out of the nearly empty lot and we headed downtown to Henderson's Fine Foods.

The bell above the door chimed as we entered Henderson's Fine Foods a few minutes later. The shop was mercifully empty, save for Georgie and Jane, who sat behind the counter, steaming mugs in hand, sharing a laugh over something. The familiar scent

of exotic spices and gourmet treats enveloped us as we stepped inside.

"Hey, y'all, come on in!" Georgie called out, her smile warm and welcoming. "Come get a cup of tea. This is a special Darjeeling I got from a new importer in Austin last week. It's amazing."

From the aroma alone, I was convinced. The tea sent up a fragrant steam, hints of grape and a subtle floral scent hung in the air as Georgie poured us each a cup. The delicate china clinked softly as she handed them over, then went over to the door and flipped the open sign to closed before locking it.

We all settled into a cozy nook near the window where Georgie had set some chairs, surrounded by shelves of colorful jars and packages. Jane's kind face was etched with curiosity and a touch of concern as we sat down.

"Thanks for agreeing to talk with us," I began, cradling the warm cup in my hands. "It's nothing official, obviously. We're just trying to understand a few things about what happened to Margie and what was going on within your book group before she died." I paused, choosing my words carefully. "I know it's probably a sensitive subject, but if you don't mind, we'd like to hear whatever you have to say about any... disagreements... Margie might have had lately with the rest of the group."

Jane's eyes flickered with emotion—sadness, perhaps a touch of guilt. She took a sip of her tea, gathering her thoughts before speaking. She sighed, her fingers tracing the rim of her teacup. "Oh, where to begin? Our book club... we've been together for so long, you'd think we'd have it all figured out by now." She shook her head. "But lately, things have been... complicated. There's been a lot of tension, especially between Margie and Evelyn."

"What kind of tension?" I asked gently.

Jane's eyes darted to Georgie, then back to me. "Well, there were disagreements about various things with all of us. But if I'm being honest, a lot of it seemed to revolve around Evelyn and her... strong opinions."

Jane took a deep breath, her eyes distant. "You know, thinking back, I realize there was always a... tension between Evelyn and Margie. They grew up together and were a little too close sometimes, maybe. But things really got more serious between them after Trevor came into the picture."

I leaned in, intrigued. "How so?"

"Well," Jane continued, lowering her voice slightly, "Evelyn was always fascinated by Trevor's work. She'd hang on his every word when he talked about his expeditions. At first, we all thought it was just her passion for history, but over time..."

She paused, glancing at Georgie before continuing. "I started to wonder if Evelyn might have had feelings for Trevor. Nothing ever happened, mind you. Trevor was devoted to Margie. But he was kind to Evelyn, encouraged her interest in archaeology. I think that attention meant more to Evelyn than Trevor realized."

Cassie and I exchanged glances. This was definitely new information.

"After Trevor passed," Jane went on, "things got worse. Margie wanted to sell some of Trevor's artifacts. She said she needed the money, but I think part of her wanted to move on, too. Evelyn was furious."

"What happened?" I prompted gently.

Jane's expression darkened. "Oh, it was awful. At our last book club meeting, Evelyn and Margie had a terrible fight. Evelyn accused Margie of dishonoring Trevor's memory, said the artifacts belonged in a museum. Margie said that Trevor would have wanted her to be taken care of, that Evelyn had no right to dictate what happened to her husband's possessions."

She shook her head sadly. "Evelyn stormed out. We were all shocked. I've never seen her so angry. I don't know if they talked again before Margie was killed."

The weight of this revelation hung heavy in the air. It wasn't proof, but it certainly painted Evelyn in a new light—and provided a potential motive we hadn't considered before.

I was hesitant to ask, but curiosity won out. I wanted to know what Jane thought about the theory that was forming in my mind. "Do you think Evelyn could have killed Margie?"

Jane sipped her tea and looked down at her lap a minute before nodding. "I hate to say it about a friend. But Margie was a friend, too. I don't know if Evelyn killed her. It's hard to imagine. But it's possible."

After a moment of heavy silence, Cassie frowned, her brow furrowed in thought. "But wait a minute," she said, looking around at us. "Trevor's already gone. Why would Evelyn care so much about the artifacts now? It's not like keeping them would bring him back or change anything between them."

We all paused, considering this point. It was a valid question—one that made the situation even more puzzling.

Jane sighed, shaking her head. "I wish I knew. Maybe it was about preserving his legacy? Or perhaps..." she trailed off, then shook her head again. "I just don't know."

I could see the wheels turning in Cassie's mind, but before she could voice any more theories, I decided to shift gears.

"What about Linda or Sarah? Would either of them have any reason to hurt Margie that you know of? Any disagreements there?"

Jane shook her head. "Definitely not Sarah. She was the peacemaker of our group, always trying to smooth things over. Actually, ever since the thing with Margie and Evelyn, she's been going back and forth between them, trying to get them to patch things up. But I'm not so sure she was able to get anywhere significant before Margie..." she trailed off.

"And Linda?" Cassie gently pressed.

Jane's eyes wandered and I could tell she couldn't decide about whether she should spill the beans on her friend's affair.

"Just so you know, I overheard y'all the other day talking about the affair, so we already know about that, if it makes any difference."

Jane sighed. "It's true. Shocking to all of us, but yes. Linda is having an affair. I only found out at the fundraiser the other day myself, and I'm pretty sure Sarah didn't know either. But from what I understand, Evelyn and Margie knew about it."

She paused, her expression troubled. "I don't know all the details, but I got the impression that Margie wasn't happy about it. She and Linda had words over it, apparently. But I can't imagine Linda would... well, you know." Jane shook her head, as if dismissing the thought. "Linda's not the type for violence. At least I don't think she is."

I glanced out the window at the people strolling by on Main Street and felt guilty that we were hogging Georgie's store when she could be making sales. I thought Jane had probably told us all she could. But I still wanted to hear Linda's story. Cassie was right. We needed to talk to her in person.

"I would love to talk to Linda, but we don't really know her. Do you have any ideas about how we could get her to talk to us?" I asked Jane as I finished my tea and set the cup down.

Jane brightened. "Why don't I call her up and have her stop by right now? Would that work?"

"Oh, I don't want to take up more of Georgie's time..." I began, but Georgie waved away my comment.

"No problem, honey! I want to know what Linda says too! There will always be more customers," she replied. Jane texted Linda and fifteen minutes later, Linda knocked on the glass. Georgie got up to go let her in.

"Hey, y'all, what's going on? Ooh, it smells delicious in here."

Georgie smiled and gestured at the teapot. "We have some tea. Would you like a cup?"

Linda nodded and sat down in the chair huddle with us. "So, what's going on?" she asked, looking at Jane for answers. Georgie opened a box of cookies imported from France and we all tucked in. They were delicious crisp cinnamon scented wafers, and I immediately made a mental note to buy a box before we left.

Jane glanced at me before explaining things to Linda. I nodded my head. "These girls are tying to figure out what happened to Margie."

Linda looked shocked and set her teacup on a nearby shelf. "Really? Are they with the police or something?" She looked at me closer as Jane explained about our relationships with the police force and her eyes lit up.

"Oh, you're the caterer! The one who found Margie..." she trailed off and her mouth turned down, sadness creeping into her face.

"We were talking about our little group, and whether any of us would have killed Margie."

"Oh! Goodness! Why would any of us do such a terrible thing?" She laughed and grabbed another cookie. My eyes darted to Cassie and then to Jane.

Jane cleared her throat. "I guess we heard some things about you having an...indiscretion...and that Margie knew about it."

"Oh, for heaven's sake," she sighed heavily. "I suppose there's no point in hiding it anymore. Yes, I was having an affair. Yes, Margie knew about it. But I didn't kill her!"

She looked at me directly, her eyes glistening with unshed tears. "I already told all this to your sheriff boyfriend. I regret the whole thing! All it's been is trouble. I thought I could keep it quiet, but with Margie's death, it's all getting churned up."

Linda grabbed a tissue, dabbing at her eyes. "Everybody's judging me. I know they are! Margie was the worst of all. But the heart wants what it wants, you know what I mean?"

She took a deep breath before continuing. "I have an alibi for that morning. I wasn't doing my hair like I told everyone. I was with Harry—he's the man I've been seeing. We were together at the Four Winds in Kerrville that morning."

"The sheriff already confirmed this?" I asked gently.

Linda nodded, blowing her nose. "Yes. I even had Harry give him the credit card receipt to prove it. My carefully kept secret has

become common knowledge." She laughed bitterly. "The desk clerk probably remembers us, too. Not many people our age check into a motel room on a Thursday morning."

She looked at us pleadingly. "I loved Margie, like all of us did. I would never have hurt her. This affair... it's ruined everything. My reputation, my friendships even! But I'm not a murderer."

Jane pulled Linda into a hug and they both let the tears fall. I could feel the pain and regret in Linda's voice. It was clear to me that while she might have made some poor choices, she wasn't our killer. Which Ryan must have already known, given that he'd checked out her alibi. I felt a little foolish walking over the same ground he'd already covered, but I couldn't have known and I felt I needed to explore the book club angle as much as I could before my mind could make sense of all that had happened with Margie.

Georgie glanced at the clock and I took that as a sign that it was time to wrap things up.

"Thank you both so much for talking with us. I know it isn't an easy subject, but I feel like things are a bit clearer now."

Jane stood and gave Cassie and I hugs. "I hope it turns out that it was someone other than a member of our group," I told them.

Linda and Jane nodded in agreement. We said our goodbyes and thanked Georgie for letting us use her shop, and then stepped out into the blast of midday sunshine. It was overwhelming after the peaceful, cool interior of Georgie's shop.

I had Cassie stop by the store on the way back to the B&B. The clerk, who clearly remembered us from the day we visited Hunter, gave us a wary look. I gave her my sweetest smile as we angled toward the meat section. I knew I wanted to do a down home meal tonight, one that screamed Texas, so chicken fried steak was a must. Mashed potatoes, creamed spinach, and a fresh salad would round it out nicely.

"What did you think about all that?" Cassie asked as we wandered up and down aisles. "I have a pretty clear guess about who killed Margie. What about you?"

I nodded. "If it's someone in the book club, it has to be Evelyn. Of course, it could be someone outside of the book group still. But it's interesting to me that Evelyn was so obsessed with Trevor's things and here the prized artifact goes missing at the same time Margie is murdered."

"I would never kill you, just so you know. Not even if you stole Ty from me," she said with a laugh. "At least I don't think I would."

"Same here, Cass. Friends for life, yeah?" We glanced at each other and smiled and then continued through the store, picking up odds and ends to make our dinner perfect.

"My money's on Evelyn, though," Cassie said, as we checked out a few minutes later. "I know it could be some random yahoo. But I don't think it is. I have a gut feeling about this."

I nodded as I paid and nodded again to the cashier. She seemed satisfied that we hadn't caused a ruckus this time, and gave me a friendly smile as we headed out.

"I think you're right. My gut is telling me the exact same thing. The question is, can we convince Ryan and Ty?"

Chapter 24

Cassie dropped me and my shopping bags at Primrose House a little after two, promising to come back after she took care of some things at her shop. Cocoa greeted me at the door and I laughed as he pranced around me all the way to the kitchen, nearly knocking me off balance as we made our way through the B&B. I set the bags on the counter, then gave him a good long pet. When I stood up, I surveyed the kitchen. It was nice and clean, ready for me to cook, and I couldn't wait to get started.

As I was unpacking the groceries, Maria came into the kitchen with a stack of hand towels and put them away. She gave me a warm smile. "Everything's been quiet since you left. Wade's been in his room the whole time, only came down once for a glass of water. I gave him your note, and he said yes to dinner."

I danced a happy jig, and she laughed. Cocoa bounced around, getting into the jovial spirit of things.

"We got a new online reservation for Friday for two rooms and I put them in six and seven, right next to each other," she continued as she grabbed a bottle of water and took a long drink.

I nodded, grateful for her update. "Thanks, Maria. I appreciate you holding down the fort."

"It's no trouble at all," she replied. "Did you find out anything new?"

I nodded and told her about all that had happened with Jane and Linda as I started to organize the food and make a plan for dinner.

"Wow, that is a lot to process. Do you think it's important? Are you going to tell Ryan?"

I nodded. "I'll tell him tonight. You're still coming, right? With Daniela?"

She nodded, and we talked a while more about Margie and her friends as I pulled on my apron and found my mallet, ready to get serious, turning some tough round steak into tenderized perfection.

"Listen," I said after we'd puzzled for a bit over what it all meant and I'd mixed a flour and seasoning concoction to dip the steaks into, "why don't you take the rest of the day off? You've been working so hard. Just come back for dinner around seven, okay?"

Maria eyed my piles of ingredients I'd pulled out. "Are you sure you don't need any help preparing?"

I shook my head, smiling. "I've got it covered and Cassie's coming back soon, so she can help if I need it. Go enjoy your afternoon, and we'll see you tonight."

"Alright then," Maria agreed as she grabbed her things and gave me a smile. "We'll see you at seven. Thank you, Abby."

I finished tenderizing the steak and then set it in the fridge until it was time to fry it. Then I went out to the backyard and walked around a few minutes. I hoped it would be cool enough that we could eat at the picnic table that sat under the big oak tree, but seeing as it was about a million degrees currently, I thought it was best to get the dining table inside prepared just in case. We'd turned the old dining room into a conference space for guests a couple of months before, but when I went back inside, it only took

me a few minutes to rearrange some things and get it feeling almost like a dining room again.

Back in the kitchen, I started peeling and chopping onions and potatoes. As I did, my brain churned on everything that Cassie and I had learned from Jane and Linda. I thought about Evelyn and how invested she seemed in Trevor. Could she have been in love with him like Jane had hinted? I'd never known the man, but from the stories I'd heard and the handsome face I'd seen in the photos at the museum, it seemed highly possible.

I didn't have too much time to think about it all though, because as I was chopping lettuce for the salad a little while later, Wade came down from his room.

"Thank you for the dinner invitation. It wasn't necessary, but I'm looking forward to it. That curried chicken salad has been playing on my mind ever since I had it, so I'm sure dinner will be wonderful."

I smiled at him. "We plan to start around seven. Feel free to make yourself at home before that." I blushed, realizing that he was still a guest at Primrose House. "Normally we do happy hour around now. I'm so sorry, with everything going on and you being the only guest I completely forgot. But we have wine and beer in the fridge and I can make you a snack plate too if you want one."

"No, I'll wait for your delicious dinner," he said as he gestured with his head at my cutting board. "But I will take a beer, if you don't mind."

I pointed him to the drinks fridge near my catering fridge where we kept the guest drinks and he chose a bottle, then headed out to the front room.

Only a few minutes later, Cassie came in. "Alright, lady! What can I do to help?"

We settled into companionable work, chatting about wedding plans and what we'd learned from Jane and Linda. I dredged and fried the steaks and Cassie mashed the potatoes with lots of butter and sour cream. Midway through our preparations, Maria came in

and fell in line beside us after telling us that Daniela was spending the night at a friend's house and wouldn't make it.

The three of us chatted and cooked and laughed. It felt good to relax and enjoy their company and the pleasant work of the kitchen. The only thing missing was Aunt Meg and when I realized it my heart sank a little. She would have loved to have dinner out under the stars, listening to an old adventurer's exciting stories.

Ryan and Ty came in just before seven. "It sure smells good in here," Ryan said.

"Looks good in here, too," Ty said with a grin as he moved around the counter and scooped Cassie into a serious smooch.

Ryan gave me a quick kiss and hug too, and we laughed when he pulled back and had flour on his shirt. "Hazards of hugging a chef," I told him.

We finished up the cooking as the guys got themselves a beer and then we all went out to the yard to decide between the picnic table and the dining room. It was warm still, but there was a nice breeze, so we decided to set dinner up out in the yard. I had Ryan and Ty pull some industrial fans out of the shed and hooked them up near the picnic table, which helped quite a bit. Maria and Cassie set out citronella candles to light the place and keep the bugs at bay and I put a pretty centerpiece of daisies in a mason jar on the picnic table before bringing the food out and setting it in the center as well.

"Alright y'all, time to eat!"

I introduced Wade to Cassie as we all found our places at the table. The late evening sun glimmered through the oak leaves. We passed around the mashed potatoes and the spinach. I'd set out a salad for each person and took plates to give each one a piece of chicken fried steak, then covered it with the cream gravy.

"My goodness, I don't know the last time I had such an incredible meal," Wade said between bites.

Ryan chuckled. "We've all gotten spoiled with Abby around. Every time she cooks for us, it's a delight."

We made small talk for a while and the company and the food were so enjoyable that the evening heat was barely noticeable. As the meal wound down, a comfortable silence fell over the table. The clinking of forks against plates slowed, and the warm glow of the setting sun covered the table with soft light.

Wade leaned back in his chair, his eyes distant, lost in thought. The mood shifted, and we all sensed the change. Margie's death invaded our thoughts and made it hard to enjoy ourselves properly. I glanced back and forth between Ryan and Cassie, wondering if I should bring up Margie's death or whether it was best not to talk about it with Wade at all.

Cassie was the one who finally break the silence. "Wade," she said gently, "we're all so glad you're here with us. But I think we're all wondering... what really happened that day at Margie's? If you don't mind telling us."

Wade's eyes refocused, meeting each of ours in turn. He took a deep breath, his shoulders squaring as if preparing to carry a heavy load. "I suppose it's time I told you all the whole story," he said, his voice low and serious.

As we all leaned in, the cozy dinner party atmosphere faded, replaced by an air of anticipation. Whatever Wade was about to share, it wouldn't be light dinner fare.

DEATH AND BLACKBERRY PIE

SUGAR CREEK MYSTERY SERIES

BOOK FOUR

NOVA WALSH

TWO WORLDS PRESS

Chapter 26

Wade left early the next morning. The sun had barely crested the horizon when I checked him out of his room. Selfishly, I didn't want him to leave. But I was happy to know he was going on to have more adventures rather than being stuck in jail for a crime he didn't commit. I met him on the porch, a travel mug of coffee in hand.

"For the road," I said, passing it to him.

Wade's eyes crinkled with gratitude. "Abby, I can't thank you enough for everything. I'm sorry having me here was so much trouble for you."

I shook my head. "It was worth it, believe me. Just promise me you'll have more adventures," I replied, surprising myself with the lump in my throat.

"Oh, you can count on that," he winked, then sobered. "I hope you all catch whoever did this to Margie."

I nodded firmly. "We will."

Maria found me in the kitchen a little while later when she arrived for work. She raised her eyebrows. "Wade's gone?"

"Just left," I confirmed, pouring myself a cup of coffee. We talked for a while about B&B business, although there wasn't much to be done now that Wade was gone. We went upstairs to survey the place and I helped Maria clean Wade's room. Despite the chaos that Brody had caused, the guest bathroom was all back to normal, minus a grey section of wall that needed to be repainted. I made a note to myself to pick up some touch up paint at the store sometime before the next gaggle of guests arrived.

As we worked, I turned my attention to the plan we'd devised the night before to trap Evelyn. Part of me thought it was crazy, and part of me thought it was genius. But as I fretted yet again over the possibility that we were wrong about Evelyn, I reminded myself that it didn't really matter. This trap was a test. If Evelyn failed, we would know that she was the killer. And if she passed, we would know she was probably innocent, at least if we understood her motivations the way I thought we did. Either way, it would lead to information that would get us closer to finding Margie's killer.

As the morning wore on, I grew more and more agitated. I was itchy to get over to Cassie's and help her set the trap for Evelyn. Finally, I couldn't take it anymore.

"I'm heading to Cassie's," I announced. "You good here?"

Maria shooed me away with a smile. "Go, go. I'll hold down the fort."

The short drive to Cassie's felt like an eternity. When I arrived, I found her pacing in the front of Divine Finds. She deftly maneuvered through the crowded space with a frown.

"Finally!" Cassie exclaimed as she noticed me. "I've been going over and over this in my head. What if we're wrong? What if we're right? What if..."

I grabbed her shoulders, halting her mid-stride. "Cassie, breathe. This is going to work. We're going to find out the truth, one way or another."

She took a deep breath, nodding. "You're right. Okay, let's do this."

The first thing we did was lock up Cassie's shop for the day.

We didn't want to give Evelyn any chance to try to visit the place once she heard about Cassie having the artifact, so she decided to lock up and send Mandy home. Next, we headed over to the museum to talk Artie into helping us. Luckily, we found him at the museum dusting one of the cases in an otherwise empty room.

"Well, hello again, ladies! What a pleasant surprise, I didn't think y'all would be back so soon! Looking to learn some more history?"

I hated to burst his enthusiastic bubble, but I figured he'd be excited about what I had to tell him. "Actually, we're here because they let Wade off yesterday for Margie's murder."

"I knew it! I knew they got the wrong person. Wade is a good man, not a murderer. You can hang your hat on it."

I nodded emphatically. "We totally agree. Listen, Artie," I started, trying to think of the perfect way to entice him into helping with our plan.

Cassie cut me to the chase. "We have a theory, Artie, and if you're up for it we would love your help running a little...experiment."

His eyes lit up, and he leaned on the front counter. "I'm all ears."

Cassie beamed. "I know this might sound a little cuckoo, but we have good reason to believe that Evelyn Brooks might actually be the one who killed Margie, and we have an idea for how to prove it."

He grew more and more enthusiastic as Cassie and I explained our plan to him. At the end of it all, he was nodding and nearly bouncing out of his hiking boots.

"You know, when you put it all like that, I could really buy it. Evelyn has always been a little...obsessed with Trevor. And you know what else is funny? Evelyn just called me up yesterday and told me she had a bunch of Trevor's things ready to donate. I guess that nephew of theirs sold her what was left of the collection. I wonder now if her plan might have been to donate the other things so she could keep that special carving for herself." He shrugged. "To tell you the truth, I don't know what that woman was up to. But I love your plan. I'm in!"

"Alright," I said as I began to pace the old creaky floor. "Let's run through what you should say when you call her. It's got to be just right to get her to try to steal the carving back. We want you to convince her that the carving that Trevor had at his house was fake and that his nephew gave the real one to Cassie to auction. And it's very important to say that Cassie plans to take them to Austin tomorrow morning to auction them..."

Artie waved his hand at us. "I know, I know. Please. Let me do this my own way."

Despite the dread that this created in the pit of my stomach, when I glanced at Cassie, she nodded to Artie. "Alright then, go ahead. You do it your way."

Artie grinned. "I knew you were a smart one," he said as he pulled his phone out of his front pocket and slipped on eyeglasses.

A moment later, he dialed and held the phone up to his ear and then gave us all a thumbs up as he connected to Evelyn.

"Evelyn, hey, hi. It's Artie over at the museum. Hey, I wanted to let you know something I heard this morning. You know how everybody's talking about Margie's carving that was stolen? Well, I was just over at that antique shop downtown, Divine Finds. They called me over to do an appraisal and you'll never believe it, but it was for Trevor's carving. Yes, the jade one from that Himalayas trip. The special one he had on display in their library."

He was silent a minute, listening.

"No, no. I'm sure. This was the real deal. A while back, Trevor showed me a specific notch pattern on one of the feet. He said not many people knew about it but that it was how he could tell the difference between the real one and the fake that he had made for his house display."

Artie pulled the phone away from his face and gave us a wink. I was thrilled with his brilliance. "Anyway, the one over at Divine Finds had the notch pattern, so I know it's real."

He listened for another minute. "No, I don't know how they got it. It sounded to me like the owner, that Cassie lady, was acting as a go-between for someone who wanted to sell them. Maybe that nephew of Margie's had it all along? I don't know. Funny that whoever stole it from Margie's place only got the replica... Anyway, all I know is that we'll have to kiss our chance of having it for the museum goodbye because she's taking it to Austin for auction tomorrow morning."

He paced and fiddled with a pocket on his vest. "Mhm. Yeah. I know. It's a shame. Trevor would have wanted it to stay here, I know. Well, there isn't much we can do about it. It'll be over at the shop until the mornin', but then it's out of our hands. Alright, I better get gone, Evelyn. I'll talk to you later."

Cassie and I burst into applause as he hung up the phone and he broke into a wide grin.

"Alright, ladies, y'all better promise me you'll let me know what happens. This is exciting! Maybe I shoulda gone into law enforcement myself, sting operations, traps. Funner than dusty old artifacts..." He stopped and threw back his head with a laugh. "Don't listen to me. I love these dusty old artifacts."

We thanked him profusely and promised to let him know every detail of what happened, and then headed back to Cassie's shop. It was time to finish setting our trap. And then we would have to wait. If we were lucky, we would catch Margie's killer. I crossed my fingers, wishing for all the luck in the world.

CHAPTER 27

The bell above the door of Divine Finds jingled as Cassie and I entered a few minutes later. The familiar scent of old books and antique wood met us and it instantly put me at ease, but then Cassie broke the spell.

"Alright," Cassie said, clapping her hands together. "Operation Catch-a-Killer is a go. Where should we start?"

I surveyed the shop. "Let's make it as easy as possible for her to get in without being obvious. Maybe leave the backdoor unlocked?"

Cassie nodded, moving towards the rear of the store. "Good idea."

As she unlocked the door, I began rearranging some of the displays. "We should make a clear path to where we're putting the 'artifact'," I suggested.

"Oh! Speaking of which," Cassie called from the back room, emerging with a dusty cardboard box. "I had this old security camera in storage. Never got around to using it before, but it should still work."

We spent the next hour setting up the camera, hiding it among the antiques so it wouldn't be noticeable, but would still have a slight view of both the front and the back doors. After a few frustrating attempts, we finally got it connected to Cassie's laptop over in the bungalow.

"Yes!" Cassie exclaimed as the grainy black-and-white feed flickered to life on her screen. "Houston, we have visual."

I grinned, feeling a mix of excitement and nervousness. "Now we just have to hope Evelyn takes the bait."

The plan was for Ryan and Ty to patrol nearby all night. They couldn't directly be involved in the trap, but we would call them as soon as Cassie and I saw any activity on the camera and they could swoop in and stop her. This way, Cassie and I could stay at the bungalow out of harm's way and still be part of the action, which should make the guys happy.

After we got the camera set up and double checked that the feed was working, I promised Cassie I'd be back soon and then headed to Primrose House to finish up a few things and get myself ready for our stakeout. As much as I hated leaving the B&B without a caretaker, it was Wednesday night and we didn't have any guests, so I decided to leave it locked tight and hope that no last-minute travelers arrived while I was gone. There was no way I was going to miss the action to babysit an empty house.

I took a quick shower and felt a little silly dressing in all black, but I did it anyway. Then I spent some time uploading pictures of my citrus cake onto my website to pass the time. But as the sun started to sink, I couldn't fight the excitement any longer. I packed my silly picnic basket full of stakeout snacks—popcorn, chips and salsa, cookies, nuts, and grapes—happy that at least this time I wouldn't have to carry the awkward thing down a mountain. I threw in several energy drinks, locked up Primrose House tight, and headed over to Cassie's place.

Cassie was nearly jumping out of her skin when I arrived a while later.

"Evelyn called me!" Cassie said. "She's worried! I think this is gonna work!"

"What did she say?" I asked as I set out the snacks on the coffee table where Cassie's computer sat.

"I didn't answer. I let it go to voicemail."

"Did she leave a message?"

"She did! She said she heard I had one of Trevor's things and she hoped she could talk to me before I sold it. She said she might want to buy it," she said, her eyes dancing.

As we were talking, Cassie's phone rang, and she glanced down at the screen before squealing and jumping up and down. "It's her again. Boy, she's worried. She stopped by the shop too, looked mighty angry when she realized we were closed," she said with a chuckle.

My eyes lit up. This was exactly what we'd hoped would happen. "This is good. You're right, she seems scared. But is she scared enough to take the bait? It's a big stretch between wanting to buy the carving and breaking into someone's shop to get it."

"If we're right, she killed one of her closest friends over this thing. I don't think a little breaking and entering is going to phase her."

Cassie had a point.

Once the sun set, we checked in with Ryan and Ty. They'd parked themselves a few blocks away, not wanting to scare Evelyn off but wanting to be close enough to help if it came to that. I hoped for their sake that Evelyn would be quick about it and that this whole thing didn't turn into a wild goose chase, because it would make for one heck of a long night for all of us if it did.

We started out full of energy, snacking and gabbing and laughing as we watched the camera where nothing happened. Cocoa kept us entertained with tricks for popcorn. But as the night wore on, our enthusiasm started to flag, and the energy drinks turned from stimulating to sickening. Cassie and I huddled over the computer, watching the static image of her store until my eyes felt like they were going cross. Now and then I caught a glimpse of movement out the shop's front window and got excited, but hours passed and nothing ever happened.

I could not believe we'd talked the guys into doing this. I felt more and more guilty as the night dragged on without any activity.

But then suddenly, just near midnight, something happened. I hit Cassie, who'd been scrolling through wedding dresses online, and she sat up and stared too. "Whoa. Call the guys!"

We watched as the back door creaked open and Evelyn stuck her head inside to survey the place. I called Ryan right away, but he didn't answer. I growled and texted him to tell him what was happening as I watched Evelyn move all the way inside and close the door behind her. Why was this man never available when I needed him?

Cassie and I continued to watch as Evelyn moved silently around the store, shuffling through display cases, at one point knocking over a spinning rack of greeting cards. She had a bulky bag slung over her shoulder and my guess was that she had the carving inside, ready to plant in place of what she thought was the real one. She grew more and more frantic as she moved through the store and didn't find any jade carvings.

I started to worry she was going to give up before the guys got to her. I called Ryan again, but no answer.

"Cassie, call Ty," I told her. She got no answer, either.

"Should we go over there?" I asked, my stomach churning with anxiety. It was a terrible idea, but I didn't want her to get away. Before we had the chance to do something stupid, though, we saw Ryan and Ty burst in the front door of the shop and I let out a deep breath.

"Put your hands up, Ms. Brooks. You're under arrest," Ryan said on the screen.

"No!" she cried as she saw Ryan. She grabbed an antique lamp and flung it at him, trying to race out the back where she'd come in. Ty jumped out and grabbed her arm, and she looked like she was about to have a heart attack as she struggled to get away from him. Suddenly, she slumped and her head fell to her chest. Ty pulled out his cuffs and shackled her as great sobs heaved from her chest.

"Let's go!" Cassie cried and grabbed my hand. "I wanna see what she has to say before they take her away!"

We raced out of the bungalow door with Cocoa on our heels. "They aren't going to let us come in," I began.

"This is my business! And that is my fiancé! Heck yes, they better let us come in!" she replied as she swung the backdoor open. Ty immediately pulled his gun and aimed it at us from where he stood next to Evelyn, and we all breathed out a sigh as he realized who it was storming in. "Woman! Do not do that to me! I could've shot you!"

Cassie trembled, and I wrapped my arms around her as we moved to the side, trying to stay out of the way while Ryan and Ty went to work. Ty opened her bag and pulled out a large jade carving of what looked like a jaguar. Evelyn looked scared for a minute, and then her face creased into an angry glare.

"Mrs. Brooks, you're under arrest," Ryan said and then began to tell her about her rights.

She scowled at him. "I don't care about any of that. What does it matter? Clearly you know I stole that," she gestured with her head at the carving. She laughed. "Margie was miss goodie-two-shoes while Trevor was alive, hung on his every word and story," she said with a sneer. "Or seemed to anyway. But when he died, her true colors showed through, like I knew they would. She just wanted to sell his things for money. She didn't really care about any of it. Not like I cared." Her voice hitched as Ryan pulled her gently toward the door.

She changed her tune all of a sudden and began to plead with Ryan as they walked toward the front. "You have to believe me! I didn't mean to do it! I was just so angry!" Her eyes flared, and I took a big step back. I could feel the negative energy radiating off of her and it was almost overwhelming.

"It wasn't right! She should never have treated his things that way. They were priceless. They were part of a legacy. And she was just going to hawk them like some cheap jewelry. Trevor would have been so upset. I knew him better than Margie did. I knew how he would feel about her selling the things he spent his entire life trying to find."

There was obsession and madness and love in her tone and it frightened me even though Ryan had her in handcuffs. As they headed out the front with her, Cassie and I sighed and surveyed the damage. Her shop was a disaster and several antiques had been damaged or ruined. But we were okay and Margie's killer had been caught, thanks to us. We both realized it at the same time and fell into a hug, big smiles on both of our faces.

CHAPTER 28

In the morning, after I'd slept in and given Maria a thorough minute-by-minute replay of what happened with Evelyn the night before, I headed over to Cassie's shop to help her put the place back to rights. The ruckus the night before had done some damage, and I knew that she'd lost at least a few antiques in the process of the guys arresting Evelyn, but I had a feeling she wouldn't be too broken up about it.

Sure enough, when I got to Divine Finds, Georgie and Ellie were there, listening in shock as she told them all about our night. Her face lit up with excitement.

I gave Georgie a quick hug, then moved over to Ellie and did the same. She was getting bigger and bigger every day, and I could tell by the glow surrounding her that she was going to be a fantastic mother. "Who's watching the bakery?" I asked her.

She beamed. "We actually just hired a bakery manager," she told me. "It had to happen eventually, but this baby is already slowing me down. And once he gets here, there's no way I can manage the bakery the way I have in the past. Our new person, Blythe, is incredible. She managed a bakery in Austin before moving over our direction. You'll have to come over and meet her soon."

We all caught up a little while longer, and then Georgie and Ellie headed out and left us to our mess. Cassie had indeed lost a few antiques, including the lamp that Evelyn had thrown, but nothing too valuable. As we swept up the glass and righted displays, we plotted yet again, but this time to make a special meal and have a quiet night, just the four of us. Now that Evelyn had been arrested for Margie's murder, the guys would finally have time to hang out again and we wanted to spend every spare minute with them, knowing that more chaos could happen at any time.

I was still in charge of the B&B, even though we wouldn't have guests until the following day, so we planned to once again meet there. After we put Divine Finds back to rights, Cassie and I hit the store once again for supplies. As we left the antique shop, I noticed dark clouds gathering in the distance and the wind starting to pick up. Looked like we might get a storm, which would be a much needed break from the grueling summer heat we'd endured for what seemed like forever.

Our joy bubbled up as we wandered through the grocery store, infecting everyone around us. We were on cloud nine, still proud of ourselves for what we'd accomplished with Evelyn. "Let's grill steaks," Cassie suggested as we hit the meat section.

I nodded. "Maybe some shrimp, too. I'll make a salad and we can do some baked potatoes."

The clouds had grown much closer as we left the store, and a storm was nearly upon us. We stopped by Cassie's bungalow on the way to Primrose House to pick up Cocoa. He hopped into the truck and sat between us, his tongue lolling, ready for adventure and maybe a mouse chase at his favorite B&B.

Just as we pulled into the parking lot at Primrose House, the dark clouds burst into an epic downpour. Ryan's truck sat in the lot and I saw him and Ty sitting in the rocking chairs on the porch, waiting for us. I laughed and Cassie and I jumped out of the car and ran toward them, Cocoa on our heels.

We were downright giddy that the whole thing with Margie was over and it felt like a day to celebrate. The rain made it even more festive. As hot as it had been over the last several weeks, the cool relief of it felt miraculous. I slowed as we got to the porch and then laughed as I twirled in the rain, falling into Ryan's arms a minute later, soaking him too. He put his hands on my face, grinned, and then gave me a kiss that I felt all the way to my toes.

The summer wasn't over, not by a long shot, but the little taste of cooler weather got me in the mood for the fall. It would take a while, but eventually we would make it through this difficult summer, just like we'd made it through the difficulty of figuring out who killed Margie Belcase.

Before we had a chance to go inside, an SUV came barreling into the parking lot, splashing up puddles and pulling close to the porch. As soon as I saw who it was, I squealed and ran back through the rain to the vehicle. Bertie and Aunt Meg waved to us as they climbed down and each gave me a hug.

"Aunt Meg! Why didn't you tell me you were on the way?" I yelled through the storm, grabbing her and hugging her as tight as I could as we walked up to the porch. My heart was nearly bursting with joy that she'd returned. Everything felt right with the world all at once.

Bertie stepped up onto the porch and shook her wet hair, then ran a hand through the grey curls. "We wanted to surprise y'all. See what kinda ship you gals have been running without Meg here," she said with a laugh. Ryan and Ty gave them each a hug, and we all laughed as we tried to get dry without success.

"Well, this sure is a surprise! Such a wonderful one!" I pulled Aunt Meg into a hug again, not ready to let her go. She smelled like ocean and sunshine and her eyes danced. The time away had been good for her, I could tell.

With Aunt Meg finally home, I could go back to focusing on my catering business. And it was a good thing because I was heading toward empty on my bank account and needed to focus hard on making Deep in the Heart a success. Not to mention, with Cassie being engaged, I had a whole new task ahead of me that would surely occupy some of my time—finding myself a place to live. As long as it wasn't the couch at Primrose House, it would be fine.

After Ryan brought Aunt Meg and Bertie's things inside and we all dried off, we fixed ourselves drinks as laughter and stories filled the air. I got a few potatoes into the oven to bake, happy that I'd bought plenty of extra food now that we would have two more at the table, and then we all headed out to the porch, drinks in hand. The rain pattered peacefully on the roof as we all sat down. The storm had cooled everything off considerably and our mood was light and jovial as we settled in to socialize.

Now that Aunt Meg was home, I could admit to myself that I'd had a difficult time running both the B&B and my catering business. It wasn't something I wanted to tackle again for a long, long time. I only hoped Aunt Meg was ready to settle back in and take over the reins again. It had been a rough couple of weeks with Margie's death and Aunt Meg gone. And a rough couple of months, if I was honest, as we'd navigated through multiple deaths and business difficulties.

But summer was on the wane, I could feel it in the air, and our little group was finally all back together. For now, at least, I could simply enjoy my friends and family and my home and be grateful that things were finally settling down in Sugar Creek.

THE END

———

**Coming October 2024, Death and Eggnog, book 5 in the
Sugar Creek Mystery series!**

Preorder Now!

**A small town Christmas pageant. A Broadway diva's
emotional homecoming. A holiday whodunit that will keep
you guessing until the very end.**

Sugar Creek's annual Christmas play takes center stage as Abby
Hirsch prepares to cater for the festive production. But when a
famous actress returns to her hometown to join the cast, bringing
glitz, glamour, and a generous helping of chaos, Abby finds herself
in the middle of a holiday mystery that's anything but merry.

Abby must sift through a cast of colorful suspects--from jealous
understudies to the entertaining but meddling Drama Mamas--to
uncover the truth. But with her quirky best friend Cassie by her
side and sparks flying with Sheriff Ryan Iverson, Abby and the
gang might just find a way to serve up justice in time to save
Christmas in Sugar Creek.

This yuletide mystery features:
- A charming small-town Christmas setting
- Theater drama with a deadly twist
- Plenty of quirky amateur sleuthing
- Clean slow-burn romance
- Recipes!

**Death and Eggnog is a deliciously festive addition to the
Sugar Creek Mystery Series. Filled with holiday cheer,
mouth-watering seasonal treats, and small-town Texas
charm, this cozy mystery is the perfect recipe for a capti-**

vating Christmas read. Curl up with a mug of hot cocoa and join Abby for another thrilling culinary caper!

Preorder Now!

Abby's Celebration Blackberry Pie

INGREDIENTS

For the crust:

2 cups flour

10 Tbsp cold butter

1 tsp salt

Ice water

Sugar for dusting

1 egg for egg wash

For the filling:

4 cups fresh blackberries

3/4 cup sugar

1/2 cup flour

1 tsp cinnamon

1/2 tsp nutmeg

4 Tbsp butter

Juice of half a lemon

DIRECTIONS

For the crust, cut the butter into small cubes then cut into the flour until small crumbles form, rubbing together with your fingers to break up bigger clumps. Add ice water and mix until it all combines—not too dry or too sticky. Cut in half and roll into 2 round discs, then refrigerate while you mix the filling. (You can also do this the easy way and use 2 premade crusts—I won't tell!)

Preheat your oven to 425 degrees.

Mix together the filling ingredients. Roll out the bottom crust and place it in a pie dish then fill with the filling. Top with the second crust and poke holes or alternatively create a lattice crust by slicing the top crust into strips and lying in an alternating pattern. Beat the egg with a little water and brush the top, then sprinkle it all with more sugar and put in the oven. (I always like to put my pie dish on a cookie sheet in case the filling leaks out to cut down on messes).

Bake at 425 for 15 minutes, and then decrease the temperature to 375 until the crust is nicely brown and filling is bubbly, about 20 more minutes. Cover with foil partway through if the crust starts to brown too much.

Cool before serving.

Lemon Lavender Shortbread Cookies

INGREDIENTS

1 stick (8 Tbsp) butter at room temperature

1/4 cup powdered sugar

3/4 cup all purpose flour

1 Tbsp cornstarch

1 tsp vanilla

Zest of 1 lemon

1/4 tsp lavender extract or 1/2 tsp dried lavender (optional)

DIRECTIONS

Mix together all the ingredients until well combined, it will start crumbly but come together more and more as you work it. Press the dough together into a disc and roll to about 1/4 inch thick then cover in plastic wrap and place in fridge for 30 minutes.

Preheat the oven to 350 degrees. Take the dough out and cut it with cookie cutters or into squares with a knife.

Place cookies on parchment paper lined cookie sheet and put back in the fridge for another ten minutes or so to firm up, then bake at 350 for 12-15 minutes, until slightly browned and cooked through. Cool on wire racks.

If you'd like these cookies a little sweeter, you can make a quick lemon icing by mixing together a little lemon juice with powdered sugar until you have a thick liquid consistency then drizzle this over the cookies as they cool.

Strawberry Ginger Chutney

INGREDIENTS

1 lb fresh strawberries
1/2 cup sugar
1 Tbsp freshly grated ginger
1 Tbsp lemon juice
2 Tbsp red wine or champagne vinegar
Salt and chili flakes to taste

DIRECTIONS

Wash and hull the strawberries and place them in a pot with the sugar, ginger, and lemon juice. Bring to a slow simmer and cook down until the moisture is about halfway gone (about 10-15 minutes).

Once the chutney has cooked, lightly mash with a fork or potato masher to create a jam-like consistency. Add the salt, chili, and vinegar and adjust to taste.

Serve this tangy sweet sauce with meats or on the side of a tangy cheese like brie or halloumi.

About Nova Walsh

Author Nova Walsh writes culinary cozy mysteries full of humor, shenanigans, and friendships that last a lifetime. She mixes in a healthy dose of amateur sleuthing, some slow-burn romance, and a pinch of comedy in every book she writes.

Nova is a former chef/caterer who still loves to cook but loves to write even more.

She's an enthusiastic, if not totally successful gardener and loves travel, wine, and hanging out with friends.

Nova lives in central Texas with her husband, son, and two delightfully crazy pups. When she isn't writing, she's often cooking, gardening, hiking, or reading a good book with a pup by her side.

You can contact Nova at nova@novawalsh.com